GETTING A RISE

"Rose, I was wondering if you'd mind giving me some practical advice about Cl— I mean men, in general." Kyra glanced shyly at the other woman.

"Sure, honey, ask away." Rose passed Kyra a wooden bowl. "Here, while we're talking you can start to make the bread. Think of the dough like a man. To rise, it needs something to trigger it. In the case of the bread, either yeast or sour starter will do the job. But it's not enough to get a rise out of the dough. You have to add just the right amount of stimulation at the proper rate, so it won't erupt in one big bubble. You do this by working—you could say massaging—the yeast through the whole of the mixture. Kneading is the key to success."

She winked slyly. "Now much the same is true with a man. It's quite easy to stimulate one—getting a rise rather easily. But if it's not controlled, his bubble will shoot off early, giving neither one of you as much pleasure as possible. The trick is to learn to handle him in such a way that you both enjoy the end result much better."

"How?"

"Honey dear, I'm sure you've heard the saying: The way to a man's heart is through his stomach?"

Kyra nodded.

"Well, I want to tell you a little secret: The quickest, most direct way to a man's heart actually exists a little lower, say about ten inches lower."

Sinfully Delicious

Lora Kenton

LEISURE BOOKS  NEW YORK CITY

A LEISURE BOOK®

June 2002

Published by

Dorchester Publishing Co., Inc.
276 Fifth Avenue
New York, NY 10001

ISBN 0-8439-5083-8

Printed in the United States of America.

To Nonno Enzo and Mom for giving me the love of writing, and to Dad for telling me I was good. Many thanks to Kathryn Fox for her kindness in critiquing, and to N. Keith Collins for expertise in weapons.

To Sharon—big sister and best friend. Thanks for our first piece of great advice—"Find your local writers' group." To HCRW—thanks for being that wonderfully supportive group. And finally to Altug—loving husband and survival partner. Thanks for always being there. Cok seni seviyorum.

Sinfully Delicious

Prologue

Tyler, Texas, Mid-June 1879

God, how he hated his job! Cliff Baldwin's black thoughts stalked him as he pursued one of the Yancey brothers, the youngest, through a forest in eastern Texas. Low scraggly bushes and overhead limbs clawed at him, but Cliff was impervious to the minor scratches. He inhaled the fresh smell of broken pine needles. The boy was close by.

Glimpsing movement a few yards to his left, Cliff softly stepped behind a tree. Young Tommy was scrambling behind a tall cottonwood. Cliff's bounty-hunting partner, Shane, already had the two elder brothers tied up and under guard back at the outlaws' shack. They'd just finished disarming Zach and Russ when shots from the surrounding woods had sent them scattering for cover. Cliff had set out alone to bring in the last Yancey criminal.

Sighing, he aimed his Colt revolver and waited for the opportunity he knew would come too soon. Endless tracking, capturing, and killing were carving wounded notches on his soul. He'd left his home in New Orleans years ago in a desperate attempt to preserve what little was left of his honor, but now stood a greater chance of losing it entirely. He'd set out to create a peaceful life, to escape his father's influence—to avoid following in the family's godforsaken path of misery and destruction.

Tommy's gun fired. Bark flew off the tree that shielded Cliff. He ducked. Yeah, he'd forged his own path, all right—one strewn with blood, pain, and betrayal. He wasn't the courageous hero others whispered about, but rather a tormented, spent cartridge of a man, hiding painful secrets, longing for something beyond his ability to attain—a happy life.

Closing his eyes, Cliff bit down on his bottom lip until he tasted blood. The pain helped him gain control and force the memories to retreat.

"Give up now, Tommy. We've got your brothers. You know you won't escape for long without them." It was a useless plea. He watched for any sign of surrender, just in case. *Maybe this time would be different.*

Even though he knew all the heinous crimes the Yancey brothers had committed for months across Texas, he didn't want another man's blood on his hands. Tommy couldn't be more than seventeen. It was unfortunate he didn't have a proper father and brothers to set a good example for him. He was simply following in his family's immoral ways—a fate with which Cliff was too familiar. He bit his lip again.

"Bastard!" Tommy shouted, and shot simultaneously.

Cliff dodged behind the tree, his excellent reflexes keeping him alive once again. Regret might flow through his veins like wildfire on an open prairie, but he had enough desire to live to defend himself. Ears straining, he took aim and waited.

It wasn't long. Still wet behind the ears, the outlaw was too young, too impetuous for the jaded likes of an older, experienced man-hunter like himself. Tommy flung himself away from the cover of the cottonwood in a rolling tumble of arms and legs, bringing up his gun to fire at Cliff, who quickly discharged his own weapon.

An unholy scream of pain echoed through Cliff's ears as a bullet whizzed past two inches from his head. He stumbled toward Tommy, who writhed on the ground, clutching at his belly, the metallic smell of blood permeating the air.

Cliff froze in his tracks, his stance stiff and uncompromising. His jaw tightened as he battled to keep down the nausea. Goddammit! He'd gut-shot the boy. He wouldn't wish such an agonizing death on his worst enemy or the vilest criminal. But Tommy's roll had thrown Cliff's usually flawless aim askew.

"Help me, Baldwin. You gotta help me." The boy's ragged voice reflected his tremendous pain, his blue eyes pleading as they looked toward his executioner. Blood covered the front of his shirt and the top of his pants, seeping through the fingers clutching at his bowels. *He doesn't even have enough hair on his face to shave!*

"God, I'm sorry, kid. Why didn't you just give up? It didn't have to be this way."

"Finish it, damn you."

Cliff bowed his head. It was the only way. There was nothing even the most gifted surgeon could do for a gut-shot wound inflicted at such close range. But his hand wavered, his determination faltering.

"D-damn your soul to hell forever, Bayou Baldwin, if . . . if you don't . . . do it now!" The garbled whisper of anguish ended in a groan as Tommy bent double, blood oozing to the ground.

Cliff fired straight at Tommy's heart. Truth was, Bayou Baldwin's soul was already damned to hell. It would take an angel to save him now. But miracles were for fools, and angels weren't strong enough to survive life on earth.

New Orleans, Ten Days Later

His informant had finally found Cliff.

As the man snatched the letter off the silver salver, his hurried movement knocked over a Tiffany ashtray. It thudded softly as it hit the thick Turkish carpet. Barely registering the fluttering spray of gray cigar ash littering the floor, or the servant silently cleaning it up, he slit the Texas-postmarked envelope and withdrew a newspaper clipping. The loud, rustling sound of the paper in his trembling hands grated on him, so he slammed it quiet against the desk. "Bayou Baldwin Saves Us Again!" was printed in big, bold headlines across the front page of *The Dallas Enquirer* dated a week earlier.

Taking a swig of bourbon, he savored the sensation of liquid fire coating his insides. A feral smile split his face. Who'd have thought his informant would uncover information so quickly? The smile faded, however, as he read.

Legendary bounty hunter "Bayou" Baldwin today brought in those nefarious criminals the Yancey brothers. Once again he has protected the good citizens of Dallas and northeast Texas from outlaws who kill our men, defile our women, and terrorize our children. Relentlessly and courageously, he tracks and captures bank robbers, cattle rustlers, thieves, and murderers. His pursuit of justice is second only to his quest for honor.

The Yancey brothers have spread terror for thirteen months, showing no mercy to anyone standing in their way. They have killed young and old alike, in ways too graphic to be described in a family newspaper. Six months ago, they robbed a train twenty miles east of Dallas, killing sixteen people on board, including the conductor and engineer, eight other men, four women, and two children—the youngest just fourteen months old. Survivors reported hearing the outlaw who shot the baby say that if the mother couldn't shut her up, then he would do it for her.

But insatiable greed took the brothers too far. A large reward was offered for their capture, dead or alive, and every bounty hunter and many law officials from three states set out to bring in the evil trio. The crafty criminals eluded the posses, however, until the most daring, bravest, and most remorseless man of all joined the hunt.

Bayou Baldwin cornered the men at their hideout north of Tyler. Reports say he and his partner, Shane Chandler, tracked the man-wolves to their lair, where they set a trap and snared the vermin. Two of the brothers were brought in alive. The third and youngest criminal lay face-down across the saddle of his horse. He will be buried in a nameless grave in unconsecrated ground—a just punishment for such an evil soul. The two older brothers await trial and then timely execution.

Who is this man Bayou Baldwin, our hero? His past is shrouded in mystery, and this reporter found no one to confirm any of the various stories surrounding his identity. Some say he is the son of a plantation owner who lost the family fortune during the War. Others say he left home after an altercation with his father, a corrupt carpetbagger. One informant was sure he hailed from New Orleans, where he attended university. He befriends Indians, half-breeds, prostitutes, and righteous men alike, but lives the life of a homeless wanderer.

Wherever you are, we, the good citizens of Dallas, salute you, Bayou Baldwin! May God reward your soul for your glorious heroism on this earth. May all the sweet innocents rest soundly in their beds knowing Bayou Baldwin is on the job.

With an angry snarl, the man crumpled the article in a tight ball and hurled it across the study, watching it roll into a corner. The sweet taste of victory was within his grasp, yet Fate insisted on playing her defiant games. "Bayou" Baldwin would *not* deny him—only force him to devise a stronger plan. He chuckled under his breath. He'd always been good at devising a plan. Real good. Clifford U. Baldwin *the Third* owed him. He could either return to New Orleans . . . or die.

Chapter One

Lost Soul Angelfood Cake: This light but flavorful cake will fill you with heaven's grace and hope. A simple but proven recipe.
From the *Sinfully Delicious Bakery Recipe Book*

Las Almas Perdidas, Texas, July 1880

She was alive. At least for the moment.

As she strode past the doors of a white-clapboarded Protestant church, Kyra Lourdes made the sign of the cross and kissed her rosary, uttering a soft prayer to the Virgin Mary for her miracle of deliverance.

She'd escaped unaided from her vicious fiancé. Now all she had to do was find the man she hoped would save her. She'd seen too much to risk going back alone.

Stopping to survey the drab, simple town, Kyra wrinkled her nose and heaved a weary sigh. The smell of dirt and refuse made her skin crawl. A bath would be wonderful. Her hurried flight across hundreds of miles and the peculiarity of both her surroundings and the people she'd encountered since entering Texas also made her uncomfortable. Without Grandpère's excellent training, she'd never have made it this far.

Determined, she once again marched down the dusty boardwalk until she saw the big Victorian house sitting at the edge of town. The gentleman she'd stopped with her inquiry had given her excellent directions. She still didn't understand the stunned look that had crossed his face when she'd asked where *Madame* Lucy lived. After all, this home was where the sheriff had suggested she would find Cliff Baldwin.

The setting sun dappled a rosy glow over the pale-pink two-story house. It had a wide front porch that ran around three sides and beckoned the visitor to come and linger in its cool shade. It was the perfect picture of domestic bliss.

Kyra gulped, a shiver running down her spine. A twinge of longing twisted her empty stomach. She visualized a large family and their daily life in such a home. They would enjoy delicious meals at the dinner table as they chatted about their day. Later they'd sit on the front porch swing and converse with passing neighbors. There would be children running and playing in the backyard, and a mother and father would share the bounty of their love for each other with all of them.

Beneath her skirts, she stamped her calf-high, kid-leather boots. What she wouldn't give to have such a life, such a home, that feeling of pure love and acceptance, of sharing and creating together with an adoring husband.

Kyra pursed her lips. Many of her mother's friends would say she'd been given ample opportunity to achieve her dream. They badgered her for being too persnickety, as well as too flamboyant and wild in her ways. But they didn't understand. She knew what she wanted, and she'd tried hard to find it by following her mother's guidance. She just hadn't succeeded. The men her mother chose for her left her feeling empty and alone, with a frustrated desire for more, or for something she'd once had, driving her to escape before her dream suffered a permanent death.

Stuffing her rosary back in her pocket, she shrugged loose her tense shoulders and lifted her chin. The fog of fear she'd lived in the past few days had retreated as she'd drawn closer to her goal. Unwittingly, she'd left the old Kyra behind and started a new life. She'd decide for herself from now on. *Please, God.*

Blowing a tendril of hair out of her eye, she ascended the steps leading to the front door. She paused before knocking. As she smoothed the heavy mass of dark hair back into the chignon at the base of her neck, she also adjusted her hat with its wilted feather plume, then fluffed the skirts of her green velvet riding habit, which clung to her legs. Then she bit her lips and pinched her cheeks for some added color. Drawing gloves out of her reticule, she slipped them back over her hands. Earlier she'd removed them before they'd turned entirely brown from all the dust she'd encountered in her travels. Now, however, she wanted to appear her best as she presented herself to *Madame* Lucy and a surprised Cliff. With her lacy handkerchief, she wiped the film of moisture beading her forehead and the nape of her neck.

Someone cracked a window to her right, and loud laughter and jumbled conversation spilled from within. Kyra worried her lip at the thought of interrupting what sounded like a dinner party, but she had to find Cliff.

She removed her matching parasol from underneath her arm, then pointing the tip on the floor, leaned on it slightly to present as refined a picture as possible.

She rapped on the knocker and waited. A muscular, rough-looking man opened the door. Instantly, his eyes widened in astonishment—just like the previous gentleman from whom she'd inquired directions. Her hand went to her hair, inspecting her chignon. Had she not wiped all the dust from her face? Did her clothes appear too travel-weary? Her riding habit was the height of fashion, but with all the dust Mr. Pip had turned up, well, it did look sad at the moment.

Deliberately she calmed her hands and tilted her chin. She was a Lourdes after all, and her mother had trained her well. This man certainly couldn't be the master of the house, dressed in dirty denims and a stained shirt. He didn't look like a butler either, but she'd already borne witness to the fact that Texans had many unusual customs.

Replacing her parasol under her arm, she held out her calling card to the waiting man, whose gaze was fixed somewhere below her face. "Hello, sir, my name is Kyra Dawson Lourdes of New Orleans. I'm so sorry to intrude upon *Madame* Lucy and her family without an invitation, especially as it sounds as if she's entertaining. But Sheriff Overby told me that a good friend of mine is possibly visiting with *Madame* Lucy this evening, and I was hoping to speak with him. Would you be so kind as to present my card to *Madame* and request a moment of her time?"

Actually the sheriff had also mentioned the Rabid Wolf Saloon, but Kyra had preferred seeking Cliff at a family home first, rather than venture into a disreputable-sounding establishment. She'd never known Cliff to drink anyway.

The butler finally recovered his voice. "You wanting to talk with Lucy?" He squinted and took her card, turning it over in his stubby fingers as though he didn't know quite what to do with it. "Are you sure of that?" His dark eyes twinkled with laughter as he scratched the top of his balding head.

"Yes, sir, I am. I do hate to interrupt *Madame* Lucy's dinner party, but I must find my friend Mr. Baldwin."

The butler choked. "You can't mean Cliff Baldwin, can you? You're looking for *the* Cliff Baldwin?"

"Yes, I am, sir." She restrained her desire to tap her foot. How many times had her mother drilled into her head that foot-tapping was simply not ladylike? *And you look like a common Cajun when you cross your arms over your chest.* She dropped her arms, reclaiming her parasol, as the remembered phrase breezed through her mind.

She didn't understand why the butler didn't do his job and present her card to his mistress. Why did he keep asking all these questions? He must be a long-time family servant to refer to his mistress by her given name. But when in Rome, do as the Romans do. She would try to adapt to these strange Western customs during the short time she was here.

"All right, missy, hold on one moment and I'll go get her ladyship," he managed to spout between loud guffaws of laughter. He shut the door in her face as he went to fetch his mistress.

"Oh, my word, she couldn't actually be a lady! Why, Sheriff Overby called her *Madame* Lucy. He didn't hint to me that there was an English title in the family!" Kyra muttered under her breath as she drew herself up a little taller and swiped the dust from her face and clothes that the butler had found so shocking. Her *grandmère* had been of the English nobility as well, and always had a strong aversion to dirt.

As the door swung open again, a wave of musky perfume tickled her nose and a tall, buxom, middle-aged woman appeared. Kyra pasted on her most charming, refined smile and dropped into an elegant curtsy that her mother had made her practice for hours before being introduced to the new Queen of Spain—Maria Cristina of Austria—during their tour. As she rose, she nearly gasped at the color of the gown Lady Lucy wore. Kyra had never seen such a shocking shade of red and, well, now that her gaze was a little higher, she blushed over Lady Lucy's décolletage. Why, her nipples practically showed! Finally, Kyra's view leveled on Lucy's face—she'd absolutely never seen so much makeup on any lady of quality, even on the servants and shopkeepers. Why, Lady Lucy was positively a painted lady!

A slight look of derision, quickly concealed, crossed Lucy's face. Gulping, Kyra closed her mouth and straightened her spine. She would *not* be so vulgar as to gape or make comment.

"Bon soir, madame—" she began in French, but Lady Lucy held out her hand and interrupted her.

"I don't speak French."

Kyra's brow creased in bewilderment. "Oh, pardon me. Good evening, Lady Lucy. Please forgive my intrusion while you're entertaining. Sheriff Overby, who sent me to you, gave me no idea you were in the middle of a dinner party. I'm in search of a dear friend of mine, Mr. Clifford U. Baldwin the Third. Sheriff Overby told me he might be visiting in your home. May I have a moment of his time without disturbing your other guests?" She was so pleased she'd gotten through her little speech without disgracing herself that she again gave Lady Lucy her most gracious smile.

"You wanting Cliff, you say?" Lucy's solemn face revealed no emotion.

Kyra's usual intuition seemed to have deserted her. "Yes, my lady, I would like him to know I've arrived." *Please let that sound like Cliff is expecting me.*

"Come on in," Lady Lucy stepped back, allowing Kyra to enter. The butler hovered in the background watching them, his eyes alight with amusement. Kyra lifted her chin a notch higher.

"If you'll wait right here, I'll fetch Cliff for you," Lady Lucy said. "Don't move from this spot."

Kyra did detect some emotion in Lady Lucy's eyes with that emphasized statement, but it was a tangle too difficult for her to comprehend at the moment.

Many times Cliff had looked at her just as cryptically—his private emotions buried beneath his calm exterior. Only the slightest flickering in his eyes had ever given him away, and then only to her. Maybe that was why she'd always delighted in shocking him out of his composure.

She suppressed a small smile, remembering the time she'd put a tadpole in his lemonade. It had been painful holding back the bubbling laughter as Cliff's eyes widened at the sight of the little black amphibian swimming among the ice. His face had remained unchanged for a full moment. Then he'd burst out laughing, and pulling the tadpole out of his drink, had come chasing after her to toss it down the back of her dress. She'd been so delighted she'd finally made him laugh that she hadn't minded how the slimy thing tickled her spine, even after it landed in her drawers.

Warmth spread through her as she grinned at the memory. Kyra pictured Cliff, his black wavy hair and clear blue eyes—his smile, rare and reserved for her, face shining with pleasure. Her heart beat wildly and her palms felt clammy. She'd see him again . . . *any second now.*

Yes, she'd come to Texas looking for a man—and not just any man from what she'd heard. Cliff Baldwin, it seemed, had earned his reputation as a dangerous, relentless bounty hunter, and was now a rancher, or so she'd been told. Most of the rumors she'd picked up about him were very unflattering. In fact, some she'd questioned had suggested she'd do well to avoid him. But she wouldn't listen to any of them. Even though she hadn't seen Cliff in seven years, he was still her friend, and nothing he'd done would shock her or make her think less of him.

Rose watched as Cliff Baldwin rolled over and sat up naked in the bed. He stared at her, waiting.

Throwing aside her shimmering pink robe, she stood beside the bed in her low-cut shift. She slumped her shoulders so her rouged nipples peeked between strands of her blond hair. Most men liked that sort of thing.

"I haven't seen you in a while, sugar," she purred.

"Just got back from taking my cattle to market. My men went over to the Rabid Wolf, but I wanted something more . . . satisfying." He pushed up against the pillows, crooking his finger at her.

"Well, I'm glad you got here early."

He winked. "Why waste my time on drink when I can enjoy a pretty wild thing like you?"

Rose shivered. Cliff Baldwin was pure Texas man—a living legend with cold blue eyes and long black hair. She eyed the ragged scar on his cheek. He was dangerous. She liked that in a man. Her gaze dragged over his long, dark legs. He was taller than most, with a wide chest tapering off to lean hips. He was sleek and dark. He was magnificent. Her gaze veered lower and she moistened her lips.

He almost made whoring worthwhile . . . *almost.*

Slowly, Rose pulled off her loosened shift, rotating her slim hips to slide it down her legs. It pooled in a puddle of satin on the floor. She stepped out of it and made her way toward him. His wicked smile sent a thrill through her body, spreading slowly, hot moisture gathering between her legs.

They'd said little since he'd swaggered in, his husky voice hinting at a faint Southern accent, suggestive and heated. It contrasted with his cool, aloof image. The few beads of sweat on his forehead gave him away. He was more affected by the show she provided than he let on. Then again, he rarely revealed anything of a personal nature to her during their times together. But she'd long understood he was a lonely man—maybe because they shared loneliness in common.

She watched his eyes savor her as she straddled his legs, his gaze running the whole length of her with mocking slowness before he took hold of her arms and pulled her to him. Her breasts felt full and heavy, the nipples erect with anticipation as he scooped up one and lowered his mouth to a rouged tip, laving her.

She knew the game he liked to play. She'd be passionate, and he'd be in control. Fortunately, it was a game she'd learned to play well.

Leaning slightly on her parasol to help hold her tired weight, Kyra glanced around Lady Lucy's home, or at least what she could see from her vantage point in the entry hall. Weariness taxed her mind, and the thick smell of tobacco gave her a headache. She pointedly ignored the butler. He hovered in the doorway of the room to her right, his gaze darting back and forth between her and the raucous guests in the adjoining room. Something wasn't quite right, but her tired brain could focus only on finding Cliff.

She looked up the elegantly curved stairwell in front of her. The mahogany balustrade gleamed, and the face of a roaring lion was carved in the elaborate newel post. She couldn't see much upstairs, except a couple of doors that opened off both sides of a hallway. Hearing girlish laughter coming from some of the rooms, she grinned. Some of Lady Lucy's young dinner guests must be gossiping and repairing their appearance in the bedrooms. She remembered many such scenes from her own experience.

Trying to distract herself from the worry gnawing at her gut, Kyra stepped toward the dimly lit room to her left. The door was wide open and no one was inside. It appeared to be an entertainment room. The candles in the wall sconces gave a soft pink glow. She'd never seen sconces that cast such a pretty colored light. Entranced, she studied the stage at the far end of the room and the piano in the back corner. Chairs were scattered throughout. Obviously Lady Lucy must not have planned entertainment, or the room would be orderly.

The butler finally left her alone, vanishing into the salon. She inched over there and peeked through the cracked door. This was the room from which all the voices came. She'd heard Texans were a rowdy bunch who enjoyed themselves without inhibitions. It must be true because their laughter and loud shouts were definitely not as refined as the sounds from her mother's home when she entertained. The same soft pink sconces lighted this room. She squinted to see better.

Oh, my! The artwork on the opposite wall caught her attention immediately. Was that a picture of three nude women draped over a reclining man? Of course she'd seen plenty of nude paintings and statues in museums on her travels through Europe before her chaperone could whisk her away, but these figures were grotesque rather than classical. And, goodness, certain body parts were greatly enlarged. What *were* they doing? The man had one of the ladies' breasts in his mouth while he caressed the second lady. As for the third lady—why, it couldn't be, could it? Could that last woman actually have her mouth around the man's unmentionable?

As she bit her tongue to hold back a gasp, Kyra's astonished gaze swung to the dinner guests. There were at least twelve people. They weren't dressed in any sort of formal attire at all, and each man had his arm around a woman who wore—my heavens, it couldn't be! Why, *they were only wearing their underclothes.* The ladies were practically naked and swinging their blessings all over the place, out in full view for any man to see and touch. She gasped. One man's hand completely covered his partner's naked breast while another had a lady pinned against the wall. Kyra jumped back and inched toward the front door.

She wasn't going to wait around and see what other strange customs these Texans had.

Doing as the Romans do had just gone a bit too far!

Cliff lay back on the bed, his arm over his eyes, as Rose performed her ablutions behind a white cloth screen. Out of all the girls at Lucy's, Rose was the most passionate. But he still felt empty.

He sighed restlessly. It was time to go. His muscles groaned in complaint as he stretched his legs toward the foot of the bed. He winced, thinking of the hour ride to his ranch following such a long trail ride. At least he was going home with a profit this time. Pride straightened his shoulders as he remembered how he'd left New Orleans with nothing. He slumped slightly. If his next drive didn't go even better than this one, he might face the prospect of poverty again.

Searching for his clothes, he slid his legs over the bed. He'd just finished dressing when a pair of slim arms twined around his waist from behind.

"Don't wait too long before you come back for a visit now," Rose murmured throatily.

Cliff clasped Rose's hands, breaking her hold. "I won't."

He grabbed his gun belt off the nightstand, fastened it around his waist, and picked up his hat. He nodded to Rose, and was heading for the door when someone pounded on it.

"Cliff, finish up and get on out here. You got trouble!" Lucy's irate voice came through loud and clear.

He jerked open the door. "What's wrong, Lucy? I didn't tire out your best girl," he said, a half grin on his face. Behind him Rose snorted.

"There's a *lady* downstairs looking for you. She presented me with her card." Lucy shoved it into his hand.

Miss Kyra Dawson Lourdes was embellished in green satin ink across the small calling card. It took a moment for the words to register, a vision flashing before his eyes of a young scamp in pigtails maturing into an impossible dream—a fantasy he'd finally put out of his mind. Kyra? Her name rolled softly in his mind, before realization struck. Oh, God, it couldn't be. She couldn't be here in Texas, in Las Almas Perdidas . . . in a whorehouse!

Cliff wrenched his gaze from the card. "Where is she?"

"I left her in the entry hall. I ordered her not to move, but you better hurry if you don't want no one to find her. Horace is with her, but he can't stop laughing and staring long enough to do his job. For some reason she thinks this is a family home, and that I'm a '*my lady.*'" But this was said to empty air, as Cliff was already halfway down the hall.

Kyra backed her way out of the house, trying not to be noticed by the butler, who still stood beyond the cracked door. She had a horrible feeling she was in one of *those* places. She was almost to the outside door, and blindly reached behind to turn the knob. Instead her hand encountered someone's coarse, rough, and warm clothing. Something moved! She gasped and whirled around. Surely she hadn't touched him there!

"Well, *wooee,* I sure do like the way you say hello!" The cowboy swung his hat off and stepped closer.

He had two companions with him. All three wore the same type of woolen, striped, dusty pants, like most of the men she'd encountered since crossing the border from Louisiana. They all had plain, dark shirts on, with vests but no ties, and bandannas around their necks. She'd dubbed this look the "Texas male uniform." Worse yet, their aroma hinted of several nights spent sleeping with cattle.

The one she'd touched also wore a huge smile on his face.

"You must be one of Lucy's new girls. I ain't seen you here before. You're a right friendly sort. Let me show you the way I like to say howdy." He swooped his face down to meet hers.

Kyra swung her parasol and clobbered the man on his head. "Don't touch me!" Unfortunately, the parasol opened and didn't deliver the mighty punch she'd desired.

"Well, why not? You touched me," the stranger said as he easily shoved her parasol out of his face.

"I'm very sorry. I didn't mean to—touch you, I mean. I was just leaving. I must have gotten my directions wrong. I'm not supposed to be here."

"You sure are a pretty little thing. Why don't you stay and play a little while? I'm Edgar Easley and these are my brothers Elton and Eugene," Edgar said as he gestured at his companions. "We'd like to get to know you better. We don't mind sharing."

The two other brothers eagerly nodded as they surrounded her, pushing in closer. They all looked alike, with long, unkempt brown hair, handlebar mustaches, and dark, leathery skin.

Blood surged through Kyra's veins, and her heart pounded in her ears. The parasol wouldn't do her any good against three grown men. She threw it on the floor and whipped out her derringer from the pocket of her riding habit, ripping the velvet in the process. "Don't move any closer or I'll shoot. And don't think I won't. My *grandpère* was a riverboat gambler, and taught me how to use this thing."

"And if she can't manage it, I can," a menacing voice said from the top of the stairs.

Kyra turned to look, keeping her gun aimed at the brothers. "Cliff!"

She stiffened. *My Lord! How he's changed.* He was so much larger, more rugged, more of a man . . . her heart lodged somewhere near her throat and she couldn't breathe. But he barely looked her way as he descended the stairs, his gun trained on the three Easleys.

"Edgar, Elton, Eugene—I think you boys had better back up now, real slow, and don't make any moves I might misunderstand," Cliff said as he approached. "This lady here is a friend of mine, and I wouldn't want to see you doing anything you might regret."

"Hell, Baldwin, we didn't mean no harm. She grabbed hold of Edgar here as he came in the door, and we thought she was one of Lucy's new girls."

That must have been Elton who spoke, but it could have been Eugene. There wasn't enough difference to tell.

"Just back on out the door. You can come through after we leave." Cliff gave the command in a soft but steely voice.

Grabbing Kyra's arm in a viselike grip, he turned to Lucy. "I'd appreciate it if you'd keep my friend's arrival here tonight a secret, Lucy. I hope I can trust you."

Lucy inclined her head slightly, and Cliff turned his attention to the three brothers.

"And boys, if I hear a word about my friend's presence here at Madam Lucy's, rest assured I'll know who started the rumor."

The three *boys* blanched at his soft-spoken warning and backed further out the door. "No, no, we won't say nothing, will we, Edgar, Elton? We didn't see nothing. We don't know nothing. You can count on us." Eugene had found his voice at last.

"Fine, just fine. Now excuse me, men." Cliff's palm, large and warm against Kyra's back, guided her out the door.

As he started down the steps with her, Kyra remembered her manners. She stopped abruptly—forcing Cliff to halt as well, turned back to Lady Lucy standing at the door, and said, "Thank you for your help finding my friend. I'm sorry to leave so soon. But if I can ever be of service to you, please let me know." Cliff abruptly covered her mouth with his hand and practically dragged her out onto the street.

Rebelliously she bit his finger, forcing him to turn her loose. She whirled to face Lucy. "And would you please tell me where you buy those wonderful pink sconces?"

Chapter Two

Surprising Gingerbread: A cake that's sugar and spice, everything *not* so nice. At first taste it's maddeningly ginger hot, but goes down as sweet as brown sugar. From the *Sinfully Delicious Bakery Recipe Book*

Cliff held on to Kyra's arm, hauling her toward the center of town, forcing her to keep up with him.

"Why are you in Las Almas? And what the *hell* were you doing in a place like Madam Lucy's?" Cliff had a hard time believing his eyes. He'd gotten the wind knocked out of him, first from seeing her pointing her small derringer while surrounded by the Easleys, and then from finding her all grown up.

Glancing over at her a moment, he took a calming breath. She pulled against his hold, her face flushed and her jaw set mulishly.

He stopped, still gripping her arm, and sighed. "Are you going to answer me?"

"If you've finished yelling at me and dragging me everywhere, then perhaps I will." Her cat-green eyes flashed. "You aren't behaving at all like a gentleman." She shook her arm out of his grasp and crossed it with her other over her chest.

His gaze followed. The full breasts she'd inadvertently thrust upward surprised him. She'd filled out the last few years, he noted as he took in the soft curves of her slim hips.

"Well?" she prodded. Her exasperation drew his eyes back to her flushed face.

"If you wanted to talk to a proper gentleman, then you should have stayed in New Orleans," he finally answered.

He narrowed his eyes, watching as she straightened her backbone and lifted her head in defiance. She'd lost her hat, her chignon spilling out glossy chestnut hair, when he'd pulled her forcefully away from Madam Lucy's. The heavy tresses cascaded in long wavy locks around her small waist, and gentle wisps of hair, yearning to be tucked behind a delicate ear, curled around her warm face. The familiar olive-skinned features and high cheekbones bespoke her Spanish and French heritage, and when she spoke, the tempting mole next to her mouth beckoned a man's eyes to her full lips.

She'd turned into a belle, not that he was surprised. The fiery little girl he remembered had emerged from her cocoon as a lovely young woman—albeit a dusty young woman. Warmth surged through his body, and his heart quickened. *Not again! He wouldn't let her drive him loco this time.*

"Well, I see I made a mistake to think you'd be pleasantly surprised to see me, so I'll just be on my way," she said.

The droop of her lips and shoulders tugged at his heart as she moved to make her way around him.

"Hell." He grabbed her elbow and pulled her along behind him, searching for a private place to talk. He couldn't remember the last time he'd been so close to losing his control. He'd always prided himself on his ability to maintain order and restraint. It was how he stayed focused and sane, and in part, was also the reason he stayed away from alcohol.

He swore beneath his breath. He hadn't felt like this since he was twenty. Shouldn't he be immune by now?

Trouble. That was all her presence in Las Almas could mean. What sort of madness had brought Kyra Dawson

Lourdes, a lady he thought he'd completely put out of his life years ago, here to this half-assed cowpunching town?

He'd managed only a few yards when she snatched her hand out of his grasp and stopped, one boot slamming with a thud on the boardwalk. "What's wrong with you, Cliff? You're dragging me like a rag doll, talking vulgar. Have you lost your manners?"

Cliff was about to respond to Kyra's accusation when he noticed the town's bakery shop behind her. A fluke really, it catered to the wives and mothers of Las Almas, who'd increased in number in the last three years—along with the churches and schools.

It was rumored that the two women who'd started the business had deliberately located it so closely to the Wolf and Lucy's in order to discreetly keep an eye on the comings and goings from the saloon and whorehouse. Any husband who entered those doors found an angry wife at home when he returned. The wives sure had perfected the small-town grapevine. Thank heaven he didn't have a wife.

Cliff returned his gaze to Kyra. She wore her "riled up" look—her right foot tapping away and her arms crossed in front of her. He couldn't help a low chuckle as he recalled this exact same expression on her face the day he'd teased her mercilessly about how she threw a baseball. She'd not been pleased at all with his comment that she threw like a blasted girl, and had practiced for hours to prove him wrong. Pursing his lips to contain his smile, he gestured with his head toward the bakery. "Come on, Kyra, let's go in there and have a talk."

Placing a hand at her back to push her forward, he strode through the doors of the Café. The smell of fresh-baked breads and spicy ginger made his stomach growl. He pulled out a chair for Kyra and eased himself into one across a small table, half expecting the delicate chair to crash to the floor.

Out of habit, he scanned the frilly room. There were a few other tables, all adorned with flowered tablecloths. He and Kyra were the only customers.

He removed his hat as a pleasant-looking woman approached the table from behind the back counter.

"What may I serve you, sir, ma'am?"

"We'll each have a lemonade and gingerbread," he answered, scanning the hand-printed menu she'd handed him.

While Cliff ordered, Kyra busied herself with restoring her hair to its proper chignon, all the while peering from her lowered lashes at the man before her. Her irritation and disappointment had dissipated to uneasiness—her stomach churning at the prospect of having to converse with this man she no longer knew. The years gone by hadn't seemed long enough to change a person so drastically—at least *she* hadn't changed that much.

The sting of tears threatened. Had she traveled all this way to entrust her life to a stranger? One who probably wished she'd stayed in New Orleans? He'd chosen to leave her and his home years ago, but she'd still expected him to be pleased to see her. Kyra was certain now, for all the excuses she'd ever made up on Cliff's behalf, that he'd never sent word of his new life because that was the way he preferred it.

She also had trouble reconciling his appearance with her memory of him. The short wavy black hair he once wore now descended in straight locks to his shoulders. He'd always been tall, but now he seemed huge, his upper body wider, more muscular. She observed the muscles in his thighs bulging against his tight jeans as he fidgeted on the chair. Blushing, Kyra quickly returned her scrutiny to his face, which was darkened by the sun, making him all the more intimidating. He still had the scar at the corner of his eye, but there was a newer one, longer and more ragged, stretching halfway across his left cheek. *How had he acquired it?* Really, the only familiar thing about him was the color of his eyes—the clearest blue.

The waitress left, and he once again pinned Kyra with his stare, making her feel even more frazzled. She dug deep for some bravado, seeking the right words.

"Hell, Kyra, I didn't mean to shout at you earlier." He leaned forward, taking her hands in his.

His big work-roughened palms felt foreign to her. Then he released them.

"You surprised me." he leaned back on his chair, his fingers raking through his ink-black hair. "When I saw you at Madam Lucy's, surrounded by the Easley brothers, I lost control. I'm afraid you got the worse end of my temper. I'm sorry."

Kyra was about to smile when he started in on her again. "Do you know what sort of place Madam Lucy's is? Do you have any idea what you walked into there?"

She was afraid she had a very good idea, but it was just too horrible to contemplate. She much preferred succumbing to safer naïveté. "Why, I know they have some very unusual customs. I did take a peek into the salon when the butler wasn't paying attention. I've never seen dresses so, well, uh, open and short, and women so, um, friendly. I could even see their blessings hanging out!" This last was whispered in embarrassment. "*Madame* Lucy is a lady . . . isisn't she?"

"Hell, right she's a lady—the *head lady of the evening* for these parts. It's Madam Lucy, not *Madame*. You just walked into Las Almas's best, and only, whorehouse."

Whorehouse! Her fears confirmed, the red heat of embarrassment crawled over Kyra's neck and face. She tried to lift her eyebrows haughtily while looking down her nose at Cliff, who thoroughly enjoyed her discomfort, mocking humor lighting his eyes and a half grin splitting his face. But all that came out was, "It crossed my mind that-that it was a . . . you know . . . but I . . . I didn't want to believe. . . . You can't mean I walked into one of those places! Why, I *never* . . ." Kyra whispered, glancing at the waitress.

"Yes, you did. You walked into a brothel, a crib, a sporting house, a palace of sinful pleasure, a—" He stopped when she slammed her hand over his mouth, shutting off his words as the waitress neared the table with their order.

When the waitress was safely back behind the counter, Kyra responded, "All right, I understand. But honestly, Cliff, I had no idea. I mean the sheriff, as well as a nice gentleman I met at his office named Luke, and the others—they didn't tell me what *Madame* . . . I mean, Madam Lucy's was. I thought she was French and assumed it was a family home. Why, it's such a pretty house with that nice wide front porch and pretty pink sconces. And her butler called her his ladyship. How was I to know? Besides, I was too tired to think clearly."

Cliff guffawed. He sounded as though he hadn't laughed in years, his voice raspy and low. "Horace isn't a butler. He's Lucy's guard." Kyra rose an eyebrow in question and he explained further. "He, um, he throws the men out if they happen to get a little too rowdy, or if um . . ." He sighed as he searched for the words.

He didn't seem particularly eager to explain what sort of things went on in a place like Lucy's, and she probably didn't want to know anyway.

She watched him as he looked away a moment and then back at her. "What are you doing here, Kyra, and why were you looking for me? Did something happen at home?"

His tenor was soft now, persuasive. When he spoke to her this way, he reminded her of the gentle and caring friend he'd once been. Oh, he'd changed. The fine-boned gentleman she'd known was now a big cowboy, emphasized by his attire—a blue chambray shirt and snug Levi's. But it was more than physical. He'd obviously seen a lot in the last seven years. She saw it in the depth of his eyes. Wildness lingered there, mingled with . . . sadness perhaps, or loneliness. But nonetheless, deep inside he was still Cliff, her childhood friend. *He had to be.*

"Yes, I-I needed to find you," she finally answered, "and, well, it's a long story. I'd prefer not to discuss it here." Now that she felt safer, with Cliff's presence, she wanted to delay the moment of reckoning. She wasn't sure how this new Cliff would react to the story she had to tell.

She squirmed in her chair, observing him with trepidation. She saw the questions racing through his mind. Before he could ask her to elaborate, she interrupted him.

"Would you tell me what you've been doing these last few years?"

He didn't seem pleased by the change in conversation. "Oh, this and that, nothing much."

She frowned, "Really?"

In the silence that followed, Kyra sensed a lock inside Cliff being clicked firmly in place.

"Really," he finally responded.

"Would you like to know what I've heard?" She sipped daintily on her lemonade. Its tart sweetness revitalized her senses, mingling with the excitement of Cliff's nearness.

"Not particularly." He shifted in his chair.

Kyra leaned over the table. "Why, you're positively a legend, Cliff—a fast-gun bounty hunter . . . the best until you quit, they say. Some people don't seem to like you much, though, and they gave me a deuce of a time getting information on your whereabouts. Why, I remember two distasteful men in Dallas calling you several vile names I wouldn't dare repeat." Seeing his unemotional response changed her mind. "All right. They called you a snake, a son of a . . . a loose woman, a piece of cow patty, a—"

"Tsk, tsk." Cliff grabbed his lemonade and thrust a huge hunk of cake in his mouth. Swallowing, he said, "I see you've learned some colorful language in the time you've been in Texas. What would people back home say?" he added in feigned dismay. "I don't want to talk about this, all right?"

Frowning, he took a long drink, set the glass down, and leaned forward. But before he could speak, Kyra glimpsed the same nice gentleman she'd mentioned to Cliff. Luke Hampton, a tall man dressed entirely in black from his leather boots to his bandanna, stepped through the doorway, removing his hat.

"Well, there you are, miss. I was walking by outside when I saw you through the window. I see you found your man." He nodded in Cliff's direction. "Baldwin."

"Hampton." His tone was soft but steely. "You met Miss Lourdes at the sheriff's office?"

"Yes, when she came asking for you. I'd intended to go look for you while she waited with Sheriff Overby, but . . ."

"Why didn't you? She marched right on in at Lucy's."

"Cliff!" Kyra intruded. "Mr. Hampton was very gallant, offering to locate you for me, but, well, I hoped to surprise you." Actually she'd been determined that she was *not* going to miss seeing his shock by sending someone else to fetch him. "Mr. Hampton, the sheriff, and a couple of other men were in the middle of a card game. I slipped out when one of the men palmed an ace and Mr. Hampton caught him."

Luke smiled, but quickly turned his attention back to Cliff. "I wasn't sure where she went as Overby mentioned both the Rabid Wolf and Lucy's to her. I set out after her right away, but checked the Wolf first."

The explanation seemed to suit Cliff. He let his scowl fade and nodded.

"I appreciate your concern, sir," Kyra declared. Really, they needn't talk about her as if she weren't there. "But as you can see, I've found Mr. Baldwin." She placed her hand in Luke's in appreciation. He was handsome with auburn hair and classical features, and Kyra smiled up at him.

Luke colored slightly, shook her hand, and dropped it. "Anytime, miss. Since you're in good hands, I'll be off now." He put his hat back on, tipped it in her direction, and left the Café.

Cliff had suppressed an unreasonable urge to snatch Kyra's hand out of Luke's. Keeping his face composed, he shot up from his chair. She had some explaining to do, and the sooner he got her to his ranch the better.

Replacing his hat on his head, he snapped, "It's getting dark, which tends to bring out no-good, two-legged creatures. We'll talk more at my ranch. Let's go to your hotel and pick up your things. I don't want you staying there alone."

Kyra started to speak, but Cliff was quick to grab hold of her by the elbow, lifting her out of the chair, as he placed a coin on the table. He nodded to the waitress, and sauntered out of the Café toward the Hacienda, the only decent hotel in town.

Kyra strode beside Cliff on the boardwalk, their footfalls and the creaking of wooden planks the only sound. He didn't look at her or speak as his glare shifted down an alley. People had emptied the streets, except for a few men. How many had headed to Madam Lucy's? She shivered and walked faster.

Kyra glanced again at Cliff. She needed to gain his attention.

"Cliff?"

"Yes."

"I'm not staying at a hotel."

He stopped in his tracks, eyebrows knitted. "And you are just now telling me this? Where are your things?"

"Well, I didn't have any"—she paused—"time . . . to get a room, and my things are . . . hidden."

Cliff puffed his cheeks and blew out softly. "You hesitated. What didn't you have, Kyra?" He surveyed their surroundings before returning his gaze to her.

As she chewed on her lip pondering her reply, she peered up at him through lowered lashes. He was eyeing her mouth with a look of yearning that confused her and made her stomach churn. Then the longing was gone, replaced by an indecipherable mask.

"Also, I don't like lies," he added, the black of his pupils intensified as if daring her to deny the fib.

Taking a breath to help steady her nerves, she looked down at her dirty green riding habit, pretending to be fascinated with the torn pocket. "Yes, well, you see I—I don't have any money."

"What?" Cliff gripped her hand and pulled her into the alley. "What do you mean you don't have any money? How the hell did you get here from Louisiana alone and without any money?" His voice was strained in his attempt not to shout.

Kyra stiffened her spine, pulling up her chin. "I *did* have money when I left home. In fact I bought myself a train ticket to Dallas . . . but there I . . . lost it." Cliff's left eye twitched. Quickly she added, "That's all part of the story I'm supposed to tell you at your ranch, remember?"

He gave a long sigh. "Why do I have a feeling I'm not going to like hearing this? Fine, so at least tell me how the blazes you got here after you *lost it.*"

Kyra blanched, feeling increasingly uneasy, her pulse jumping erratically. "Yes, well, as it turned out, I couldn't get on the stage in Dallas, and had to . . . ride here, *hence* the riding habit I'm wearing."

"You rode here by yourself? Do you realize that there are all sorts of dangers out there—animals, snakes, cattle rustlers, thieves . . . need I say more?"

"No!" she shouted back. "You needn't. I managed to get here, didn't I?" She stamped her foot, her arms crossed tightly across her chest.

Cliff lowered his voice. "By God, I hope your reasons are good for trotting off halfway across the country alone. I can't wait to hear what you have to say." He grabbed her elbow, pulling her out of the alley. "So where are we going? I assume you have a horse somewhere?"

Kyra hesitated. "Mr. Pip is tied up behind the livery."

"Mr. Pip?"

"Yes, Mr. Pip."

"Hell, I don't want to ask. Let's go." He led, or more precisely dragged, her toward the stables. "My horse is at the livery; we'll get him first."

Another minute passed, Kyra again struggling to match Cliff's long stride. The man was exasperating when he gave in to his temper. Well, she could give as good as she got. Maybe it was time she refreshed his memory. She'd wanted to bring it up anyway, and she'd always enjoyed shocking him.

"Cliff?"

"Yes."

Pulling on his elbow, she looked up at him. "Did you say you don't like lies?"

Her sugary-sweet tone got his attention. She was up to something.

"Yes, I did," he confirmed warily.

"What if it's a good lie, say, to avoid hurting someone's feelings?"

He turned to judge her disposition. She smiled that sly smile of hers. He'd seen it upon many occasions when they'd played chess, just before she shouted, "Checkmate."

"I think it's better to say it like it is," he said, forcing some conviction into his voice.

They continued their path to the livery. He saw the sky in the distance had finally turned black, the moon yet to show.

"Cliff?" She pulled his elbow harder.

"What?" he answered in his most exasperated tone, hoping to stop her from talking, which seemed impossible to do. He didn't remember her being such a magpie.

"I was thinking back to our meeting at Madam Lucy's and realized that you weren't in her salon. I did peek in there, and you *did* come from upstairs."

He glanced sideways at her as she peered up at him a little too innocently.

"I do believe I heard a few girls laughing upstairs. I wonder, what was so amusing, and what could you possibly have been doing?"

Cliff couldn't believe he actually felt himself flush. He opened his mouth, only to shut it again. He'd been with her less than an hour and already the reins of his control were slipping. It was like old times. Suddenly, he felt more lighthearted than he had in months. Tweaking her nose, he winked and said, "That's none of your business. Now hurry up, cat-eyes, it's getting late."

The pungent smell of horses, hay, leather, and sweat greeted them as they reached the livery stable. He introduced Kyra to his stallion, Blackjack, a name befitting his dark coat and frisky temperament. Blackjack tossed his head and reared back on his hind legs as Cliff pulled open the stall door.

"Calm down, you spoiled baby. I didn't leave you here alone that long. Besides, I know you were busy eyeing that pretty mare across the way the whole time." Cliff prepared him to ride.

"We're ready; now where's Mr. Pip?" He turned to Kyra, trying not to roll his eyes at the name. She pointed to a clump of black willow trees a short distance away.

Reaching the stand of trees on the banks of a gurgling stream, Cliff dismounted and made his way behind the foliage, stopping abruptly. "What the . . ." He turned to find Kyra behind him, biting on her cheek to keep from laughing. The scene was suddenly all too familiar.

"Kyra?" A hard edge laced his voice.

"Yes?" She broke into a big, bright smile.

"Do I not recall you being quite a good horsewoman, even at the age of fifteen?"

"Yes."

"So, tell me. Do you see the difference here between my animal and yours?" Cliff pointed between Blackjack and Mr. Pip.

"Yes, of course I do." She put her hands on her hips, no longer smiling.

He shifted his weight to his other leg, stabbing his finger toward Mr. Pip. "Then you realize that this Mr. Pip of yours is *not* a horse, but a goddamn *mule?*"

"My, Cliff," Kyra retorted, "I don't believe you used to get so angry all the time. Why you never . . . except for that last evening I saw y—" She halted.

Regret swept over him, strong and fierce. He brought his arm down in defeat, bent his head, and reached back to massage his neck. "I hoped you'd forgotten about that."

She whispered, "How could I? That was the same night I received my first kiss and you walked out of my life."

He couldn't help but look at her lips, her words evoking a sweet memory. It seemed he was about to apologize for the second time in one night. Amazing, considering that before today he couldn't remember the last time he'd done so. "I'm sorry. I don't mean to be angry. But the thought of you out there, all alone in the wilderness on nothing but a stubborn mule . . . God, Kyra, I don't think you realize how lucky you are, good shot or not."

"I'm sorry, too, but I can assure you Mr. Pip was a fine mount. As soon as he understood I cared for him, why, he was completely obedient." Again that ludicrous heartwarming smile lit up her features.

"He was, huh?" Cliff stated skeptically as he strode over to the mule and patted its neck. Mr. Pip tossed his head in appreciation, nuzzling him for more.

"Why, just this morning it was so hot he lagged behind, so I gave him some water and a hat, and he perked right up!"

"You gave him a hat?"

"Yes, see?" She pulled out of her saddlebags one of her fancy plumed French hats. "I fashioned two holes here for his ears. See?" She smiled at Cliff again—proud of what must have been an utterly ridiculous sight.

Obviously rustlers or thieves hadn't accosted her because they'd been too busy laughing their asses off.

"God, Kyra, I don't know if I should kiss you or put you over my knee. Let's get going before I do something we'll both regret." *Like kiss you . . . all over.* The thought brought a groan of surprise to his lips—surprise that Kyra could still drive him wild with desire. *Oh, yeah!* Seven years hadn't killed his lust after all.

But she deserved better—better than him.

"Come on, Squirt." He recalled his old nickname for her as he pulled her toward Mr. Pip's saddle. "We've got a ways to my ranch, and I can't wait to hear what you have to say. I especially want to know how you went from a train to a mule."

"My name is Kyra, not Squirt." She poked Cliff in his chest to emphasize her point. "I have never liked that nickname, and I do wish you wouldn't call me that now." She poked him once more to drive her point home.

A raspy laugh rumbled from the depths of his chest. "Kyra, honey, I sure have missed you." He wrapped her in a warm bear hug, then quickly released her to help her mount.

Kyra leaned down from her seat on Mr. Pip and stared Cliff in the eye with a devilish tilt to her lips. In a syrupy sweet voice, she said, "Cubby Bear, I sure have missed you, too." She patted his cheek, then kicked Mr. Pip into a fast trot down the road, her laughter floating behind her.

Cliff mumbled under his breath about stupid nicknames made from people's initials—which was why he'd never told anyone since Kyra that his middle name was Ulysses.

Chapter Three

Lucky #7 Ranch Soufflé: An unusual soufflé recipe in that it is considered good luck if it falls. But the taste is unexpectedly uplifting.
From the *Sinfully Delicious Bakery Recipe Book*

From a rise above Cliff's home, his ranch sprawled before her in the valley below. The moon had risen, giving enough light for her to see the outline of buildings, stable, and corral. It all appeared rustic to her untrained eye, but then everything she'd seen since leaving Dallas had looked rustic to her. The buildings were made of wood and stone with terra-cotta roofs. A few trees dotted the landscape, but mostly it was bare.

Kyra threw a sideways glance at Cliff. He'd removed his hat, and his dark hair glistened blue in the moonlight. He observed her carefully, as though gauging her reaction to his home.

"It's nothing like your plantation, Belle Celine, or the town house. I know it's not the luxury you're accustomed to."

Surprise lifted her eyebrows. *He was worried about what she would think.*

"I think it's wonderful, Cliff. It seems warm and inviting."

"It's called the Lucky Number Seven. I bought it last year when the owner decided to sell and move back East."

"What made him leave?"

"Maybe it was the long stretch of bad luck he had." At her laugh, Cliff expounded. "Really. He bought this place thinking to turn it into a resort and health spa after some old Indian told him there were healing hot springs on the place."

At his pause, Kyra prodded him. "Well, what happened?"

"Never could find any springs." His eyes twinkled as she laughed. "So then he decided to open up a rest stop and trading post for the cattle drives coming through."

"What happened to that plan?"

"There's no cattle trail anywhere close to here. Besides, most ranchers don't go so far to carry their cattle to market anymore with the railroad nearby."

"So how did he make a living?"

"Well, that's the thing. He never did. He ranched the place, but when one of his greenhorn friends planted locoweed on the rangeland and poisoned most of his cattle, he finally gave up."

Kyra laughed so hard her eyes watered. She wasn't sure what locoweed was, but she understood what had happened nevertheless. Cliff reached out and nudged her arm, bringing her attention back to him. She was surprised by the determined set to his face.

"One man's disaster is another man's blessing. The Lucky Number Seven is mine. I *will* make it a success."

As her agreement seemed important, she gave it quickly. "I'm sure you will."

He nodded. "I've got lots of men depending on me," he mumbled, his vision focused on his ranch. When his gaze returned to her, his shoulders straightened and his jaw tightened. "Over there are my stables and corral." He pointed to a large structure to their left and the fencing surrounding it. "To the right you can see the bunkhouse, chow hall, and barn. Straight ahead is my house." He hesitated a moment. "I do have two bedrooms."

Kyra bowed her head, a blush crawling hotly over her cheeks, her laughter forgotten. "Uh, I hadn't thought out the details. Is it, um, all right for me to stay with you? I mean, what will people say?"

"I just saw you at Madam Lucy's whorehouse, your gun cocked and your eyes blazing, and now you're hesitant and embarrassed over staying alone with me?" He chuckled.

"It's not funny. I had no choice but to go to Lucy's. At the time I thought it was safer than the Rabid Wolf," she said with a grimace.

How could I have been so naïve? Kyra prided herself on the unusual education she'd received from Grandpère—the same education that had made her mother despair of ever making a proper lady out of her. Unfortunately, while Grandpère had taught her all about guns, cards, and riding, he hadn't deemed it fit to educate her about brothels.

"Look, Kyra, don't worry about what anyone else will think. You're in Texas now, not a New Orleans ballroom. Folks mind their own business here, and standards are more relaxed. After seeing the reaction you inspired in the Easley brothers, I'm sure not going to let you stay in a hotel all alone. Women out here need to have a man to protect them, or they're considered fair game."

Butterflies fluttered warmly in her stomach at his words, his offered strong arm making her want to kiss him—until he spoke again. "Besides, you won't be here long enough to socialize with the women of Las Almas, who'd be the only ones to snub you for staying out here with me unchaperoned."

Instead of a kiss, she glowered at him, but he ignored her and prodded Mr. Pip downhill toward the stables. "I don't know if we can house Mr. Pip"—he'd actually said the name without laughing that time—"in the stables with my horses. I'm afraid he might get his tender muley feelings hurt when they all laugh at his hat." His face was sober, serious, not a sign of a smirk. "I guess we'll have to let him stay in the corral."

"We will not," Kyra thundered. She patted Mr. Pip on the neck, his coarse hair prickling her fingers. "Don't you worry, honey," she drawled softly. "I won't let that mean old man abuse my baby."

Cliff flinched ever so slightly, but enough for her to notice. Surely he had to know she was jesting.

"Mr. Pip is as courageous as I am. He won't let a few laughs puncture his skin," she continued.

But Cliff's face was hidden back behind his mask, solemn and immobile. He no longer seemed in the mood for joking.

"*Hola,* Boss, who you got there with you?" a melodic deep baritone called out.

Kyra peered into the darkness and saw a cowboy standing with the stable doors open for them. It was too dark for her to make out his face clearly, but she assumed he must be Mexican from his use of Spanish.

"Paco, let me introduce you to an old friend of my family back home. This is Miss Lourdes."

Kyra reached down from the back of Mr. Pip, extending her hand to the smiling man. "Truly, sir, I'm not as old as I look. I celebrated only my sixtieth birthday last week. *Mucho gusto a conocerle.*"

Paco laughed and shook her hand. "*Señorita,* truly I would say you do not look a day over fifty, and I am charmed and delighted by your Spanish."

As Paco and Kyra shared a smile, Cliff reached between them, removing her hand from Paco's grasp. He'd dismounted from Blackjack, and now reached up to swing her down from Mr. Pip.

For a moment, her breasts brushed against his chest. A sharp breath caught in her throat, and he backed away, his hands dropping to his sides.

He turned back to Paco after retrieving her satchels. "Miss Lourdes will be staying here for a few days. I expect all the men to show her respect. As for her mount here, well, their tolerance will do. I can't demand the impossible."

"*Sí, señor,* I will pass the news." Paco chuckled as he led Mr. Pip and Blackjack, who seemed to dwarf the man, into the stables to tuck them in for the night.

She searched out Cliff's imposing body in the moonlight. The only sound was the shrill accompaniment of crickets to the bass of bullfrogs. "What a nice man. I think Mr. Pip will like him."

"Well, that's certainly a load off of my mind," Cliff responded drily as he guided her arm in his and led the way toward his house. It had a wide front porch that wrapped around two sides.

He swung open the front door, and she walked in, looking around the main room. She was eager to see how he lived, what he'd chosen over La Belle Époque plantation.

There were two fireplaces on both the left and right ends. One of his ranch hands must have been in the house as an oil lamp on the table beside the door was lit, giving the room a warm and glowing ambiance. Mantels above the fireplaces held oil lamps that flickered light on the gleaming wooden stocks of rifles on the walls. In the center of the room was a stuffed leather sofa, a high-backed wing chair, and surprisingly, a delightful rocking chair. The smell of burning lamps reminded her of home, making her feel both at home and homesick.

Shaking her head to ward off the twinge of nostalgia, she focused on one wall, behind the furniture, at what appeared to be an Indian-painted hide, stretched and worked into supple buckskin. The tapestry apparently told a story, the lovely dyes of orange, red, blue, and green adding to the cozy feel of the room. She could make out trees and bluffs overlooking a raging river and human figures on horseback, possibly warring.

"Oh, my, how beautiful! What an interesting work of art," Kyra exclaimed as she walked closer to get a better look. "I don't know when I've ever seen such warm, vibrant colors. Where did you get it?"

Cliff smiled, and she was caught by the beauty and warmth on his face instead of the buckskin painting. She had a feeling he still didn't smile much.

"It was a gift from the mother of a good friend of mine, Shane Chandler," he said. "She was thanking me for something I did."

When she was about to question what he'd done, he quickly plopped his hat down and picked up a lamp, directing her attention to the door on the left. "You can sleep in here. Shane uses it when he visits on occasion."

They stepped into the room, and she was enthralled with the fireplace. "How wonderful, a two-sided fireplace. I don't think I've ever seen such a thing before."

"Yes, well, it gets rather cold here on winter evenings, so I had the original changed. The one at the other end of the living room opens up into my bedroom as well."

Kyra moved toward the four-poster bed, catching a glimpse of herself in the mirror above a simple, golden chest of drawers. Oh, dear. She did look a sight.

Cliff set her bags in a corner, and hurried out the door. "Let me show you the kitchen."

She smoothed her hair back, then rushed to follow him.

It was as large as the living room, with a huge wood cookstove taking up the back wall. A sink with a water pump was on the wall to the right, below a large window. A table with four chairs occupied the left side of the kitchen.

"Where do those two doors lead?" She pointed behind the kitchen table.

"The first leads to the pantry, and the second to the back porch. The outhouse is back there."

Once again, Kyra's face burned at discussing such personal matters in front of a man, especially Cliff.

"I wish I could offer you better. I know you're used to water closets. I just haven't gotten around to installing plumbing yet."

Kyra saw from the corner of her eye that he was uncomfortable as well, although she doubted it had anything to do with delicate sensibilities.

As she turned away, a tall cabinet drew her interest, and to cover her embarrassment, she pulled one of the doors open to see what was inside. She'd honestly never spent much time in a kitchen, and was curious. Inside, was a box attached to the pull-down door with a metal object on the bottom.

"It's for storing and sifting flour." Cliff spoke behind her, his voice lowered an octave.

She imagined that if she leaned back, ever so slightly, she'd feel his chest against her back. His breath warmed her neck when he said, "I do have a cook, Miguel, but he had to leave a few days ago for Mexico. He got news his mother was very sick."

"Maybe I can cook for you while I'm here," she whispered as she turned around, finding herself nearly in his arms.

She looked up to find him staring at her. Her heart hammered a little, the piercing blue of his eyes burning through her. She stepped back to allow more space between them.

"How domestic of you." His voice was tight and his gaze contained something akin to desire, or maybe it was longing. His eyes narrowed with doubt. "Do you know how to cook?"

"Of course I do," she bluffed, hoping Cliff wouldn't see through her fabrication the way he had earlier that evening. "Mama thought it was important that I should learn in case, um, in case I was ever in a situation where I didn't have a chef." Having started the lie, she might as well make it sound plausible. It was important to her to repay his hospitality.

His gaze bore into her. He stood beside her, imposingly tall and wide, a large hand on the kitchen counter. The space around her got smaller as he studied her, and she felt pinned by his scrutiny, like butterflies on velvet.

"I think it's time for you to go to bed." His voice was smooth and husky at once, making her stomach lurch. "I imagine you're tired after your long trip and adventures in town. We can have our talk in the morning."

"Is something wrong, Cliff?" She cocked her head to one side.

"No," he sighed. "I'm just not used to sharing my house with a woman, and a pretty one at that." His perusal swept over her as he spoke, and again something rippled inside her stomach.

"You think I'm pretty?" She lowered her eyelashes in embarrassment, but lifted them again a moment later, her gaze meeting his. The blue of his eyes became darker and more intense.

"Yeah, pretty enough to . . ." He waved his hand. "Never mind. It's been so long since I left New Orleans, I'm afraid I've become a little rough around the edges."

They entered the living room again and Kyra grasped his arm. He froze, and she was a little taken aback by the solid feel of him. Was the rest of him as hard and warm? She quickly withdrew her hand at his searing look, suddenly feeling shy.

"I—I'm sorry. Your chess set. The one we used to play with. I just noticed it under your lamp stand." She smiled. "It brought back memories."

"You mean the times I was forced to lose." He smiled devilishly.

"Now that's not true!" She put her hands on her hips. "I was always the better player."

"A sore loser, you mean, which is why I let you win."

He had a twinkle in his eye along with a heated smile. He'd always liked toying with her. But she could tease him just as mercilessly.

"Well, I'm sure I'll have ample opportunity to prove you wrong. I hope you've had time to improve your game, Bayou Baldwin, because I'm even better than before," she called over her shoulder as she flounced off to her bedroom and opened the door.

"Wait, Kyra, that's the wrong room."

She was amazed at the bed. It was huge, taking up most of the room. She turned to find Cliff to her left, in front of the nightstand. "You couldn't do without the luxury of a big bed, I see," she said. Her cheeks burned. This wasn't proper at all.

"No, but it's about the only thing I still wanted from the *good life.*" The sarcasm in his voice dripped with ice, but it was the unreadable darkness in his eyes that made her shiver.

"I—I'm sorry. I didn't mean to come in here."

He had turned to guide her out of the room when she gasped at the sight of a tintype picture sitting on his nightstand.

"Oh, my, Cliff. I haven't seen this picture in years!" She saw him roll his eyes. He obviously wasn't happy she'd seen it. And come to think of it, he'd stood directly in front of it. Maybe he didn't want her to think he'd been homesick.

Cliff watched as Kyra smiled at the tintype. It was a picture taken of her as a bridesmaid at her cousin's wedding the year before she started finishing school. Both their families, including him, surrounded her, their fathers and Cliff on one side and their mothers on the other. Her smile was bright and her eyes wide with laughter. Kyra'd never grasped the prevailing wisdom that one should look serious in pictures. Her beautiful, dark hair was arranged in an artful style on top of her head with soft tendrils framing her face. She wore an innocent bridesmaid dress, which showed off the tiny waist of her child-woman figure. She sure had filled out. Her face didn't seem as naïve either, or as happy, for that matter. Damn, she looked like she was about to cry. Hell, she was crying; that was a tear gliding down her cheek.

"Kyra, honey, what's wrong?" He reached out to her.

Unexpectedly, she whirled and threw herself into his arms, sobbing into his chest. Her sobs seemed torn from the depths of her soul, as if a dam inside her had broken.

As Kyra wrapped her arms tighter around Cliff, the picture frame in her hands struck the side of his head. He grimaced, and removed it from her grip. Carefully, he set the picture back on his nightstand, Kyra still clinging to his chest. Hell, he was going to have to do it. He wrapped his arms around her small body, a shudder passing through her and echoing into his own. He couldn't get over the feel of her, her smallness fitting into his protective hold so perfectly, his chin resting on top of her head.

He patted her back, rocked her gently, and let her cry. A memory came to mind of his mother crying while he, a four-year-old, patted her on the back. He bit his lip, forcing the image aside, and concentrated on the woman he held in his arms.

"I'm s-sorry, Cliff. I-I don't know what c-came over me. Seeing that p-picture brought back old memories. I was s-so innocent back then."

"And you're not innocent now?" His hands gently cupped the sides of her face as he brought her gaze up to meet his. Her skin was like silk beneath his touch.

Her eyes shuttered and she lowered her arms from around him, gripping her hands tightly. She walked away toward his bed.

She glanced over her shoulder. "You may not want me to stay after I tell you what's happened."

Cliff grabbed her elbow and steered her out of his bedroom. It was time they talked. Obviously she'd referred to what had brought her here. He'd concentrate better in the living room. If she needed comfort, he didn't want to be providing it from his bed.

He seated Kyra on his sofa. "Would you like something to drink?" She shook her head, so he sat beside her.

"I ran away from home, Cliff. I came to ask for your help. Please don't turn me away! I had nowhere else to go."

"I think you better start from the beginning. And while you're at it, tell me how you found me. I don't remember giving anyone back home my location."

"I witnessed a murder. I saw my fiancé kill a woman."

Chapter Four

Fickle Chocolate Hearts: For those who can't decide—six petite chocolate truffles, each with its own special filling.
From the *Sinfully Delicious Bakery Recipe Book*

"You saw what?" The words exploded from Cliff. *"You have a fiancé?"*

Kyra bounced off the sofa and paced. "I've had six fiancés over the last six years, Cliff. With each engagement that I broke, my parents got angrier and angrier, and less understanding." She stopped for a minute to face him, then continued pacing. "They swore this time I'd have to go through with it. If I tried to break this engagement, they promised to disinherit me. Mama was especially mad because half the legacy Grandmère left me I can only inherit at my marriage. You see, her will stipulates that it must be split among various charities if I don't marry by the time I'm twenty-five." Her eyes beseeched him, pleading for him to understand. "I could handle the lack of money. But I couldn't handle my parents denying me their love and support. How could they do this to me?"

He reached out to her, offering her comfort. But she was so wrapped up in her pain, her memories, she didn't see him. She kept pacing, hugging her arms around herself.

"Several days ago, I went to Jacques' town house, to plead with him to end the engagement. I knew our marriage was a bad idea; I knew we wouldn't suit. I wanted to make him see reason. If *he* ended the engagement, my parents couldn't blame me. His house is two doors down, on the other side of your . . . your father's. I went through the back lane to his garden because I didn't want anyone to see me visiting him unchaperoned."

At this Cliff's jaw tightened, but he kept silent. He wanted to hear it all.

"He was in a secluded area, behind the gazebo, arguing with a woman. I couldn't make out who she was or what they said. Without warning, Jacques went crazy and stabbed her in the back. Over and over. The woman was in a-a crumpled heap, down and bleeding. She had to have been dead, and Jacques kept on stabbing her. He was like an animal. I ran away as fast as I could."

Instant, unwelcome memories of his father and life at La Belle Époque plantation flooded his mind at the violent picture she described. Predominant were the images of his father, a snobbish member of Boston society, who'd transplanted himself to New Orleans after the War Between the States. Nobody knew it, not even Kyra, but his father—the *gentleman*—in actuality had been nothing but an abusive drunk, making Cliff's life a living hell until he was big enough to fight back and ultimately leave.

Kyra stepped closer and hesitantly touched his arm, bringing his attention back to her. "I didn't know what to do. I thought about speaking to the authorities, but I was too afraid." She shivered at the memory. "The next morning I read that a woman was found in a nearby swamp stabbed to death."

Seating herself beside him, she continued. "Cliff, Jacques is a Delacroix. I don't know if you knew him or not. He only bought the town house on the other side of your father's two years ago. But surely you've heard of his family and remember all the political ties they have?"

Cliff shifted a little in his seat. "Yes, I know of his family. I vaguely remember hearing my parents talk about Armand and Paulette Delacroix. They must be Jacques' parents?" An uncomfortable sensation washed over him at the childhood memory, although he couldn't imagine why.

"Yes, and Jacques' grandfather was a senator. Jacques has aspirations of a political career all the way to the White House. What good would a woman's word be against his, especially a fiancée's word? He could say I made it up over a spat. Besides, my parents wouldn't believe me. I've told outlandish tales in the past about my suitors to end the engagements. They'd simply say I was up to my old tricks."

He took her hands in his, seeking the words to console her.

"Wait!" she ordered. "Let me finish."

"Go on." His hands rubbed hers, feeling their softness, small in his own.

"That same evening, after I'd read the newspaper article, I was to attend a soiree with my parents at Laetitia Gressin's home. Although I didn't want to see anyone, I also didn't want to stay home alone or upset my parents further." Kyra stood up again, only to lower herself, kneeling at his feet. "Cliff!" Her eyes were doelike with fear. "Jacques unexpectedly showed up at the soiree holding the cameo locket that Grandmère gave me on my sixteenth birthday. He told me he'd found it near the gazebo." Her eyes watered again into deep green pools.

"You're safe, Kyra. Take a breath." He placed his hands on her shoulders and massaged them.

"I-I told him I must have lost it the last time I visited, but I could tell he didn't believe me. I knew I was in danger. I could see it in his eyes . . . I was terrified, Cliff . . . I remembered all the blood. He was so violent, like he was insane. I didn't know what to do! I simply had to find you. I knew that you'd help me." Kyra swiped at the tears streaking down her cheeks, her wet lashes and trembling lips stirring a mixture of undefined emotions in his gut.

He stroked her hair, marveling at the silky feel, her chignon having spilled some of the tresses during her despair. He couldn't remember ever seeing her so distraught. The Kyra he remembered was a little hellion who rarely allowed herself to be dispirited. Although loneliness used to drive her to be his little brat, she'd always found a way to see the positive in all things. He'd admired that about her, maybe because it was a characteristic so alien to his own nature. She enjoyed life and tried new things with gusto, rarely afraid of the consequences. With her passionate approach to life, she reminded him of his mother in her younger days, before . . . A strong, familiar desire to protect welled in his chest, making him feel at once powerful and weak.

Shaking his head, Cliff brought his attention back to Kyra's bowed head. Grandpère had been proud of her courage and zest, of course. It was one of the reasons that crazy old coot relished teaching his only granddaughter all manner of things her parents disapproved of. Nonetheless, the old man had taught both him and Kyra how to shoot a gun, how to play and even cheat at cards. To Cliff he'd also taught the definition of a true man and father.

Cliff fingered a lock of Kyra's hair, tucking it behind her delicate ear, the fear and sadness in her eyes eliciting a shudder of rage within him. Anger rolled through his body like thunder, threatening his taut control. He wanted to kill this Jacques with his bare hands, but he didn't want to frighten Kyra with the truth of the violence he felt. Instead he kept his emotions leashed as he soothed hers.

He tilted her chin to face him. "Look at me, Kyra," he said to console her. "We are going to take care of this."

"We are?" She sounded like a lost child.

"We are," he affirmed. "Does Jacques have any idea where you are?"

"Not really, but he's close."

"Why do you say that?"

"I'd need to continue my story."

"All right." He leaned back against the sofa. "Go ahead."

She took a deep breath, lifting herself to her feet, again pacing, Cliff watching her.

"Later that night, in my room, I remembered about the trip my ex-fiancé Quinton took—"

"Quinton who?" Cliff interrupted, somewhat disturbed. What had he expected? That she was still unmarried at her age was uncommon.

"Your friend . . . Quinton Green. I-I was engaged to him for almost a year, but . . . well, we just weren't suited."

Cliff bit down hard, clenching his teeth at the thought of Kyra in Quinton's arms, or Jacques', for that matter. Again, what had he expected—that she become a nun? Why he should feel anything, he didn't understand. He'd left years ago fully expecting he'd never see her again. That was for the best, at least for Kyra.

She continued pacing. "Well, Quinton—"

"You've had *six* fiancés?" He winced at his own tone of voice, but *six* fiancés? She'd said so earlier, but he seemed to suffer from a case of delayed reaction.

"Yes, six. Now may I go on with my story?" She glared defiantly at him.

Well, at least she wasn't crying anymore. Cliff much preferred this Kyra; all fired up when pushed into a corner, strength in her stand.

"So, where was I? Oh, yes, Quinton—"

"Why six fiancés in six years? Wasn't there even one that suited?"

Her hands flew to her hips, and her foot tapped away, but a betraying twinkle lit her eye. "Oh, I can see you're going to be just like my mama and papa about this."

"No, but I'm curious why you've had so many fiancés."

She snorted, tossing her head. "I can't help it if I was engaged to six of the deadly sins."

Now he was truly confused. "The what?"

"The seven deadly sins—surely you've heard of them, even though you're not Catholic," she sniffed. "And I have one more to go, I suppose. Let's see. I don't remember the order, but there's greed, gluttony, pride, sloth, anger, envy, and lust. Yes"—her eyes looked up to the ceiling in thought—"and I've had six fiancés to whom I can attribute six of these sins."

"Which one was lust?" he asked harshly.

"Actually, I haven't met that one yet," she answered. "Now may I go on with my story?"

"Yes, I suppose you can tell me about your fiancés at another time," Cliff replied gruffly, strangely relieved. However, he had every intention of finding out the details. *They'd probably all suffered from lust, but she'd been too naïve to see it.*

"Oh, heavens, that would take forever. Besides, it's not any of your concern."

"Yeah, well, we'll see about that." He leaned his arms on his knees. "So, something about *Quinton.*"

"I remembered that night, after the soiree, that Quinton had traveled to Dallas on a business trip a year ago and brought back a newspaper, the *Dallas Enquirer,* I think it was. In it, there was an article and illustration depicting the true story of a certain bounty hunter named 'Bayou' Baldwin bringing in those awful bank robbers the Yancey brothers, if I remember correctly." Kyra stopped as if to gauge his reaction, her hands in fists at her side. "The cartoon looked so much like you, only you were bigger." Her gaze traveled a slow path down his body. "Then the name and the description they gave . . . well, it had to be you. Of course, Quinton didn't believe it. He kept saying that your name wasn't that unusual and that you weren't the type to go into bounty hunting . . . that you were a refined gentleman, after all. But I had a feeling. I also remembered the time you'd told me about your dream to go out West, and, well . . ." She shrugged.

A minute of silence passed.

"Anyway, that was when I decided that I needed to leave and find you, so I packed a satchel and took the first train to Dallas. Once there, I made several inquiries as to your whereabouts, discovering a wall at every turn. No one wanted to divulge any information."

Cliff had to grin at that. "Payback," he explained.

"What?"

"It's a code in the West. You mind your own business if you don't want retaliation from some man who doesn't want to be found."

"Oh."

"So what did you do?"

"Well, I had some savings with me, and so I hired a private detective. A few more days and I knew that Cliff Baldwin was probably living near Las Almas Perdidas. The investigator said you'd left bounty hunting and might be ranching in these parts. There was nothing confirmed, but I took a chance and headed to the depot to buy a ticket on the stagecoach to Las Almas, and that's when I saw him."

Kyra stared at him. He attempted a calm facade, although a storm brewed inside.

"Who is 'him'?"

"I don't know," she gulped. "I was waiting for the next stagecoach here when this awful-looking man started asking people at the depot about me. He had a paper, but I couldn't see what was on it. I heard my name and hid."

At that, Cliff lurched forward, sitting on the edge of the sofa. "Christ, Kyra! What did he look like?" His taut control snapped.

"Well, he was very tall, blond, and had a scar from left to right on his neck. I didn't see any more because I needed to hide."

He exhaled. "Oscar Wade! That *bastard*," he barely whispered.

"You know him?"

He grimaced. "Bounty hunting's a rather small profession. He's a real son of a . . . he's mean and conniving. I had some run-ins with him, mostly because I cheated him out of some big prizes, or so he says." The disgust in his voice was clear. Cliff saw he was frightening her. Time to move on. "So what happened next?"

Kyra took a breath. "Well, I ran away from the depot as fast as I could, and ended up in an open marketplace. That's when I ran into a young boy leading a pack mule . . . Mr. Pip." She paused.

"Go on."

"Yes, well, I offered him an exorbitant amount of money for Mr. Pip, which he accepted with profuse praise for all my ancestors." Kyra grinned with the memory. "Unfortunately, I didn't realize I was being watched. A crowd of women selling Mexican blankets and trinkets came and surrounded me. They wrapped the blankets around me as if they hoped to sell me some clothing. It was later that I realized they'd stolen all my money. Thank God it wasn't all that far to Las Almas, although I was afraid I might not find you." Kyra returned to the sofa and gracefully settled herself next to him. "I got on Mr. Pip and rode here. The rest you know." She shrugged.

Cliff chewed on the information she'd given, imagining all the possible ramifications. Was Wade a private hire? If he was, then it would take more time to find Kyra than if a whole force of bounty hunters were out there trying to get the prize. More likely, Jacques had hired only one man to keep it as quiet as possible. It wouldn't have been difficult to find out she'd taken the train to Dallas.

How much time was there? Kyra had certainly not come to town quietly, which meant he had to get moving and find out what the stakes were. He had to get a message to Shane.

Kyra's yawn brought him back to reality. He would have to figure out a strategy later. First he needed to reassure her and then send her to bed. He turned to gaze into eyes like giant orbs, filled with hope and something else. Trust. Strange, yet there it was, even though he'd been the one to leave all those years ago without so much as an explanation. He remembered his mother's saying about true friends being there no matter what. And here was Kyra, seeking him out when she needed him, the way she had as a child. He'd been her big brother then. One didn't forget a brother so easily.

She'd missed not having any siblings, and although her parents cared for her, they'd always been somewhat confining with their pompous society airs. Kyra had wanted to romp around, while they'd wanted her to be a lady. If it hadn't been for him and that black-sheep maternal grandfather of hers, she probably would have become just a pretty porcelain doll for some future husband. Cliff was glad she was not.

By strange coincidence, he'd also been an only child, finding companionship with the little girl next door. Their parents had often entertained together, so they'd gotten to know one another quite well. Soon enough, he had a little girl in pigtails tagging along after him like a bratty little sister. Eventually, he'd grown accustomed to having her around, even needing her around. She became the bright light in a dark world nobody knew he lived. She'd thought nothing of the tintype he kept in his bedroom, but in reality it was perhaps his most precious possession, reminding him of all he'd left behind, of the good and evil shown in that one picture. He'd often looked at it and wondered which one he was—good or evil. That question was also part of the reason he'd left bounty hunting, finding the ease with which he could kill a man disconcerting.

Shane had never batted an eye for the lowlifes they chased, but then again Shane was Shane. He was still out there, roaming the lands in search of wanted men. Every so often he stopped by for a visit on his way to somewhere else.

Shane hadn't been by in a while, meaning chances were good Cliff would find him on his doorstep soon. But probably not with Cliff's luck. He'd have to get a message to him.

Cliff sighed, pushing his worries away. He needed to take care of Kyra.

"Kyra, I don't want you to worry about anything. If there's one thing I can do, it's protect you. You probably don't want to believe this, but most of the things you've heard about me are true." He paused for a moment; she stared at him wide-eyed. "I've seen a lot of ugly things in my life and I've learned how to deal with them *my* way . . . too well." He remembered the day he'd decided to quit bounty hunting. He averted his gaze, not wanting to divulge too much of what was in his heart to Kyra's understanding eyes. He sighed again, lacing his fingers together in thought.

"Dallas isn't that far from here. . . ." He trailed off. "Listen, it's getting late and I think we should continue our talk in the morning over breakfast. Can you fix up some ham, biscuits, grits, and red-eye gravy?"

"Ham, biscuits, grits, and red-eye gravy?" Kyra asked, her mind obviously racing to see if she had any clue as to how to make them.

"Yes! Doesn't that sound good, and so *easy*?" He couldn't help but smile suspiciously.

Kyra bristled. "Don't you worry! I'm sure I can fix that just fine. But I'm a little concerned about the stove, you know. Every stove is different, and well, I—I hope everything comes out the same on yours, that's all."

"Come on, Squirt, I'm sure you'll want to wash up before going to bed."

"Oh, yes. That sounds divine."

"I hope you don't mind a pitcher and bowl for tonight. I promise you can take a proper bath tomorrow."

New Orleans

Damn! She'd gotten away. Jacques Delacroix pulled the thick drapes back on the bedroom window of his town house and peered through the glass at the Delta storm raging outside. A sharp crack of lightning lit the room, making demonic shadows dance in the recesses. The low rumble of thunder echoed his inner growl of anger and frustration.

His hand tightened on the sash. Who'd ever have thought that his prim and proper fiancée would've had the gumption to run away like she did? But she wouldn't escape him for long. Although he didn't think he had anything to worry about now that the other bitch was dead, he couldn't risk Kyra damaging his future plans by arousing whispers and rumors.

He'd have to stop her. But he didn't think he'd have to kill her. She was important to him. Her generous nature was like a healing balm, providing him comfort.

Thanks to his informant, he already had an idea as to where she'd headed. He smiled with perverse delight, then closing the drapes on the storm that raged outside, picked up his tumbler and poured whiskey on the one that raged within.

Chapter Five

Hardtack Biscuits: These are good biscuits for the novice because they don't require bread-making skills. They're supposed to be hard anyway.
From the *Sinfully Delicious Bakery Recipe Book*

Cock-a-doodle . . .

"Ugh," Kyra complained as she shoved a pillow over her ear and burrowed deeper under the covers.

Cock-a-doodle-doo.

It was no use. She could still hear it. She cracked one eye and looked toward the window. Dawn was breaking over the horizon. She'd left her window cracked last night. The sweet smell of summer morning drifted in along with the sounds of the noisy rooster. She was definitely not used to being awakened at the crack of dawn—or should she say the "cock" of dawn?

Kyra heard low voices outside her room at the front door. Two men whispered to each other. Well, she might as well get up. Her stomach did a small dive as she recalled her boast to Cliff. He'd better not be expecting too good a breakfast this morning, or he'd be in for a rude awakening.

"How do I get myself into these situations?"

She pushed up and swung her legs over the side of the bed, then reached for her satchel. It didn't contain much, just the few belongings she'd managed to pull together in her hurry to escape. She hadn't unpacked last night, so exhausted she'd simply put on her nightdress, climbed into bed, and basically died. She rubbed her tongue across her teeth and combed her fingers through her hair. Ugh, she needed a bath.

What had Cliff said—something about a pitcher and bowl for last night and a bath for today? Kyra wrinkled her nose. She wouldn't bother him right away with a bath, but certainly didn't want him to see her looking like a fright. She poured cold water from the pitcher into the bowl and shivered. Maybe later she could indulge in a tub full of hot water.

After conducting a hurried toilet, she arched an eyebrow at the minor display of clothes she'd brought with her. They wouldn't last very long. Why, at home she'd changed several times a day.

What were Mama and Papa doing right now? Her stomach churned with the knowledge that they'd worry about her. She should have left them a message, but her flight had been so frantic and hurried. Oh, why had Mama insisted on pushing her into marriage? She knew the family legacy was important—but wasn't her happiness important as well?

Heaving a frustrated sigh, she fumbled through her clothes until she caught sight of the bright yellow morning dress. Her spirits were still down from recounting her story to Cliff. Maybe the sunny color would help lift her disposition. She donned her camisole, then extended her corset in front of her, and flung it out of the way. She hated the blasted thing, and avoided wearing it whenever possible, which was rare. But now she had an excellent excuse—she didn't have a maid to help tighten the stays.

After slipping on her stockings and petticoat, Kyra pulled the yellow dress on over her head. It was one of her favorites. Besides being a cheery color that suited her, it had a pretty crocheted white lace trim edging the round neck and short sleeves, as well as a three-inch lace flounce at the bottom. Mother-of-pearl buttons fastened down the front all the way to her waist. Which pointed out another good reason to wear it—she'd be able to do it up by herself. The dress was wrinkled from spending time in her bag, but, oh, well, it was the best she could do for the moment.

Pulling her satchel wide, she found a yellow ribbon in the side pouch where she'd also tossed her journal, and tied her thick hair in a simple ponytail. She'd need it out of the way to cook. She winced—what had she gotten herself into?

Finally, Kyra hooked the rest of her clothes on the pegs or laid them inside the chest drawers. As she was walking out the door, she glanced at her bed. Hmmm. She didn't think Cliff had any maids. He hadn't mentioned any last night anyway. Should she make her own bed? Surely it couldn't be that difficult.

After several attempts to make the bed appear as smooth as her maid did back home, Kyra threw up her hands, deciding that just a little rumpled was all right.

She was ready to face Cliff.

But Cliff was nowhere to be found.

Where was he? Stepping into the kitchen after visiting the outhouse, she saw no trace of him anywhere. He was probably giving work to the ranch hands.

"Well, I guess I'd better do my share," she mumbled as she surveyed the kitchen. "Just because I've never cooked before doesn't mean I can't do it. I'm smart, aren't I? I've eaten plenty of food all my life. I'm as intelligent as Marie," she said, thinking of her family's chef.

Marching forward like a novice soldier into his first battle, she explored the kitchen, opening cupboards and studying shelves. Plates and bowls made of blue enamelware sat above cast-iron pots and skillets and below glasses and pottery coffee cups.

She stepped into the pantry. Shelves running the length of two walls were filled with boxes and bags of foodstuff. She saw rice and beans, cheese and butter, some canned items and smoked meat. There was even a bag of potatoes and a small barrel of pickles.

She gazed out the window at the end of the small room and looked for Cliff, but he was nowhere in sight. Nor did she see any of his hands. Surely, he had more than just Paco to help run things, didn't he?

With a resigned sigh, knowing she could delay no longer, Kyra turned her attention back to the task at hand. First she pulled the ham down from a hook in the pantry and lugged it back into the kitchen, dropping it on the counter with a thud. She rifled through a drawer until she found a sharp knife.

"My goodness, this is hard to cut!" she exclaimed after several minutes had passed and she'd only sawed off two thick pieces. She persevered until she had six more. "I'm glad that's over. Surely it has to get easier now."

That, however, was wishful thinking. What was she supposed to do with the ham now that she'd cut it? She'd eaten breakfast ham numerous times, but never had to cook it.

She pulled a heavy cast-iron skillet from the cupboard, and plunked it down on the stove. A very cold stove. Well, that simply wouldn't do. Everyone knew one needed heat to cook. She'd have to start the fire since Cliff was hiding somewhere.

She remembered seeing a pile of chips and wood out on the back porch. Several armloads later, she searched the kitchen for lucifers. Aha, there they were on a shelf beside the stove.

She lit the match and threw it in. Nothing happened. She waited. She threw another match. A little smoke this time. Hmm, she needed something that would start quickly. There were a couple of newspapers sitting on a small table near the stove. That should do it.

Soon she had a big fire going, its warmth seeping into her bones. She watched it for a minute. Hmm . . . the fire probably shouldn't be so big. Then again, maybe the food would cook more quickly that way. She shut the door and flung the ham into the skillet.

What next? Oh, yes, Cliff had wanted biscuits. Armed with an enamelware bowl, she marched back into the pantry and hunted out the flour. After dumping quite a bit in the bowl, she was stumped. What else was supposed to go into biscuits?

Once again, she'd eaten plenty, but never thought much about what went into them. Well, they had to have something to make them doughy. So she went to the pump to add some water.

The pump was hard to work. She'd never had to use one before, as water was always brought to her in glasses whenever she wanted it. She kept pumping the handle until she got a trickle. Was the dough supposed to stick to your hands so thoroughly? She tried removing it from her fingers, but it just clung to the other hand. Irksome stuff. Maybe she needed a little more flour. Now, that was better. But shouldn't there be something else in biscuit dough besides flour and water? It needed something for . . . flavor. Yes, that's right—lard. She'd seen a bucket of it sitting in the pantry. Since she wanted her biscuits to be very flavorful, she added lots of lard. Then she had to add more flour. Finally she had the consistency she wanted.

She found a flat pan hanging on the wall in the pantry. Not knowing how to roll out biscuits, she pinched off pieces of dough, rolled them in her palm, and dropped them on the pan. Where to put them? Kyra examined the stove and discovered a door adjacent to the fire door with racks inside. She shoved the biscuit pan in. Now that hadn't been so difficult. Really, people who made cooking seem mysterious and hard didn't know what they were talking about.

What next? Something smelled. Oh, no. The ham. It was burning! Kyra seized the handle to move the pan. "Oww. Stupid, stupid. You should've known that would be hot," she muttered, putting her mouth to her burned palm. She hadn't touched it but a second. The sting wasn't too bad. Grabbing a dishcloth, she moved the pan. The ham didn't appear too burned. "It's just good and brown," she said as she turned the pieces to sizzle on their other sides.

Now she was ready to start something new. Coffee. Spotting the coffeepot, she reached for it on the back burner and headed for the pump.

She had trouble getting enough water again, but then she noticed a full pitcher hiding underneath the sink. That would work a whole lot easier than the perverse pump. She poured enough to rinse out the coffeepot, filled it, and searched for the coffee. Not knowing how much to use, but figuring Cliff probably drank a lot of coffee to help him wake up so early, she dumped in three handfuls.

After checking the ham again, Kyra turned her attention to making grits. She emptied most of the water from the pitcher into another pot, contemplating how many grits to use. Well, if Cliff would be thirsty, he'd certainly be famished, so she dumped a mound of grits in and set it on the stove beside the coffee.

That should just about do it. She had everything under control, of course. Ham sizzling, coffee brewing, grits cooking, and biscuits baking. Wouldn't Cliff be proud of her?

Oh, she'd forgotten to flavor the grits. Marie made wonderful grits in a variety of ways. Kyra loved them with cut-up vegetables such as peppers, onions, and tomatoes along with a little meat. But her favorite recipe utilized shrimp. However, she seriously doubted Cliff had any fresh shrimp out here in the middle of Texas. She'd just add some seasoning and serve it with the ham. Finding the pepper, she gave the shaker a colossal shake, and then searched for the salt until she found a tin of white crystals. Actually, she'd need sugar, too, for the coffee. Finding another tin of unlabeled white crystals, she tasted each with a touch of her finger to figure out which was which.

The tantalizing aromas made her stomach growl.

"Good morning, Kyra."

She jumped. "Oh! You scared me, Cliff. Why must you move about so quietly?"

Cliff smiled despite the frown on her face. She sure did look fetching in that yellow dress with her hair up. He smiled even wider when he noticed the flour dotting her face and all down her front.

"I didn't know you were so jumpy. I hope you slept well." He reached into the pantry and pulled out an apron hanging behind the door.

"Here, put this on. It'll save you messing up that pretty dress." He dropped the neck piece over her head and then pulled the fabric around her, wrapping it twice to make it fit. Miguel was quite a bit bigger. His appreciative gaze ran up and down her slim figure.

She smiled at him over her shoulder as he finished tying the bow at her back, her green eyes sparkling. "Thanks so much, Cliff. I slept as sound as Grandpère after a night on Bourbon Street. I was exhausted. Breakfast is almost ready. Are you hungry? Where have you been this morning? I didn't see anyone outside."

"Whoa—slow down. One question at a time." He laughed. It was good to see her feeling well this morning. Life would never get her down. She'd been very upset last night, but here she was the next morning, bright and chipper and back to her usual sunny disposition. He loved her zest for life, but . . . it scared him, too. Turning, he said over his shoulder, "Yes, I'm ready for breakfast. Let me go clean up. I've been working with the men."

She didn't need to know the details. He'd had his ranch hands up at dawn to go over the extra safety precautions they'd need to take until the threat against Kyra had passed. He wasn't going to take any chances with her safety. The men had been fully cooperative. He hadn't expected any less. They were all good loyal men.

As Cliff passed through the kitchen door, he called out, "I hope you made some gravy to go with those biscuits and ham I'm smelling. I sure do love red-eye gravy."

"Oh, my goodness." *She'd forgotten the gravy.* How did one make red-eye gravy anyhow? And what was that smell? The biscuits! Smoke billowed out of the oven. Kyra flung open the door, once again forgetting to use the dishcloth. "Owwwww . . ." She snatched the blasted cloth, and then pulled the biscuit pan out, casting it on the counter beside the sink. "Oh, no," she moaned as she sucked on her burnt finger. The biscuits were perhaps a tad too "good and brown." Well, it was too late to do anything about it now. At least they weren't black.

Kyra heard a splattering, and twisted toward the stove. The coffee boiled over. Remembering the cloth this time, she pulled the coffeepot off the fire, then quickly removed the pan with the ham as it was getting overly done as well. The grits seemed fine—thank heavens she hadn't messed them up. Oh, but she'd forgotten the salt. She turned to the counter and grabbed a tin. Wanting everything perfect when Cliff returned, she hurriedly spooned the salt and added a huge shake of pepper. She reached for the other tin and added sugar to the coffee.

Now, all that was left was the gravy. All she knew about red-eye gravy was that it was made from either whiskey or coffee and poured over the ham. She grabbed the coffeepot and poured out about half the liquid onto the ham. Hmm, it looked a little runnier than she was used to seeing. Actually, she wasn't used to red-eye gravy. Her parents considered it beneath their taste, so she'd only had it on a few occasions when visiting Grandpère.

Well, that was it. Since Cliff wasn't back yet, Kyra set the table to have everything pretty for him.

Cliff strode through the door. Perfect timing.

"Boy, am I hungry. It sure does smell good. I never would've thought you'd learned to cook. But you've proven me wrong."

"Well, just remember this lesson, as I always will—prove you wrong, I mean," she teased.

Seeing her bright smile, Cliff knew she had to have slept better than he did. He'd tossed and turned the whole night, alternately worrying about Jacques and what he was doing to find Kyra, and frustrated by thoughts of her in a bed in his house. He sure had never expected *that* dream to come true.

"It's hot in here," he complained as he tried to tear his thoughts from the sensual path they traveled.

"Cooking, you know," Kyra said with an airy wave of her hand. "I always heat up the kitchen when I cook." This said with the demeanor of a professional cook. "Come on, Cliff. Sit here at the head of the table and let me serve you."

"All right, honey. Bring it on." He eased into his usual chair, and watched as she loaded his plate, filled his mug, and presented them to him with a flourish. The smile on his face froze numb with dismay.

"What's wrong? Don't you like my food?" She frowned with worry.

"Oh, no, no. That's not it. I haven't even tasted it yet. I'm sure it's delicious," he hastened to reassure her. "I'm not used to biscuits so, well, brown, and gravy that's so, umm, soupy. But I'm sure it'll taste just fine." To prove his point he picked up a biscuit and bit down on it.

Jesus, had he lost a tooth? He'd never tasted a biscuit so hard. It was all he could do to break off a piece. But Kyra observed him, her eyes wide and shining, so he smiled as he chewed . . . and chewed . . . and chewed. "I've never eaten a biscuit with quite this texture." He forced a smile through the bread crumbs he still gnawed, hoping it would make his words a compliment.

The ham had to be better. He'd try that next. Why, all you had to do was fry it. What could go wrong?

You could burn it! That's what you could do. He swallowed the overly thick ham even though it left a bad taste in his mouth. But he didn't want Kyra to get upset. "Your ham sure has a unique flavor to it." She smiled tentatively in response.

Well, he may as well sample the grits. He knew better this time than to ask what could go wrong. The grits sure did seem to have a bad case of rigor mortis. Usually grits lie softly on the plate. These fairly stood up on their paws and barked. But, oh, well, maybe their appearance was deceiving. He hesitated, then swallowed quickly.

"Pshhwwhh." Grits flew halfway across the table. He started choking and coughing. Kyra flew to his side, brought his coffee cup to his mouth, and encouraged him to drink.

Coffee splattered all the way into the living room along with what must be rocks in the coffee.

"Water, water," he croaked. She ran to the cupboard, grabbed a glass, and poured the last of the water from the pitcher under the sink. After a couple of minutes, Cliff's throat eased and he was able to breathe.

"Kyra, honey, what did you put in the grits and coffee for flavoring?" He used as gentle a voice as possible with his throat still raw and coughing.

Her eyes watered. "I'm so sorry, Cliff. What happened? I only put salt and pepper in the grits and sugar in the coffee."

"I think you got your tins mixed up . . . and added a tad too much pepper as well." He closed one eye to better peer into his coffee cup. She'd forgotten to grind the beans. Well, at least they weren't rocks. "Remind me to buy the regular brown sugar from now on." *And grind a pouch of coffee,* he added silently.

Kyra's eyes rounded. "Oh, my goodness . . . I'm so sorry. I tried so hard. I wanted everything to be perfect for you. I wanted to show my appreciation for your help."

"Hey, come here." He set his coffee cup down and reached for her hands, drawing her closer to his side. "You don't have to show me your appreciation. We're friends, remember? There's nothing I wouldn't do for you. Just like you've done for me in the past."

He pulled Kyra down to sit in the chair across from him. "Do you remember that time when I was fifteen and you were ten and I wanted to run away and live on Bug Island? You helped me name my island, make my fort, brought me food for ten days, and kept my whereabouts a secret, even though I know you were constantly getting in trouble with your mother for your muddy clothes and disappearances."

"My arms are sore just remembering all that rowing," she said. "You never did tell me why you wanted to run away all of a sudden. I know you probably got a switching when you finally went home. I didn't see you for at least two weeks after that," she added in a whisper.

Cliff's guts twisted when Kyra's perceptive, questioning gaze cut through him. He needed to change the subject. "Yeah, well, you do see what I mean, don't you? You were my friend then and helped me out. You've always been there for me, when you weren't busy being a brat"—he winked, just so he didn't get too sentimental, then winced as she kicked him under the table—"and now is the time for me to help you. I don't want you to feel indebted to me at all. I would love for you to cook, but only if it's because you want to, not because you owe me."

"But I failed. I can't even make a simple breakfast, and I practically poisoned you. I must be too stupid." She slumped in her chair.

"That's not true. You're just untaught. Do you think I knew how to do anything when I first came out here? Hardly. But I met a good friend. Shane taught me. And now I can teach you."

He rose, pulling her with him. "Come on. Let's start all over and we'll do it together. I'll show you how to make a good breakfast and then you'll know next time. All right?"

Kyra's smile was back in place. "Oh, what fun . . . I always did enjoy playing with you."

His heart skittered at her choice of words, but slowed down again at the innocence he saw reflected in her eyes. *Get over it, fool.*

He picked up his breakfast plate and eyeballed the contents. Maybe the biscuits and grits would soften up in the soupy gravy. Nah, it'd be best to chuck it all.

"Come on, you can see what a slop bucket's for." Holding onto his plate and grabbing the bowl of grits, he headed for the back porch. When she followed, he pointed out a gray metal bucket and dumped the food in. "I think the pigs and chickens will relish your donation this morning." He grinned at her, hoping she'd catch on to his teasing spirit. She smiled in response. Leave it to Kyra to be able to laugh at herself—unless she was losing at chess.

Cliff taught Kyra the proper way to fix breakfast. First he showed her how to make a good steady fire that wouldn't burn the food. He also snatched the coffee grinder off the counter and helped her grind some beans.

He grinned to himself when he thought about her first cooking attempt, until he went to fill the coffeepot with water and found the pitcher empty and a pump that hadn't been primed. Good thing he kept an emergency jar of water in the pantry. He retrieved it and held it up for Kyra to see. "Let me teach you how to prime a pump."

"Prime a pump? What's that?"

"A pump doesn't work very well when it's dry. In fact, you can damage it if it's not in good shape. That's why I keep the pitcher of water below the sink. Before you use the pump, you want to pour a bit of water into the top here." He poured in the water and worked the pump—up and down, up and down. Water spat and sputtered, and then gushed out in streams.

"How interesting!" Kyra exclaimed, moving closer to see, her gentle body pressed snug against his hard side. "But why does it need water to get started?"

Cliff bent toward her sweet face, so close to his own, his eyes seeking the sexy mole at the corner of her mouth, and felt almost dizzy as her small pink tongue licked her full, round lips, leaving them shiny and sleek. He smelled the scent of jasmine in her hair, and watched her breasts rise and fall with her breathing. He didn't think he had the fortitude to explain how friction and pressure were necessary for pumping a strong gush of liquid. "Trust me on this, Kyra."

"Of course, Cliff." Her brow wrinkled as if perplexed.

He exerted iron control, and turned their attention back to his cooking lesson.

After they had the grits simmering and the ham sizzling, he taught her the proper amounts of lard and flour to use for biscuits, along with the saleratus and salt to make them rise. He showed her how to use the sifter in the cabinet to make the texture smoother. Then he brought in the pail of fresh milk, which sat on the back porch. "This will give the biscuits a better taste than water."

"Oh."

She delighted in learning how to do it right, and was a very quick learner. But he could tell by her constant flush, she was still embarrassed at all the mistakes she'd made. "Actually, Kyra, you did quite well for it being your first time in the kitchen. I'm surprised at how you figured out how to do things without any training at all. You should have seen all the meals I messed up when Shane first taught me." He laughed at the memories.

When the coffee had brewed and the ham was nearly ready, he showed her how to add just enough coffee to the skillet to make the gravy and soften the meat. After seasoning the grits properly, everything was done.

As they sat together to enjoy their meal, he reached for the newspaper he'd brought from Las Almas yesterday. "What happened to my paper? I thought I'd left it here last night."

Kyra wrung her hands. "I believe that's another thing I did wrong. I used the paper to start the fire in the stove."

"Oh, well, don't worry. I'll get another. I've got to go to town anyway."

"Would you mind if I go with you?"

"I don't think that would be wise. We don't want people knowing you're here, in case Wade shows up."

"But what about the people I saw in town yesterday?"

"I know Lucy won't talk, and the Easley brothers should heed my warning if they know what's good for them. Today I'll talk to the sheriff as well."

"What are we going to do, Cliff? Am I going to have to run from Wade and Jacques all my life?" Worry lurked in her eyes.

Cliff covered her hand with his. "Trust me, Kyra. You did the right thing when you came to me. I know all about the type of men who harm gentle women and defenseless children, and I've learned how to stop them. I'll make sure nobody ever harms you."

It was a pledge.

Chapter Six

Open-Heart Sandwiches: Covered with a variety of savory delicacies, these sandwiches are served uncovered and unprotected to reveal their tasty toppings.
From the *Sinfully Delicious Bakery Recipe Book*

Cliff reined Blackjack to a halt in a whirl of dust on Main Street of Las Almas. The horse guzzled from the water trough while Cliff tied him to the snortin' post.

"I know I ran you hard, boy, but I have to get a message to Shane as soon as possible." With a final pat on his horse's neck, he headed toward the telegraph office.

He had three jobs in town before hurrying back to the Lucky Number Seven. Worry ate at his gut, even though he'd instructed his men about extra precautions for Kyra's safety. But he felt uncomfortable having her out of his sight. He had far more personal experience in dealing with bounty hunters and criminals than any of his men—although every last one of them had been affected by violence in some way or another.

As Cliff entered the telegraph and printing office, the smell of ink assaulted his senses. He anxiously tapped his fingers against his leg. He had no idea where Shane would be at any given moment.

Cliff didn't know if Shane completely understood why the thought of endless tracking, capturing, and sometimes killing didn't appeal to him anymore. Although they'd both witnessed extreme violence as children, it had been in vastly different ways. To Shane, violence was a way to achieve justice. To Cliff, violence destroyed homes and families.

After settling on a couple of likely locations, Cliff sent the messages and then made his way to the sheriff's office, his mule-eared boots clopping on the boardwalk. Sheriff Overby was tacking up a wanted poster to the bulletin board outside his office door.

"Morning, Sheriff."

"Baldwin. Glad to see you. Hope your lady friend caught up with you yesterday without no harm. Hampton was fit to be tied when he realized she'd gone to find you alone. I hope you know I had no intention of sending her into the Wolf or Lucy's. Never thought she'd consider going into one of those places on her own being as she's obviously a lady."

"She caught up with me. Actually, Miss Lourdes is why I'm here. I need to talk to you a moment in private."

"Well, step on in. Oh, by the way, Baldwin, you ought to take a look at this new wanted poster. You recognize them boys?"

The Yancey brothers' picture glared back at Cliff. "They escaped a week ago," said the sheriff, "six days before they were scheduled to hang in Dallas. You might want to be on the lookout for trouble, Cliff, seeing as how you were the one that turned them in—and killed their little brother."

"Great, just what I need. More trouble," Cliff mumbled as they walked into the sheriff's office.

"So, what other trouble you got on your mind this morning?" The sheriff sat behind his desk, the chair groaning under his heavy weight.

Cliff leaned his arms on the back of a chair and lowered his voice, "Miss Lourdes is in danger. She witnessed a murder back home in New Orleans and ran away. From the story she told me, I think the murderer has sent a hunter named Wade and maybe some others on her trail. As soon as I have Miss Lourdes protected here, I plan to find Wade and persuade him to hunt someone else. But I'd—"

"A murder! Why, I'll need to question her and telegraph a warning to the New Orleans police."

"You're right, of course, and I'll bring her in to talk to you . . . but only *after* I'm assured of her safety."

"You best tell me exactly what's going on if you expect me to wait to question a murder witness." The sheriff stood up and leaned across the desk, his face as determined as Cliff's, only a few inches from his own.

Cliff didn't back down; he clenched his jaw and moved in even closer. As succinctly as possible, he outlined Kyra's story.

"So you can see why I'm anxious to protect Miss Lourdes first. This Jacques sounds like a madman, and he has money and power."

The sheriff rapped his fingers on his desk, his expression serious. "You can let up your death grip on that chair. I agree to your plan because I don't want any harm to come to her. I'll tell the others that were here yesterday to keep quiet."

"Thanks, Sheriff."

"All right, Baldwin. Considering all you've done in the past to help the law, I guess the law can help you out this time. I give you one week before I'll ride out to your ranch to talk to her myself. Is that understood?"

"Two weeks."

The Sheriff shook his head. "Ten days . . . not one day more."

With an abrupt nod of appreciation Cliff turned to go, then paused. "I'll talk to Hampton myself," he added before he shut the door behind himself.

Now where in the world, or more specifically where in Las Almas, would he find Luke Hampton? As he clomped down the boardwalk, he looked in shop and office windows hoping to catch a glimpse of him. He didn't know all that much about Luke, who was more or less an enigma around town.

He was liked well enough, but no one knew who he was or what he was doing here. He'd lived in Las Almas less than a year, and often disappeared for weeks at a time, sometimes appearing in town only long enough to stock up on supplies before heading out again. It was whispered he was involved in everything from swindling to gold mining to oil speculation.

But Cliff had to have some reinforcements if Wade did indeed come looking for Kyra. And he'd always relied on his gut feelings with regard to judging people's characters. His instincts had saved his life more than once, and he wouldn't be dismissing them now. Whereas he trusted Sheriff Overby for his honesty, and indeed that was by far the most important requirement of any lawman to Cliff's way of thinking, Overby was not the most adept or intelligent person in his job. He needed someone else to be on the alert in town, and his instincts told him he could trust Luke. The question was where to find him.

As he passed by Adams General Store and Mercantile, he remembered the newspaper he needed to replace. He sauntered through the door, bells jingling over his head. Adams peered at him from behind a counter.

"Good morning, Baldwin. How you doing today?"

"Fine, just fine. You got this week's *Dallas Enquirer*?"

Adams nodded his head. "Over here."

As Cliff walked forward, he caught a glimpse of movement out of the corner of his eye. He turned toward the back corner, finding Luke Hampton examining shovels and pickaxes. "Hampton, I was looking for you," he announced as he left the newspaper on the counter and approached the other man. "Can I talk to you a moment?"

Luke peered at Cliff curiously, then nodded. Cliff gave Luke a once-over, wanting to verify one final time that his instincts were on track. Luke was dressed in his customary black, from his Justin boots to his suede hat. The only color showing was a bright orange and blue geometrical hatband, which seemed to be of Indian origin. He was tall and strong, with a whiplike physique. His gaze was straight and steady, with no hint of weakness or deceit—just an air of privacy and aloofness.

With much fewer details than he'd given the sheriff, Cliff quietly repeated Kyra's story and asked for Luke's vigilance in town as well. "I'm asking for your help because I'm going to be gone for a couple of days to track Wade. While my hands are capable of handling things at the ranch, I need to make sure someone in town can waylay Wade, or anyone else, if he shows up here before I get back. I wouldn't want to leave such an important matter only on Overby's shoulders. You understand?"

"Sure, sure." Luke grinned knowingly. "Can never hurt to have more eyes on the lookout. Don't worry. I plan to be in town for a week at least. If I hear of anyone inquiring for Miss Lourdes, I'll make sure he doesn't find her. She kind of reminds me of my sister. Wouldn't want to see her harmed."

Cliff didn't show his surprise. This was the longest conversation he'd ever had with Hampton, and the first he'd ever heard of any family of his.

"I'm much obliged for your help. When this is all over, I'll owe you one."

Now Luke chuckled. "Well, you know, I might take you up on that. I hear you're friends with Shane Chandler. I'd be interested in an introduction. Might have a business proposition for him."

Cliff nodded and ambled back toward the counter. He was curious, but wouldn't prod for information.

"Would you be wanting anything else, Mr. Baldwin?" Adams asked from behind the counter.

Supplies, supplies . . . he glanced around the store. He couldn't think of anything they needed back at the ranch. Paco had stocked up yesterday. But then his gaze lighted on a couple of cookbooks resting on the shelf directly behind the counter.

"I'll take one of those cookbooks." *Lord, please let Kyra be pleased and not offended.*

Cliff arrived at the ranch house to find Kyra sitting on the front porch drying her long hair in the sun. The hair was still damp, and the blazing light picked out red highlights in the glossy chestnut locks. He longed to know if her hair felt as soft as it looked, to smell once again her sweet jasmine scent. A smile of welcome lit her face as he reined in Blackjack. Cliff dismounted and slapped his horse across the rump, sending him trotting off to the stables.

"Did you enjoy your bath?" he asked.

"Yes, thank you for helping me heat the water and fill the tub before you left. I hope your trip to town was successful."

"I got a message off to Shane to get here pronto. I hope he receives it."

"Did you get a newspaper as well?" she asked, her face a pale shade of pink.

He tossed the paper onto her lap. Then he laid a brown paper-wrapped package on top of it.

Wide green eyes stared at him in surprise. "What's this?"

He couldn't help but smile in response. "Just a little something I picked up in town. I hope it doesn't offend you."

She opened the package carefully, slowly, finally making Cliff reach out and finish tearing the wrapping himself. *Mrs. Featherstone's Guide to American Cookery* stood out in gold letters on a black leather binding.

"A cookbook! Thank you, Cliff. I do believe this is the sweetest present anyone has ever given me."

And with that, letting the book and paper tumble from her lap to the floor, she stood on the tip of her toes, tugged his head down, and planted a soft peck on his cheek. He was awash in a field of jasmine.

Cliff's face burned as he breathed a sigh of relief and pride. "I'm glad you like it, but I can't imagine it comparing to the gifts those six fiancés probably gave you, much less those I remember your parents giving you every year at Christmas." He reached down to pick up the paper and book and handed them back to her.

"Oh, but it does. My mother always gives me what she thinks I ought to have—new formal clothes, guides to proper etiquette, ribbons and combs and other such nonsense. All to make me acceptable to some man. And my fiancés, yes, they gave me gifts, but nothing with imagination . . . just the typical flowers and candy. You thought about what *I* might like . . . something to help me learn and grow . . .

a new experience to conquer. It was extremely considerate and I appreciate it."

"Or I could be selfishly interested in my own stomach."

Kyra's head bobbed up from skimming through her new book. She caught his grin, and then laughed out loud. He would have joined her if his throat hadn't tightened. It had been a long time since he'd heard her really laugh, and he'd forgotten how delightful it sounded. Her mother had tried for years to teach her a softly trickling ladylike type of laugh, but she'd never gotten the hang of it. Her laugh was silly, loud, and full-bodied. It made people want to join in.

"Well, I guess I couldn't blame you if you did. I mean, that breakfast I served this morning would make me go out and buy myself a cookbook as well. I thank you, Cliff."

"How about we put the cookbook away, pack a picnic, and I'll show you around my ranch a little."

"I'll race you to the kitchen." And off she flew, the screen door slamming behind her.

Cliff shook his head, picking up the paper again. At least she'd carried the cookbook with her this time. He followed along behind her.

Soon they were on their way, heading toward the river. Cliff took Kyra's hand, and tucked it under the vibrant muscle of his arm. She sighed at how safe and feminine it made her feel. She could picture so clearly the time when he'd been, in her worshipful eyes, a Southern gentleman like no other. If it weren't for his gun belt jabbing her hip, she'd almost believe he still was.

From the corner of her eye, she studied his lean figure in tight jeans until her glance collided with his mocking, knowing smile. Flustered, she riveted her gaze toward the river. He knew his effect, the horned toad. Now that she was older, she wasn't so naïve. She understood the masculine appreciation in his eyes. But what confused her was the turbulence and longing he tried hard to hide. His desire, it seemed, bore great unhappiness as well.

She faced him shyly, her heart skipping a beat. "What?"

"You've grown into a beautiful woman." His voice could have melted butter.

Something fluttered in her stomach. "You exaggerate, Cliff." She shooed him away with her free hand.

He turned his gaze back toward the shallow river they approached. "I never exaggerate," he said with finality.

Finding a shaded spot under a tree, Cliff spread out the blanket, placing the picnic basket on a corner to help hold the blanket down. Kyra sat, folding her legs beneath her yellow day dress, her hands primly on her lap.

She watched him plop down beside her, and followed his gaze toward the river. It glistened, snaking through slickly smoothed rocks. She observed the small crashes of whitewater as it beat a constant humming rhythm, which she found soothing. The rippling water journeyed beyond the bend, to where the sun sat lower in the western sky. She leaned back, enjoying the feel of the breeze caressing her, relieving the heat. The smell of prairie grasses made the world seem fresh and clean.

Kyra turned her attention once again to Cliff. His ebony hair blew back with the breeze; his face was clean-shaven and smooth. He loomed big sitting beside her, nearly taking up the rest of the blanket. My, but he was handsome—even more than she remembered, his profile resembling one of those Greek statues she'd seen in Europe. *Society* might not see him as handsome, with his long hair, scars, and rugged features, but to her he was an Adonis.

She wondered if the rest of him looked like a Greek god, and blood rushed to her face as she remembered the scandalous statues, many of which hadn't even sported a fig leaf. However, she had to admit they'd been beautiful, the marble and bronze exhibiting the fine details of the male anatomy. They'd seemed so powerful, overwhelming the visitor with the strength of their form. In fact, the small appendage between their legs went almost ignored. Would it be the same with Cliff? Gulping, Kyra fanned herself with a hand. Where did such thoughts come from? Her mother would have chastised her up one side and down the other for her impropriety. Some conversation was needed, something to take her mind off his body.

"Your ranch is impressive, Cliff. It's wonderful."

His searing blue gaze found hers. He smiled, and a wave crashed deep in her belly. What was wrong with her? Yes, he was handsome and had been her childhood friend, but she felt like an infatuated sixteen-year-old again. He'd left her then and she shouldn't be feeling like this now—not after so many years.

Kyra swallowed, watching as he pulled his blued Colt out of his holster, laid it to his side within reach, and twisted to face her.

"Bounty hunting can be profitable if you're any good at it." His expression took on a faraway look. "Once I earned enough, it was a matter of getting a good deal, which this ranch was," he added, gesturing behind them. "I've got a mortgage on it, but after one more season, I should be able to pay it up. You know, even though I didn't finish my university studies, my education still came in handy for running this business."

"Do you regret not finishing at the University of Louisiana?" Would he tell her more about why he'd left so abruptly? She'd always wondered if she'd played any part in his decision to leave. Once, she'd suggested he go out West, since it had been his childhood dream, but he was supposed to have said good-bye first. He hadn't done that. She placed her fingers to her lips, remembering the kiss they'd shared the last evening she'd seen him. Realizing what she was doing, she hurriedly dropped them.

After staring at the rushing water for a while, Cliff turned to regard her. "No. Sometimes . . . but mostly no. I never wanted to go back," he said, sounding more convinced.

Her heart thudded to a stop. She saw the pain in his eyes—the determination in his words, wounding her in the process. She hung her head, studying her hands.

"Was it me?" she asked.

Cliff gaped at Kyra, taken aback. She looked so forlorn at the moment. He reached out and tilted her chin, his thumb caressing her cheek.

"No, you had absolutely nothing to do with it. Not in any way that counts. Please don't tell me you thought you were at fault."

She licked her lips. "I—I thought that in some way you wanted to get away from me . . . the kiss we shared . . . the argument we had." She shrugged.

Throat tight, he closed his eyes a moment. "Kyra, no. Yes, it was wrong of me to kiss you. You were too young for me and I should have restrained myself. We certainly shouldn't have argued the way we did. My temper was atrocious. It . . . well, it brought out the worst in me . . . made me act in a way that reminded me . . . I wish I could explain it all, Kyra, but I can't. Not to anyone. Not now. Just believe me, you had nothing to do with it."

She cocked her head to one side, a smile on her beautiful face. He was glad to see the sadness leave her.

"Do you think you'll tell me one day?" she asked.

His mouth twisted. "Maybe, when I'm ready." Like when armadillos run races and cows ride in coaches. He reached for the picnic basket, placing it between them. They filled their plates with sandwiches and cheese, eating in companionable silence.

"I take it that your visit to Madam Lucy's means you don't have a special woman in your life," she blurted out.

He choked on a piece of cheese. Proper ladies didn't talk about such things with a man, but then again, he wasn't just any man to Kyra.

He had no choice but to laugh. "You are full of surprises, aren't you? No, I don't have a special woman."

"Why not?"

His chest lurched. "Do you think any decent woman would want a man with my reputation or would be willing to risk being with me?" His gaze returned to the river, before those sensitive eyes of hers perceived his loneliness, his distrust. A part of him longed to hear her say, "I would." But that was nonsense. Even if Kyra were willing, he could never make her his wife. It wouldn't be safe.

"Besides, I've never wanted to marry." He said the words with finality.

"I think a woman would be very lucky to stand side by side with a man like you. You're a good and honorable person, Cliff, deep inside where it counts."

Her shyly spoken words made him scowl even more. "You don't know that, Kyra. I am *not* the good person you believe I am. You don't know half the things I've done. You just have a bad case of hero worship. You have ever since the first day we met when I stopped those boys from drowning your puppies in that washbasin. Besides, there are plenty of men out here who don't appreciate what I used to do for a living. Any family I might have would be put in danger because of my past." With that, he stood up and started putting away the food. He needed something to do.

"You sure don't like talking about yourself or answering questions, do you?"

"You're blame right about that. I guess I've gotten too accustomed to the Texas way of life. Out here a man's privacy is something worth fighting and dying for. No one has dared ask me questions about my past. Except Shane."

"How did you meet Shane?"

Kyra continued eating from her plate, forcing Cliff to stop putting the food away and sit back on his haunches.

"I was his partner. He's how I got into bounty hunting."

"Oh. Actually, considering how accident-prone you used to be, I find it amazing you managed bounty hunting so well."

Hell, she made his palms sweat. He loved being with her, but couldn't she leave the past alone?

Abruptly she reached out and touched the small white scar next to his eye. He remembered telling her that he'd been thrown from his horse. Her touch was whisper soft, her fingertips so electrifying he nearly jumped. Grimness overshadowed his face.

She pulled her hand away, flustered. "Do—do you care for a game of cards? I found some on your mantel," she murmured, head down, staring at her hands, safely back in her lap.

God, she was a pretty little thing. She was probably about the only person he could stand interrogating him, and even that wasn't easy. He smiled. "Only if we can bet on something."

"Hmmm. All right, what shall we wager?"

"I win and you have to tell me all about your fiancés."

"Absolutely not! They're none of your business."

He studied her outraged face. Her sultry lips were inviting, the mole above her lip begging to be kissed. "Afraid you can't win? Is that it?" That was sure to get her.

"What's in it for me?"

"What would you like?"

"If I win, you have to tell me why you left New Orleans."

That stopped him cold. He would never share that part of his life, even with her. But he wanted to hear about the six fiancés, and if he picked the right game, he was sure he could win. Her grandfather had taught her many card games, but she didn't have much practice with the ones designed purely for betting.

"All right. It's a deal, but I get to pick the game. Monte. You remember how to play, don't you? We bet on the top two and bottom two cards of the deck. We'll play five rounds."

"Of course I remember how to play. It's just that I haven't played this game very often. Hand me the cards, Bayou Baldwin. I'll deal first."

Kyra snatched the cards from him, dealing them the way Grandpère had taught her. Unfortunately, as it turned out, she was distracted from her game, what with Cliff talking to her, his devilish smile giving her body the shivers. In the end he won three hands out of five.

What was wrong with her? She rarely ever lost; she was good at games of chance. She threw her cards down in disgust. "Well, I suppose you won this time."

Cliff grinned and stretched out on the blanket, his head held up by his arm. "I see you're still a sore loser."

Kyra, feeling somewhat disgruntled, quirked her lips at his lazy smile. She slid her gaze down the length of his body and back to where his hand rested on the blanket in front of him. *If only I were brazen enough to touch it.* He finally interrupted her wayward thoughts.

"So, you were going to tell me about your fiancés, the six deadly sins?" he reminded her with a triumphant smirk.

"Oh, heavens, Cliff, I couldn't possibly tell you about all of them now. We would be here all night," she complained as she smoothed out her skirts.

"So just start with the first one, and tell me about the others when I get the urge. Deal?"

She threw him a look of true annoyance. He stared intently at her, those predatory eyes . . . waiting.

"Deal," she whispered. She toyed with the grass on the edge of the blanket. "It's rather embarrassing, you know."

"Is it?"

He gave her his best amused look now. Well, she wasn't going to let him ruffle her feathers. Kyra straightened her spine. She'd tell him everything. After all, that's what he wanted to hear, wasn't it?

"Yes, well, my first fiancé was *Greed*—or Torvill Knox, if you wish. His father made it big with the railroad. He was a university graduate, quite savvy in business. My parents were the ones who introduced him to me after my debut."

"Why were your parents set on him?"

"Well, my being their only child, and a female at that, they wanted someone who could run my inheritance properly. Unfortunately, I soon resented him for the miserly little man he was. All he ever wanted was my land and money."

"Little man?"

"Yes, he was beady-eyed, had small ears, and reminded me of a greedy mouse."

"If you didn't like him, then why did you accept the engagement?"

"I didn't have much choice, of course. I wanted to please my parents. They pressured me in a not so subtle way to accept, and were so happy when I did." She paused a moment, studying a ripple in the water where a frog had dived in. More quietly she added, "It wasn't long before I was miserable." She turned her gaze once again to Cliff. "He never showed once that he cared for me, only for my financial standing. He didn't have a romantic bone in his body. Flowers, the opera, or the theater, among other things, were frivolous according to him. He practically had a cash register for a heart. I soon grew tired of his long lectures on spending. Why, I became an expert myself at investing and the economy."

"So you broke it off right away?"

"Oh, heavens, no. I still wanted to please my parents, and you know how ostracized one is for breaking an announced engagement. It was as we approached the actual wedding date that I finally found the courage. I kept imagining the wedding night and . . . well, that was enough to push me."

Cliff had a picture in his mind of Kyra on her wedding night with a miserly beady-eyed mouse of a man. He was glad she'd ended it. However, he did find it amusing that she seemed afraid at the prospect of lovemaking. Hell, it had been a while since he'd spent much time around any woman who didn't make a living on her back. Most refined ladies had more delicate sensibilities. He smiled to himself.

"Yes, I could imagine him ooh-ing and aah-ing." She threw back her head, moving it from side to side, her hair spilling out of her chignon. "*'Ooh, your money is so wonderful, aah, your dowry will make wonderful investments, ooh, I can't wait to get my hands on everything else you'll have'*—and it was enough to make me ill. I will *not* give myself to any man unless he . . ." She stopped in mid-sentence as Cliff sat up, scowling.

Well, she'd certainly shocked him this time, and just as he was thinking about her supposed delicate sensibilities.

"Oh, goodness, I've overstepped propriety again, haven't I? I always did forget myself whenever I was around you."

"Do you *care* to explain what you know about 'ooh-ing' and 'aah-ing'?" his voice thundered. He wouldn't have been surprised if they'd heard his roar all the way back at the ranch.

Chapter Seven

Heavenly Hash: Give your taste buds blissful peace with this mixture of fruits and nuts. A delightful dish to share with someone special on a warm summer's eve.
From the *Sinfully Delicious Bakery Recipe Book*

"Why, Cliff, I'm not ignorant, you know." Her tone was a little too coy for him.

"Kyra, answer the damn question. Has any man taken advantage of you?"

She shooed him away with her hands. He grabbed hold of them in a steely grip. "I mean it." He made his tone as threatening as he could. He'd sent many a lowlife running with less.

"Oh, Cliff, it's not what you think."

"Well, explain it then." Hell, she didn't seem the least bit intimidated despite all his efforts.

She shrugged. "I just happen to have partially seen, but mostly heard, my maid coupling with the groom, that's all."

"You what?" His voice was hoarse.

Her eyes downcast, she continued. "After you left, I took to going up in the loft in the stables whenever I wanted to write in my journal. One day I was up there, nearly asleep, when I heard this piercing scream followed by a cacophony of heavy breathing, rantings and ravings . . . *oohs* and *aahs,* basically," she explained, raising her eyebrows and hands. "Why, it was quite the exaggeration. I'm sure that if it were supposed to be like that, I would have heard my parents in my own house at least once, don't you think?"

He shook his head now, a smile on his lips. "God, Kyra, I can't believe you sometimes. Have you no shame?"

"About what? Hearing what I did or telling you?"

"Both." He shook his head again.

"I'm sorry. It's not as though I could have let them know I was there. I suppose I'm not a proper lady to tell you all this," she said, facing her lap again.

"No, Kyra, you are in every way that counts."

At that her chest jerked with laughter. "Yes, I'm not so ignorant, see? I know all about men. Why *I* have even seen what a naked man looks like," she admitted in a conspiring whisper. "Europe was full of Roman and Greek statues, their unmentionables in plain view. It was quite the shock." Her face was scarlet now.

"Now, Kyra, don't go basing your knowledge of men on those statues," he warned.

"Why not?"

He started to say something about real men, and then shut his mouth. "I think that is for you to find out with your future husband."

"Well, at this rate I may never get married."

He didn't know what to say. Her life was certainly in turmoil at the moment, and he doubted anyone would want to be fiancé number seven. *He* certainly wasn't going to apply for the job, no matter how tempting he found her.

"I think we should be getting back now," he said.

They collected their things and ambled toward the ranch house, each sunk in their own thoughts—Cliff worrying about the devil tracking Kyra, and Kyra pondering what demons stalked Cliff.

* * *

Alone that night in his bedroom, Cliff lay propped in his bed with a book on livestock management. He'd just read the same sentence for the twentieth time. Cursing, he rubbed his eyes once again and started over. Used to living alone, he found it distracting to have a woman under his roof—especially when that woman was Kyra.

An image of Kyra as he remembered her in New Orleans hovered in the back of his mind. The truth was, she'd scared him then and she scared him now. It all seemed so long ago, the time when his affection had gradually changed. Leaning against the pillows, he tried to remember when it had happened exactly, but couldn't put his finger on it. One day he'd seen her as a pesky little sister . . . and then he hadn't. He puffed air in his cheeks, exhaling in a frustrated whisper. God, in some ways it seemed like yesterday. Clearly, he hadn't forgotten the pot of turmoil she'd stirred in his heart. And now, there she was in the other room, more woman than child and more beautiful than a woman had a right to be. She was a belle, sultry, designed to plant fantasies in a man's mind. He'd seen it then, as innocent as she'd been; he saw it now.

Cliff sighed, snapped the book closed, and plunked it on the night table. He'd do better to get some rest. But a picture of Kyra down by the river kept invading his mind. Her head was thrown back, a look of passion on her face, her mouth partly open. He'd wanted nothing more than to kiss her luscious lips, stroke her body with his heated touch, thrust her beneath him and make hot love to her under the sun. He groaned, shifting restlessly.

God, please let Shane get here soon. He wanted to take care of her situation and get rid of her. Sure, he cared for her. How could he not? But they were grown now and it was just too . . . dangerous. Too dangerous for her. He was not a man she could trust.

He doused the lamp and shifted to find a comfortable position. The perspiration beaded on his forehead, his sex swollen painfully. How was it possible she could still affect him this way—this suddenly? It had been the same, years before. One year he'd gone off to the University of Louisiana, and returned to find she was no longer a child. After three years of seeing her sparsely, he'd found himself more and more attracted to her each time. But he'd known she wasn't for him. Foremost, she wasn't yet available for courting, and even if he'd waited for her debut, he wouldn't have called on her as a beau.

He'd mastered the art of hiding his emotions, but that had never been Kyra's forte. It hadn't been hard to understand that she was infatuated with him. But he'd always pretended he didn't see it—or her. He'd been determined not to ruin her life by tainting her with his. It hadn't been easy.

Cliff's lips thinned as he remembered that Christmas Eve when he'd given in to his urgings and kissed her. God, her unschooled lips had been his undoing. Maybe, if he hadn't abruptly left New Orleans that night, he would have given in to his heart. Instead, he'd managed to protect it. It had only been a few months before that he'd been consumed with despair at his mother's death. His guilt and sense of betrayal had been so overwhelming, he had almost welcomed death for himself.

Remembering that time brought a lump to his throat. Kyra. Maybe she was the reason he'd survived, until he'd decided it was easier to make a life elsewhere and start over.

Blowing out a spew of pent-up air, he saw her again in his mind the last time he'd really spent significant time with her. It was after his mother's funeral, and prior to that fateful Christmas Eve. The university had closed for a two-day break, and because the weekend followed, he'd decided on a four-day visit with Kyra's grandfather. He knew he'd probably see her as well, but he'd convinced himself he bore nothing more than brotherly affection for her.

It didn't seem that long ago.

He'd been let in to Grandpère's town house only a few minutes before he saw Kyra rush down the stairs in a swirl of skirts. She'd obviously been notified of his arrival.

"Cliff . . ." She stopped herself short at the bottom of the stairs. Giving him an impish grin, she straightened her skirts slowly and then moved across the foyer in a graceful walk.

She wore her hair down in soft ringlets around her exotic face. Her deep emerald-green day dress matched the color of her eyes, hugging her body in a way that tugged at his imagination. Every time he saw her, she got prettier . . . and older.

With a bubbly laugh she threw herself into his arms. God, she felt good, way down to his soul.

She pulled back to study him, a hint of shyness to her smile. A moment later she frowned.

"Oh, Cliff, you don't look so good. You've lost weight. Are you all right?"

He made an attempt at a smile. She was the first person to care enough to ask. "I'm fine," he said gruffly. "We had a few days off . . . and well, I hoped Grandpère wouldn't mind a guest for a few days. What do you think?"

"I take it you don't want to go home?" she whispered.

He looked away. "No, I don't want to go there. I'd rather spend my time with an ornery man and a scamp like you. Are you here for the day?"

"Actually, my parents had some business in Baton Rouge, and so I'm staying here until they return. Grandpère's teaching me a new card game. I'd love to play with you."

Later that evening, Grandmère rocked in front of the fireplace with her needlepoint as he, Kyra, and Grandpère played *scala quaranta.* Grandpère had picked up the card game during a recent visit to Italy.

After a few rounds, the older couple decided to retire for the night, but Kyra wanted to play a little more. Kissing Kyra's cheek, Grandpère cautioned, "I know you're in trustworthy hands." He'd emphasized the word *trustworthy.* Cliff knew Grandpère thought of him as a grandson, but still needed to convey the message for Kyra's protection. Not that Cliff had any lascivious plans—at least not outside of his mind.

After the final card had been thrown, Cliff pushed up from his chair to head for bed. But Kyra abruptly grabbed hold of his hand, pulling him along behind her. He followed her up the stairs, until they reached the threshold of her room.

"Cliff, go get your coat, and meet me back here."

"But . . ."

She disappeared inside her bedroom, and so he did as she asked. He returned with his coat to find her waiting, wrapped in a white woolen shawl.

He grinned. "Whatever the mischievous plan is, it's a bad idea. It's too late to go out on the streets. I'd prefer to turn in for the night." *Rather than spend another aching moment in your presence.*

"Oh, Cliff, I don't see you all that often. How about some fun? Come on."

"I don't like 'fun.' "

"Well, *I* do." She pulled him into her room.

"What are you doing?" he whispered. "Are you out of your mind? If Grandpère finds me in here, he'll skin me alive."

"Oh, I'm sick of all this propriety and morality constantly being shoved down my throat. One day I'll end up married to some stuffy Creole and . . . well, I want to enjoy some time with you, Cliff. Don't ruin it."

Her gaze clung to his, pleading green pools, *full of trouble,* he reminded himself. He wished he could tell her he'd call on her when she came of age in another year. That *he* wouldn't be a stuffy Creole. But he remained silent.

She turned then toward the window. He pushed aside the thoughts of her marrying some other man and reminded himself again who she was. She was just Kyra, the pesky little girl in pigtails who used to follow him around like a shadow.

She raised her window high and motioned for him to come forward. Quickly, she crawled out onto the roof. He ran forward. "Are you crazy?"

From the other side she flashed a devious smile. "Come on. The stars are beautiful from here. I want to show them to you."

A while later he had to admit she was right. For some reason, the river always smelled stronger, and cleaner, during the night. The stars were beautiful. *She* was beautiful. How was it that she enjoyed life so much? What was her secret? And would it make her more vulnerable to being hurt one day?

Silence loomed between them for a long time as they lay back watching the sky. It was infinite and grand, its secrets calling to him in whispers from the October breeze swirling above him.

"Do you believe in God, Kyra?" He wasn't sure where the question came from, but the peace of the moment seemed to inspire such reflections.

"When I see a sky like this, I feel a sense of grandeur and yet simplicity—a powerful force that connects us and draws us together. Yes, I believe there has to be." She turned, holding his gaze. "Do you?"

"No . . . I don't know. If there is a God, why does He allow good people to be hurt, to suffer, and evil to prosper?"

"Why do *people* allow others to be hurt, to suffer, and evil to prosper? It's a question of responsibility and free will . . . choice."

"For whom?" Her eyes shone with starlight and he was mesmerized.

"For all of us. Father Le Blanc would say that God is the healing love available to us all—ready to pick you up when times are hard . . . to carry you through them, if you ask. But we have to act, to respond, as we are God's hands of change . . . of love." She giggled. "Wouldn't Father be surprised? I did pay attention at Mass after all."

He shrugged. "I don't know why I brought it up."

"I'm glad you did. Don't you have any dreams, Cliff?"

"Dreams? No, I suppose not."

"Why?"

"I don't know. Dreams are for those who deserve . . . for those who have time to spare thinking about them, I suppose." A knot formed in his belly.

"You are so lucky, Cliff, and you don't even realize it."

"Why would you say that?" Her eyes were wide, her lips moist in the moonlight. He wanted nothing more than to kiss her. "What makes me so lucky, brat?"

"I do wish you'd stop calling me that. I've grown up if you haven't noticed."

"No, I haven't." Even in the dark, he saw the hurt flit across her face. It was better this way.

She seemed to recover. "Yes . . . well, you're a man, for one thing. You can do anything you want, follow any dream. Me? I'm limited to dreaming about what man will ask me to marry him, to hoping it's someone I love and who loves me. Even so, my freedom shall be greatly fettered. I doubt any man is willing to put up with my 'spirited' ways, as Mama reminds me constantly. I'll die from boredom."

"I'm sorry, Kyra. But when you eventually fall in love, maybe you won't find those things you like now as attractive. Anyway, I'm sure you'll find a man who loves you. If I didn't see you as my little sister, I'm sure I'd fall in love with you myself." There it was again. Pain etched on her features so honestly, he wanted to take back his words. But he wouldn't.

She gave him her profile as she gazed at the stars. "Think up a dream right now, Cliff."

"I can't . . . and it's silly."

"Yes, you can. Come on."

He sighed. "Crazy . . . all right. I'd leave New Orleans, and head West somewhere . . . maybe buy myself a nice ranch, and spend most of my time outdoors. No more formal attire, no conventional anything, no continuing the family fortune and name."

She lifted up on her elbow. "Then *do* it. You can. If I could, I would. Do it for me too. But don't forget to say good-bye before you do."

He stared at her for a long while. His heart was beating stronger than it had in four long months. It was a crazy idea, but she made it sound simple. Just maybe, after he finished his studies, if the opportunity or need arose, he would . . .

The creak of the door to Kyra's bedroom jarred Cliff out of his recollection. He listened as she pattered toward the kitchen, and a few moments later returned to her room. She must have needed some water. Would she remember to prime the pump? He grinned wryly. His own pump was fully primed and ready. He closed his eyes and concentrated on the ranch duties he'd planned for the next morning. Maybe that would deflate his ardor, and he'd get some sleep. Nah, not likely any time soon.

"Blasted buttons," Kyra complained to herself the next morning as she tugged on the best dress she'd brought with her. It was in the Princess Polonaise style with the green overskirt draped up to form a slight bustle in the back, revealing her white lacy underskirt below the hem and up the front slits of the skirt. The lace was repeated at the V neckline. She'd always thought the dress flattering to her figure and coloring, and for some reason she wanted to look her best for Cliff this morning. She'd fixed her hair à la Concierge, pulling her regular chignon up to the top of her head, and letting tendrils float down around her face; no easy task for someone used to having a maid. But the blasted buttons were impossible to reach—why any dressmaker thought putting fastenings on the *back* of a dress was a good idea, she couldn't understand. She'd have to get Cliff's help with the top ones. All she'd accomplished was turning herself into a knot.

Once Kyra finished her morning toilet, she hastened to the kitchen to start her second attempt at breakfast. Yesterday, thcy'd lived on pretty simple fare the rest of the day, and she wanted to do right by Cliff at least once.

She'd set out some eggs, and was reading how to scramble them in her new cookbook, when a shadow crossed the wall.

"Oh, Cliff, is that you? Would you mind finishing the buttons on my dress? I had trouble reaching the top ones earlier," she explained, her gaze never wavering from the recipe before her.

"I'm not Cliff, but I'd be happy to oblige," said a low, unfamiliar voice.

Kyra froze, her heart slugging wildly against her chest. She closed her eyes; Wade had found her! Inhaling once, she searched the area around her, noting the cast-iron skillet she'd left on the stove. Taking another big breath, she cautiously turned.

Her eyes widened with shock. Leaning against the kitchen table was the biggest, most ferocious-looking Indian she'd ever seen. He stood there, dressed in the usual cowboy garb, his muscular arms and legs crossed, and an expression of faint amusement on his face. She hadn't even heard him come in!

Kyra backed up alongside the counter, toward the stove. Her heart raced. Was he another one of Jacques's hires, or a renegade thief looking for trouble? Cliff had introduced her to all his ranch hands the day before on their return from the picnic, and this man positively was not one of them.

"Now y-you listen to me. I'm a guest here on Cliff Baldwin's ranch—*the* Cliff Baldwin. You—you'd better leave before he finds you here and—and does something horrible—like kill you and feed you to his hogs."

"You think he could manage that?" The stranger raised his eyebrows, obviously not believing he had anything to worry about.

She observed him warily, his amusement seeming to increase, bordering on a mocking sneer. His black hair hung even longer than Cliff's, but was tied together with a leather thong, rather than hanging loosely as Cliff's did. His pulled-back hair emphasized his sculpted features—the high cheekbones, elegantly straight nose, and dimpled chin. *If he weren't so savage-looking, she'd almost consider him handsome.* The irrelevant thought flashed through her mind as she inched away.

"Yes, I should know," she said. "After all, I'm . . . I'm . . . his woman and—well, he would *not* take kindly to you mistreating me. He's friends with the Comanche, you know" Maybe that would win some points in her favor. This man might be a Comanche himself.

The stranger flashed his teeth, the white of them contrasting with his dark, swarthy skin. "Do tell."

What was she to do? Kyra's back hit against the stove, her hands behind her groping for the skillet. She glanced down the length of the stranger, taking in the short-sleeved faded blue cotton shirt leading down to the two big guns he had strapped around the waist of his dark pants; the holsters were tied to both of his massive thighs. Instead of boots, he wore moccasins that reached his knees. He was near enough that she caught a whiff of him. He smelled vaguely of an herb she knew, but couldn't name. It surprised her.

"Yes," she said, "and Cliff has learned all about torturing men, skinning them alive after they roast in the hot sun for agonizing long hours, their hands and feet tied to stakes on the ground. He's even cut off their unmentionables if he's angry enough," she warned, her gaze lowering to the man's middle. She lifted her head back up to find him smiling ear to ear. "You don't strike me as the sort who wants to part with his *you know what.*" Seizing the skillet, she swung it toward the dark man. In an instant, she found herself divested of the skillet, his big body pinning her to the stove, her arms up in the air, held by one of his big hands.

"You were saying?" the stranger asked, his onyx eyes staring darkly into hers.

Chapter Eight

Comanche Corn Pudding: A spicy version made with Indian corn soaked for long hours to soften. The endless color varieties of the kernels give this dish an unusual but appealing appearance.
From the *Sinfully Delicious Bakery Recipe Book*

Cliff was working in the barn with two of his hands, repairing branding equipment damaged in the recent roundup, when he heard Kyra's ear-splitting scream. God! It must be Wade. Heart hammering and six-shooter in hand, he ran to the house in a matter of seconds. Flinging open the front door, he headed for the kitchen, his blood coursing wildly through his veins. As he crossed the threshold he stopped in his tracks, surveying the scene before him. Shane was bent over on his knees, and Kyra was making a run for the back door. At the sight of Cliff, she turned, running toward him instead and placing herself behind him.

"What the *hell* is going on here?" Cliff roared.

Holding on to the back of his shirt as if for dear life, Kyra yelled in his ear, "Do something, Cliff! Tie him up."

Shane was still bent over on the floor, in obvious agony.

Ears ringing, Cliff turned to Kyra and holstered his gun. "What the *blazes* did you do to Shane?"

"Shane? Shane who? Shane Chandler? You mean that this obnoxiously rude, savage-looking man *is your friend*?" Her spine straightened as she pointed to the man on the floor, the one writhing in pain.

"He used to be, at least. What did you do to him?"

Taking a step away from his back, she pointed again to Shane. "Well, it was *his* fault. He could have told me who he was instead of frightening me to death, the ill-mannered lout. He deserved to be brought to his knees. Grandpère told me that if a man ever got too close and I felt threatened, to knee him in his unmentionables—and *he* got too close," she explained, her voice prim and prissy, then crossed her arms over her chest.

Cliff's mouth hung open.

"I guess you think I should apologize, but Mr. Chandler deserved what he got. I suppose it would be ladylike to say I am sorry right away, but I'll do it when I'm good and ready and only after I've accepted his apology first."

Cliff turned the shocked look on his face toward Shane, who now lay sideways on the kitchen floor with his legs bent toward his chest, his eyes closed, his face almost white. Cliff felt a pain of sympathy in his own groin.

Then, out of nowhere, he erupted in a fit of laughter. He laughed so hard it forced him to bend over and lean on the table, tears welling up in his eyes. He finally stumbled back, then thudded down on one of the chairs.

Shane pushed up unsteadily on his knees, his countenance angry enough to kill with just one good stare.

"I never thought I'd see the day *you'd* fall in a fit of laughter. Nice company you keep," Shane added, his voice higher-pitched than normal, his glare directed at Kyra. It intimidated her enough to send her retreating two more steps.

Cliff still laughed. "Well, I never thought I'd see the day you'd be bested by one tiny woman." It was useless. He couldn't stop the laughter that rumbled through his chest. "Shane Chandler . . . this is Miss . . . Kyra Dawson Lourdes . . .

of . . . of New Orleans." Cliff's deep rumble was still echoing heartily.

Shane again gave Kyra a menacing stare. "*Pleased* to meet you, I'm *sure*," he replied in a most sarcastic tone of voice.

Slowly, Shane got up, bracing his arms behind him on the kitchen counter.

Cliff stood as well, continuing his introduction on a more serious note, although he couldn't wipe the smile off his face. "Kyra is visiting for a short period of time. I'll explain it all to you. Did you get my message or are you just stopping by?"

"Got your message," he answered, his black eyes still focused on Kyra. "This she-cat claims to be your woman and that you're liable to roast and skin me alive before you cut off my *unmentionables*."

At that, Cliff took a good look at Kyra, noticing for the first time how lovely she was in her green dress with her hair piled high on top of her head, the escaping tendrils softly framing her reddened face. His heart tapped out a rapid dance. God, if only it were true. If only he could make her his woman in reality. He forced his attention back to Shane. "Well, I do believe she almost took care of that herself." He sat down. "She's not my woman. She's an old friend from back home . . . but she absolutely must be left alone," he warned Shane, his tone final.

"Here you go again," she said. "Talking about me as if I'm not even here. I can speak for myself, thank you, and I can assure you, I have no intention of being charmed by Mr. Chandler."

Shane seconded Kyra's protest. "Hell, Cliff, I pretty much find that most decent white women absolutely must be left alone, or have you forgotten how dainty white ladies turn their noses up at a half-breed savage?"

"Oh, I've seen the effect you have, even on *decent white women*," Cliff answered dryly.

"You're a half-breed?" Kyra asked. "Well, that explains your name and your European-looking features."

"I'm half Comanche, and you were wrong. First I skin them and then I roast them over a spitfire. That includes pretty women who try to destroy my manhood."

She took out her poking finger and actually had the gall to poke Shane on his shoulder. "If you hadn't been such a rude lout, trying to frighten me, it would've never happened. You got what you deserved," she said, her hands finally resting on her hips.

Cliff was impressed. Shane was right. Usually white women went out of their way to hide when Shane was present. But not Kyra. Hell, Shane probably wished she would hide!

Shane turned to Cliff. "You say she's a friend of yours? Since when do you have a woman *friend*?"

Cliff looked at Kyra, ignoring his friend's sarcasm. "She used to be the knock-kneed, freckled, pigtailed girl next door."

"What a charming picture you paint, sir," Kyra replied tartly.

Shane observed Cliff and Kyra for a moment. Judging by the vibrations he sensed between the two, he was sure that Miss Kyra Dawson Lourdes was more than just the girl next door. But it wasn't any of his business to delve into Cliff's past. Cliff tended to keep that part of his life quiet, a decision Shane respected. However, if there was one thing Shane did well, it was sensing people's feelings and dispositions for what they truly were. There was more here than met the eye.

Shane's thoughts were cut short when Cliff spoke, his serious facade returned. "Now, you two, I hope you'll apologize to one another and try to be friends, especially if we're going to spend some time together." Cliff glanced from Shane to Kyra and back again. He obviously expected Shane to apologize first.

Shane figured he'd better get it over with, and extended his hand to Kyra, making sure to hold up his other hand before she got too close. He wasn't taking any chances with his *unmentionables.* "I apologize for scaring the sh—bejeezes out of you. I didn't expect to see you in Cliff's kitchen, and your wanting him to button up the back of your dress was a tad too tempting."

She gripped his hand graciously, while Cliff hurriedly fastened the few top buttons. "I apologize then for hurting you. Had I known who you were, I certainly would have given you a proper welcome, but let me do it now. Would you please join us for breakfast?"

Shane nodded, and slouched into a chair next to Cliff. "So what's going on?"

Cliff spent the next fifteen minutes recounting Kyra's story as they waited for breakfast.

"So Wade is after her?" It was more a statement than a question as Shane furrowed his brow in thought. "I don't recall any posters with Kyra on it, and I'm sure I would have noticed," he said, giving Kyra the once-over. He turned back to Cliff, finding him scowling at him.

"For just a piece of calico," Shane added, "you are mighty possessive, aren't you?" At the sight of Cliff's eyes turning a frosty blue, he lifted his hands up in defense. "Calm down. I'm just poking you."

"Wade must be Jacques' private hire," Cliff speculated. "We'll have to make some plans over breakfast. You *are* going to hang around a while, right?"

"I've got nothing better to do at the moment . . . and I do believe I'm starved."

"Well, don't get your hopes up. She isn't much of a cook." Cliff whispered.

Their plans were made. Cliff was leaving her at his ranch while he hunted Wade. Shane would stay with her. She'd pleaded with Cliff to reconsider, but to no avail. He was determined to take the offensive against Wade, and Shane was the only man he trusted capable of protecting her in his absence.

She didn't want to be left alone with Shane. It wasn't that she didn't trust him—not now that she knew he was Cliff's friend. But, well, they hadn't exactly gotten off to a good start. And he was a stranger. Also, she was anxious about Cliff's safety. He'd had a lot of experience hunting down criminals, but Jacques had probably put a huge price on her head. And money made men do desperate things.

Kyra swallowed the lump in her throat. Cliff would head out before noon for Dallas. And nothing and no one could change his mind now. It was frustrating. Here she thought she was on the verge of starting a new life, of being a new woman, and yet here Cliff was making decisions "for her own good." She might as well be back in her mother's house.

Hearing a door squeak, Kyra turned to face Cliff as he stepped out of his bedroom, fastening his gun belt around his hips. He was dressed in dark denim pants and a blue shirt, with black leather leggings and a black vest, his hat tilted over his left eye. He was tall, lean, and incredibly virile. A heated blush crawled over her face at the thought. Her blood raced through her veins and her stomach felt like she'd swallowed a bowl full of fish. Then she noticed the two guns at his sides and the cartridge belt across his shoulder. She raised her eyes to his in alarm.

"Now, honey, it's nothing to get upset about. I know how to use these guns, and Wade isn't going to get the drop on me. You just don't venture out on a manhunt without a lot of protection. Trust me, I know what I'm doing."

"I trust you, Cliff, but I'll still worry over your safety. Please, please be careful. Don't take any unnecessary chances." She turned from Cliff, guilt-laden tears in her eyes. "I'm so sorry. I've been selfish. I was thinking only of myself when I came to you. I didn't realize the danger I'd be putting you in."

A strong arm turned her around to face him, drawing her close—her body a scant inch away from his. "Never let me hear you're sorry for coming to me again. You did the right thing. I would never have forgiven you if you hadn't come to me for help. I'm your friend, remember, and not a fair-weather friend." He pinned her with his gaze, his eyes blue fire, as though to reassure her with the intensity of his stare alone. "Ahh, honey, come here." He pulled her the remaining inch into his arms. "Don't worry. Nothing's going to happen to me. I'll be back in two days at the most."

Cliff continued holding Kyra, feeling her need for comfort. He also felt some other things as well—namely two firm well-rounded mounds pressing into his chest. Blessings, she'd called them, remembering her reference when she'd described what she'd seen at Lucy's. She was definitely well blessed! A tremor of desire crawled down his belly to settle in his groin. He set her away from him.

But as soon as he pushed her away and looked into her wide, appealing eyes, he found himself pulling her back against his chest. He squeezed her strongly as if to mold their bodies into one, his hands pressed against the small of her back, his fingers itching to travel lower. His gaze sought the mole at the corner of her mouth. He would taste it now. His mouth covered hers as his lips sought to claim new but familiar territory. A gasp escaped from her, and he tasted the sweet nectar of her breath. He tried to be gentle, but found it difficult. The sensual scent of Kyra, her luscious lips under his, her hips crushed forcefully against his solid arousal, all sent him over the edge. He lifted her in his arms, her feet dangling, as his tongue slid smoothly between her teeth. A shiver tingled through her body, and surprisingly, she wrapped her arms around his neck and pressed even closer. Impossible! He couldn't hold her any tighter.

His tongue traced the inside of her mouth, around the corners, licking her mole, before delving deep again, seeking out her sweet inner core, wishing he were seeking out her other, even sweeter, inner core. When her tongue met his and tasted him for the first time, a shudder shook his huge frame and he groaned deeply. Oh, Lord, he had to stop this. It had already gone way too far. He set her away from him and took a deep gulp of air. God, he'd meant to reassure her, not ravish her.

He glanced into her eyes. She looked bemused, and shook like a leaf.

"I'm sorry," he said. "That was uncalled for. I got carried away."

She didn't say anything, staring at him, questioning.

"Uh, I need to go," he went on. "Don't think about what just happened. It was a mistake. I promise you it won't happen again." And as if pursued by a pack of matchmaking mamas, Cliff picked up his hat where it had fallen on the floor, walked around her, and nearly ran out the door.

"Coward," she said to his hastily departing back. But he was already gone. The door slammed shut behind him. Suddenly, Kyra's knees gave away, and she sank onto the sofa, smiling delightedly, her hands shakily brushing through her tousled hair. *How typical of him—just when things are becoming interesting, he gets scared and runs away.* Exactly like he'd done years ago.

Men—they were inferior sorts of creatures. They weren't able to handle the deeper emotions as well as women. But with Cliff, well, there might be a good reason why. She pondered the dilemma. She wasn't sure what secrets he held close to his heart, but she had a strong suspicion.

Sighing, she remembered his kiss. Then unbidden came memories of the first one they'd shared—seven years ago, the day before his departure. It was the same day of their horrible fight. How many times had she relived that last kiss since then? Too many times to count, surely. Cliff's had been her first kiss, and was without doubt her best. She'd compared his kiss always to the few she'd received in the years since. Some of the kisses had been nice, but none had seemed to hold the same excitement for her as his. Maybe that was the luster that had been lacking in her engagements. Maybe she hadn't only been trying to thwart her mother's plans to marry her off and preserve the family legacy.

But this kiss! Well, there was exciting, and then there was *exciting.* The kiss of a twenty-year-old Cliff would have made any young girl blush whenever she remembered it. But the kiss of the grown man had been enough to make the grown woman want something more—something that involved that hard form pressed against her belly. Something that involved a lot of *oohs* and *ahhs. Maybe her maid hadn't exaggerated after all!*

Cliff stepped outside onto the porch. He took a deep breath. God, what had come over him? Green eyes and an attractive mole, that's what. Along with a nice set of *blessings.*

Oh, hell, he didn't have time for this. He had more important things to do. Turning, he caught sight of Shane leading Blackjack out of the stalls toward him, saddled and packed with Cliff's gear and favorite Winchester rifle. Cliff stepped down to meet him.

"I appreciate this, Shane. I trust you to keep Kyra safe."

"Don't worry, friend. I'll keep her safe for you . . . in all ways."

Shane had the gall to smirk at him. Cliff reached out and pounded his friend hard on the back, sending the big man crashing to his knees. Shane's laughter rumbled in deep waves as Cliff vaulted onto the saddle and rode away at breakneck speed.

"Fly away, friend. Fly as fast as you can. But you can't escape your destiny." And then Shane laughed all the harder, sitting in the dirt.

Cliff slumped in his saddle as he peered down the dirt streets of Dallas. It was hot and dusty, but he'd made good time, arriving before dusk. A local saloon was the perfect place to start his search, and he needed something to wet his throat anyhow.

He still had a couple of contacts from his bounty-hunting days here. He didn't want to confront Wade until he had all the facts. He needed to know how many men were searching for Kyra, but he didn't want to tip any of them off to her whereabouts by asking directly about her.

Normally, when hunting criminals, Cliff would've started out at the sheriff's office, finding out as much information as possible. But he dealt with the darker side of bounty hunting now. This wasn't the legitimate hunt for a known criminal, but stopping a hunt for an innocent victim. Wade wouldn't have done anything to draw the attention of local law enforcement. Cliff would have to start with the seedier side to seek out the information he needed. He headed toward The Evening Paradise.

He'd been to the saloon several times before, of course, as it was the center of Dallas's growing crime rings. It was more than a mere saloon, including a gambling hall with tables for roulette, faro, poker, and keno. It also sported a small restaurant, a dance hall, and of course the rooms upstairs for traveling men and working women.

Dallas made Las Almas look like a small country town. It was expanding its boundaries and getting to be quite a city. And like all growing cities, it attracted business to the area—which meant more businessmen. His lip curled. Where businessmen arrived, greed and corruption were soon to follow. He knew from personal experience. That was the main reason he'd chosen to settle in Las Almas rather than Dallas. He had no patience for city life and all that it entailed, having had enough of that growing up in New Orleans. He much preferred the wide-open spaces, the privacy, and the simple life away from too many people.

By and large the people of Las Almas were honest and straightforward. People whom Cliff could trust and live amongst. He was building a good life for himself. One that was a far cry different from that of his father and what his father would have created for him. *Just as it should be.*

Cliff forced his attention to the matter at hand as he entered The Evening Paradise.

He surveyed the crowd. The air was heavy with curling smoke and musty with perfume. There had to be two hundred men scattered throughout the building—a larger crowd than normal. They were playing craps, pool, poker, or drinking beer and whiskey. Women in short skirts that reached only their knees and barely covered their breasts danced with cowboys, served liquor, or entertained at the gambling tables. He didn't see anyone he knew, so he headed toward the barkeeper.

"Root beer," he ordered, leaning nonchalantly against the bar. The barkeeper poured a large glass and slid it toward Cliff, who stopped it with his hand.

After guzzling half the drink, he examined the few men lounging against the bar. Most were busy watching the singer on stage. The blond, voluptuous beauty with plumes woven in her hair wore a seductively short gold evening dress. In a low, sultry voice she belted out "You Naughty, Naughty Men" from the play *The Black Crook.* He had as much privacy as he was going to get.

He tilted his head toward the barkeep and speaking in a low voice, said, "I'm looking for a couple of friends. Wonder if you might have seen them this evening. Pete Jones and Carlton Harris. I think they hang around here often. Do you know them?"

"Sure, I know Jones and Harris. They're regulars here. Can't say as how I've seen them around this evening. But you see the room. Our new singer's drawn quite a crowd."

Cliff glanced at her, nodding. He didn't care about the entertainment, but it always paid never to appear too desperate for information. People didn't like to give it then.

"Well, I guess I'll look around for myself. Appreciate your help," Cliff said as he turned to go. Then, as if a thought had suddenly occurred to him, he added, "Oh, I forgot one other friend, Oscar Wade. Have you seen him here, if you happen to know him?"

The barkeeper wasn't smiling. His eyes were suspicious. "Yep, I know Wade. But if you're a friend of his, you best be moving on along. Wade headed out of town this afternoon, and he might not be around much longer. He's got a posse out hunting him. Seems he wasn't able to pay up on some huge debts he racked up at the tables over the last two weeks. If that posse finds him, you might not have a friend left."

Cliff smiled coldly. "Well, there are *friends,* and then there are *friends.* Wade is the type one doesn't mourn too much, if you know what I mean."

"Then you might want to talk to Mr. Carmichael. He's standing over there to the side of the stage with the three-piece suit. He's the owner of The Paradise and didn't take too kindly to Wade's lack of funds. He's the one who sent the posse after him. Maybe you two could strike up an interesting conversation."

Cliff nodded, flipped the barkeep a coin, and headed toward Carmichael. *God, please let the posse get to Wade.* But he still had to make sure no one else was on the case. And then he had to do something about Jacques back in New Orleans. One problem at a time, though.

"Mr. Carmichael, I'd like to talk to you about a mutual acquaintance," Cliff began.

Carmichael turned toward Cliff, a brow rising faintly in question. He was dressed impeccably as a businessman—matching coat, waistcoat, and pants—the works. Just the type Cliff trusted the least. But when you dealt with rats, you sometimes had to talk to weasels as well. "Who, might I ask, is inquiring?" Carmichael questioned haughtily.

"Name's Baldwin. I'm looking for Oscar Wade."

"If you're a friend of Wade's you'd better be praying for his life. If my men catch up to him and he doesn't have the money he owes me, his life won't be worth much."

"Wade isn't a friend. He's an old rival. I have a debt I need to collect. Do you have any idea where he's gone?"

"You'll have to wait in line to collect that debt. Mine comes first, if he's able to repay. I have no idea where he's gone, but I've sent my best trackers on his trail. Last time I saw him, he was sputtering off about all the money he was due because of some exclusive rights he had." Carmichael turned back toward the stage, watching the singer. "Personally, I think he was out of his mind. Probably the fear of death made him snap. I did have five guns trained on him at the time. He muttered something about catching a Creole angel and finding his soul before he passed out. Do *you* have any idea where he went?"

Cliff had a gut-wrenching, gnawing, terrible fear he knew exactly where Wade had gone. Finding his soul . . . Las Almas Perdidas in Spanish meant "the lost souls." Somehow Wade had found out where Kyra was! The question was, did he know *where* in Las Almas? Cliff had to get back to the ranch.

He allowed none of his thoughts to reflect on his face, however. Experience had taught him not to let anyone know what he was thinking or feeling—except Kyra, it seemed. "No idea. I hope your men get him. I would consider my debt paid with his death as well." Cliff turned to go, but remembered one more question. "How and when did he get away from you?"

The saloon owner scowled. "I let the doctor attend him. Hoped to bring him around enough to determine if he had a prayer of repaying me the twenty thousand dollars he owes. He pulled a fast one, all right. He must have been pretending all along, because he knocked the doctor over the head and escaped out the window. Must have been at about three o'clock this afternoon."

As Cliff left Carmichael, a ball of fear formed in the pit of his stomach and gnawed its way up his chest to lodge in his throat. He had to get to Kyra before Wade found out she was at the Lucky Number Seven.

Twenty thousand dollars in debt and a posse on his tail! There was nothing that would stop a man that desperate except death. He prayed the posse got to Wade before he did, because Cliff was afraid he might be too late.

Chapter Nine

Christmas Eve Eggnogg: This recipe goes great with a little mistletoe to celebrate the giving spirit.
From the *Sinfully Delicious Bakery Recipe Book*

After Cliff left, Kyra became restless. She had to get away from the house. She didn't want to be alone with Shane in such close quarters. And besides, she wanted time to reflect on what had happened with Cliff, on his kiss and her feelings.

She went to her bedroom, picked up her journal and fountain pen from the side compartment of her satchel, and a wide-brimmed hat from a peg on the wall, then headed out the back door just as Shane entered the front.

"Kyra," he called.

She ignored him. Where to go?

Spying the stables, she ran toward them, entering the open front doors. The place was spotlessly clean and huge. There had to be stalls for twenty horses, at least. Cliff was doing well for himself. Noticing a ladder in the back, she hitched up her skirts and climbed to the loft above. She nestled deep into a thick pile of hay, inhaling the sweet, clean smell, ignoring the way it lightly scratched her arms and face.

She placed her journal down by her side as visions of Cliff floated through her mind. She saw his eyes the way they'd last looked at her, alight with passion, then masked with frustration and vexation.

It was a similar reaction to what had happened seven years ago with their first kiss. She was sure he'd been enjoying it as much as she had, when he'd abruptly pushed himself away.

The memories were real again in her mind. . . .

It was Christmas Eve and Cliff was home for winter break from his final year at the University of Louisiana. They'd both been invited to attend Laetitia Gressin's annual Christmas Eve party. She'd seen him less frequently since he'd started his university studies, and every time they were together, something fluttered inside her. The sisterly affection she'd always held for him had changed slowly with every meeting to deep infatuation. He, on the other hand, as far as she could tell, didn't reciprocate her feelings. Maybe this time he'd see her as a woman rather than a childhood friend. She'd even dressed for the occasion, or at least as provocatively as her mother would allow. She'd loved the soft white dress with lavender velvet trim the moment she'd seen it. The high-heeled shoes, however, pinched her feet.

All evening she'd watched Cliff as he conversed with other women—including that catty widow Mrs. Redford. What did he see in them that he didn't see in her? He never flirted with her the same way. She was determined to change that. She hadn't had her debut yet, but it wouldn't be long.

"Please let him see me as a woman," she pleaded in prayer.

During a lull in the festivities, she found her chance, and asked him to step out onto the veranda with her so she could give him his Christmas present. He was so handsome in his black evening attire, she couldn't help but gawk.

The night air breezed cool against her skin, and the full moon illuminated his blue eyes and made his short black hair glisten. Somewhere in the garden below, a water fountain trickled gently, sounding a soothing lullaby to her ears. She'd waited all evening to have him to herself, and now she didn't know what to say. Cliff leaned against the balcony balustrade, one of his rare smiles lighting his face, and her heart skittered.

He broke the silence. "You're very pretty tonight. There's something different about you, but I can't put my finger on it."

"It's my dress. I—I had it made just like one I saw pictured in *Harper's Bazaar.*"

"No, that's not it, Squirt."

"Kyra. My name is Kyra. The shoes then? They make me taller because of the heels."

He shook his head. "No, brat, that's not it either."

"Kyra. Please call me Kyra." Her eyes threatened tears, and so she looked down at the veranda floor.

"Hey . . ." He swatted her shoulder playfully. "I'm sorry, Kyra. I didn't realize you don't like my nicknames anymore."

It was useless. He'd never see her as a woman. "Here's your Christmas present." She handed him a wrapped box.

There was a moment of silence. "Thank you. I have something for you, too."

"You do?"

He pulled out his hand from behind, giving her a small white package. She never could resist a present. Quickly, she unwrapped it, gasping with pleasure when she lifted the lid. Inside was a beautifully ornate miniature musical box. She lifted it out in awe and pried open the lid; Beethoven's "Claire de Lùne" tinkled sweetly.

"It's beautiful, Cliff. Thank you."

He smiled, unwrapping his gift. He seemed surprised with the framed picture of them with their families. He appeared even more surprised when she pulled out a twig of mistletoe from her reticule, laughingly dangling it above her head.

His eyes filled with warmth and incredible longing as he moved toward her, bestowing on her a brief and chaste kiss. When he lifted his head, he peered deeply into her eyes before his mouth descended on hers again with a growl from deep in his throat. His lips were soft and smooth, gentle and caring, but his kiss was scorching. Her heart melted and she pressed closer, her fingers raking through his hair and closing into a fist. His hand glided down her back, and his fingers splayed over the swell of her buttocks. She moaned, about to hold him tighter, when he wrenched himself away, then retreated. Utter frustration was etched on his handsome face.

Kyra's breath caught and her pulse galloped. She couldn't believe he'd actually kissed her. Maybe he did see her as more than a "little brat." Her heart raced with joy, but she contained her elation at his look of mortification. "Cliff, what's wrong?" She moved closer, lifting her face to his. "That was nice. Would you please kiss me again?"

"God, no, Kyra!" he exploded. "Don't you know what you're doing?" His tone quieted when he saw the hurt on her face, the tears gathering. "You've only just turned sixteen, remember? You're too young. You should know better than to stand out here in the dark kissing an older man."

"But, Cliff, you're my best friend. You'd never hurt me. I trust you."

"You don't know anything about me, Kyra. I'm not the man you think I am. I'm not the boy I used to be. Hell, you should trust me least of any man here!"

She wasn't daunted by his words, but saw through to the pain he hid. She stepped closer. "Try it, Cliff. See if I can trust you. Kiss me again." Once again she raised her lips to his. But he backed farther away from her.

He was rejecting her. Although she understood his reasons, at least on the surface, her infatuated heart cried out with the pain, until all she wanted was to lash out at him. "I didn't realize you were such a coward," she said, moving forward as he retreated.

Cliff stopped, an angry glint in his eyes. He shoved her away, stopping himself immediately as she fell backward and reached for the rail to catch herself. Hoarsely he cried out, "My God," then ran off the balcony, away from the house, and out of her life.

One of the horses at the far end of the stable whinnied, pulling Kyra away from her memories of the past. She rolled over onto her stomach, thinking about all the years that had passed. It didn't seem all that long ago, but after that night, she hadn't seen Cliff again until he'd walked down the stairs at Madam Lucy's.

Kyra shuddered at the memory of Cliff's father. He'd been so angry when he'd found out his son had left without a trace, she'd secretly prayed for Cliff not to show up any time soon. Of course, she'd never dreamed he'd run away for good. In the years that followed, she'd never heard from him once. She thought his father hadn't either, but couldn't be sure as he refused to ever mention Cliff's name again. His mother was fortunate to have been dead six months already, avoiding the pain of her only son's disappearance.

Kyra shifted onto her back again, trying to get comfortable. She thrust a piece of straw between her lips, remembering again that first kiss. However, its memory didn't thrill her as much as the memory of her most recent one. She'd sensed the passion in Cliff's kiss—but also the powerful resistance. What was the cause? Fear? Why would he resist a relationship with her if he desired one?

As always when perplexed, Kyra poured forth her feelings and experiences into her journal, hoping to make sense out of her confusion. She was almost finished recording her thoughts when a thump from below caught her attention. She grimaced. Perhaps one of the cowhands had returned from the fields to work in the stables. She rolled over and inched flat on her belly to peer from the loft to the ground below. A strange man slinked inside the door and hid behind a barrel in the corner!

"Kyra!" Where was that foolish girl? Shane frowned as he cupped his hands and shouted again. "Kyra." Still no answer. He left the barn and headed to the henhouse. Maybe she went to find some eggs for supper. Or maybe she was acting like a brat and hiding from him. He'd left her alone when she'd first disappeared, but now she'd been gone long enough.

"Kyra." No, no sign of her in the chicken pen either. Surely she hadn't wandered off. She knew the danger she faced.

He scanned the perimeter of the ranch, looking for places he hadn't checked. He couldn't detect movement anywhere. All the hands were either riding the fences or posted at lookouts. He was alone guarding the home fort. And what a fine job he was doing! One hour into his post, and he couldn't find his small female charge anywhere.

He was sorry about that. Obviously, Cliff's interest in Kyra was more serious than his friend might like to admit. But Shane couldn't change the color of his skin, and he wouldn't even if it were possible. He knew he'd frightened her when he'd snuck up on her initially, but he hadn't figured she was so set against him she'd run off as soon as Cliff disappeared.

Shane frowned when his gaze fixed on the stables. Maybe. It was the only place left to check. He headed there, whistling lightly. He didn't want to be accused of sneaking up on her again.

As he opened the door, he heard a faint rustling inside. A slight grin lit his face. He'd found her hiding place. He couldn't wait to see what excuse she'd come up with to explain her actions. If she thought he wanted to bask in the sunshine of her smile, she had another think coming. White women were much more trouble than they were worth.

The door swung closed behind him as he stepped inside. His eyes hadn't yet adjusted to the dimness when he caught a swift movement behind the barrel in the corner. He expected it to be Kyra, and his reflexes were just a fraction too late. The gunman had a bead on him before his hand reached his holster.

"Put your hands up, Baldwin, or die now!" a raspy, low voice threatened.

That voice sounded familiar, but he couldn't place it.

Gradually, he raised his hands, palm sides forward. Either the other man didn't know Cliff, or it was too dark for him to recognize he had the wrong man. Of course Shane's hat also shadowed his face. Either way, he needed a diversion.

"Didn't think me and my brother would get loose, did you, Baldwin?" The man stepped out of the shadows. "Oh, it's Chandler, is it?"

Shane recognized Russ Yancey's fair-headed countenance. He remembered his brother Zach, too. Where was he?

"That's just fine; we planned to kill you, too," Russ continued. "In fact, Zach is out hunting you right now. Seems like I'll get to take care of both you and Baldwin. Thought you'd sent us away for good, didn't you? You and your partner made a big mistake when you captured us and killed little Tommy. We Yancey brothers always take care of our own. And I'm here to take care of you now."

The click of a hammer tightened Shane's muscles. A dark shadow dropped from the loft as he dived for Yancey.

"Kyra!"

The gun barked. A sudden pain followed by a strong burning sensation lodged in his left shoulder. It knocked him backward.

Instantly, he rolled over and drew his Schofield revolver. Damn, Kyra was in the way. She'd landed squarely on top of Yancey and knocked them both to the ground. Yancey, no fool, quickly grabbed her to use as a shield. He scrambled to his feet, dragging Kyra up with him, struggling to level his gun on Shane. Kyra clawed and struggled in his arms.

"Let me go, you filthy, odoriferous slug!" she panted.

She twisted all over the place, her face as red as a chili pepper, and her temper even hotter. If she'd move just a little to the right, he'd be able to get a shot off without any risk to her.

"Silence. Be still and shut up, bitch, before I shoot you right now!" Yancey threatened as he fought to gain control of her. He tightened his grip around her chest, trying to hold both her arms down with one of his, while his other arm focused the gun once again in Shane's direction. "Drop it now, Chandler, or I'll shoot your slut right between her tits!"

Kyra gasped, the insult appearing to have offended her more than the brutal treatment she received. Shane watched, amazed, as she bit Yancey's arm, and stomped on his foot with the sharply pointed heel of her riding boot.

"Bitch!" Yancey exclaimed as he slapped Kyra across her face, knocking her down.

Shane's bullet nailed him through the heart. Kyra screamed as the bastard slammed against the stable wall.

Yancey's gun went off one final time before his body slid into a heap on the hay.

Shane felt a searing pain across his temple, but extended his hand toward Kyra. He wanted to ask her if she was all right, but black spots swam into his line of vision and the world blurred. He was on the precipice of a deep black hole, ready to swallow him into its depths. As he reached for Kyra again, the ground rose to meet him before total darkness set in.

Chapter Ten

Prickly Ash Root Powder: It'll cure what ails you, with the fire of purification. Apply with caution and respect.
From the *Sinfully Delicious Bakery Recipe Book*

Shane was dead! Kyra was terrified. She ran to him, then knelt over his body, lifting his head and feeling for his pulse. But she was too traumatized to find it. Gradually, she noticed the small but steady rise and fall of his chest. Then she put her fingers below his nose and felt, to her relief, the slight wind of his breath.

"Thank you, God," she murmured heartily. What was she to do? She'd never had any experience in dealing with wounded, bleeding men. Surely he shouldn't be lying in the muck of the stables.

Help—she needed help! She dropped Shane, flinching when his head hit the ground with a thump. She berated herself on her carelessness, hoping he wouldn't remember any of it when he awoke. Then she raced for the bell-pull outside the mess hall, and rang it as hard as she could. *Please let someone come quickly.*

She rushed back to the stable, found a saddle blanket, then with strength she hadn't known she possessed, maneuvered Shane's body onto it. Doggedly, step by slow step, she dragged the blanket out of the stables and toward the ranch house. She reached the base of the porch stairs, and frowned with dismay over how she'd drag him up the steps. Then she heard a thundering of hooves. Twirling, she faced what might be new danger, placing her body directly in front of Shane, trying to protect the unconscious man as best she could.

Paco! And he had another cowhand with him.

"*Señorita,* we heard the bell and came as quickly as we could. What happened?" Paco vaulted off his horse and headed to the body behind Kyra. He stopped in shock when he saw Shane and his wounds.

"A man . . . with a gun . . . hiding in the stables . . . I jumped . . . but too late . . . shot Shane . . . grabbed me . . . Shane killed him . . . but got shot again. He fainted! God, help me. I don't know what to do." She was panicked, but so relieved to have someone there to help.

Paco turned to his young companion, whose light hair contrasted sharply with the black eye-patch he wore. "Ride quickly, Sammy. Spread the news among the others what has happened. Have someone go for the doctor and two men come back to the ranch pronto to help guard. Tell the others to tighten their watch. Someone got through!"

Sammy kicked his mount, turning about.

"Wait a minute," said Paco. "help me get Mr. Chandler inside first." Sammy doubled back and dismounted; both men gently moved Shane into Cliff's bedroom, laying him on the mattress. Then tipping his hat quickly to Kyra, a slight blush lighting his boyish features, Sammy left. His horse's pounding hoofs galloped swiftly away.

"Oh, Lord, Paco. I don't know anything about gunshot wounds. Do you?" Kyra gulped, trying to calm her rapid heart.

"*Sí, señorita.* I have tended such wounds before. Do not worry. This man is a tough one, no? Here, help me take off his shirt. We need to remove the bullet."

She blanched, but stiffened her spine. She would not be a coward. She could handle this. She must help Shane recover . . . She must!

Together, Paco and Kyra stripped Shane's shirt off and cleaned his wounds. Shane's unconscious body jolted in shock when Paco poured alcohol over his shoulder. Kyra wanted to cry. He'd lost so much blood and was extremely pale. He looked more dead than alive when they finally bandaged him. The smell of blood nauseated her, but she bit her lip and forced the feeling down.

"*Señorita,* I think I will go get the saddlebag doctor myself. He's lost a lot of blood, no?" Paco said.

"Saddlebag doctor?"

Paco studied her, obviously judging whether she'd be all right by herself. "Yes, he roams the range and doctors to the *vaqueros.*"

Nodding, Kyra drew herself straight and plastered on a calm, determined facade. "I'll be fine. Please hurry and get the doctor. What should I do while you're gone?"

"Sit by his side, *señorita,* and if he awakens, try to keep him calm. That is the best you can do."

And with that he left her feeling helpless and alone.

"Don't be such a baby!" Kyra said with ill-concealed annoyance.

"I'm not being a baby. I'm simply explaining that genteel Southern ladies faint, *not* a half-breed Comanche warrior. I think the shot to my temple is the better explanation for why I passed out." Shane's voice sounded weak but surly, even to his own ears.

Kyra fluffed another pillow and placed it behind him. The movement caused the gouge at his temple to ooze more blood. The final shot Yancey had gotten in as he'd dropped to his death had only grazed Shane, but caused enough trauma to knock him out.

Shane suffered through Kyra's ministrations, biting back a retort about preferring less bleeding to fluffier pillows. He didn't mean to sound short, but wasn't amenable to being weak and vulnerable—not that this was the first time he'd been hurt.

He eyed her expensive green gown, covered with his blood and totally destroyed. She had saved his life. He owed her.

"If you think you can hold something down, I'll get some food for you," Kyra said, interrupting his thoughts.

At his eager nod, she left the room.

The light filtering through the window was turning dusky when he caught a whiff of chicken. His stomach growled. Kyra entered, dressed in a clean skirt and blouse, and set a tray on the night stand next to him. He looked hungrily at the tray and saw it was laden . . . with a bowl of *broth.* It seemed she was bent on starving him into further weakness.

"How are you feeling?" she asked.

"Like a stampeding herd of newly castrated bulls just ran over me."

Kyra didn't even blink. "Is there anything else I can get you?"

"Yes. You can go back and make me some real food."

She ignored him, placing her hand over his forehead. He wanted to tell her that she needn't bother checking every five minutes, but kept silent.

Her eyes marred with worry, she said, "I hope you're not getting a fever."

"Prickly ash root will do the trick. I have some in my gear. If you bring me my supplies, I'll find it for you. You'll need to seep it in some hot water." He tried to sit up higher so he could eat, but had trouble even lifting his arms to push himself up.

Kyra sat on the bed next to him. "I'd be happy to do whatever you need. How about this broth first?"

At his nod, she placed the tray in front of him, and to his surprise, leaned closer and placed a spoonful of broth between his lips. Maybe he'd been wrong about her.

"Paco's gone to get the saddlebag doctor."

Shane grimaced. "He can't do anything I can't do myself."

Kyra rolled her eyes. "That nice young man with the eye patch, Sammy, went to warn the others and have a couple of Cliff's men come help guard."

"That's good," he nodded. "Cliff's men are very loyal to him. Every single one of them he saved from violence of some sort."

"What do you mean?"

"Well, a few are actually criminals we tracked. Cliff was able to persuade them to try a different path."

"Paco, too? And Sammy?" Her brow wrinkled. "Neither look like criminals to me."

"They aren't." Shane scowled. "Most of the men are victims of violence. Sammy's father got killed by bandits one night. Wrong place at the wrong time. The poor kid tried to protect his papa and lost his eye in the process."

"How terrible. And Paco?"

He tightened his jaw. "The Yancey brothers killed his wife and baby daughter on a train."

Kyra's eyes widened as she gasped. "The newspaper article," she whispered. "I read about that, a year ago."

He shifted uncomfortably and abruptly changed the subject. "I'm going to give you instructions for treating my wounds. It's my mother's way. It'll rid my body of any poisons and prevent fever and infection."

She was silent as she continued to feed him. When she focused on him again, she said, "I'd love to learn more about medicine and healing. Do you know much?"

"Yes, my mother is a *puhakut.* Medicine woman, in English. She's also called an eagle doctor, as was her mother before her. Usually Comanche women pass their healing knowledge down through their daughters, but since she had sons, she taught me. Of course, that was before I went to live with my white father."

"How wonderful to have the gift of healing. I wish my mother could have taught me something as useful as that." She spooned another mouthful of broth into his.

"She must have taught you other things."

"Yes. I'm very good at balancing a book on my head, and using the proper fork at dinner," she answered sarcastically. "Please tell me more about your mother's healing and your people. Do you have any other gifts? How long have you been away from her?"

Shane chuckled weakly. "You sure do like to ask a lot of personal questions, don't you?"

She shoved another spoonful into his mouth. "I'm sorry. You don't have to tell me anything. I'm curious, that's all." She sighed. "It's one of my greatest flaws."

"You aren't flawed. You have a strong spirit—for a white woman."

Kyra smiled. "That's my Grandpère's doing, I'm afraid. He indulged me."

"Reading people."

"What?" Kyra's brow wrinkled in confusion.

"You asked about gifts. I have the gift of extra sight. I'm not sure if it's something I've always had, or developed from my line of work." He paused to rest, his voice raspy with exertion.

"Do you ever visit your mother?"

Shane nodded. "Every once in a while I head up to Oklahoma to see her."

Quiet lay between them. What had possessed him to tell her so much? She had a sympathetic manner about her. Then again, maybe he was just grateful to her for saving his hide.

"Well, besides the tea I'm to make, what else should I do?"

"I have powdered prickly ash root you should sprinkle over the wound. You should also mash the root into a cocktail of mixed herbs I have in my medicine bag. We'll make a poultice to put on later. Take off the bandages so I can see the damage," he ordered.

She did as he asked, and he saw that the deep laceration in his shoulder still pooled blood.

"I'm afraid you'll need to sew a few stitches."

"You have to be out of your mind! I've never done that before."

He did his best to grin. "No? You've done needlework before, haven't you?"

"Yes, but this is your flesh we're talking about. Please tell me you're trying to aggravate me."

His strength was ebbing. He couldn't spar with her any more. "I know it's a lot to ask, Kyra. But I didn't think the woman who jumped off a loft on top of a gunman would be so squeamish."

A few minutes later she rifled through his belongings, pulling out his medicine bag. She held out the different medicines, watching for his nod when she pulled out the correct ones.

"Before you set the stitches you'll need to cover the wound with the prickly ash root powder."

"M-maybe we should wait for the doctor."

Shane grimaced. "I'll lose too much blood if we do that. I'm sure you make very pretty stitches. Just don't make any frilly patterns, all right?"

She was queasy at the idea of what she'd have to do. To top it all, no matter how weak he was, Shane seemed to enjoy her discomfort—the demented sick weasel.

She shot a meaningful glance in his direction. The demented sick weasel managed to grin mischievously.

In retaliation, she grabbed a pinch of the powdered prickly ash root and sprinkled it over his wound.

Shane hissed, his eyes watering to streams.

She immediately relented. "Oh, Shane, I'm so sorry. Did I hurt you?"

It took him a moment to respond. "I'm fine. Did I tell you my mother also calls this 'fire medicine' because it burns like hell? Anyway, it had to be done—maybe without so much gusto, though." He paused a moment. "You'll need to repeat the motion three more times. My mother does everything in four motions or doses. Don't forget to put some powder on my temple as well."

After she was through treating his wounds, and had sewn his laceration to the best of her ability, she added some herbal poultice she'd made under his direction and bandaged him. She stepped back to view her handiwork. Shane was white and looked weak, yet he'd continuously sparred with her as if nothing were wrong. It was all bluster.

"Shane?" she whispered. "Are you in pain?"

Eyes shut, he murmured, "The peyote buttons you can make into a tea for pain . . . and willow bark for fever."

She turned to leave, but was stopped short by Shane's weakened voice. "Thank you, Kyra. I'd thought you a little prejudiced, but am honored to call you friend now. . . ."

Kyra inhaled a shaky breath. "Thank you. I'm honored to call you friend, too."

Later that evening, Kyra, in a modest nightdress and robe, sat at Shane's bedside. She watched as he drained his third cup of willow bark tea. He was still weak, but the doctor had come and gone, declaring there was nothing more he could do, that they had already done everything he would have prescribed and more. Many of Cliff's men, including Paco and his son, Emilio, had stopped by to check on Shane and see what help they could be.

Shane shakily set aside his teacup. "Tell me about Cliff as a child. Sometimes I believe he came out full-grown, as serious and solemn as he is now."

Kyra laughed. "Cliff *has* always been serious. We grew up as neighbors, at least when our families were in town. His family moved to New Orleans from Boston after the war, and his father established a factor house for the cotton growers."

"Factor house?"

"Most factor houses charge the planters incredibly high interest rates and then turn around and make a high percentage as sales agents. I never understood as a child why his family was so ostracized by the rest of New Orleans society, but since I've grown older I've come to understand how his father was mistrusted and accused of being a carpetbagger."

"Then how did your families get to be friends?"

"Cliff's father bought a tax-forfeited town house directly beside ours on the Vieux Carré. Also, both his parents had been prominent socially in Boston, and that made a lot of difference to my mother. The bluer your blood and the better the family connections you have, the better friend she is. But beyond our family and a couple of others, the Baldwins didn't have many friends in the early years. I think Cliff was rather lonely, and that's the only reason he allowed me to tag along—especially since he was so much older than me. After all, he was eleven and I was six when we first met. Plus, I don't think he had a very happy home life. His father was boisterous whenever I visited, but his mother was timid and solemn. I don't think I ever saw her smile." Kyra shivered, rubbing at her arms.

"How do a boy and girl so far apart in age play together?"

"Oh, Cliff had a wonderful imagination. He'd create all sorts of games that we'd act out. Sometimes he was the pirate and I was his cabin boy. He'd make me fetch him things, like sneaking cookies and lemonade from Cook. And if I didn't do it, he'd make me walk the plank, which was a fallen log over a creek in the woods. He always was in charge. If we played Indians, then he was the chief and I got scalped; if we played Conquistadors, then he was Cortez and I was Montezuma. Come to think of it, he's still telling me what to do today! He's out hunting my tracker, while I wait here alone. That's not fair, is it?" Kyra slapped her hands against her lap.

"I know I didn't live up to my fierce Comanche reputation and do a very good job protecting you today, but you aren't alone." His eyebrows were raised high with sarcasm, but his pale face was also tinged pink.

"Oh, I know. I meant it figuratively. And by the way, I don't understand why you thought I'd be prejudiced. I'm part Indian myself, you know."

He looked surprised, then disbelieving.

"It's true! At least I think it is. My Grandpère has always claimed his grandmother was Natchez. But I was honestly never sure if he said it only to aggravate Mother. He always likes to ruffle her feathers. But even if it weren't true, I'll have you know that I've lived amongst people of mixed blood all my life. I descend from a mix of French and Spanish myself . . . and some English on my grandmother's side—that's where 'Kyra Dawson' comes from. I've had friends with English, Portuguese, Indian, or African blood mixed in. That's quite common in New Orleans. Why, our public schools allowed all different backgrounds in the classroom together for a few years back in the '70's."

"And did you go to those schools?" Shane's lashes fluttered drowsily.

"Well, no. My parents hired a tutor when I was younger, and then I went to a private finishing school. My mother was always, and still is, concerned about maintaining appearances. I've never understood why that was so important to her, but I know I've been a great disappointment because I have such a hard time remembering all the rules she lectures me on."

"I've heard you mention your *grandpère*."

She laughed softly to herself, awash in some of her favorite memories. "Yes. Cliff and I were allowed to visit Grandpère frequently. He's more Cajun than Creole and an awful lot of fun. Still is. Cliff really took to Grandpère. He told us about his exciting life as a riverboat gambler, something Mama never let him talk about in her presence. And he taught us how to shoot, play cards, and swim. He even took us canoeing in the bayous."

She fell silent for a moment, and glanced at Shane, who watched her from under lowered eyelashes, totally still, his breathing even. Good. Maybe she was helping him relax. She continued on, in a softer voice. "Sometimes one of our mothers would send us down to the French Market. We gave the hawkers such a hard time mocking their cries. I can still hear Cliff: 'Craaaawwwdaaads, craaaawwwdaaads, buy 'em before they crawl back to Daddy.' And then there was the time we worked in a Carnival krewe. It was the winter before Cliff left. My mother would never have let me help build the float and join the parade if she'd known. But Cliff helped me sneak away and participate. He didn't let me go to the krewe ball afterward, though, and I was furious for days. He claimed I was too young.

"Oh, I wish he hadn't gone away. I was just getting old enough to really start having fun when he left. We could have gone to balls together, danced, taken afternoon outings to the ice cream parlor, or played tennis. Why, I've become quite a good tennis player. I play to win, not like those other silly girls who play just to show off their tennis dresses. I bet I could beat Cliff, too. In fact I know I could."

Suddenly, Shane's head dropped heavily, interrupting Kyra's ramblings. Her eyes focused on him better. He was asleep. Well, goodness. She'd annoyed her fiancés many times, but didn't remember having bored a man to sleep before.

She stood and stretched her tired, stiff limbs, then carefully reached out to cover him better. She would stay with him tonight, in case he came down with a fever. After dousing the lamp, she settled into the rocking chair, which she'd pulled into the room earlier, and drifted off to sleep.

* * *

A few hours later, Cliff stood in the darkness outside his home, watching, his heart racing with hot seething anger. His chest compressed with the pain of betrayal, an icy-hot sensation slowly ripping through his body. The lamp was lit in his bedroom, casting shadows against the shade, outlining a woman bent over a man in bed. Kyra and Shane were together, alone, *in his bedroom.*

Chapter Eleven

Son-of-a-Bitch Stew: This mixture of calf brains and other animal innards goes down smoothly, but is sure to get you back later.
From the *Sinfully Delicious Bakery Recipe Book*

Cliff didn't know how long he stood outside, watching the shadows through the window, waiting for his limbs to find the strength to move. Shane had always been a man of his word, but then again Kyra was as tempting as a siren . . . a betraying siren. Cliff hated deception—he'd had his fill growing up.

Memories of his father haunted him. He'd been one man to the world and another at home. Cliff remembered clearly the nights his father would leave his study after having had too much drink. He believed drinking in secrecy meant he wasn't a drunk, but Cliff had long understood, as had his mother. Granted, they'd both denied the illness before, until the ugliness was too much to ignore. His father, on the other hand, had never stopped denying it. He recalled the times his father had knocked him around, just to *keep him in line.* The next day he'd apologize profusely, sometimes buying him trinkets or extravagant gifts. All the while he'd explain to his son how Cliff had really tripped, causing his own injury. *Right?* his father had always asked. For years Cliff had been forced to lie about his injuries, even to himself, for he'd always hoped his father would love him enough to change. But that had never happened. Meanwhile, his own sense of reality had become distorted, and he was often unable or perhaps unwilling to separate fact from fiction. He closed his eyes, forcing the past to retreat.

The pain Cliff had felt as a child now burned inside him. Shane and Kyra had betrayed him. Kyra's betrayal cut deeper than Shane's for some reason. She and his mother were the only people he'd ever allowed to own a piece of his heart, and in different ways they had both abandoned him. His mother he could forgive because she'd lived the same hell that had been his, going from a passionate woman to one with a broken spirit. But Kyra's betrayal he couldn't understand, and he would not accept it. Why had he been so gullible to believe she'd remained untouched after six fiancés? A memory of her recounting the story of her first fiancé found its way to the heart of his anger, building itself to a smoldering blaze. He shouldn't care what she did and with whom. She was not his, and yet . . .

Cliff's strides, now intent, brought him to his front door. He turned the heavy iron latch and walked in, the door clicking shut behind him. The house was dark, with shadows playing on the walls from the light of the moon coming through the windows. He turned toward the kitchen, where he heard Kyra moving about, muttering to herself. The thought of Shane in his bed waiting for Kyra served only to feed the fire smoldering within. He'd take care of Shane later.

Kyra prepared another cup of medicinal tea for her ornery patient. Shane was being impossible again—his pleasant mood of the early evening spent. She desperately needed him to recover, and worried she'd go mad if Cliff didn't relieve her from the obtuse man. Cursing Shane's savage manners, she pulled up the sleeve of her long silk robe and pumped some water into a blue enamel kettle, then heard the faint rustling of clothing from the doorway.

"Shane, for God's sake, you are too . . ." Kyra was about to say *weak* when she saw it was Cliff who stood there—looking anything but weak. Something was very wrong. The flame in the oil lamp she'd lit danced, the flickering of light and darkness playing upon the planes of his face. But it cast enough light to see this wasn't the same man who'd left her only yesterday. The man standing before her now was the cold, angry Cliff who'd walked down the stairs at Madam Lucy's, only this time his anger was directed at her. There was something else, too—longing perhaps. For a moment, she likened him to a wounded panther, his dark locks of hair falling around stormy blue eyes. His lips were spread thin with deadly determination and his muscular arms flexed in reaction to the tight fists he formed at his sides. She took in the rest of him, noting the gun belt he wore, his dusty chaps, blue denim pants, and dark shirt. He'd obviously ridden hard.

Instinctively, she backed away, uncertainty shooting through her at the frightening aura he presented. Was this *the* Cliff Baldwin everyone had warned her about? Was this how a cornered criminal had felt when confronted by this big man?

"*Cliff.* You're back." Her voice sounded weak and nervous to her own ears.

He said nothing. He continued to stare at her, his glare icy and intense. A minute passed, and finally he moved, walking over the threshold, slowly unbuckling his gun belt and laying it on the kitchen table.

"What's the matter, cat-eyes? Aren't you happy to see me?" he asked, a dangerous chord to his voice.

"Wh-what's wrong, Cliff? Are you angry about something?" She backed up another step, anxiety rising within her.

"Such innocence . . . such wariness." He moved closer still. "But I know the truth."

"The truth? Cliff, please . . . you're frightening me. What's wrong?" she pleaded once again. She wanted to tell him what had happened to Shane, but her voice was lost as he pressed against her until her back hit the kitchen counter.

She looked up into his smoldering eyes, hoping to understand, but found herself even more alarmed. *Dear Lord,* this wasn't anger, but a boiling rage. Her pulse quickened. Would he actually harm her? She couldn't believe that he would, and tried desperately to speak, her breath coming in short gasps. As he braced his arms on the counter behind her, a suffocating sensation swallowed her.

"Since I won the wager, please do tell me more about your fiancés. For example, how many have you allowed into your bed?" His voice was dark and raspy with suppressed emotion.

Kyra was shocked, delaying her reaction as she lifted her hand to slap him across the face. Cliff grabbed her arm in a steely grip and smiled. It was a smile that didn't reach his eyes. A feral smile meant to intimidate. With his other hand he lifted her chin higher before his head descended, taking her mouth in a savage kiss, his tongue possessing her with brutal punishment.

His wild invasion was so unexpected, she didn't know how to react. Her lips trembled beneath his, and she heard the sound of her ragged breathing. She pushed her hands against his chest, but to no avail. He was much too strong for her. It scared her knowing how much power he had over her if he chose to use it. As panic overtook her struggle, he paused, breaking the kiss, to peer into her eyes. Kyra froze then at what she saw—his demeanor changing from rage to betrayal and finally vulnerability.

"Cliff?"

He searched her face with tormented eyes, finally resting his gaze on her parted lips. With a groan, he plunged his velvet soft tongue again into her mouth. This time, she slowly responded, kissing him back, her tongue darting between her trembling lips to meet his. She trailed one hand along his shoulder, finding his hair. As she grasped the cool silky strands, he continued his relentless invasion—his tongue drifting in and out, stopping only to flick at the creases of her mouth. Kyra's senses were overwhelmed by Cliff's ardor, her nipples hardening as he pulled her tight against his chest. His musky scent, a curious mixture of horse and man, tantalized her, making her want more.

The teakettle she still held in her other hand dropped to the floor, sounding a clattering echo as she moved to curl her hand around his other large shoulder. The feel of her hands on him seemed to ignite Cliff's passion further, and he moved to cup her bottom with both his palms, pressing her hard against his arousal. Kyra gasped, her breathing hard, for he felt huge and so hot against the softness of her flat stomach.

"Cliff? Pl-please stop," she blurted out in between his kisses.

He ignored her, his wet tongue gliding over her throat and his hands climbing the rung of her ribs to her breasts. His deft fingers found her nightdress beneath the silk robe, unfastening several buttons, his hands fumbling. Shoving the opening to one side, he reached in to lift a full globe over the neckline. His fiery kisses burned a path of destruction from her throat down to a rose-tipped nipple, his mouth now suckling her with intense hunger.

A wavelike sensation Kyra didn't recognize started low in her belly, frightening her back to reality. She had to stop this madness before it went too far. This was not how she'd ever expected it to be with him, not with anger between them. "Cliff, stop. Please," she again pleaded, her voice breaking.

At the sound of her voice, Cliff wrenched himself away from her breast, his hand still cupping the mound gently. It took all his willpower to find a measure of control as he stared intently into her sad eyes, a sliver of guilt snaking into his conscience. Reluctantly, he put her night clothing back together and forced his hands aside.

"I suppose, then, you find my touch more abhorrent than your other lovers', including Shane's?" His mouth quirked into a painful half smile. "I think you'd better hurry, he's been waiting in my bed long enough." With that, he stepped aside to allow her escape.

"Shane?" Her voice was soft, questioning.

Silence was followed by the sound of slow shuffling footsteps coming from the living room.

"Kyra? Are you all right? Are you growing that tea yourself?" Shane called weakly. "I thought I heard something hit the floor. . . ." Shane halted as he approached the kitchen. "So you're back."

Cliff inhaled once, then twice. He was afraid to face Shane—afraid of what he'd do to him, and yet he'd have to face him eventually. He turned directly to Shane, his breath stopping midway at the sight of Shane's naked torso and the big bandage wrapped around his left arm and shoulder, and another around his head. All coherent thoughts fled as he finally rested his gaze on his friend's pale face.

"What the hell happened to you?" Cliff croaked. He had an inkling that maybe he'd jumped to conclusions.

Kyra answered from behind him. "Shane was shot. He lost a lot of blood and I was afraid he'd die. Paco and I p-put him in your room so we could t-take care of his wounds." Her voice broke in a half sob.

Cliff's heart sank. He watched, stupefied, as she shoved past him and Shane, the sound of her receding footsteps patting against the wood floors, and then . . . the screeching thud of a slamming door. Something inside him died and his eyes slid closed.

After Kyra left the kitchen, a strained silence descended. Cliff and Shane warily observed each other.

"How about making that willow bark tea Kyra was starting? I need to sit down." Shane's words broke the tension as he headed for one of the chairs around the kitchen table.

"Yeah, sure." Cliff sighed, then removed his leggings and bandanna and draped them over a chair. Quietly, he headed for the pitcher and bowl on the counter, and washed the dust off his hands and face. He searched for a towel, and spied the teakettle on the floor. Regret washed over him. Hell, he'd acted like a true bastard, hurting the one person who didn't deserve it. He glanced at Shane, whose face was white as he carefully adjusted his arm to a comfortable position.

"Who shot you?" Cliff picked up the kettle.

"I was wondering when you'd get around to asking." Shane grimaced and leaned back.

"My mind was elsewhere." Seeing that Kyra had already stoked the stove, he placed the kettle over an eye and searched for the willow bark. He found a pouch of it on the counter next to the stove and opened it, waiting for the water to come to a boil.

He turned to face Shane. "You obviously took care of the situation," Cliff said. It dawned on him then that this could be serious. Maybe Wade had already made it to the ranch. Cliff had been so busy feeling like an idiot, it hadn't entered his mind what Shane's injury signified. Worried now, he stepped toward his friend. "Was it Wade?"

"No, it was a goddamn Yancey brother. Russ. He thought I was you at first. But he and his brother Zach were out looking for both of us. He took me by surprise, and Kyra was in the way. I had to kill him." Shane groaned as he shifted once more.

"Why don't you go sit on the sofa and I'll bring the tea?" Cliff got a mug from the cupboard.

"I can make it till the tea's ready."

"So, where's Russ's body?"

"A couple of your ranch hands took him to town."

"Damn! Well, that leaves Zach, and he's probably coming after us soon."

"You're right. I'm sure as soon as he hears about Russ, he'll come gunning." Shane paused a moment, then stared carefully at Cliff. "If he finds out about Kyra, he'll use her to get back at you."

"Hell. To make matters worse, I believe Wade will be here soon. He's got a posse after him. I trailed them on my way here, and Wade took a detour to lose them." Cliff fell silent a moment, pondering his options. "I think I'm going to have to head out of here with Kyra until the posse catches up with Wade and Yancey is stopped. There's just too much danger coming from too many different directions for me to feel safe with Kyra at the ranch. I'm counting on your help."

Shane nodded. "What did you find out in Dallas?"

Cliff told Shane what he'd uncovered, stopping only to take the kettle off the stove to pour the tea.

"Let's go sit on the sofa." Cliff could see how tired Shane was.

Shane stumbled to his feet. Cliff sighed and ambled over to him, holding Shane up on his right side. They walked to the sofa, and Shane plopped down like a sack of potatoes. Cliff handed him his tea and sat opposite him on the chair. He raked a hand through his hair. His body felt achy and tired, and he wanted nothing more than to turn in for the night. But he had to make amends to Kyra. The problem was how and when. First he needed to figure out what to do about Wade and Yancey.

"Kyra seemed upset."

Leave it to Shane to bring up the obvious, not to mention a topic he didn't want to discuss.

Cliff glanced at Shane, who sipped his tea, his onyx eyes reading him like a book. Cliff hated it when Shane did that.

"I acted like a real bastard. I jumped to conclusions, thought the worst of her . . . and you. All I could think about was what I thought I saw through my bedroom window." Cliff shot up from the chair and strode over to the fireplace, resting his forearm on the mantel. His head bent low, he said, "I don't know what came over me, but I . . . Let's just say I was a complete ass."

"Sounds like jealousy to me, which is what I'm going to accept as the reason for you doubting my word." Shane laid his cup on the side table, his silence speaking eloquently. "I think we should get some sleep. I'll stay here on the sofa."

Cliff turned back to Shane. His friend wasn't happy with him at the moment. He couldn't blame him. Jealous. Maybe he was. What it meant as far as his feelings for Kyra, he didn't know. He'd thought that he'd gotten over his attraction for her over the years, but then again, he hadn't seen her all grown up. No matter how he circled it, she was special and always would be. It was insane to think he could just put her aside, but what did it mean?

A relationship with her was out of the question. Having a wife and family wasn't in the cards for him. He could easily end up like his father, and his father before him, and treat Kyra the way his mother had been treated. This evening was a perfect example. True, he hadn't hit her, but he *had* mistreated her. And what about children? He didn't want to risk hurting his child the way he'd been hurt. Trying to prevent a pregnancy from occurring wouldn't be easy with Kyra in his bed. It also wouldn't be fair to her even if he could prevent her from receiving his seed. She deserved children. She was a passionate woman, so much like his mother. It would kill him to see her end up . . .

No. Angels needed protecting. They weren't strong enough to survive relationships with demons like him. He had a bad temper most times, and occasionally, when riled, lost control. He'd first seen the warning signs on that Christmas Eve seven years ago. He needed to resolve her situation as soon as possible, before he did something they'd both regret. Now that he'd tasted her, he didn't know if he could keep his hands off her.

He sighed. After what had happened in the kitchen, she probably didn't want anything more to do with him. He should be happy she'd finally seen him for what he was. But he was still going to have to apologize. *Again.*

Cliff walked over to his friend and grabbed Shane's good arm, hauling him to his feet. "Go back to bed. I'll sleep on the sofa. You need some room with that arm of yours." Shane protested, but was too tired to argue for long. Cliff continued. "We'll figure out what to do tomorrow. I don't want to be an easy target for Wade or Yancey. They're too desperate right now, and that makes them unpredictable. Even with my men helping, I don't want to take the risk. I'm going to have to take Kyra somewhere and lie low for a while."

Shane refused Cliff's help, and staggered toward the bedroom.

"I'll be stronger tomorrow, and I can watch out here while you take her away," Shane said. "I'll get help and handle Yancey and Wade. If I can lead the posse to Wade, then we won't have to worry about him anymore."

Shane paused when he reached the bedroom, and moaned as he dropped onto the mattress. "Zach Yancey is another story," he hissed through his teeth. "I've got to speak to the sheriff about Russ, so I'll make sure to discuss his brother as well. One thing we can count on is that desperate men make mistakes. Maybe I can send him on a family reunion."

"Well, not in the shape you're in at the moment. I may be able to get Luke Hampton to help. He seems trustworthy. You can decide for yourself."

Shane lay weakly against the white sheets, his face nearly as pale. Cliff, again, felt remorse over what had happened with Kyra. *So stupid.*

"There's my cabin outside Athens," Shane suggested. "I haven't been there in a while, but you're welcome to use it."

"That's a good idea. Let's talk about it more in the morning. I'm beat." Cliff doused the lamp, turned, and left.

The next morning Luke Hampton, in his usual dark garb, rode in on his palomino stallion as Cliff directed his ranch hands on the day's work. After he finished instructing Paco about taking over some of his own duties, he strode over to where Luke waited by the main house.

"Good morning, Hampton," Cliff said as he shook his hand.

"Baldwin," Luke acknowledged with a nod.

"You saved me a trip to town." Cliff led the way into the kitchen. He saw that Kyra still hadn't come out of her room. "Coffee?" Cliff lifted a pot he'd brewed earlier.

Luke nodded and turning a chair backward, sat resting his arms on the backrest. "I came to tell you there's a strange man in town asking questions about Miss Lourdes."

Worried, Cliff handed him a mug and excused himself so he could get Shane. He didn't want to discuss anything without him.

A few minutes later, with the aroma of Arbuckle Coffee filling the air, Shane and Luke sat around the kitchen table. Cliff faced them, leaning against the counter.

"The stranger you said was asking after Kyra, what did he look like?" Cliff began.

"Like Lucifer after a saloon fight with Jesse James. He's got a big scar across his neck." Luke narrowed his eyes, as though envisioning what he'd observed. "He came in the saloon in the early morning hours, while I was finishing up a high-stakes poker game. He made his rounds, including my table, discreetly offering money to anyone who could give him information as to her whereabouts." Luke shrugged. "I gave him what he wanted before hightailing it over here. He should be halfway to Pikes Crossroads by now."

Shane slapped the table, chuckling.

Cliff nodded his appreciation. Luke's ploy had bought them some time, but they had to hurry and make tracks.

He needed Luke's help, and Shane seemed to like him, so he proceeded to explain the situation in more detail.

A few minutes later, Luke nodded. "Sure, I'll help Shane. Never been one to deny a little adventure. We can take care of both Wade and Yancey. You'd figure the brothers would have run when they got away from the noose, rather than come after you."

"Revenge," Cliff replied, shifting on his feet. "When we went after them a little over a year ago, I shot the youngest Yancey. He didn't die nicely." He left the rest unsaid. He'd never forget the boy's look of resigned horror when he'd had to shoot him again to end his suffering.

Luke left to get some of his things. He'd figured it was better to stay with Shane, at least until Shane got the rest of his strength back. Maybe by the next day, they could head out and help the posse find Wade, if the posse hadn't already. In the meantime, Cliff would take Kyra to Shane's cabin near Athens and wait for either Shane or Luke to come with news.

Cliff wanted to take care of Wade and Yancey himself, but he didn't want to risk leaving Kyra with someone else. He grimaced. Kyra was not going to be happy spending any time with him. Well, he'd give her a few more minutes. If she didn't come out of her room by then, he'd have to force her. They needed to get going.

Cliff sat across from Shane at the kitchen table, going over their plan one more time, as Kyra stiffly swept into the room murmuring a greeting. She headed toward the coffeepot and poured herself a cup. Cliff recognized the yellow gown she'd worn at the picnic, and felt a twinge of remorse, recalling how nice that afternoon had been. Now she wasn't even looking at him.

Kyra fixed herself a plate of food, glad to have at least forced Cliff to do the cooking this morning. Flinging her hair back, she caught Shane observing her and felt a pang of guilt. He was injured, after all.

She faced them squarely. Shane wore a loose gray cotton shirt, which meant he had to feel a little more comfortable. He didn't appear as pale as he had yesterday, and she breathed a sigh of relief. She smiled at him, ignoring Cliff.

"Shane, I'm so glad you seem better. I'm sorry I wasn't up earlier to help you. I was more tired than usual," she lied. She'd actually woken with the rooster's crow and spent the morning writing in her journal. She glanced at Cliff. *Snake* was right.

Cliff stared at her, in his dark green shirt and snug denim pants looking as imposing as ever in the small kitchen. She pointedly focused her attention back on Shane.

He winked at her. "I think that by tomorrow I'll be back to my old self, rude savage and all."

"Oh, Lord. Please, no. I don't know which is worse, Shane the ornery patient or Shane the obnoxious tyrant."

Cliff glanced back and forth between them. "I'm glad to see that yesterday's events have helped you find a liking for each other," he said wryly.

Kyra turned to the window to peer outside. She could barely stand looking at him. *How can he speak to me as if nothing happened?*

"I guess it's too much to hope you'll part with one of your smiles for me today," Cliff said gruffly to her back.

She whirled, deciding to eat elsewhere, as Cliff called to her in that low voice of his.

"Kyra, you need to get your riding habit on and pack for a few days, possibly longer."

She stopped in her tracks, turned, and headed back, plunking her plate on the table. "Where are we going?" she asked icily.

Cliff let out a long sigh. "Somewhere safe. Wade—"

She interrupted him before he could elaborate, laughing sarcastically. "Oh! And I'd be safe with you?" Then grabbing her plate, she fled back to her room, the door slamming behind her.

Cliff glanced at Shane, who wore a knowing smile. Cliff glared at his friend and pushed up from the table. "If you weren't injured, I'd knock you flat."

"You could try," Shane replied, his eyebrows lifting with skepticism. "You must have been a really bad boy last night," he continued, another mischievous grin splitting his face.

Baring his teeth, Cliff shot him an obscene gesture.

Shane threw back his head, laughing heartily. "Well, at least she didn't knee your *unmentionables*."

Cliff ignored him and hurried over to Kyra's door. He paused a moment before knocking.

"Kyra! I need to talk to you." She didn't answer, so he knocked again.

"Kyra, we don't have much time," he said, exasperated. She still didn't answer.

"I'm coming in." Cliff opened the door, finding her sitting on his rocker in front of the window. She looked like an angel with the sunlight wrapped around her. He shifted his feet, finally resting his weight on one leg.

"Kyra, if we had time I'd sit here and grovel for your forgiveness, but we have to leave immediately. We can talk about last night later."

More silence.

"Don't take more than ten minutes to get changed and gather what belongings you'll need for a few days away, all right? I'll be outside getting Blackjack and Poker ready. We'll take Mr. Pip along to carry provisions. Oh, and don't pack too much because we'll move fast." He watched for a reaction, then shut the door and left.

Ten minutes later, Kyra stepped outside. She wore her freshly brushed green velvet habit, had her derringer at her side and satchel in her hands. She saw Cliff down at the corral getting the horses ready and instructing Paco. As she studied the length of his lean body, her cheeks burned at the memory of the shameless things he'd done to her last night. She was about to examine her feelings further when the door behind her squeaked open. Shane stepped beside her, squinting as he observed Cliff in the distance.

Kyra stared at his strong profile. Funny how she didn't find him so frightening anymore. "Is your arm paining you?"

Shane stared down at her for a full minute before answering. He seemed to weigh something in his mind.

"No, it's better. It's not the first time I've been shot."

"It isn't?" Kyra frowned at Shane's nonchalant tone.

"No, I've been shot and bruised up in more ways than I can say. They aren't very pretty stories for a lady to hear." Shane riveted his gaze back on Cliff, who was strapping the last of his provisions on Mr. Pip.

"I suppose that in your line of work it comes with the territory."

"Yeah," Shane replied, his dark bottomless gaze boring into hers. "Cliff saved my life once. That's how we met."

Kyra's eyes widened. "He did?" She couldn't shake the feeling he was trying to tell her something.

He gave her his profile. "Cliff's been beaten and bruised a lot as well."

Kyra's stomach knotted. "Well, he used to be in the same business, I suppose."

"No." Shane shook his head. "That, too, but he'd been bruised and beaten inside and out—before meeting me." He paused, watching her intently. "He just doesn't talk about it."

Kyra started to say something, but Cliff approached them with the horses.

"This is Poker," he said, patting the beautiful roan gelding he held out to her. "Are you ready?"

He seemed so somber she couldn't help but feel sad for him, even after what had happened between them.

"Do you name all your horses after card games?" She saw surprise flit across his face, as if he'd expected her to continue ignoring him.

"Pretty much. Either I name them after games or the cards themselves."

He watched her as she moved forward to pat Poker on the nose.

"I've got a horse named Queen of Hearts or Queen for short," he said, "and another favorite of mine is Eight of Spades, or just plain Spades, and so on. When we come back I'll introduce them all to you. I just haven't had time."

"Why?" Kyra asked curiously.

"Why what?"

"Why the names?"

Cliff hesitated. "It reminded me of your *grandpère,* I guess." He shrugged, cocking his head away.

But Kyra had caught the naked loneliness on his face. Instantly she understood what his life must have been like the last few years. He'd missed Grandpère enough to name his horses, years later, to remember him. It didn't surprise her, now that she thought about it, because in many ways Grandpère had treated him like a son. Cliff had missed Grandpère. *Maybe he missed me, too.* Kyra's breath caught in her throat at the thought, and the next words tumbled from her mouth before she could stop them.

"You never wrote to me, or your father." She wanted to wipe out the hurt she heard in her own voice, but there it was—her heart out in the open for him to trample all over.

Cliff sighed, his gaze darting at Shane for a moment. Kyra glanced at the half-Comanche as well. The man seemed to thoroughly enjoy their conversation, ignoring both their pointed hints to leave. Kyra locked her gaze with Cliff again. He observed her intensely, sending ripples of heat throughout her body. She caught a hint of his scent—a masculine mix of horse, leather, and sweat. She found it intoxicating.

"Yeah, well, at the time I thought it was better for you to forget about me," he said. She noticed he didn't mention his lack of contact with his father. "Besides, I figured you'd have been married by now rather than leaving a trail of six fiancés."

At that revelation, Shane exploded with laughter.

"Wooeee, why doesn't that surprise me? What's the matter, Kyra? Can't keep a man?"

Obviously, Shane was back to being obnoxious. She poked his good shoulder. "Listen here, Mr. Chandler, I was never left! I have always been the one to break off my engagements, to the despair of all my former fiancés."

Shane held up his hand. "All right, all right. You sure do pack a mighty finger for being so short."

Again Kyra drilled a hole in his shoulder. "I am not short! You two are just abnormally oversized mongrels." She finished with her hands on her hips, her satchel hanging from one side.

Grinning, Cliff prodded Kyra forward, putting an end to the attack so they could get moving. "Hampton should be here soon."

"Don't worry, we'll be fine," said Shane. "Expect one of us in a few days."

Cliff helped Kyra mount Poker and handed her the reins.

"Where are we going and why?" she asked.

"We're going northeast, near Athens. Shane has a cabin up there. Wade's in town. I'll explain on the way."

Paco nodded his greeting as he came over with Mr. Pip. Cliff added Kyra's satchel to the mule's load, then retrieved the animal's hat and placed it on his head. Mr. Pip didn't seem pleased with his proximity and twisted, using his big teeth to nip at him.

"Why, you knothead . . ."

Kyra giggled, and reached down to pat Mr. Pip on the head. "He *is* a mule after all, Cliff." She crooned to the animal.

Before Cliff could retort, he was interrupted by the exuberant shouts of a little boy running toward Kyra from the stables. It was Paco's son, Emilio. She must have met him while he was gone.

"Hola, señorita!" He turned to Cliff. *"Buenos días, Señor Baldwin. Como está usted?"* he asked formally.

Cliff greeted the boy and proceeded to mount Blackjack.

The boy turned back toward Kyra. *"Donde vas señorita?"*

As Kyra explained about her trip, Cliff watched the ease with which she spoke to the child. He'd never been good with children, almost afraid of them. Kyra didn't share his problem. She was comfortable around most people, drawing them out with her openness and honesty, her genuine interest in them. He glanced over at Shane, usually a serious man with a deadly demeanor, and there he was grinning like a simpleton. Emilio was equally enchanted by her.

Kyra wasn't aware of it, but she provided comfort to the little boy, still vulnerable from the deaths of his mother and baby sister. Yes, she was a bright star standing out in a dark sky. If only she were his bright star to wish upon. But those were only dreams.

Chapter Twelve

> **Pemmican:** A dried meat, mixed with berries and toughened by pounding and kneading. As a result it is highly nutritious and will keep for months. Prized by many Indian tribes.
> From the *Sinfully Delicious Bakery Recipe Book*

They rode hard for several hours. Kyra got used to seeing the back of Cliff's broad shoulders through the dust his horse kicked up. It was a good thing she'd put on her hat and bandanna. Every once in a while he'd twist around and make sure she was still there. Mr. Pip was tied to her mount, which slowed her down, but the mule was a good sport, even at the pace Cliff set.

They stopped only briefly to water the animals and have a drink themselves. Cliff explained a little about what he'd found out in Dallas as well as what he and Shane had planned, and then they were on the move again. She really shouldn't let him take charge completely, telling her what to do, but he was just so good at it. Old habits were hard to break.

As the hours passed, Kyra reflected on what Shane had tried to tell her earlier. It was obvious the man understood far more than Cliff realized. Her gaze caught on a hawk's descent from the sky, and she thought back to her childhood years with Cliff. She'd always suspected the truth about his life at home, but had ignored it because he did. He'd never spoken of his pain. *Never.* Her heart twisted. What a disservice she'd done him. But she'd been young and naïve. It had been easier to put such horrors aside and pretend they'd go away. Instead it was Cliff who'd gone away.

Kyra looked at him now, sadness leaching through her. Had she let him down all those years ago? She felt guilty for feeling sorry for herself and her plight when she'd had caring parents wanting what they believed was best for her. At least they loved her. Cliff had lost his mother as a young man, after living a childhood of pain and lies. Even last night, when he'd frightened her, she'd seen the longing in his beautiful eyes. The fear he harbored within himself—fear of her. She pushed down the lump in her throat and continued to stare after the dark-haired man ahead of her. The time had come to talk, and she intended to use the next few days of privacy to do so.

Sighing, she took in the countryside in the hopes of diverting her thoughts. The land sloped in the direction of its grasses, bent by the will of the wind. Mesquite grass spiked upward amid the taller shrubs and black-eyed Susans, and prickly pear dotted the road they traveled. In the distance, clumps of sumac and groves of honey-mesquite trees offered shelter from the sun to the indigenous creatures of the area. Gradually, the terrain changed to a darker color, orchards of trees growing thicker and larger.

Lost in thought, she was surprised when Cliff called a halt, stopping next to a stream shaded by the large crowns of cedar-elm and sugarberry trees. Kyra mused it was a good thing she'd kept herself in riding shape or she'd surely suffer from sore muscles tomorrow morning.

Cliff was already dismounted and surveying the area by the time she pulled on her reins.

"Are we stopping?" she called, removing her hat and bandanna.

Cliff sauntered toward her. He'd acquired a Western swagger since living in Texas. He fixed his blue gaze on hers. "I think this is a good place to camp for the night. We could push it, but we skipped the midday meal and I'm sure you'd prefer to eat and rest. We'll only have a few hours ride in the morning before we arrive at the cabin." He reached to help her off her horse, and she gladly accepted his assistance, although she didn't really need it.

"I can manage a longer ride if you think it's necessary," Kyra replied, her hands gripping his strong biceps as he brought her down. Her pulse quickened and she leaned on him a moment, allowing her legs to grow accustomed to standing again. He felt so good, and she was disappointed when his arms flexed to push away from her.

"Yeah? As I recall, when your eyes turn a leafy green color, like they are now, it usually means you're dead tired."

"What?" She squinted at him indignantly.

"I remember a chubby child on horseback trying to keep up with me."

"I was never chubby!"

"You were compared to now. If I remember it right, I'd have to tell you several times that we could stop racing and that I knew you could best me. But no, you had to beat me at least three times before you were satisfied you were the better rider—or player for that matter." He shook his head, grinning. "You were the sorest loser I'd ever known to play cards or chess, not to mention bad-tempered. Just like Grandpère."

Kyra crossed her arms, tapping her foot. "You do have a tendency to hyperbole, don't you? And I could keep on riding if we need to."

"Uh-huh."

"Oh, you—you're impossible!" She turned, brusquely brushing off her habit, muttering to herself about Texas and all the dust. Feeling observed, she twisted to gaze behind her, finding Cliff still there with a wide smile on his face.

"What now? Do you want to poke more fun at my expense?"

"No, it's just that you really can look a fright when the occasion warrants."

"Are you finished?" She saw that he wasn't as he continued to peruse her with an amused look on his face. Well, he was right. Her usually perfect chignon was a mess and her face was dirty with dust and perspiration, but he didn't have to make her feel self-conscious over her appearance. She observed Cliff as he gazed up at the sky, the sun seeping into the western horizon. He too was dusty and wet with perspiration, but it just made him more rugged-looking and handsome.

When Cliff turned to take care of the horses, Kyra bustled over to the stream. She knelt to wash her hands and face. After shaking her hands dry, she worked on her chignon, but found she'd lost several pins during the bumpy ride. Sighing, she opted for a braid instead. Finished taking care of her needs, she walked back toward Cliff, who was busy setting up camp. He'd already laid out their gear and collected wood for a fire.

"What would you like me to do?" She swallowed nervously. The prospect of spending an entire night so close to him made her skin tingle.

Cliff glanced up, stacking another piece of wood on his arms. "There's a bag over there by the sleeping gear. Maybe you can choose what you want for supper, not that there's much selection."

Kyra found the bag and took out tins of beans and fruit. Well, it was better than nothing. There was also pemmican, flour, and a few other essentials.

By the time Cliff had a small fire going, she had biscuit dough ready. Taking out the skillet, she set out to cook their supper over the open fire.

Cliff let out a raspy laugh. "You've adapted well, considering your upbringing."

She narrowed her eyes at him, pursing her lips in thought. "Is that a compliment, Mr. Baldwin?"

"Yes." Then he smiled so brightly, her heart hammered in response.

When the food was ready, she ate as fast as Cliff. Goodness, she hadn't realized she was famished.

"Are we racing?" Cliff teased.

"If I had a mind to, I could probably eat you under the table."

"Hm, I'm glad you're not one of those stuffy society ladies who feigns a lack of appetite."

She seconded that.

The next few minutes were silent, each eating while deep in thought. Her gaze darted to Cliff when she saw him set aside his plate. Kyra continued to nibble nervously. He was thinking about something—something scalding, judging by the heat in his eyes. She gulped down her food, remembering how his hair had felt through her fingers and the hard contours of his shoulders. Maybe he was remembering their embrace as well. Her forgotten anger welled up again.

"Kyra, I'm sorry about what happened last night," he began, his hand raking through his dark hair. "I didn't mean to—"

"Treat me no better than one of your loose women," Kyra finished for him.

At that, Cliff became quiet.

She blinked back the misty sensation washing over her eyes.

"That I did not do," he finally ground out. "It may have seemed that way to you, but I was angry, Kyra. And I—I care for you. It shouldn't have happened, but believe me I didn't treat, or mean to treat you like a . . ." He stopped, seemingly unwilling to utter the word.

"How was it different?" she asked, daring him to explain.

Cliff pulled up one of his knees to hug and closed his eyes. "Kyra, I don't think this is something we should be discussing. It just wasn't like that for me, trust me."

"The conversation may be inappropriate, but kissing me the way you did and making me feel your-your, well, you know, and my-my front in your-your mouth, while I'm thinking you want nothing more than to hurt me . . . that's fine?" she blurted out, her face feeling like scarlet flames.

Cliff bent his head toward the ground, his finger drawing in the dirt. Quietly, he answered, "I never really kiss any of them. It's just cold sex without any of the heated feelings you provoke in me with just one kiss. I can't explain it, Kyra, because you haven't experienced such things. It's ridiculous for me to even try." He continued to draw in the dirt, his head low.

"Well, you seemed to think I was experienced yesterday. You may as well have called me a whore to think I could have been with Shane after only knowing him two days."

He lifted his head. "Don't say it, Kyra. I know I behaved badly and that you're not that sort of woman. I wasn't thinking straight and I—I suppose I was jealous," he spat out.

Kyra's spirits soared. He'd apologized, said he cared for her, that her kiss had affected him, and that he'd been jealous. What more could she want?

She stared into his wide eyes, clearly etched with apprehension, for a full minute before she came to a decision.

Cliff swallowed—not once, but twice. The sound resonated in his ears. He watched Kyra come to her knees, hitch up her skirt, and scoot her way toward him. His heart beat loud and clear. When she was directly in front of him, she stared at him. What did she see? Could she see he longed for things he couldn't have?

Tenderly, she placed her hands on his face, her eyes wet and naked with emotion. A long moment passed before he quietly mouthed, "What?"

"Kiss me, Cliff, without the anger this time. Please?"

Cliff closed his eyes. The feeling of her hands was a balm. He'd known she was too good a person not to forgive him, but this? He didn't know if he could handle it, if he could deal with just one kiss. She shouldn't want it from him. All he could ever give was pain and suffering.

He opened his eyes, amazed at the small woman in front of him, still there, with her hands on his face, watching him expectantly.

"Cliff, I'm not asking you for more. Just one kiss."

"Kyra . . ." Cliff started to protest, but she placed her finger on his lips. She wore one of her dazzling smiles as she leaned forward, her forehead on his, and her emerald gaze holding him captive. As if his hand had a will of its own, he raised it to her face, caressing her as gently as a butterfly's whisper, then moving to stroke her hair. He leaned back then, a little, to observe her.

"I want to see your hair," he whispered as he unraveled the thick silky rope. He combed through her locks with his fingers, until the strands descended in long waves to her lap. He brought his head forward, cradling it against the side of her head. Inhaling, he caught the scent of jasmine again. She smelled so good—too good for him. He started to pull back, but she lifted her arms into an embrace, clutching him against her. Her face was now buried between his neck and shoulder and he was loath to let her go.

"Ah, Kyra, what am I to do with you?" Cliff asked, more to himself than to her. He pulled back a little, gazing again into her eyes. His thumbs moved up to touch the softness of her petal-smooth pink lips. She was so pretty. He shifted his hand to cup her chin, not knowing how to proceed. He wasn't sure what she expected, and he didn't want to frighten her again with the ardor he'd shown last night.

Gently, he moved forward, touching his lips to hers.

Cliff watched as Kyra closed her eyes at the feel of his lingering mouth. *Lord,* her lips were like berries, so sweet, full, and warm. She swayed and he held her steady against his body as he explored her mouth, placing feather-soft kisses at the corners, occasionally tugging her lower lip to suckle. Seeking the mole nearby, he moved to kiss it, then her nose and her eyes. Pausing, he stared at her, waiting for her to open her eyes and searching deeply into them when she did. Kyra smiled, kneading his shoulders with her hands. Feeling his control vanish, he invaded her mouth, prying it open with his tongue and searching for her softness.

Cliff continued plundering Kyra's mouth, the sound of their breathing progressively more intense and labored. Cupping her ribs with a hand, he gloried in the racing pulse of her heart. She pressed closer to him, her chest leaning heavily against his as her lips moved over his, her teeth nipping him. He pulled her in even closer, if that was possible, swallowing her with his big body, and wanting nothing more than to let go and make love to her as he'd dreamed of so many times. He raked his tongue across her teeth, then deepened the kiss again. The fantasy of her assaulted his mind when she gasped, causing Cliff to pull back. He took a deep breath, hoping the torture he felt didn't show on his face.

"Are you all right?" he whispered.

Kyra drew herself away a little. Her eyes stung with thick emotion, and she blinked a few times in an attempt to regain some control. Looking back into his torment-ridden eyes, she took a deep breath and lifted her hands to travel across his shoulders. She measured their width—and finally, with one hand, she tauntingly traced a trail down his chest. His muscles bunched in reaction, and his intake of breath was raspy and deep.

"Kyra, I think we should stop now, before this goes too far." Cliff's voice was taut and restrained.

He was right, but all she could see was Cliff as a child, bruised and alone. Now he was a man, still bruised and alone. He'd named his horses after a deck of cards, in honor of Grandpère, also a part of her, for they'd shared those times together. She remembered the tintype in his bedroom, a reminder to her of his homesickness. She thought about Shane, and what he'd insinuated, and fought the horrid pictures of Cliff in New Orleans she'd tucked away in the recesses of her mind. All the times he'd had odd bruises, all the times they'd both ignored his obvious physical pains. She closed her eyes for a moment, and when she opened them again she trained them on the white scar to the side of his eye. How many others had he hidden away?

Kyra's heart broke for him. He'd known so much heartache, and believed that somehow it was what he'd deserved, but she knew better. She made a decision. She would show him a way out of the darkness, if he would let her. With that in mind, she reached to grab hold of one of his big hands. It was warm and callused, reminding her of how hard he'd worked since leaving New Orleans. Slowly, she raised it, swallowing hard as she placed it against her aching breast.

"Touch me, Cliff," she said, her stomach churning partly with anticipation and partly with fear. Cliff's hand curved around her breast, his thumb cautiously brushing its crest. An unexpected rush of pleasure shot through her. She'd give herself to him if he wanted her, no matter the consequences.

Kyra slid her eyes closed at his caress, waiting to see what he'd do, not sure herself what she expected. He groaned as if in pain as his hand left her, the heat of his body suddenly gone. She opened her eyes to find him walking toward the stream. It had become darker now, and she could see only his outline as he sat on the bank and leaned over to wash his hands and face.

Kyra watched him a while, trying to decide what to do. How far could she push him? Should she? She needed to understand what was in his mind, but how could she if he didn't talk to her? Maybe he didn't want her, but the way he'd kissed her and the things he'd said denied that possibility. Well, he'd run away before, and he wasn't getting away so easily this time. Her resolve strengthened, she lifted herself to her feet and made her way to where he sat.

Cliff sensed Kyra behind him. *Damn*, why couldn't she just let him be? Did she want to find herself compromised by a man who couldn't offer her anything? He certainly couldn't use her and discard her afterward. Not her.

He groaned low in his throat. If she weren't there, he'd have plunged himself into the cold water by now to relieve the pain in his groin. Instead, he was going to have to stand the torment of her nearness, as he watched her sit next to him and hug her knees to her chest. She rested her chin on her upraised knees, and they sat side by side, in quiet companionship, for a long time, listening to the night sounds, being comforted by the smell of the campfire carried on the breeze.

Cliff tried to concentrate on the chirping hum of the cicadas and the sound of water in the creek gurgling on its way downstream. A chuck-will's-widow bird called out in a loud whistling song, but no matter the distraction, he could only think of her.

When he finally glanced her way, he found himself admiring the perfection of her sweet profile. Maybe if they talked about something, he could forget about how much he wanted her. "Would you tell me about your second fiancé now?"

Kyra seemed a little surprised by the request, and considering all that had occurred, he couldn't blame her. She knew, he could tell, that he was playing a game, trying to pretend nothing had changed between them. He could see her mind working. Yes, she would play, but she wanted to win. He just wasn't sure how.

"Frederick Idle," her voice whispered in the night air.

"Which deadly sin was he?" He threw a rock into the water, watching it skip a few times before plunging into the stream's depths.

"Sloth."

Cliff grinned. "That bad, huh?"

"Yes, another one of my parents' arrangements. For the life of me, I still don't understand what they saw in him, except that he was as rich as Midas."

"Most parents think that way, especially for their daughters," Cliff replied dryly. What would his father do with his assets now that his only son had disappeared? He bit his lip, forcing the thought aside because he didn't want to care.

"Yes, well, this man was so rich he never had to lift a finger his whole life, and in fact it was obvious he never did." Kyra paused to smile at Cliff. "I wish I could have put him side by side with you. He was such a dandy."

Cliff had to laugh at that. "I suppose that wins me points or something. Not being a dandy, I mean."

"Oh, Cliff, he rang a bell for everything, was driven wherever he needed to go, and carried an awful lace handkerchief, which he constantly used to dab his face and nose. His other hand always held a cane, which he didn't need. He used it to lean on when he exerted himself with a walk in the garden," she continued with her usual gusto.

He shook his head. Kyra always did like to tell a story.

"He doesn't sound at all like the man for you."

"Not at all. Passion and romance would have been too much work for him. I don't think I would have gotten any 'oohs' and 'ahhs' from him on my wedding night."

A burst of laughter shot from Cliff. When would he remember to expect the unexpected from Kyra?

He stopped laughing when she said, "If I ever get married, I want a *real* man on my wedding night."

Cliff groaned at the thought of being that man, his arousal painful again. "Do you even know what that is, Kyra?" he whispered.

"After six fiancés, I have a fair idea." Her eyes shone with the truth of her feelings.

Feeling uncomfortable, Cliff sighed and picked up a stick next to him on the bank. He dug into his pocket and pulled out a small paring knife, which he used to carve on the wood. It was safer to keep his hands busy.

"I shouldn't have kissed you. Please don't ask me to again." Cliff gripped the branch and sliced from the bottom and out, flecks of wood flying into the stream.

"Why not?"

He sensed she'd stiffened her spine, ready for battle. "God, Kyra, what sort of question is that?" He paused to look at her. "I'm a man, Kyra, with needs, and your testing them doesn't help. All I want to do is thrust myself into you and make love to you till we both can't walk. Is that what you want to hear?"

His admission of lust should have sent her running, but instead she searched his eyes, reading the naked desire in his with a steady gaze of her own. Then, as though it were the most natural thing in the world, she said, "Then do."

Cliff's eyes widened with shock and he jumped to his feet, pacing in long strides. "Do you have any idea what you're saying? Are you out of your mind?" He stopped to face her. "Do you think I could just make love to you and move on? No," he answered for her. "And I won't chain you to me for the rest of your life."

Cliff saw the hurt that sprang to her eyes, and his gut twisted. "Kyra, it's not that I don't want you. There are things about me you don't know." He slapped his thigh with his hand, his gaze riveting on the star-studded sky.

"Tell me."

"I don't want to talk about it. Just understand that you'd be miserable and I'd end up hurting you more than you've ever been hurt before."

Kyra narrowed her eyes. "Well, well, I can't believe it, but it sure sounds like *the* Cliff Baldwin is nothing but a coward." Her hands were balled up in angry fists at her side.

Cliff swallowed, then redirected his gaze to the stream, and with a defeated slump to his shoulders said, "Call it what you will."

Kyra twisted onto her knees. "You were punished as long as I can remember, and even now, if your father isn't here to do it for you, then you'll do it yourself!"

At that, Cliff flinched. "What do you mean?"

Kyra jerked up to face him and whispered, "I mean, Cliff, that either you were really clumsy growing up, or I was really stupid. Which was it?"

The blood drained from his face. Time stood still. She *knew,* and had probably always known, his shame. He couldn't find the words to respond, for they were lodged in his throat. He watched as she stepped closer to him, a tear rolling down her cheek.

"Cliff, I was too young to understand completely or to know what to do then. I'm sorry I wasn't a good friend."

The life went out of his legs as he dropped to the ground with a thud, staring intently at the stream, his heart hammering an erratic tempo. His forehead beaded with perspiration, and his hands felt clammy. It had finally gotten dark enough for the moon to show its reflection on the water. Funny, how one could notice such things during moments like this.

"My father was a drunk," he croaked. "Oh, he was good at hiding it in public, but at home he made life a living hell. And my mother . . . he flaunted his women to her, mistreated her. Things happened. When I was old enough to fight back he stopped, but the damage had been done, and my mother . . . after she died . . ." He took a deep breath as he sought Kyra's sweet features. "I knew I had to go away and not turn back. I knew it even before I kissed you that night. I was always afraid, and still am, of being just like him."

Kyra crouched low beside him. "You are *not* like him."

"No? How would you know? I lost control with you last night and did things I shouldn't have, didn't I? My grandfather was just like my father. It's my inheritance."

"Only if you let it be. You didn't really hurt me last night and I know you never would. You're not them. You've learned from their mistakes. I've never even seen you take to spirits."

"Just because I don't drink doesn't mean I'm not capable of being mean. I could hurt you or any child that came along. You don't know me, Kyra." He sighed deeply. "Do you know why I left bounty hunting?"

"No."

"Do you remember what I told you about the Yancey brothers?"

"Yes."

"I fatally shot the youngest Yancey, except the wound was such that he could have lingered in agony for hours." He looked straight at her, swallowing. "I put him out of his misery, just like I would a horse." He fought to gain control, a sheen of wetness stinging his eyes. God, he couldn't remember the last time he'd allowed his emotions to take over like this. "That's who I am."

Kyra touched his arm. "Oh, Cliff, don't you see? You did what you had to do in self-defense and still found a conscience for someone else's suffering, an enemy's suffering. I don't think your father ever had a conscience when it came to you. He was too busy being sick. You are not the same."

Cliff found the strength to climb back on his feet. "You're wrong, and you shouldn't wait around for me to prove it to you. I've lived a life of violence for too long. It's part of me now." He glanced down at her. "I think we should get some sleep." Then he walked away toward the camp and the fire that had almost burned out. He'd said all he was going to say.

She was about to rise when she saw he'd left his carving knife on the ground. She picked it up and put it in her pocket, then followed along, the night ahead looking glum.

When Kyra reached the campsite, she saw Cliff had not only put sand in the fire, but had also put their bedding together. He'd done it for safety. She observed the rigid form of his body under his blanket, an arm over his eyes in silent retreat. Sighing, she dropped on her bedroll and removed her boots. She was dealing with a mule. He was stubborn, but then again, so was she, and capitulate he would. What did he have to lose but his fears? And he had a lot to gain—peace, love, a sense of self-worth, and maybe even a smile.

She remembered earlier when he'd given her a genuine one. He was so handsome when the smile reached his eyes. She prayed he would find one to keep. She stared at him a moment, then got under the covers, searching for a comfortable position on the hard ground. At the sound of her next to him, Cliff turned on his side facing the trees.

Kyra tossed and turned half the night until slumber eventually overtook her. Toward dawn she had the strangest dream. Cliff had his arm wrapped protectively around her body and whispered in her ear. She felt the sweet vibrations of his breath and turned in his arms to get closer. His hand squeezing her arm a little too hard jarred her awake. She found his blue gaze fixed on something behind her.

"Don't move," he whispered. "We have company."

Chapter Thirteen

Scrambled Brains and Eggs: An Old South recipe sure to keep the mind oiled and sharp with ideas. Better than Dr. Hogan's famous elixir.
From the *Sinfully Delicious Bakery Recipe Book*

Cliff watched the two men on the other side of camp as they quietly searched through his gear. The early rays of dawn outlined them clearly. They looked like no-good drifters to him. It was possible they only meant to steal, but they whispered to each other, gesturing in his and Kyra's direction. He wasn't taking any chances. He reached for his Colt revolver.

One man turned and walked into the woods, leaving the other behind. *Shit,* there was no telling where the son of a bitch was going. He had to act fast.

"Kyra, do you have your gun?" he whispered carefully.

"No! I wasn't thinking last night. I . . ." Her eyes were wide.

"Shh. Don't move," he ordered. "If something happens to me, run to the horses as fast as you can." Then he slithered on his belly toward the bushes behind the remaining thief.

Cliff stealthily watched the man rifle through the bag of provisions. He was slightly built, with greasy hair curling around his shoulders. Silently, Cliff rose and approached him, whacking the man over the head with his gun. With a moan, the intruder dropped to the dirt. Cliff dragged him behind the bushes, and was about to tie his hands when Kyra screamed.

"Where's your man, lady?"

Kyra almost gagged from the stench the stranger emitted. His hold was brutal and his gun jabbed in her side.

"I see my partner's gone. Your man do that?"

He pulled so hard on her hair her eyes stung with tears. She'd left it unbound last night, too tired to braid it again.

"Hey, man," he yelled out for Cliff to hear. "I got your woman, so you better come out if you don't want nothing to happen to her."

Kyra swayed against her captor. She hadn't even gotten a look at him. *Dear, God, please let Cliff be all right.*

The deafening silence continued.

The man continued to shove his gun against her ribs as he lifted his other hand to her breast and squeezed painfully. She tried to grab his hand, but he yanked at her hair again.

"Frisky little woman you got here," he yelled, "and nice titties too."

The stranger proceeded to drag her away from their camp, and a well of panic surged in her chest. She trusted Cliff. But what if he was hurt? Maybe the other man had gotten to him. Her throat clogged as she choked down her anxiety.

Then she felt it. Cliff's paring knife was still in her pocket. She debated her possibilities. She couldn't bear the thought of this man's slimy hands on her body. It was better to die trying to escape than not to try at all. He'd probably kill her anyway.

Kyra edged her hand into her pocket and grabbed the smooth walnut handle. When they reached a clump of rocks jutting forth between a stand of sumac bushes, she took a breath and purposely tripped, dragging the stranger down with her. He was forced to let go of her for a moment, and she seized the opportunity, turning and stabbing him in the gut. He screamed, aiming his gun at her as she scrambled away from him. She stumbled, the sound of gunfire ringing in her ears before everything went black.

Cliff watched the bastard teeter, then fall back, a bullet between the eyes. From the corner of his eye he saw the man he'd left behind the bushes stare at him a moment before making a run for it. Cliff fired a shot after him, but missed. Muttering an obscenity under his breath, he ran to Kyra.

She lay on the ground, scarcely a foot from the dead man. "Kyra . . . Kyra! Are you all right?" Cliff reached for her and shook her gently, but she didn't move. What was wrong with her? He turned her over, his gut knotting with fear. Nothing visible. He felt for her pulse and found it strong and steady, drenching his insides with pure relief. She must have hit her head on a rock.

"Kyra! Look at me," Cliff demanded.

With a flutter, she opened her eyes. Everything spun in front of her, and she found it difficult to distinguish top from bottom. She fixed her gaze on a treetop to orient her vision.

"Are you all right?"

She diverted her gaze to Cliff's worried face. "Cliff?"

He smiled with obvious relief. "How are you feeling?"

She lifted a shaky hand to her head, some of the haziness leaving her. "I must've hit my head."

"Let me see." He brushed her hands aside so he could examine her. "Does it hurt when I touch you?" He felt the rising lump on the right side of her head.

"It doesn't hurt too badly."

"You'll probably have a bad bump. You gave me a scare there." His voice had lowered an octave.

"Actually, when you didn't come out for so long, I was afraid something had happened to you." She allowed him to pull her to a sitting position. She took hold of his arm as a wave of dizziness hit her.

"I was waiting for the right moment, which you gave. What you did was risky."

"Well, I didn't think I had anything to lose."

"Probably not." Cliff looked behind her. "It seems I didn't knock the other one out enough. I also didn't have time to tie him up. He got away."

Kyra worried her lip. "Do you think he'll come back?"

"I doubt it."

She turned to stare at the man sprawled a few feet away. Blood. She hated the smell. Her stomach lurched, and she fought to swallow back the rising bile in her throat.

"You killed him."

Cliff said nothing. She saw he'd shuttered his expression, and her stomach clenched with remorse. It wasn't as if she saw dead people every day, especially killed dead people. Lately, she seemed to be seeing her fair share of killed dead people.

"Cliff. I—I didn't mean . . . You saved my life." Her eyes held his unwaveringly.

Cliff seemed to consider that a minute, and then scooped her up in his arms as he stood to his full height. She let out a cry of surprise, grasping his neck. "Where are you taking me?"

"You should rest, while I take care of the body."

"All right," she agreed, resting her head on his shoulder.

It was nice, being in his arms like this, even if it was only for a short walk. She glanced at him from half-closed eyelids, her body a tangle of nerves from the violence she'd witnessed. Cliff had kept any sentiment from his face, and the unshaven shadow of his morning stubble added a sinister aura to him. She could see how people might mistakenly believe the cold reputation he had.

Cliff set her down on her bedroll. He searched her eyes a moment longer as if to reassure himself that she'd be fine. Then he went back to the body.

A while later Cliff sauntered into sight and washed up at the stream. Water dripped from his hair when he sat next to her.

"How are you feeling?" he asked.

"A little nauseous, but otherwise fine."

He reached for her, the concern obvious in his face as he examined her once more. "That's not good. Your head injury could be worse than it looks."

Kyra closed her eyes, enjoying the feel of his gentle hands. It was very similar to the way he'd touched her last night. Then she stiffened, her lids flying open. She arched an eyebrow and smiled as a *very* devious idea formed in her mind. He seemed to have no qualms about touching her as long as he thought she was injured. Could she maybe . . . Of course she couldn't feign illness too long, but as long as she felt a twinge of something, she could exaggerate it a bit. It wasn't exactly being deceitful, as long as she did feel injured to some degree, which at the moment she did.

The more she thought about it, the more her burgeoning plan had merit. She pursed her lips as she watched him study her head. He'd never experienced a peaceful life, nor the contentment a trusted relationship could bring—and was afraid of allowing her to get too close because he'd never faced his fears. Maybe she just had to help him overcome his doubts.

You fell? Get back on the horse, chèrie, her grandpère had always told her. Well, as far as she was concerned, Cliff hadn't even gotten on the horse in the first place. In his mind he'd fallen before he'd even tried riding. Yes! She was going to have to seduce him. What a gloriously spectacular idea.

Oh, dear. *Seduce him?* Now, just how did one go about doing that? Her conscience needled at her honorable self. If she won at this, Cliff would probably feel compelled to marry her. It wasn't fair to force him into a marriage with someone he might not truly want, but then again, if she didn't, he might never heal his childhood wounds, nor experience the healing balm of a loving family. He'd said he cared for her, and was even jealous the other night. That was a step to love, wasn't it? He also desired her, didn't he?

As for herself, she was practically a spinster at the age of twenty-two, and it was doubtful she'd ever find another man—not after six fiancés. Besides, she'd always been infatuated with Cliff, and she thought she could easily let that emotion blossom into the love married couples shared.

Seduction. It couldn't be that difficult, although honestly, she was very nervous about lying with a man. Then again, if Cliff treated her the way he did last night, it would probably be very nice.

Two hours later, Cliff's lips spread thin. If she wiggled one more time he'd . . . He inhaled deeply as he steered Blackjack. Poker and Mr. Pip followed behind, attached by a rope. His stallion didn't seem to mind Kyra's extra weight as much as Cliff did. She'd said she felt too dizzy to ride by herself, so he'd done the only appropriate thing. It would slow them down, but there was just a few hours ride left anyway—a few hours of sheer hell if she didn't stop pressing her soft backside against his crotch. How long had it been since he'd visited Lucy's? Obviously too long if his manhood couldn't behave itself with an injured woman on his lap.

Then there was the matter of her hair. She hadn't braided it, and the smell of jasmine rose in waves, inviting him to bury his face in her silky mass. How much longer before they reached the cabin?

He thought about their conversation last night; he wasn't sure what to make of his feelings. He still couldn't believe Kyra'd not only realized his family secret, but had had the courage to confront him about it. In some ways he felt liberated to have told the truth about his childhood. He'd often felt a strong sense of shame for what had happened within his family, and guilt.

But Kyra didn't see it the way he did. She certainly didn't seem to hold him responsible for what had happened or to think any less of him. Hell, she'd apologized for not helping him out more when they were younger. She'd even had the gumption to offer herself to him twice. He still couldn't credit it, especially after the way he'd treated her the other night. Cliff slid his eyes closed at the memory of her resting his hand on her breast. It hadn't been easy for her, but as usual, she'd had guts. He, on the other hand, for all the black reputation he had among people, was a coward in disguise. She'd even said so, and she was right, or he wouldn't have run away from New Orleans in the first place.

He was right about one thing, however. She should stay away from him. The problem was that she wasn't a very good listener when she wanted her way, and here they were, almost at Shane's cabin, where he'd have to resist the torture of being alone together for God only knows how many days. He should have sent her with Shane. She should have married one of her fiancés. Could the other four be as bad as the two she'd already described?

"Kyra, how close did you get to all these fiancés? Physically, I mean." The question popped out of his mouth before he could think.

"He speaks!" Kyra exclaimed with a giggle. "Is that really any of your business?"

"No. I guess not."

"A kiss here and there, although Torville Knox did try to stick his tongue down my throat once. It was *disgusting.* It was nothing like your kisses."

Cliff grimaced as she wiggled her backside again. "It wasn't?"

"Oh, heavens, no! Why, with him I wanted to gag. With you I got the most . . . Well I'm not quite sure how to call it, but it was a different sort of feeling. Kind of like having butterflies in the pit of your stomach when you're nervous about something exciting, and then there was this ripple that started deep in . . . well, somewhere . . ." She turned her head slightly, and he could see her blush as she searched for the words.

"That's enough, Kyra. Please don't explain it any further." His voice was now strained and strangled.

"Are you all right?"

"Yes. I'm fine." Nothing a cold bath wouldn't fix. "How are you feeling?"

"Better. But still somewhat dizzy," she added. "I'm sure I'll be fine by tomorrow. I suppose it's a good thing I don't have a maid these days. Otherwise, I'd be wearing my corset. Then I'd be sure to faint, don't you think? This way, at least I can breathe easily, although I do feel rather loose in my bodice."

Cliff groaned as she followed with another good wiggle. "Kyra! Do you think you could find the right position and stay put . . . please?"

"I'm sorry. Are you sure you're all right? You sound funny."

"I just want to get to the cabin." His breath rushed out through clenched teeth. He needed to find another topic of conversation.

"How is Grandpère?" he said. "I haven't asked you yet, although I've meant to." That was a safe question.

Kyra waved her hand in front of her. "Oh, causing controversy as usual. Ever since Grandmère died he opened up the dam, so to speak. He used to restrain himself quite a bit on her account, believe it or not. But that is no longer the case, to the dismay of my mother. He loves mischief, and is now painting naughty pictures, caricatures that reflect his low opinion of high society."

"That doesn't surprise me." Cliff grinned at the memory of the ex-gambler. He knew exactly from whom Kyra had inherited her penchant for trouble. "I'm sorry about Grandmère, by the way."

"Thank you. She suffered a great deal, and we were relieved when she was finally at peace. She died five years ago."

"I wish I'd known, not that it would've done any good."

"Oh, Cliff, it was such a lonely time. You were gone without a word for almost two years, my parents were pushing Torville Knox on me, and then Grandmère died. I felt about as lost as a seventeen-year-old can feel."

Cliff tightened his hold around her in sympathy. "If it's any consolation, I was living my own hell at the time. I'm sorry I ran away. I wish I could explain it better, even to myself."

"You don't have to. I understand." With that, Kyra pulled her leg over the horse's neck to sit sideways so she could embrace him. Cliff stopped the horse a moment to pat her on the back. When she rested her head against his shoulder and obviously had no intention of moving, he nudged the horse forward again. Maybe this way she wouldn't be wiggling on his crotch any longer.

He glanced down. Her eyes had drifted shut and she seemed asleep. He sighed. Well, it wasn't much further, he told himself as he studied the softness of her sleeping face.

No, she wasn't squirming over his crotch any longer, but she was sure worming her way into his heart.

An hour later, Cliff saw the outline of Shane's one-room log cabin nestled between two big cottonwood trees. The prairie grass was thick, bushes and trees dotting the landscape around the dwelling. A nice-sized brook scurried along behind, the wild grass lusher and greener at its banks. On the other side of the brook, Indian paintbrush waved in the breeze, and butterflies danced to the same rhythm.

Passing the stables, he headed to the cabin first to divest himself of Kyra, as well as their gear, before taking care of the horses and Mr. Pip. He glanced down at Kyra, still leaning against his shoulder, her arms around his waist, in obvious slumber. He didn't want to wake her, but didn't have any choice. He nudged her twice on the shoulder, and her lashes fluttered. He smiled down at her with a mocking curl to his lips. "We've arrived."

Sitting up, she looked around, her gaze still sleepy. When they arrived at the doorstep, Cliff dismounted first, then pulled Kyra down into his arms, bouncing her weight to get a better hold.

"I can walk."

"I know, but given your injury, I don't think you should for now. I want you to rest."

He turned to take her into the cabin when a soft mewling sound stopped him. Kyra shifted her head to see as well, and her eyes lit like a child's in a confectionary shop. "Oh, Cliff, it's a kitten, and he's all alone. Let me get him. He's so sweet—don't you think so? Look at that thick black fur."

"I'm sure he'll stick around. Let's get you inside for now." His mule-eared boots clopped up the front steps, the kitten right behind.

"Look, he's following us. I think he's hungry." Kyra strained to peer over his shoulder.

Cliff studied the animal. It was scrawny and meowing to wake the dead. He'd never liked cats. But judging from the look on Kyra's face, he was going to have to find a liking. She struggled to get out of his arms, her hands scooping the kitten up as soon as her feet touched down.

"Hello, you precious baby." She scratched behind the kitten's ears, and it purred ferociously.

Cliff watched as it nipped at her fingers with its tiny, sharp teeth. Kyra giggled with delight, petting the thick dark pelt back toward the tail. If only he could trade places with the black devil.

"You remind me of someone. Hmmm . . ." she pondered, her forehead ridged in thought. Cliff's pulse beat a little faster in response to the gleam brightening her eyes as she directed an impish smile his way. "I think I'll name him Bayou Kitty."

Then, holding the kitten close to her chest, she turned around and walked through the front door, stopping suddenly as though she'd forgotten something. She swayed, and he quickly lashed out his hand to steady her. That was interesting. She'd seemed so much better a few minutes ago. The excitement of finding the kitten must have made her forget she wasn't feeling well.

Cliff got Kyra settled on the bed inside, snuggling with the blasted kitten she refused to give up. He went outside to grab their satchels, dumping them on the floor inside. With an order for her to stay put, he finally maneuvered the kitten out of her arms so he could feed it. Unfortunately, they didn't have any milk, so he settled for giving it some softened bacon left over from their lunch. Satisfied he'd taken care of his two charges for the time being, he strode out the door.

"To seduce or not to seduce. That is the question."

Kyra held the kitten up to gaze into its green eyes as she paced back and forth in front of the fireplace of Shane's one-room cabin. Then she studied her temporary home, noticing it clearly for the first time since their arrival. Shane's furnishings were simple and basic. It was obvious he spent little time in residence. She walked to the lone window beside the door, and opened it to let in a little fresh air. The musty smell inside gave her a headache.

Cradling Bayou Kitty to her cheek, she enjoyed the soft tickling of his fur as she paced toward the small cookstove and table with four chairs taking up the back wall. There were two shelves in the whole place—one holding a few cans of food and kitchen implements beside the stove, and the other holding some lamps and candles above the fireplace. Craning her head, she studied the small loft overhead, accessible by a rung of stairs.

Bayou Kitty let out a high-pitched meow, pawing at her hair, and Kyra turned her attention back to their conversation. "So if to seduce Cliff is the answer to the first question, then the second question is—how? Even after six fiancés, I don't know much about seduction. Creole society is so extremely rigid. Why, I've never been out of sight of a chaperone when one of my suitors is present. Oh, I know well enough what's supposed to happen. It's *how* to make it happen I don't know. Somehow I have to get more intimate with him.

"What would make *me* feel more intimate with *him?*" Nudging her hand for a caress, the kitten meowed again, then settled in a soft purr. "Thank you, Kitty, you're right! Talking. Yes, that's it. Talking intimately with a close friend always makes me feel more open and loving. Surely it'll work with Cliff as well. Why, the times we've been the closest the last few days were when we talked personally." Kyra snapped her fingers in satisfaction, content with her brilliant plan. Now all she had to do was figure out the details.

She sat on the bed, her hands stroking the kitten. "I don't think I should start off strong from the start. We're bound to be here at least a few days. I'll use my injury to soften him and get him close to me. Then after I've worn him down, I'll get him to talk. He'll be like biscuit dough in my hands."

She stood, chin extended, and with a purposeful stride went to the window to seek out her victim. Where was Cliff? And why wasn't he here when she was ready to put her plan into effect?

But speaking of her plan, she'd better act like she was injured if she wanted Cliff to help heal and comfort her.

She put Bayou Kitty on the floor, swatted at his backside, and headed for the bed. She'd try acting like she had a severe headache. Lying down, she uttered a practice moan or two. Hmm, sounded a bit too loud. What she needed was a soft moan, as if she truly didn't want to worry Cliff, but her pain was just too strong to be contained. She let out another practice moan. Yes, that was better, lower and softer but with a hint of despair. She practiced a couple more times until she had it just right. Then she tossed and turned on the bed a bit to make it look like she'd been distraught. The process loosened her chignon and made her hair tumble down. That was good—she didn't want to seem to be too much in control.

Finished with her preparations, Kyra didn't know what else to do. She longed to start supper as her stomach growled louder than Bayou Kitty's purr, but Cliff could catch her out of bed, and it wouldn't help her to seem injured to be able to cook. So she lay there staring at the wall until she drifted off to sleep.

Chapter Fourteen

Oyster and Octopus Gumbo: Aphrodisiacs to be sure.
The victim of your affection will be none the wiser.
From the *Sinfully Delicious Bakery Recipe Book*

Kyra was snoring lightly as Cliff walked into the cabin. The late afternoon shadows from the nearby thicket of trees engulfed the cabin with a dusklike sheen of darkness. Cliff had scouted the area, refreshing his mind with the terrain, and building up ideas for possible defense.

Leaning toward Kyra, he smiled at the slight smile on her face. She lay sprawled across the bed in complete abandon as if she hadn't a care in the world, her body relaxed, her expression peacefully innocent. Unwittingly he reached out to caress her cheek and capture a loose tendril to place behind her ear. Her breath came out in a louder snore. Cliff chuckled as he set about emptying their satchels and starting a quick supper. She must be feeling well to sleep that soundly.

From the corner of his eye he caught a twitching movement. It was the kitten curled up on a chair, claiming the one spot of sunshine left shining through the window. It also was fast asleep, soft little purring snores huffing through its tiny nose. Cliff shook his head. He must be going soft—his gaze shifting toward the person to blame. She'd had the gall to name the damn thing Bayou Kitty, saying it reminded her of *him.* Nobody had ever compared *him* to a helpless kitten before. Hell, she had to be crazy.

When Cliff had cooked up the rabbit he'd shot, a pot of frijoles, and some biscuits, he walked over to Kyra and tapped her on the shoulder. She looked up at him with a dreamy expression on her face and murmured, "Cliff." Suddenly her eyes widened with alarm. A pained expression crossed her face and her mouth twisted.

"Oh, Cliff. Where have you been?"

"I've been inside for a while now, but didn't want to disturb you. You were sleeping so peacefully." He was too much the gentleman to tell her she snored. Besides, he thought it was cute.

"I was? Oh, I mean, I wasn't. Truly I wasn't. I don't feel well at all. My head is pounding so."

"Are you sure? Maybe it started hurting when you woke up."

"Well, I really don't know. All I know is that it's hurting now. Would you see if the bump has gotten bigger?"

Cliff gently slid his fingers through her hair. He carefully caressed her lump, which didn't seem as swollen as the last time he'd examined it.

A low, soft moan escaped her lips.

"I didn't mean to hurt you. Is it still that tender?"

"No. I mean, yes. It's still hurting, I think. But your fingers feel good. Please don't stop."

Cliff massaged through her hair, trying to relax her and help ease the tension of her headache. How bad off was she? He'd seen his share of head injuries, and hers didn't seem that bad. But it was true that it was hard to properly gauge a head injury. The slightest bump could leave a person addled for days, and sometimes the wounds that bled terribly really weren't serious at all. He'd just have to watch her carefully.

"I guess you'd better not eat all this food I fixed then. With a head injury you have to eat lightly, so your stomach won't rebel. I've cooked a rabbit and some beans and biscuits. But for you I'll take some of the rabbit drippings and make some broth. You can have that with a biscuit. How does that sound?"

"Don't you think I could eat a little more than that? I'm very hungry actually." She ended on a whine.

"No, I don't think it would be wise. Maybe by tomorrow morning you can have a full meal." Hmm. She seemed a little paler and more fretful.

After serving Kyra her broth and biscuit in bed, Cliff sat at the small table nearby and thoroughly enjoyed his meal. Fresh rabbit and biscuits was one of his favorite meals. The coffee smelled as delicious as it tasted too.

Cliff looked up from wiping the last crumb off his plate. Kyra stared at him wistfully. "Cliff, don't you think I could just taste the rabbit or the coffee."

"I'm sorry, honey. I shouldn't have eaten in front of you, I guess. I didn't realize the food would appeal to you. But trust me, with a head injury, you'd pay for it later if you ate."

She sat up, her hair cascading around her face and shoulders, her body rumpled and cozy from lying in bed. He'd better leave before he started something he'd regret.

"Ah, Kyra, I need to step outside for a second. I'll clean up when I get back. Why don't you get ready for bed while I'm gone."

"All right." Her voice was subdued enough, but there was a hint of cheer rippling through it. Something was going on with her, but he couldn't quite put his finger on what it was.

As soon as Cliff was out the door, Kyra hopped out of bed and scurried over to the cookstove and the last of the rabbit and coffee. Hurriedly she tore off pieces of meat, shoving them into her mouth. She didn't want Cliff to come back and catch her eating, but her stomach was growling enough to mock a summer thunderstorm. There was no way she would last until breakfast with no more than broth and a biscuit.

She was frantically taking a last bite of rabbit and a quick gulp of coffee when Cliff knocked on the door and walked in. He stopped in surprise.

Kyra unobtrusively swallowed while surreptitiously wiping the grease off her fingers on her gown.

"I thought you were getting ready for bed."

"I—I, um, didn't know where you put our stuff." She opened her eyes as wide as possible.

Cliff's gaze went to the only trunk in the room, at the foot of the bed.

"There aren't many places where I could hide it." His tone was slightly sarcastic.

She had to turn his attention quickly. "That brings up another question. Where are we going to sleep?"

His body jerked to attention. Drawing himself up straighter, he cleared his throat. "I am going to sleep down here on this bed, and *you* are going to sleep up in the loft."

Kyra looked up to the narrow, small, dimly lit loft above the kitchen area. She turned in question to Cliff. It wasn't like him to be ungentlemanly, or at least it used not to be.

He rolled his eyes. "It's not that I mean to give you the less comfortable place to sleep, but I think it's safer. It's entirely possible we could have unwanted company this evening. And I want them to have to get through me to reach you."

His words filled her with warm elation, even though spoken in a gruff, somewhat surly tone of voice. He truly did care about her, and suddenly her guilt vanished. She didn't like manipulation, but she was seducing him for his own good. If only she knew how long it would take . . . and what it would be like.

Cliff lay in bed, his obsessive gaze fixed on the loft, squinting to see as much as he could of the woman making him throb with unspent lust and anticipation. Bayou Kitty had planted his small body against his side, and no matter how many times he'd shoved the animal away, he kept coming back. Finally, Cliff had given up, allowing the purring devil to snuggle up to him like a woman. If only it really were a woman—namely a small green-eyed temptress who didn't have the sense to understand her appeal. Was she deliberately trying to drive him mad, or did it just come naturally to her?

All evening she'd flaunted her delectable body at him. First by having him put together a quick screen made from some wood posts and a blanket for her to change behind—while he pictured her every movement as she removed her clothing and put on her nightdress. Then that outrageously seductive nightdress of hers, covering every inch from the bottom of her chin to the tips of her toes, but firing his imagination with images of what lay beneath. All he'd wanted was to lift the hem and throw the blasted rag away. Finally she'd had the audacity to climb up into the loft, giving him an eyeful of what actually lay under the gown as he'd held the ladder steady for her. All that white, creamy skin; it had taken all of his strength not to grab her off the ladder and fling her on the bed, pounce on her, and thrust himself as deep inside her as he could. God, he was hot just thinking about it. But the worst thing she'd done was to lie up there, on her side, hips outlined in the moonlight, beckoning. It was as if they whispered, "Come to me. Make love to me."

Jesus, he had to be absolutely crazy to lie here, imagining hips talking to him.

Logically, he knew Kyra wasn't to blame for his feelings. She couldn't help the intimacy of their environment, and he'd been the one to insist on holding that ladder for her, even though he'd seen her climb any tree in New Orleans whenever she'd wanted as a child. And she wasn't to blame for the moon shining through the window, outlining her every curve to his hungry gaze.

He was going crazy. That was all there was to it. He wanted something he shouldn't have. He had to protect her from himself. Hell, that wasn't even the complete truth. It was at times like this, in the dead of night when all things were silent, still, and dark, that his mind was determined to torment him with the truth. *He wasn't protecting Kyra; he was protecting himself.* He never wanted to experience again the pain of betrayal and loss he'd experienced as a child . . . and again as a young man. Never.

He could never open his heart to Kyra, because she was one of the few people who could destroy him.

His gaze flew once more to the loft as he heard her thrashing on her makeshift padding. She moaned in her sleep. Could she be having a nightmare? He didn't think it was likely since she'd only been asleep about ten minutes. He didn't think deep dreams started that early. Could she be in pain? He waited longer to see what she'd do. He didn't want to get any closer to her pallet than he had to, because the way he felt, he couldn't be trusted.

Her moans got louder and her thrashing harder. Hell, he was going to have to go up there. The loft was too narrow; she could easily roll over and fall off.

Dragging his feet, he grabbed hold of his shirt and threw it on. He climbed the small ladder—amazed she hadn't woken herself with the racket she made.

Kyra's skin was luminescent in the moonlight, her moans a little louder. He reached out from his perch on the ladder to touch her shoulder, but she jerked away as she moaned and rolled in convoluted agony. Her foot swiped one of the ladder rungs. The ladder swayed precariously, as he wildly grabbed for an anchor, then crashed to the floor with a loud agonizing thud.

"Cliff! Are you all right?" Kyra's eyes, filled with shock, peered at him from over the loft edge.

He took a couple of deep, rasping breaths—trying to fill his lungs once again with air. His back felt as if it had shattered into a hundred pieces. He couldn't get enough breath to speak.

Kyra hung from the loft's edge and jumped down, flying to his side. She bit her lip as she knelt on the floor beside him and smoothed the hair out of his eyes. "Oh, Cliff. Speak to me, please. Tell me you're all right. I shall never forgive myself if you're truly hurt."

With a final painful gasp, his lungs filled with air. As he struggled to sit up, he pushed Kyra away. She lay practically on top of him in her concern, clinging like a vine.

"Let me help you, Cliff. You're hurt."

"I'm fine . . . just need some air . . . give me some space." After a couple more breaths, he could sit up unassisted. "Please, Kyra. Back up a little. I can't breathe with you right on top of me."

"I'm sorry, Cliff. I just wanted to help. It's my fault you got hurt."

"How do you figure that? I know you didn't mean to kick the ladder. You were having a nightmare. I was trying to wake you." Cliff fell silent, puzzled by her guilty demeanor, her cheeks suffused with red. His eyes squinted in suspicion. "What's going on, Kyra? Why do you feel responsible? And how did you realize what had happened so quickly?"

"Why—why nothing, Cliff. I can't remember what happened. Truly. I was having a bad dream. I can't remember it exactly, but there was a lot of blood, and Jacques, I think. The next thing I knew I heard this loud crash. I looked down and saw you lying under the ladder. Somehow I knew I was responsible."

Cliff eyed her warily. Her story sounded convincing. But he had a gut feeling that something wasn't right. Ever since arriving at the cabin, she'd acted peculiar. She was up to something, but he couldn't for the life of him figure out what it was.

His gaze drifted from her face to her breasts, which rose and fell with her excited and uneven breathing. His mouth opened and his hand lifted and reached out to her. Her eyes closed and her tempting body leaned closer.

He flung himself away from her, jumping up. "Please go back to bed. Now. I'm going outside for a moment."

The door slammed shut behind him.

A low creak from a closing door woke Kyra the next morning. The cabin was flooded with light. A pleasant dream still filled her mind, though she couldn't remember the details. She could feel the lasting sensations, though, of warmth, hope, and gentle caresses. Her body tingled. *Cliff must've played a leading role.*

She rolled over and looked down from the loft to the cabin below. His bed was made and he was nowhere to be seen. She rolled back onto her pallet and stretched, languorously reaching her arms as high above her as she could while pointing her toes in the opposite direction. With a loud yawn, she sat up and flung her hair off her face. She could see out the window to the blue sky and glorious day awaiting her. She couldn't wait to get outside and start exploring with Cliff.

She hadn't fallen asleep until very late after the excitement of nearly killing him. Plus, she hadn't been sleepy, as she'd slept so much during the day. "Enough of acting sick," she said aloud. "That plan sure didn't work out. I almost got Cliff killed, pretending to have a nightmare so he'd come to me. What a fool I've been."

She searched for her clothes and climbed down the ladder, going behind the makeshift screen to sponge off. While she dressed, she spotted Bayou Kitty eating by the cookstove. Cliff must have prepared him some breakfast.

She called out to the kitten. "You'll need to go outside soon, hmmm? No more lying in bed for me. I'll start the next part of my plan and hope it gives me better results. Maybe if I can talk Cliff into walking with me and showing me around, I can open up some good conversation. Then, when we get back, he'll be all ready to be seduced. What do you think?"

Kyra reached down to pick up Bayou Kitty, who rubbed against her calf. Cuddling his soft fur against her cheek, she said, "Yes, I'm sure this plan will work much better." Giving the kitten a final tickle under the chin, she set him down so she could start breakfast.

Kyra was pleased with her culinary efforts. Even with limited supplies, her skills were improving. The aroma of salt pork and johnnycakes wafted to her nose, making her stomach growl. Goodness, but she was hungry. After all, she had eaten hardly anything last night. She nibbled on a piece of pork, wondering if she should wait for Cliff or start without him. If she didn't miss her guess, she was turning out to be quite a good chef. And what surprised her even more was that she enjoyed it.

"What are you smiling about?"

Cliff's question broke into her inner musings. She jumped, sending a plate clattering to the floor.

"You startled me! How does a man as big as you are move so quietly?" As he pulled out a chair and sat down, she picked up the plate and placed the food on the table. "I was imagining the next time I see Mama and how surprised she'll be." She sat across from Cliff and dished out the food.

"Yes, I can guarantee she'll be surprised at how you've been living since you left New Orleans. I imagine I'll have a shotgun planted in my back and a preacher in my face quicker than young Sammy can hog-tie a calf."

"Oh, Cliff, that's not what I meant. I was talking about my new ability to cook. My parents would never force you to marry me. I'm sure they'll understand. My life is in danger. They'll have to accept that you were protecting me."

"Maybe. We'll see. A lot could happen between now and then. If your reputation hasn't been tarnished back home, your parents may very well understand. It's Grandpère I'm worried about."

"Maybe Grandpère won't find out. Since Grandmère died, and he's been consumed with his art, he doesn't come to Mama's house as often as he used to. It's possible he'll never know."

"Impossible."

"How can you know that for sure?"

"Because before I left Dallas, I hunted up one of my old contacts and wrote out a message for him to take to your grandfather. He should have received it by now."

"Why didn't you tell me? Why did you do that?"

"Because someone in your family needed to know where you were. Or do you want them to worry about you?"

Kyra blushed. "Yes, I suppose you're right. I've been pretty selfish, haven't I? I've been so filled with my own worries and fear, and then with the pleasure of being with you, I didn't think seriously of what my parents might be going through. But why send the message to Grandpère rather than to Papa?"

"Because I trusted him not to overreact, and I also trusted him to take care of Jacques."

"Take care of Jacques? What do you mean?"

"Kyra, it's not enough for us to simply get rid of Wade. He isn't the source of the problem; Jacques is. I had to start an offensive against him, and since I couldn't do it myself, I turned to someone I could trust. Grandpère was the answer. He's quiet, reliable, and he knows how to deal with lowlifes."

"But—but he won't try to do anything to Jacques, will he? I don't want him to get hurt."

"You don't want Jacques to get hurt?" Cliff flung himself up from the table, his face red. He leaned toward her and thundered, "How dare you tell me you don't want Jacques to get hurt? Do you mean you're in love with the man, even after what he did? Then why the hell did you come running to me? Are you so fickle you have to have every man in your acquaintance panting after you?"

Kyra flung her water in his face. She stood up, and ran for the door. But before she went through it, she lashed out. "How can you be so hateful, Cliff? Don't you trust anyone, or is it just me? I was referring to Grandpère. I don't want Grandpère hurt. He's an old man now, Cliff, seven years have changed him, and Jacques is truly evil. If anything happens to Grandpère, I will never forgive you!" She slammed the door behind herself as she fled.

Cliff found her an hour later, lying in the tall grass of the prairie, gazing at the sky. Bayou Kitty had given her location away as he chased a cricket nearby. Cliff hadn't come after her immediately. He'd needed time to calm down, to get his runaway emotions back under lock and key. What was it about her that made him lose total control? He'd prided himself for as long as he could remember on masking his emotions—first with his father, and then later as a bounty hunter. He hadn't wanted to give his father the pleasure of knowing the pain he inflicted through his words, fists, and belt. When he'd become a bounty hunter, he'd learned that the colder, less passionate a man was, the better chance he had at survival. Emotions could get a man killed quicker than a bullet. That was one of the main reasons why he'd left the business. His emotions had started sneaking out into the open.

But ever since he'd bought his ranch, and hadn't had to look death in the eye on a daily basis, his emotions had once again been under his control, until the day Kyra had walked into Madam Lucy's and back into his life. Why couldn't he just treat her as a sweet childhood friend from his past who needed his protection for a few days? Why did he have to be roused with lust one moment and distrust the next? How did she manage to crash the lifetime of walls he'd fortified around his heart?

Hell, he owed her an apology, but he just couldn't do it. It would mean explaining his actions, and he wasn't prepared for that, even to himself. And to be honest, he was sick and tired of apologizing all the time. She'd have to understand, and if she didn't, then that was fine as well. Maybe if she was angry with him, she wouldn't be so enticing.

"Kyra." The word floated away on the breeze. He moved closer, calling out again.

She didn't face him, but she spoke. "I'm sorry I threw water at your face. I shouldn't have done that."

"I've had worse," he murmured. She flinched, and he felt like a bastard. Hell, he'd deserved to get his ass kicked.

"Cliff, would you please sit beside me? I want to tell you a story."

He let out a beleaguered groan, but sat about three feet from her. He wasn't taking any chances getting too close. "What is it?" His voice was gruff, and he tried to modify his attitude. Even if he wasn't going to apologize, he still didn't need to be grouchy.

"I want to tell you about my third fiancé, Vance Goodbody."

"Which sin was he?" He shoved a blade of grass in his mouth.

"Pride. Vance was, and still is, an extremely handsome man—thick blond hair, clear blue eyes, tall, and nicely formed. All the girls flirted outrageously with him. Some would send him gifts, messages, or wave to him openly in the streets. He was very proud of himself and became . . . well . . . rather vain. I guess I got carried away with pride as well when he started paying attention to me. I mean, the best-looking man in New Orleans was coming to call, and then he asked for my hand in marriage. I was flattered. I couldn't understand why he'd chosen me when he could've had his pick of any marriageable debutante. But I figured maybe my wealth and social position influenced him in my favor."

Kyra paused, and Cliff reflected on how naïve she could truly be. She seemed to have no sense of her sensual beauty and the lust she could inspire in men's bodies—especially his.

"What made you break off the engagement?"

She smirked. "Yes, *I* broke the engagement off. Do you know how tiresome it is to constantly have another woman batting her eyes at your fiancé? Or to have your fiancé more concerned with his appearance than your feelings? He couldn't drive with the carriage top down because it might blow his hair, we couldn't go on picnics because it might stain his clothes, and we couldn't even dance at the Fourth of July Ball because he might perspire. I couldn't take it anymore. I wanted to have fun. I wanted more freedom than that. It was like being engaged to my mother—except he was more concerned with *his* appearance than mine—though he did comment frequently on how I looked as well. He didn't want to see one hair out of place or a dress even slightly out of vogue."

"It must have made you proud to be the one to break up with New Orleans' most eligible bachelor."

"Yes, there was that as well," she said with an impish grin on her face.

Cliff felt uncomfortable. He didn't like thinking about Kyra with another man, much less a very handsome man who was also her fiancé. He lashed out to break his mind of the images forming. "So, why are you telling me this? You want me to feel low knowing you can have any man you want? Is that it?"

Her mouth tightened, but her eyes softened. "No. I'm telling you this because I want you to understand that I've had the chance to love and marry many eligible men. They haven't all been idiots. But I didn't. I didn't want any of them, no matter how rich, handsome, or important they were. My heart was already betrothed."

Her eyes implored him to understand the message beneath her words. But his heart wasn't ready yet to hear it.

"Cliff, tell me what you're thinking. What you're feeling. I want to understand what's going through your mind."

Like hell. There was no way he was going to share his thoughts, especially right now, with her. "Why? Why do you need to know what I'm feeling?"

"It would help me understand you better."

"You don't need to understand me better."

They were at a stalemate.

Kyra stood up and bent down to grasp his hand. His forehead furrowed questioningly as she tugged him upward. "Please come with me. I want to show you something."

She led him back into the cabin, then reached into her satchel and pulled out a thick, well-worn book. He felt befuddled as she shoved it into his hands. "What's this?"

"It's my journal—or at least my current one. I've been keeping this one for about nine months. It contains all my innermost thoughts, feelings, and most of the things that have happened to me. I record it all here. It helps me understand what's going on in my life, to sort out any confusing emotions so I know how to deal with them."

"Uhh, that's nice. What do you want me to do with it?"

"Well, I thought you might like to read some of it. Then maybe you could start keeping one yourself."

"Like hell!"

She looked taken aback, as if she'd offered him a prize jewel—only to have him toss it back in her face. "But—but I don't understand. Why wouldn't you want to write in a journal? Surely you can see how important it is to analyze your feelings."

"Let me get this straight. You want me to record everything I'm experiencing, my 'innermost feelings,' on a piece of paper that *anyone could find and read?*"

"It's not as ridiculous as you're making it sound, Cliff."

He snorted.

"It's a great tool for acquiring self-knowledge."

"I don't need to understand myself any better than I do right now."

"A journal can also help you reconcile your past with your present. I often read something I wrote years earlier and gain a new perspective."

"I have no desire to understand my past. What happened then is better left dead and buried."

Kyra blew out air in a loud harrumph and threw up her hands. She was vexed. There was no way to reason with such illogical arguments. And how was she supposed to seduce him if he wouldn't cooperate? Maybe he just didn't like writing.

"All right, Cliff, you don't have to put anything in writing, but I'd like it if you'd tell me a little bit more about what's been happening with you these past few years."

"And *I* would like for you to stop asking so many questions. Just leave it alone, Kyra. I'm not you. I have no desire to explore my past. Today is what's important. If I don't make any mistakes today, then I won't have to worry about understanding my past tomorrow."

Well, that was it then. It seemed like she wasn't going to be able to arrange an intimate conversation with Cliff. And she didn't have any other plan formulated. So what was she to do? She wasn't about to give up. Cliff was right in that regard; she was a very sore loser.

She turned from Cliff, walking to peer out the window, her thoughts scrambling. That left flirting. Of course she knew how to flirt; it was just that she never enjoyed it. It seemed so fake—so superficial. But she was determined to seduce him, and maybe all those other women throughout history hadn't been totally wrong when they'd used their beauty and flirtatious ways to their advantage.

Turning back to Cliff, she smiled at him from under her long eyelashes, and said in a soft voice, "Fine then. Why don't we go for a walk, and you can show me around? I'd like to see more of Shane's land."

Kyra had finished her sponge bath behind the privacy screen and slipped into her nightdress when the front door slammed, signaling Cliff's abrupt departure. She quirked her mouth in annoyance as she shrugged into her white silk wrapper and slid on her black kid slippers. Cliff had been sullen and moody since yesterday, and his mood was affecting hers. She wanted to write in her journal and go to bed early.

Sighing deeply, she tapped her fingers together in thought as she paced, at a loss as to what to do next. Flirting hadn't worked either. Maybe her campaign to entice him into a caring relationship had been a mistake. He was more distant than ever, and he didn't seem to want her help—or her, for that matter. She bit down on her lip, then exhaled, studying the white fog it placed on the window. Leaning forward a little, she peered outside. Cliff sat under the big tree out front, his head tilted back against the trunk. One would think he was in prayer, but he was probably fighting the demons in his mind.

"Oh, Cliff," Kyra couldn't help whisper. He was so big, so strong of body and brave in the face of danger and all sorts of ugliness, but when it came to himself, he was weakened by the torture he meted out to his soul.

Digging deep to find some courage, Kyra twisted her hair into a knot. Bayou Kitty clawed at the door. She gave his ears a good rub and followed him outside, making her way to where Cliff sat. At the sound of her footfalls, he moved his head forward to meet her gaze. The evening air was cool and the wind had picked up. She looked at the darkened sky, seeing the clouds that hovered, and turned her attention back to Cliff. The air had that peculiar smell of the calm before a storm.

"I think it's going to rain. Maybe you should come inside," she said, unnerved by his dark expression. His eyes flashed blue fire as he rubbed a denim-clad thigh with his large hand.

"You shouldn't have come out here," he said in a contained voice as he scrutinized her appearance. "You look like you're ready for bed."

Her cheeks flamed. She was in her nightclothes, but was properly covered from her feet to her neck.

"Yes, I was about to go to bed, when I heard you go outside . . . and, well, you seemed lonely. I—I thought that perhaps you'd like some company. You've hardly spoken to me all day."

His piercing gaze narrowed, and his body became rigid. She could see his chest moving with each breath beneath his dark blue cotton shirt, but other than that, he was dangerously still. The wind picked up, blowing his black strands back, giving him an even more ominous appearance.

His tone harsh, he answered, "Maybe I don't wish to speak with you right now. You'd do better to return to the cabin rather than bait me with your scantily clad body."

She swallowed, stiffening her spine. "I am *not* scantily clad. Should I sleep fully dressed just to please you?"

"No. You should leave me alone when I ask it."

"I just wanted to be with you, Cliff," she explained, the hurt obvious in her tight voice.

Cliff leaped off the ground, and grasped her shoulders in an almost painful grip. "Do you? Right now there is only one way I want to be with you, and that is to relieve this godawful pain you've caused my body since we got here. Is that what you want? It seems that it is, for all you've done is entice me with your wiles like a wanton. Do you think I'm so stupid not to understand what you've been trying to do? You forget, I've known a few women in my time searching for the same thing, except most of them just come out and ask for it."

Kyra gasped at the venom in his voice and the burning passion in his eyes. Shrugging herself out of his strong grip, she whirled around and ran back into the cabin, slamming the door behind her. She flung herself onto the bed, shaking with anger, embarrassment, and the pain of his hated words. Her eyes burned with hot tears as she tried to keep them from falling down her cheeks. A few escaped, and she swiped hard at them.

"I've tried to tell you what a bastard I am, but you just haven't believed me," Cliff said with a sigh behind her.

She stiffened. She hadn't even heard him come inside.

The bed sagged beside her as he sat. Then his strong fingers found the nape of her neck, massaging her tension away.

"Go . . . away, please! You were right. I've been nothing but a wanton. Just leave. I can't bear to look at you. I'm too ashamed." Her breath shuddered, ending with a sob as she again swiped at her tears.

He pulled her chin back to meet his gaze. She closed her eyes, and felt him wipe away a leaking tear with his thumb.

"Look at me," he ordered. "I should be the one ashamed for talking to you that way. I didn't mean it. . . . I'm just so frustrated I can't think straight."

She opened her eyes, finding his blue ones boring down at her. Something sad flickered in them, and she wanted to lift her hand to rake back the curtain of his hair hovering over them, but didn't dare. He clearly hadn't wanted her to get near him, much less touch him, earlier.

"I'm sorry, Cliff. I didn't mean to cause you pain. I just wanted to be with you."

"I know, but it's not so simple for me. I want you too much," he said with a groan, his breath ragged.

"Oh, Dear Lord. Won't you hold me . . . please?"

He shook his head no, but dragged her up toward him, crushing her to his chest. She clasped her arms around his neck, enjoying the feel of his strong arms.

"I never wanted to hurt you, Cliff. I—I care for you so much." Then more softly: "I think I love you." She heard herself say it, and she knew it was true. It had to be, for she'd never felt this way for any other man—ever. Maybe she had always loved him.

His arms slowly lost their hold on her as he pulled back. Tortured. That was the only way to describe the look in his eyes, the depth of emotion turning them into the gray-blue color of a sea in the midst of a storm.

"You don't know what you're saying."

"Why not? I'm not a girl any longer. I'm a woman who knows her mind. I've had six fiancés to compare, and the fact is you've always been the beau ideal, whether I realized it at the time or not."

He continued to shake his head. "Haven't you understood anything I've told you? I could never risk ruining your life. It would kill me to see your passion snuffed out, your dreams lost, your life . . . I care for you too much."

"If you care for me, then show me! Don't hide from me." Her voice breaking, she added, "I'm not a fragile china doll that needs protecting. I'm a strong woman who knows now what she wants. Let me love you."

She extended her hand to him, which he stared at for a full minute before he got up to pace. He stopped his pacing a few times as if battling a decision, then finally walked to the window.

His shoulders seemed heavy with burden as he gripped the window ledge and stared outside. Kyra rose from the bed and strode toward him. Facing his back, she spoke. "I can't say I understand what you've been through. I can't because I don't. But if I know one thing, it's that your fears are based on the unknown and the belief that you're worth what you were made to believe. If you were really the person you're afraid of being, you wouldn't have the conscience to worry about ruining my life. Your father never worried about ruining lives because he was sick. You instead worry so much, I can't fathom how you'll ever allow yourself to be free to make mistakes. When it comes to me, your conscience is misplaced. I know what you are because I can see what you can't. It's *my* choice, not yours, to ruin my life if that's your main concern. Unless, of course, you truly just don't want me . . ." She paused. "But earlier you said you wanted me. *And I want you . . . now.*"

Chapter Fifteen

Red Rose Petals Dipped in Dark Chocolate: A taste of sweet passion to sate the body and soul.
From the *Sinfully Delicious Bakery Recipe Book*

Cliff turned from the window, searching every inch of her face. He pushed back his ebony locks, his eyes shining with emotion, then let his arm hang loose at his side. "This is so damn hard for me, Kyra. I have no experience in relationships. I can only try. But the fact is that if I make you mine, damn the consequences, I will never let you go. Never! Do you understand what I'm saying?"

"I don't want you to. I—I remember how I used to dream of you this way. That you'd finally look at me the way a man does a woman. When you went away, I—I was crushed. I thought I'd forgotten all those feelings, but I haven't, and I never will. Maybe breaking my engagements was my way of stalling, no, hoping I'd see you again." She stared at her feet before meeting his gaze once more and whispering, "I love you, Cliff Baldwin. Please don't turn away."

Evening's shadows rendered Cliff ominous as his gaze clung to hers. Kyra counted every heartbeat—each lilting boom like thunder to her ears. Swallowing, she jerked her gaze from his tense face to the rigid set of his broad shoulders, reading the blatant hesitation. She leaped when he rushed to her, seizing her shoulders and hauling her to his hot and solid body. His mouth found hers in an exhaled release of pent-up frustration, his smooth tongue gliding sensually over hers. A swimming sensation, deliciously tingling and foreign, ribboned from her stomach to her womb, pooling and throbbing between her legs. His assault made her feel mindlessly dizzy with need, but also with fear. Fear of this unknown passion surfaced within her—fear of his own ardent need. Kyra squeezed her eyes shut, wishing he'd slow down, but leashing the thought, afraid to lose him again.

With trembling hands, she pressed against Cliff's chest, the heaving rhythm very like her own. His breath was warm, the taste of the coffee he'd drunk with dinner sweet and heady, his smell totally male. Her senses reeled as large hands freely roamed over her body, callused fingers kneading her buttocks, a cupping palm forcing her hips up and against his arousal. The feel of it was her undoing, and she whimpered—a small sound filled with fearful wonder. But it was enough to stop him. Panting, he stepped back, his head shaking as he swore under his breath.

"God, Kyra, I'm sorry. I didn't mean to go at you like a hungry wolf."

"It—it's all right. You weren't hurting me. I'm just a little nervous. I—I haven't done this before."

He inhaled deeply, surveying her pale expression, striving to calm the drumming beat of his heart. Her big eyes sparkled like emeralds beckoning him to their treasure. All these years, never would he have believed she'd one day be his—that she'd truly want *him*. God, she was more beautiful than all his dreams combined, and he was nothing but a bastard thinking only of his raging need. This was her first time, and although he had no experience with virgins, he should make it special for her. The last thing he wanted to do was frighten her, which she clearly already was. She just didn't want him to know, which didn't surprise him.

He bent down to lift her into his arms, then carried her to the bed and placed her gently in the middle. He turned away a moment to pull off his boots and unfasten his gun belt. Resting it on the nightstand, within reach, he twisted back to face her.

She watched him, apprehension evident in her features as he loomed over her. Rubbing a hand over his head, he debated his sanity one more time, forcing the second thoughts aside.

"This is your last chance, Kyra. I don't know if I'll be able to stop later."

Her throat bobbed as she swallowed, her tongue licking her lips, making him groan with his craving to taste it again. Her eyes shimmered with rich emotion as she extended her hand to him.

"Make love to me, Cliff" she whispered, her words blazing through his already heated body.

He came to her then, sitting beside her, his head descending to capture her lips in another heart-wrenching kiss. He caressed the side of her head with his palm, as his tongue twined hotly with hers. Pulling her lips into a pout, he broke away to plant soft kisses over her precious features—her cheeks, her nose, and her eyes. His hands itched to rip off her wrapper and nightdress, but he suppressed the urge. He was glad that he did when her arms tugged around him, one dainty hand clutching at his hair as she, too, rained kisses on his face. It was too much—sweeter than anything he'd ever felt. She touched him lovingly, cherishing him with timid passion. Could he be so lucky? Was God dealing him a fair hand for once? Fear welled inside him, and he drew back, pulling her hand from his scalp to kiss her palm. Her hand shook a little, and she shuttered her eyes from his stare. He would protect her. He wouldn't let what happened to his mother happen to Kyra as well.

"Are you all right?" His voice tightened with the control he exerted.

She looked down. "I'm just a little uncertain as to what to do. I—I hope I don't disappoint you."

He smiled tenderly. "You could never disappoint me."

He caressed her hand with his thumb.

"Are *you* all right?" she asked.

Cliff laughed low—painfully. "No. For the first time I'm not sure how to proceed." He chuckled again and planted another kiss on her palm.

"Well, wh-what would you normally do?"

Her doelike eyes reflected her innocence, and it humbled him that she'd placed her trust in him so completely, that she would gift him with her body—and her heart.

"It's just that I'm afraid of shocking you with something you won't like. Maybe even lose control and hurt you. I—I don't know what a woman who's never been with a man expects."

"Oh, Cliff. I—I only expect to be close to you, and well, I'm not sure what else, so just make love to me the way you want to. I'm sure nothing you do will shock me."

He threw her a wicked smile. "Care to wager on that, Miss Lourdes? This is one bet I'm sure to win."

"No," she whispered, "but you're torturing me by doing nothing. It's just making me worry more and I don't want to think right now."

Sighing, Cliff leaned down to kiss her nose. "I'm sorry, sweetheart." Then he kissed her with all the feeling he possessed, the hunger for her intensifying with every shy touch of her hands trailing over his upper body.

"Cliff! You feel so wonderful. I—I want to see you." Her trembling fingers sought out the buttons on his shirt, but she shook so much she couldn't open them.

"Let me help you."

When the last button was undone, he slid his shirt off, letting it drift to the floor. Kyra pushed up against the headboard, extending a wavering hand toward his flesh. Cliff closed his eyes as her fingers tentatively ran through the dark curls on his chest. Her sweet hands explored a trail, tickling down his arms, his muscles bunching with restraint. Sucking in a breath, he opened his eyes again to find the marvel in hers.

"Cliff, you are so hard—just as I imagined. So beautiful."

"I'm a man. I can't be beautiful."

"No. You are more man than I believed. More beautiful even than Michelangelo's 'David.' "

Then her forehead ridged, a questioning gaze darting to his, and he knew what she'd finally seen. Her "David" was covered with imperfect scars.

Reaching out to trace a long one that ran above his left nipple, she asked in a barely audible voice, "How?"

"Joe Thomas. He was wanted for . . . well, all sorts of things. He was real mean with a knife . . ." He left the rest unsaid, not willing to talk about killing a man at a moment like this. His throat tightened as she bent to place feather-soft kisses all along the scar. When she was finished, she lifted her head, running her fingers down his left side. His gut tightened at the sensation. The next scar she found was round with uneven edges.

Quietly, he explained, "Compliments of Dave Rollins and his gang. They shot me as I was diving for a boulder."

He watched her, his jaw clenching, anticipating the balm of her soft lips. Strangely, he felt soothed in a way he never would have expected, the pain of his scars long gone.

She moved to his other side, finding another scar—the one that was round and puckered like a badly healed burn. She caressed it, a sadly curious expression flitting across her face.

"And this?"

Cliff's voice croaked in response. He couldn't bear the humiliation of explaining that one. "My father. He put out his cigar . . . I don't really want to talk about it."

Kyra's eyes shimmered with obvious horror and sadness. "You don't have to explain." And she proceeded to kiss it as gently as she had the others. When she raised her head back to face him, he thought she'd ask about the scar on his cheek, but instead she whispered, "Kiss me, Cliff. Please."

She didn't need to ask twice. Desire curled deep in Cliff's gut as he closed his mouth over hers, holding her up to him with one arm as his hand went to free her hair. He loosened the knot that held it in place, the long tresses landing silkily around her and over his hand. Breaking the kiss, he continued to finger her gorgeous locks, studying their fiery shimmer.

"You are so exquisite, I can't believe you want to be mine." Then his hand drifted lower to the belt that held her wrapper in place, yanking it loose. He shoved the silk off her shoulders, letting it slip onto the bed. Then more desperately, he undid the buttons on the front of her nightdress and tugged it down around her waist. His breath lodged in his throat, nearly strangling him, at the sight of her.

"My God, you are beautiful," he whispered fiercely as he laid her against the pillow, spreading her hair in a frame. Her rose-tipped breasts were full, her nipples like rubies, and he couldn't wait to drag his tongue over them. He smiled as he noticed her crimson cheeks.

"Don't be embarrassed. You're so incredibly sweet." Then he moved to stretch out beside her, pulling her into his arms and kissing a hot blistering path down her neck to her breasts.

Kyra held on tightly to his hair as his mouth explored and finally closed over her throbbing nipple. Incredible warmth swept over her, tingling streamers from her breast down to the core of her womanhood. She panted with pleasure when he nipped at her crest—his tongue and breath doing wicked things at the slight sting his teeth had left behind.

"Do you like this? I want to know what you like. God, tell me you want me."

"I want you. I've always wanted you," she managed feverishly.

Cliff's dark head bent lower to nibble at the flesh surrounding her belly button, and his hands followed. Finding the nightdress at her hips, he shoved it over them, sliding it off her legs to add to the pile on the floor. Then like hot brands, his fingers slid up her trembling leg, skimming her skin on their way to her core, his mouth back at her breast suckling her with frightening intensity. When his explorations found her folds, she bucked from the blaze of heat roaring through her body. A glimmer of renewed fear struck her, the new sensations more powerful than she'd expected. Kyra whimpered when his finger sunk inside her, whether from desire, fear, or embarrassment, she wasn't sure. Her eyelids flew open, and she found him watching her, his naked hunger causing her to shiver visibly. Swallowing, she closed her eyes again.

"Don't close your eyes to me," he said in a low husky voice. "I love the feel of you." His finger slid in and out, stretching her. Then, with gentle strokes, he searched out her sensitive bud, and she gasped at the erotic pulses flowing through her.

"Cliff? I don't understand . . ." She struggled then to grab his arm and stop what he was doing.

"Easy," he said. "I only want to pleasure you." Her face flamed again and he chuckled.

"I'm sorry, honey. What can I do to ease your embarrassment, or is it fear?"

His voice was so tight with his restraint, she almost pitied him. Grinning, she answered, "Maybe it would be fairer if you were as naked as I am."

At that, he smirked, a wicked gleam in his eye. "I don't know, darling. That might scare you more. I'm as rock hard as I can get and nothing like those Greek statues you mentioned."

She gulped. "Yes . . . well . . . I've already gotten that impression."

His expression turned serious. "I'd thought to make love to you without you seeing me first. Just sort of surprise you. Are you sure you want me to take off my pants?"

She nodded, unable to utter the words.

Bestowing a soft kiss on her lips, he stood up, unbuttoning his fly, his gaze never leaving her face. When he was ready to pull off his pants he turned, the rippling play of muscle on his buttocks stealing Kyra's breath. Slowly then, he circled back around and her eyes widened with disbelief.

"Oh, dear!" She sat up, her hands bunching the sheets in her fists.

Quickly, Cliff joined her, gathering her in his arms. He rained soft kisses on her face and neck, reassuring her. "It's all right. Shh, it'll be fine, I promise you." Then he tilted her back, plundering her mouth yet again.

She was oblivious to everything but the deliciously sweet torture of his lips and hands on her body. The soothing sound of his voice caressed her, telling her how beautiful she was.

Kyra floated on air. Feeling like mush, she searched, disoriented, for the shadow of his face. Only he wasn't above her anymore. She blinked, concentrating on the movement of his heavy thigh that pinned her legs and the weight of his scalding sex rubbing against her side.

Shock coursed through her at the sensation of his teeth tugging her nipple. She cried out then, and he flicked her pebbled hardness with his tongue.

Just as quickly, he disappeared again. Kyra was paralyzed with anticipation, suspended in time, until he ringed her navel with his tongue, his hands pushing at her legs. She resisted until he called out to her, his voice raspy and breathless with contained need. "Kyra, open up for me."

He dipped to lick the flat plane of her stomach as he again pushed at her thighs. This time he met no resistance, shifting to gently stroke the inside of her thigh with a stubbled cheek.

"Cliff? What are you . . . ?" She was cut short, the feel of his wet tongue laving her folds with gentle precision, robbing her of breath.

"Oh, God, Cliff . . ." Kyra screamed, struggling to grab his hair. She was appalled, had never imagined . . . Somehow he managed to take hold of her hands and pin them beside her as he continued to have his way with her, his burning-hot tongue delving into her and his silky lips placing tender kisses at her center. When he dragged his mouth to the sensitive spot he'd touched earlier, she shuddered—the tingling boneless feeling overwhelming.

Relentlessly, he lapped and suckled, creating a pressure so sweet she thought she'd die. Then she splintered apart. Her limbs shook and her fingers dug hard into the bed as she cried Cliff's name.

She was vaguely aware when he positioned himself between her thighs, his mouth drugging as it moved over hers, his words telling her again and again how sweet she was and how much he wanted her. As gently as possible he stretched her with his shaft, the discomfort penetrating the fog in her head.

She flashed open her eyes, finding heated blue eyes inches away—perspiration on his brow. Regret and some other emotion she couldn't decipher flickered in his eyes before he leaned his forehead against hers.

"Kyra, I don't know how much longer I can hold back. I'm afraid I'm going to have to hurt you. God, I'm sorry."

Seeing his pain made her forget her own. She brought her hands to his face, cupping it gently, and kissed him. "It's all right. Just do it. Quickly, please. It's worse this way."

That seemed to be all he needed to hear, for he surged forward, imbedding himself as far as he could, his mouth covering her scream. He froze, levering his weight off her, as she dug fingernails into the bunched muscle of his arms, her breath coming out in deep spurts.

"I'm sorry, so sorry," he whispered against her temple.

A few moments passed, the sting lessening until she breathed more normally.

"Are you all right?" His face was tense.

"I think I'm fine now," she whispered.

"I can't . . . wait . . . any longer." He pulled away, before thrusting himself back in, a groan escaping him. "Kyra?"

In response, she thrust her hips up against him, giving him the encouragement he needed to continue. And then it was like a torrential downpour had begun, with no way to stop it. Cliff withdrew as far as he could, leaving her empty and wanting—only to surge forward, filling her, as he ground his pelvis against her core, so she could receive every last bit of him. Kissing her hotly, he set a rhythm that left her feeling utterly possessed and his alone.

Kyra was spiraling out of her mind, another deep wave building within her, heightened every time he ground his hips against the sensitive bud at her center. When she thought she could bear it no longer, he squeezed his hands under her buttocks to lift her, forcing her legs to wrap tightly around him, as he quickened the force and pace of his deep thrusts. Her limbs trembled uncontrollably, the fire inside her so hot it sent licks of flames throughout her body until she exploded with sweet, shuddering pleasure. Surely she'd died and gone to heaven.

She was mindless to everything then. The dimness of her surroundings blended with the misty daze of her vision. Kyra watched as if from afar as Cliff threw back his head, his chest emitting a fierce grunt as his release spurted warmly within her, the pulsing of his manhood clamped tightly by her own contractions of pleasure.

And then there was no sound but the thud of Cliff's head as it hit the pillow, followed by the burgeoning silence of their shallow breathing. It reminded her of the calm after the storm, and tears leaked down her cheek from the beauty of it. She held on for dear life to Cliff's recovering body, his weight a little overwhelming, their bodies wet and sticky, but she didn't mind. When he tried to shift off her, she wrapped her arms more tightly around him.

His husky chuckle broke the silence. "I'm going to crush you if you don't let me roll over to the side."

She released him and he rolled over, taking her along. Snuggling to him, she rested her head on his shoulder, as he caressed her hair and kissed the top of her head. She smelled the result of their lovemaking then. It was new to her, but intoxicating.

"Did I hurt you much?" he asked gruffly.

She squeezed him hard. "Only at first. I had no idea it would be so overwhelming, so powerful. Is it always?"

"No. Not always."

For a while they held each other quietly. Cliff couldn't help but think how perfectly Kyra fit him, and a swell of protectiveness rushed through him at the feel of her small body. Never had he felt so whole and warm after sex, but something held him back from telling her. He worried still about their future and didn't know how much of his heart he could give her. God, he was scared.

But she was his now, and he would never let her go.

"Cliff?" she asked with a great deal of uncertainty. "Are you having regrets?" Her voice quivered.

What a bastard he was. Any woman who'd just given her virginity would want to hear special words, wouldn't she?

"God, no. How could I when you've given me such a special gift? I just hope I don't let you down."

"Oh, Cliff, you never know. I could let you down, too. But I don't believe you will, and I'll certainly try not to."

They were silent a while longer, Cliff caressing a path up and down Kyra's arm.

"Did you mean it? What you said earlier?" he asked, his chest thick with more emotion than he'd felt in a long time.

She kissed his flesh where her head lay. "If you're referring to my feelings for you, then yes. If I didn't know for sure then, I know it now. I love you. I've always loved you, except that now . . . Well, it's different."

At her words, Cliff tightened his embrace even more. "I've never heard those words before, except from my mother." *The one person I've ever allowed myself to really love.*

He thought back to his mother and the pain of her death. He had felt such betrayal, he'd closed himself off from ever feeling that strongly again. He'd avoided serious relationships with women ever since. But now, he held a woman who gave him her love, and whom he'd cared for more, perhaps, than any other person besides his mother. Although his feelings were strong, he was afraid of opening himself up to such pain. Loving her would mean entrusting her with his heart. He didn't know if he possessed that much courage. His heart was scarred, as was his soul, but if anyone could heal it, it would be Kyra.

"If I don't say the words now, please don't hold it against me. You know my feelings are deep. You know—"

She grabbed hold of his arm. "I understand. You don't need to say more."

He squeezed her closer, kissing her temple as she fell asleep.

The sound of thunder and the flash of lightning woke her later. Disoriented, she looked around, finding him watching her as he lay beside her.

"I fell asleep?" She lifted herself up a little, the sheet he'd put on her drifting down to her waist. Right away, Cliff's body reacted to the sight of her beautiful breasts, bare and there for the taking. As if she understood his heated gaze, she quickly covered herself, and even in the candlelight, he could tell she was flushed with embarrassment.

He grinned tenderly. "I've been watching you sleep. I don't think I've ever watched a woman sleep before." He'd never spent a whole night with one, but she probably didn't want to hear that.

"I take it that in places like Madam Lucy's you pretty much *hurry up and hurry out.*"

At that, a deep rumble of laughter erupted within him. Leave it to her to contradict his last thought. When he gained control of himself again, he planted a kiss on her nose.

"Do you do that on purpose, Miss Lourdes?"

"What? Say something shocking to make you smile and laugh?" She laid her head back down on the pillow. "I like it when you smile. All the years I've known you, you've always been so serious. I suppose I discovered that the unexpected tends to bring out a smile." She lifted her palm to his face. "You are devastatingly handsome when you do."

He nipped at her lips. "You, darling, are not only beautiful and sexy, but a real treasure." Then he kissed her again with ardor, his hands urgently gliding over her body. His lips drifted downward to kiss and then capture her nipple between his teeth, ending with the gentle pull of his mouth.

She gasped.

He tilted his head up. "You were the one who convinced me to have my heart's desire."

"I'm sorry. I just didn't expect you to want to make love again so soon."

At that, he smiled, grabbing her hand and placing it on his hardness. "Oh, my," she exclaimed as her fingers curled around him, moving to feel the length and span of him. It was the sweetest torture he'd ever suffered. He held her hand still, before she made him lose control.

"I've been this way practically from the time I saw you at Lucy's. Believe me when I say it's not too soon." His voice was strangled. "However, you're probably too sore, and I should let you rest."

He pulled back from her, but she wrapped her arms around him, tugging him toward her. "I don't feel sore. . . ."

Cliff opened his mouth to protest, only to have it filled with the sweetness of hers.

In the early morning hours, Cliff awakened to the continuous cry of Bayou Kitty. The kitten must have weathered the storm outside during the night. Reluctantly, he threw his legs over the side of the bed and went to let the animal in. Weren't black cats bad luck anyway? He shook his head at the sight of the fur ball darting indoors and rubbing itself around his bare legs. He lifted Bayou Kitty to eye level and peered into his eyes.

Shaking his head, he set the kitten on a chair and headed back to bed. Once under the sheet, he pulled Kyra in his arms and grimaced as she snuggled her sweet bottom against his crotch in her search for warmth. He sighed, gathering her closer in his arms, only to find he couldn't fall asleep again. She'd managed to stir his manhood to a full morning salute. His appetites had always run strong, but he suspected she'd be the death of him. His fingers reached down to caress her intimately. God, she felt good. He slid them back and forth till she moaned in her sleep, her passage slick with need.

"Yeah, I definitely need to learn some control," he whispered as he slipped his shaft into her one more time.

She stiffened at first, and then molded herself to him as she recovered from the heated surprise of his invasion, and suddenly he felt like a cad not to let her sleep.

"God, Kyra, I just couldn't help myself. I'm sorry," he whispered, "but this time I'm going to love you nice and slow."

Chapter Sixteen

Red Velvet Armadillo Cake: Help your man kiss his bachelor days good-bye with this velvety chocolate cake. The surprising red interior reflects the loss of innocence.
From the *Sinfully Delicious Bakery Recipe Book*

Kyra awoke to bright sunshine. She'd never felt so sated or elated with life. It had to be love. Stretching, she gasped at the sting that flashed through her body. She was horribly sore—all over. She turned, seeking Cliff, but he wasn't there, or anywhere in the cabin for that matter.

She sat up when he walked in from outside. Frantically, she pulled the sheet to cover herself. He looked well rested and ruggedly handsome in his dark pants and green shirt. He smiled at her and she blushed hotly. His gaze roved over her in burning appreciation before he moved toward her and leaned down to kiss her flaming cheek.

"Good morning, sleepyhead."

"Good morning." She sounded grumpy, but couldn't help herself.

Cliff chuckled. "Somebody isn't in a good mood."

"Well, one of us is quite a bit sorer than the other."

"Oh, honey. Is it bad?" He sat down to rub her shoulders. "I knew I shouldn't have taken you that last time, but I couldn't help myself."

She flushed even more. He chuckled again. "You're so sweet when you blush like that." He kissed her nose and got off the bed. "I've got some hot water going since I figured you'd want a bath, and it'll help with your soreness. I also have some salve Shane makes—if you need it, that is. It's good for abrasions—that sort of thing."

"Yes, thank you," she answered with lowered eyes.

As if he understood her embarrassment, he shuffled his feet a little, then turned away to search his satchel.

"Yes, well, you probably want to be alone, so I'll just go back outside."

"Thank you."

"Here's the salve," he said, placing it on the nightstand before walking back out the door.

They spent the rest of the day getting used to their new relationship. After supper, Cliff suggested a stroll before sunset. They walked until they came to a nice grassy spot by the bubbling brook, and sat under a willow tree. She sensed the rising tension in him. It wasn't solely from the change in their relationship.

"When do you think Shane will come?" She smoothed her yellow dress around her and thrust her chin over her upraised legs, tilting her head to view Cliff.

"It's hard to say, but not much longer, I hope. I'd like to get this situation taken care of." He plucked a blade of grass and shoved it between his teeth.

"I'm sorry. I've caused you nothing but aggravation."

He frowned, his eyebrows knitting. "Don't even say it. I wouldn't have it any other way. You did the right thing in coming to me. I've told you that already."

Then he was quiet for a while, his gaze on the horizon, thoughtfully chewing on the grass. He was holding back something from her, she could tell. He'd probably hold back a lot for a long time. She had no illusions about him opening his heart to her all at once. It would take time before he was ready to do that, but thankfully, she could be patient when she set her mind to it.

"Cliff?"

"Hmm."

"Is something wrong? You seem preoccupied."

He sighed. "No. I was just thinking about you."

"What about me?"

"You and your life back home." He searched her features before hesitantly continuing. "New Orleans is very different from Las Almas."

"Yes, it is."

"You had quite a social life there—balls, soirees, theater. . . ."

"Yes?"

He opened his mouth to speak, but sighed instead, his gaze on his lap. Then he raised his head, his expression unreadable.

"Your parents had a lot to offer you and expected you to marry well. Had I stayed in New Orleans, I would've had a lot to offer you as well, but the fact is I didn't, and I don't know if my father has disinherited me." He paused as if to observe something in the water. "I don't know if I can or should go back there, Kyra. Everything inside me rebels against the idea, but I can try it, if that's your wish."

She reached for his hand. It felt so warm and strong, and her stomach lurched at the memory of his touch.

"I don't need to go back there," she said softly. "I've grown fond of Texas now, and I love your ranch. Do you remember how stifling I used to find New Orleans society? I feel so much freer here, and I'd rather be where we can both be happy than somewhere only one of us will feel good. I just ask that we visit there occasionally. I miss my parents and Grandpère, even now."

His hand squeezed hers and he smiled. "Are you sure? Ranch life can be exhausting, and I don't want you getting worn out. I still want you to pamper yourself, and as soon as I get this mortgage paid off I'll hire some maids and—"

"Cliff," Kyra said with a giggle, "I'm sure it'll be fine." She leaned over to place a kiss on his cheek, but he turned his head in time to capture her lips with his own, giving her such a long drawn-out kiss, she felt the pull down to her toes.

"Gotcha," he said with a devilish gleam. Then he dragged her onto his lap, and she had no choice but to put her arms around him.

"Well," he said somewhat nervously, laughter in his eyes nonetheless, "I'm sure if Grandpère were here to see how badly I've dishonored his granddaughter, he'd have me quaking in my boots with his favorite shotgun pointed south about now."

Kyra chortled. "I do believe you may be right about that, but I wasn't exactly fighting you off."

"No, but to him it wouldn't matter, and actually, it would probably be easier with a shotgun pointing at me."

"What would be easier?"

"Asking you to marry me," he said gruffly. "Would you do me the honor of becoming Mrs. Cliff Baldwin?"

She placed a feather-soft kiss on his lips, her eyes misty. "Yes." Then she flung herself into his embrace, her throat too clogged to speak. He seemed to feel it, too, for he held her quietly for a long time. Then a rumble of laughter erupted from his chest.

She pulled away, smiling at the twinkle in his eyes. "What?"

"Nothing. I'm just simply holding you and my body is already hotter than a blue flame. I just wonder if you can keep up with me."

She blushed but grinned. "Oh, Cliff. You know me. When have I ever declined a challenge? Once my body adapts to this aspect of marriage, why, it'll be just like any other race or game we play. I'll beat you in stamina and whatever else is needed, hands down."

The coy look she gave him made Cliff laugh even harder. Finally, he stood up with her still in his arms, and set her down on her feet.

More seriously, he said, "I know I've changed a lot, become rougher around the edges. I'll try to remember my manners, not swear so much, be the gentleman you remember."

She cupped his face with her hand. "Hush. I love you just the way you are. If you can swear less around me, fine, but don't drive yourself mad trying to be some image of a gentleman from New Orleans. I've had plenty of those . . . and left them behind."

"Have I told you how wonderful you are?" He turned into her hand, placing a kiss on her palm. "It's getting darker now. We should head back."

When they entered the cabin, Kyra went behind the privacy screen to change for bed. She came out to find Cliff waiting for her. She tightened the belt on her robe. "Do you need to speak to me?"

He seemed larger in the small cabin. He also eyed her hungrily, leaving no doubt in her mind as to his thoughts.

"Yes, speak to you," he answered huskily. "Do you have your little parlor gun around?"

She blinked. "You mean my derringer? I always carry it when I'm dressed. It's in my satchel now. Why?"

"Oh, I just want you to take it to bed with you. Until Shane gets here, I'm a little worried about who might show up. If something happens to me, I want to know you still have something to defend yourself with."

"I was about to go to bed." Her voice sounded somewhat high-pitched and shrill, even to her.

He glanced over her appearance, pools of heat in his eyes. "I can see that. I think for tonight you should sleep up in the loft where you'll be safer."

"You didn't worry about someone coming here last night."

Cliff sighed, air seeping through his teeth. "No. I mean that you'll be safer from me. You're still sore, aren't you?"

"Oh, yes, a-a little."

"Then up in the loft you go, Miss Lourdes." He pointed toward the loft. "Don't worry, I won't give you more than one reprieve. Upstairs, and good night."

Kyra headed to the stairs, then halted. *Why not have a little fun first?* She sashayed back to Cliff.

"It's proper to kiss your fiancée good night, Bayou Baldwin." Then she stood on the tip of her toes, and dragged his head down with her arms, making sure to plant a wet and steamy kiss on his lips. "Sweet dreams, my love." Turning around, she climbed up the ladder to the loft, holding back her laughter at his grunt of pain.

The next morning over breakfast, Cliff felt the coil of tension growing in his gut. It was time to take the offensive. He needed a clue, some direction as to how to strike at the forces lined up against Kyra.

"Do you have any idea why Jacques killed that lady?" he asked.

Kyra shook her head and flung her arm in frustration. "No. I've thought about it many times, running the scene through my head, but I still can't figure it out."

"Why don't we talk about it? Maybe I can help you remember something."

"Good idea."

"First, tell me what she looked like."

She pursed her lips, her gaze leaving him. "She was tall and slim. I couldn't really see her face, but she wore a most indecent dress. It was a very bright purple and the material was shiny. The bodice was cut extremely low for a day dress . . . and then it was covered in blood. Oh, Cliff, it was so horrible. I should've done something to help that poor woman. I could've screamed or tried to stop him somehow. But I froze. I was paralyzed with fear until I managed to run away."

He tightened his hands into fists, laying them on the table. "No, honey, that's not possible. When a man is out of control like that, nothing will stop him from killing. He would have murdered you, too. Promise me you'll never do something as crazy as trying to stop a madman with a knife or a gun."

Kyra looked startled by his intensity of emotion, but she whispered, "I promise."

The knot of fear in his stomach unfurled. "Good. Now let's get back to Jacques. Did you pick up any clues that would help us figure out who the lady was?"

"All I heard was Jacques saying, 'You'll never betray me again.' He repeated it over and over as he stabbed her. I—I can still smell the blood—and the fear—in the air." Kyra's voice was shaking. Cliff covered her hand with his, hoping to help steady her.

"Go on. Can you remember anything else, even before that day, anything that might give us an idea of what happened that night? Why Jacques killed that woman?"

An expression of thoughtful determination flitted across her face. She was quiet for a few minutes. Then her eyes widened. She snatched her hand out of his grasp, pushed back her chair and rushed to the loft.

"What are you doing?" He followed her, waiting at the base of the loft stairs, enjoying the view from below. He was allowed now. She was his.

She climbed back down, holding a book.

"Shortly after I got engaged to Jacques, there was a rumor going around that he had a mistress. I was furious and wrote quite a lot about it in my journal. Maybe I described something in more detail that could give us a clue."

They returned to the table. Her feminine scent tantalized his nose. He had to work to focus his attention on her writings rather than the memory of her on the bed a short distance away. Would he always be this horny around her? More importantly, was she still sore?

She rifled through her papers until she stopped and pointed. "Here's my notes! I was so mad about it, but Mama kept assuring me it was nothing to worry about."

"What was nothing to worry about?"

"That Jacques was keeping a mistress at the time he got engaged to me. I was furious and wanted to break the engagement. But Mama wouldn't hear of it. She said all gentlemen keep mistresses before marriage, and it was no reason to break an engagement."

"Well, there is some truth in that. But a decent man would've gotten rid of his mistress before proposing, especially if he was concerned about your feelings." He leaned down to follow her finger through her writings. "You're right, though. This information might be helpful. The dress you described sounds very much like the type a mistress would wear."

"Yes, and I remember how enflamed he was. It was *not* a dispassionate murder."

"The question is, how did she betray him? It's unusual for a man to feel that strongly about a mistress having an affair. You knew Jacques. Could he have killed her for that?"

She looked up. "No. I don't think so. The rumormongers described a long line of mistresses. He seemed to pick them up and discard them easily."

"She must've betrayed him in some other way. I wonder if she knew something about him and blackmailed him?"

Kyra pursed her lips. "I bet you're right. You know, there was another rumor going around. One about Jacques being a bastard. I mean a *real* bastard. A few brave people had the audacity to suggest that his mother'd had an affair. Mama said it was an old rumor that didn't matter anyway. As long as he had the name and inheritance, that was all she cared about. The talk made a lot of sense to me, because Jacques's father had always treated him like the lowest of Mississippi River scum, especially when he was drunk. I think that's why Jacques moved out on his own so young—even before he finished university. He was never in his father's presence if he could avoid it."

Cliff squirmed in his chair. This conversation sounded a bit too familiar. Not that he was worried that *his* mother'd had an affair, but he knew how rough it was to be abused by a drunk father until one had to leave home. He didn't want to feel sympathy for the black-hearted man.

Of course, no one was born evil. Evil was embedded in children at an early age, usually, in a home that wasn't nurturing and loving. But ultimately an adult made decisions for himself. Most of the criminals he'd tracked and caught hadn't gotten a good start in life. He could sympathize with them, but he also knew an equal number of good, law-abiding, productive people who hadn't had the best of starts, and they lived well without hurting others. When he'd hired his ranch hands, he'd chosen men touched by violence in some way, some even former criminals, but men who'd taken responsibility and altered the course of their paths. They depended on him now, and the success of the Lucky Number Seven. Actually, the dependency flowed both ways. He wouldn't let them down.

"Where are you? Are you hiding?" Kyra leaned close, pretending to peer inside his eyes, then his ears. "No, nothing in there." Then she giggled at her own joke.

He smiled, the tension easing from his chest. He grabbed her hand and placed a soft kiss on her palm. "You have such a good effect on me."

Her eyes softened and she placed a tender kiss on his cheek. "Thank you. That's the sweetest thing you've ever said to me."

Hell. This emotional stuff made him sweat. "Right. Let's get back to your journal. Maybe we should read it through and see if you've forgotten anything."

They pored over the journal for the next couple of hours. Cliff was amazed at how intensely Kyra examined her every thought. Surely such analysis was completely unhealthy. He didn't want to hurt her by informing her of that. If this was what she'd been trying to get him to do the other day, she'd been completely out of her mind. Most things were much better left forgotten, to his way of thinking.

On the other hand, the journal was helpful in giving Cliff a better idea of Jacques' character and business and political dealings. She'd recorded some of the meetings Jacques had attended with famous leaders both in New Orleans and Washington. He seemed on his way up in the political world. Kyra was right to have feared his power and believe no one would listen to her story.

There were no clues, however, connecting the politics to the murder. Maybe it was as simple as blackmail. Bastardy could be a disaster for a political candidate, and if she'd had proof, it could've seriously damaged his chances for a high career.

He and Kyra discussed the different possibilities. It felt good to work in partnership with her. He admired her quick mind, grown sharper over the last few years. He'd already seen how she used logic and reason when in unchartered territory—tracking him down, learning how to cook, and then taking care of Shane. She sorted through a lot of information to give him the pertinent facts surrounding her relationship with Jacques and paint a picture of her ex-fiancé's character.

Her descriptions confirmed Cliff's initial impression that Jacques was an extremely angry, volatile man who used his power to hurt others. Kyra pointed out in her notes how uncomfortable she'd been with the way he treated his servants and people lower than his station in life. She'd found his actions almost abusive. In fact, most of the comments Kyra had made regarding Jacques were negative. She'd most certainly wanted out of the relationship as soon as her mother had formed the alliance.

By contrast, Cliff pieced together a powerful need Jacques seemed to harbor for Kyra. It appeared Jacques had pursued her with single-minded determination that almost bordered on desperation. Cliff understood the power of need—he felt it himself—but obviously Kyra had been uncomfortable with it. Could it be as simple as a man seeking out the love he'd been denied as a child from a woman who exuded vitality and compassion?

Cliff paused a moment, then glancing up, noticed Kyra staring at him. "Maybe with time, some of this will make more sense. As soon as I've got Wade out of the way, I'll contact Grandpère and see if he's made any progress."

He leaned forward to finish reading the final entries, but she pulled the journal away.

"What?"

Kyra lowered her gaze. "Nothing. I'd forgotten about the entries I've written since finding you. I don't think you should see those."

She peeked back up at him. Cliff's face expanded in a slow grin, a devious glint lighting his eyes. "You said you trusted me with your *most personal thoughts.* Did you record your daydreams about me?"

He reached for the journal, and she jumped out of her chair, rounding the table, the book clutched tightly to her chest. He pursued.

"Actually it's the entries where I call you a snake and . . . and other things I don't want you reading," she said, tossing her hair.

He arched a dark, sculpted eyebrow, then sprinted forward, his long arms grabbing her around the waist. She squealed, struggling to escape him.

"You're better off saving your energy. When I catch my prey, they never escape."

Her body went limp in surrender. "What do you do after you catch them?"

He nibbled on her ear, making her breathless and dizzy. "I toy with them a while, and then I enjoy my feast," he growled low. "Are you still sore?"

She gasped. "You-you couldn't possibly mean to-to . . . *now.* We just had breakfast. It's daylight."

"Hmmm. I'm still hungry. All night long I dreamed about how to satisfy my appetite, and my fantasies didn't have anything to do with biscuits and bacon."

He'd already unbuttoned her blouse, her breasts peeping at him from beneath her shift. He lowered his mouth, suckling her through the thin material.

"You didn't answer my question. Are you still sore?"

His breathing was hard and his sex pressed against her through her skirts. She searched for her voice, but only managed to moan, his fingers already doing wicked things inside the open crotch of her bloomers. How many hands did he have anyway? And how did they move so quickly?

"You're so hot and wet. Tell me you want me inside you."

She pushed her hips hard against his hand, seeking him. "I—I want you . . . now, please."

He chuckled beneath his breath, lifted her into his arms, and headed for the bed. "I'm going to get my revenge and torture you with desire—until you understand how I've felt since your arrival, until you beg me to come into you."

She shyly averted her gaze. "You better watch out. I'm a sore loser—remember? I might never give in, and we'd both lose."

He let out a raspy laugh. "Maybe."

Two hours later, Cliff stretched out his legs. Kyra was sprawled on top of him, her head resting on his shoulder. He tightened his hold on her and said, "Let's get dressed and go outside. I need to get some chores done, and you can watch me." He grinned. "I'm sure you'll enjoy that."

"I'm enjoying watching you right here," she replied lazily.

His fingers skimmed down her back before he flipped her beneath him, kissing her deeply. "As much as I'd like to live out the day in bed, the horses and Mr. Pip need feeding, and I thought I'd help Shane by repairing the stable roof. Come on, let's feed the animals first and then I'll start on the roof."

"Oh, *all right*."

Cliff held her in his arms a while longer, before moving to get dressed. When Kyra sat unmoving, he glanced back at her. She was deep in thought—probably overanalyzing things again. "What?"

She sighed. "Jacques."

"What about him?"

"I was wondering. Why? Why has he done such horrible things?"

He wasn't sure he wanted to answer. "He's angry, honey. It makes people crazy to be angry so long. All they want to do is lash out at the world in revenge."

"But why are people so angry they kill?"

His heart slowed its beat, anxiety clawing at his insides. "They're angry because . . . because they were born. They're angry because they're empty inside, because love isn't what it should be, because life isn't fair . . . sometimes because it seems there's no other way to be."

Kyra smoothed the hair at his brow, then leaned forward to kiss him. "Are you angry, Cliff?"

He stared at her, frozen, his chest tight. "I have been. I've felt those same feelings for a very long time." Shaking himself, he smiled and placed a kiss on her forehead. "When I'm with you . . . you make me forget so much." He hugged her tight. "Come on, let's get busy."

As they worked together, cleaning the stalls and feeding the horses and Mr. Pip, Kyra felt a sense of comfort in spite of the weather. It was hot and the air deathly still. A few more hours and it would be evening.

Finished with the animals, she went to the creek to wash their clothing, while Cliff worked on the stable roof. She hummed to herself, thinking about her newest—and *last*—fiancé and their future together. She raised the sleeves to her white blouse, then leaning down, pulled her blue skirt to the side as she placed one of Cliff's soapy shirts on the washboard.

Lifting her damp hair away from her face, she admired the pretty wildflowers on the other side of the bank. They were an assortment one found on the Texas prairie, but never had they been so inviting before. She finished the wash, and spread it on the clothesline Cliff had hung between two trees. Satisfied, she searched out the flowers again. She would pick some for the cabin. Cliff wasn't so far away she couldn't stray a little, although he wouldn't like it. She'd just go over to the other side, quickly pick the flowers, and be back before he realized it.

Crossing over the brook, she stepped carefully on the scattered stones and bent to gather the pretty blooms. Inhaling their heady fragrance, she spent a bit of time admiring the different varieties and creating a colorful bouquet, until a shadow suddenly covered her view.

"I've caught you now!"

Chapter Seventeen

Amish Friendship Cake: Share the starter with friends in need, and your loyalty will be reciprocated.
From the *Sinfully Delicious Bakery Recipe Book*

Kyra jumped at the sound of Cliff's voice. He'd practically growled at her. "Must you always sneak up on me?"

"I wasn't sneaking. What if I'd been someone else?" He flung his hand wide. "How can I protect you if you wander off?"

She smiled apologetically and held up her floral arrangement. "You know, fresh flowers aren't only cheery, they're good for the soul. Why, I've read—"

"Come here."

His exasperated look made her a little wary. "Why?"

The rigidity in his shoulders relaxed and his face softened. "I just want to kiss you."

"Oh." Kyra walked over to him and he lifted her off her feet so he could look her in the eye.

"Don't wander off again or I'll have to punish you."

"How would you do that?" she asked skeptically as she ran her hand through his black hair.

"Let's go back to the cabin and I'll show you."

Kyra giggled. "We just spent the morning making love. Are you sure this is normal? I think you're insatiable."

Cliff grinned. "I warned you of that."

And then he kissed her long and deep, sliding her down his body, so she could feel his hardened manhood against her. When he ended the kiss, they were both breathing erratically.

Kyra stepped away and ran, calling back to him. "I'll race you to the cabin."

It didn't take Cliff long to catch up to her. Then suddenly he yelled at her to stop and shoved her behind him.

In what seemed a blur, he had both his Colt six-shooters out and cocked. It happened so fast, she hardly had the time to understand what was happening. From behind Cliff's back, she saw who he had drawn his gun on, and stifled a scream. She would never forget the man she'd seen in Dallas, or the awful-looking scar on his neck. He had company too—another ugly specimen of mankind, one who sent a nauseating stench with the breeze. In contrast, Wade wasn't unkempt, but everything about him emanated evil, a look of madness in his eyes, his dark and dusty clothing amplifying his aura. The two men's guns were still holstered, which struck her as curious. Did Cliff notice it as well?

In a low, harsh voice, Cliff barked, "Kyra, I want you to veer toward those trees to the right. The stable isn't that far. Then I want you to get on Blackjack and ride as fast as you can. I'll catch up to you later."

"No, I'm not leaving you."

"Dammit, Kyra, do as I say *now.* Don't distract me."

She couldn't see his face, but knew he was serious. She sighed. "All right. Please be careful," she whispered. Then she did as he asked and ran toward the trees, feeling Wade's stare boring into her back.

She'd had every intention of doing as Cliff asked, but no sooner had she headed for Blackjack, than she turned around and hid behind a tree to watch. She just couldn't leave Cliff unprotected, and she wanted to see and hear what they said. It was time she made her own choices. Taking out her derringer, she checked her pocket for extra ammunition.

"I want that lady, Baldwin."

Wade's voice was deep, sounding like a man who'd smoked and chewed too much tobacco in his lifetime.

"I have to say," he went on, "I was mighty surprised when I ran into my friend here, and he told me he came upon a woman of Miss Lourdes' description with a man that matched yours." Wade spat to his side, wiping his mouth on his sleeve. "Don't know any other man with my mark on their cheek fitting your description. Somebody else hire you?"

"Yeah. *She* has."

Wade seemed to blanche at that piece of news.

"Let's not forget how I came by this mark, and how close to dying you were, you son of a bitch," Cliff growled. "What's your game, Wade? You face me with your guns holstered. What's to stop me from leaving your carcass to the vultures?"

"Well, that's one thing I know about you, Baldwin. You don't care to shoot a defenseless person. I figured I could negotiate with you on the little lady. I'll give you a fair share of what I'm getting paid."

"You wouldn't have enough money in the world to make me hand her over to you." Even from a distance, Kyra could see the rage that Cliff contained. It made her shudder, and she hoped had no less effect on the men.

Wade continued. "She's got a man back home who wants her returned really bad."

Cliff put on his most feral smile. "Yeah, well, you can go back and tell him he isn't her man any longer. Now, I suggest you take your guns out of your holsters and throw them out to me . . . and watch it. I better not see anything that looks like you're cocking them. You got it?"

The two men didn't look very happy to do Cliff's bidding. Wade, in particular, seemed angrier than he was willing to let on. Kyra had a feeling he was up to something, and it worried her. She watched as Cliff kicked their guns well out of the way, and all she could think was that it was just too easy.

Cliff mirrored her thought. "What are you up to, you slimy whoremonger? Whatever it is, you'd better hop to it."

"Nothin'. Just hopin' to negotiate. I ain't gonna harm the lady now. I just wanna bring her back to Mr. Delacroix."

"Just like you didn't harm that woman in San Antonio? I hope that scar I left around your neck reminds you every day of the justice you should've received. If no one had interfered, I can assure you, I wouldn't be having to face you here now."

"Yeah, well, never could understand you going to all that trouble for a whore. The stupid bitch deserved the beating I gave her for laughing at me." He spat again to his side.

"If you can't get it up, it's your problem. The way I see it, only a coward raises his hand to a woman. I gave you a fight with a man. There's nothing I hate more than a man who picks on a woman. It makes me real sick."

Wade set his shoulders more rigidly. He fought a terrible anger, Kyra could see, but wasn't willing to unleash it . . . yet. In the meantime, Cliff set his sights on the other man.

"I had a feeling you'd be trouble . . . I should have sent you to the devil along with your friend."

The man seemed taken somewhat aback by the icy edge in Cliff's voice. Kyra had to admit that she'd certainly not like to have to face Cliff in this demeanor, and especially not with two guns pointed at her.

She chewed on her lip. Then a flash of light nearly blinded her. She noticed it again: a flash of reflected metal in the trees behind Cliff. It struck her then that there was a third man there, with a gun. Everything stopped as if frozen, fear gripping her. The distance was too much for her derringer, but she could still use it for distraction.

Her heart slamming against her chest, she screamed out to Cliff to look behind him as she shot her gun toward the trees. Her first shot still rang in her ears when Cliff rolled onto the ground, aiming and shooting his Colt in the same direction. Kyra instantly reloaded and fired again. An awful curdling scream of pain seared through the trees, and wade's unkempt companion wasted no time jumping on Cliff. Wade, on the other hand, spotted her, and quickly chased after her.

There wasn't time to reload. She glanced at Cliff, who struggled with the other man. He yelled at her to run. She did as he said, sprinting as fast as she could toward the stables—Wade behind her. Her heart beat madly and blood pounded in her ears, the rush inside her giving her feet wings, but her skirt hindered her flight. She peeked behind her a few times, finally tripping. Wade was getting closer. She got up and ran until she hardly had any breath left, then halted in her tracks, the thunderous sound of galloping hooves confusing her.

Relief poured through her like a waterfall when she saw Shane and Luke riding hell-for-leather. Shane bore down on his pinto, in what could only be Comanche fashion. His moccasin-clad feet hugged his horse as he rode bareback. Together, man and beast seemed one being, their aura as wild and dangerous as all the stories of Indians she'd ever heard. Luke, on his palomino stallion, looked not as savage, but just as hard and dangerous, an impression enhanced by the intimidating whip he carried coiled around his shoulder. Kyra felt gripped with awe . . . and relief.

A movement distracted her, and she saw Wade reach in his boot and remove a gun. Quickly, he aimed it at Shane, who defied him by leaning completely over the outside flank of his horse. Shane's intent was clear. He was coming for her.

A moment later, the air whooshed out of her lungs as he scooped her up and placed her face-down in front of him. She twisted to look behind them, and saw Luke lash out his whip, knocking the smoking gun out of Wade's hand. Then Luke coiled the snakelike object around the man, jumped off his horse, and smashed the flat of his hand against Wade's face in a peculiar way she'd never seen before. When Wade still staggered, Luke kicked sideways, knocking him unconsciousness.

The horse beneath her ran swiftly, and Kyra tried to catch her breath, relieved when Shane finally pulled his horse to a rearing halt. Shane shifted her into a sitting position as the dust settled around them, and turned back to look for Luke. Satisfied, he returned his attention to her.

"Are you all right?"

"Yes," she answered breathlessly. "Oh, my God—Cliff. We have to help Cliff," she screamed.

"Where is he?"

"I'm right here."

She watched, relief sagging her shoulders, as he came out from the trees. He seemed a little battered, but *alive.*

"Cliff."

"You little fool," he thundered. "Why didn't you listen to me? You could've been killed."

Kyra plastered her back against Shane. "I'm sorry, but I couldn't leave you, and I'm glad I didn't or you might have a bullet in your back right now."

Sounding surly, Cliff spoke to Shane. "You can let her down now."

Shane smiled. "I don't know, friend. According to the Comanche way, she's my captive fair and square. *I* scooped her off the ground, not you."

Kyra could see Cliff was on edge with his temper, so she wiggled down from the horse and threw herself into his arms.

That seemed to render him speechless. He returned her embrace, then whispered, "Don't you ever do that to me again. You scared at least ten years off my life."

She leaned away a little. "The feeling is mutual."

He let her go and pulled her to his side as Luke ambled toward them. Behind him, he dragged an unconscious Wade by the shirt, stopping to drop him at Cliff's feet.

"Cliff." Luke nodded to him after greeting Kyra.

Cliff nodded back. "Thanks. I owe you." He glanced down at Wade, scowling. "If the pig weren't already unconscious, I'd knock him out all over again."

Kyra turned to Luke. "What on earth were you doing back there? I've never seen anyone punch or kick that way before. It looked awfully strange."

Luke nodded, his face placid but his eyes intense. "It's an ancient fighting art I learned from a wise man in Asia."

"What about the others? We tracked three of them," Shane said, changing the subject as he glanced toward the tree line.

Cliff answered, "I believe the one in the trees is dead. Lucky shot on my part. The other is knocked out. I tied him up hastily because I was worried about Kyra. He's a thief we ran into on the way up. He got away then, and unfortunately Wade found him. I don't want him getting away again."

"You want me to walk Kyra to the cabin?" asked Shane.

"Yeah. Luke and I will take care of things here. I want to snap Wade out of his stupor so I can find out about Jacques." Cliff bent toward Kyra. "Do you mind going with Shane?"

"No. What are you going to do to him?" She pointed to Wade.

"Nothing to worry about. I just want some answers."

Kyra could tell by the icy stare directed at Wade that she didn't want to know the details. She shuddered a little and stepped away with Shane.

Cliff and Luke strode into the cabin a while later. Cliff held Bayou Kitty in his hands, even rubbing the kitten behind the ears. Hell, he *was* getting soft. He saw the person to blame heading his way to take the burden away from him. Kyra cooed at the black ball of fur, introduced the animal to Shane, and went to fix it a plate of food—with the varmint purring loud enough to start an avalanche.

"Bayou Kitty?" Shane smirked.

"Yes, doesn't he remind you of Cliff? You sweet little precious baby." She nuzzled her nose against the kitten's.

"Oh, yes, I can see the resemblance . . . sweet baby," Shane added for Cliff's benefit as he rubbed the little devil behind the ears.

Luke laughed, and ignored the glare Cliff shot him. When Shane joined in, Cliff gave up and parked himself on a chair, pointedly ignoring the pair.

Over supper, they shared their stories. A day after Cliff and Kyra had left the Lucky Number Seven, the posse had shown up at the ranch having followed Wade's trail to the vicinity. Shane and Luke had joined the posse, and together they'd continued tracking Wade until his trail disappeared about ten miles south of Shane's cabin. At that point they'd agreed to split up, with the posse heading farther west.

Shane and Luke, knowing Wade was on Cliff and Kyra's trail, had hightailed it for Shane's cabin, arriving in time for a heroes' welcome.

"Wade says that Jacques is on his way to Las Almas," Cliff said as Kyra shivered. He wanted to comfort her, but he wouldn't do it in front of Shane and Luke. He continued. "He was supposed to meet him sometime later this week, but he didn't know when or where. Delacroix told him he'd be in touch when he arrived." He took a long sip of his coffee before setting it back down on the table. "What about Yancey?"

Shane spoke up. "Didn't see hide nor hair of him. No telling where he is."

Kyra chimed in. "What about the sheriff?"

"I'm afraid that as decent a fellow as he is, he just isn't as capable when it comes to men like Yancey," answered Cliff. He added to Shane and Luke, "I promised Sheriff Overby that I'd bring Kyra in to report the murder she witnessed. I don't know how long he'll hold out waiting . . . he gave me ten days." He glanced at Kyra. She chewed on her lip, worry marring her face. He sighed. "Kyra, would you prefer if we don't discuss this in front of you?"

Her eyes widened. "No, don't keep anything from me. I'm not a child and this is my problem."

Shane cleared his throat. "A telegram from your father came after you left, Cliff. He demanded you return to New Orleans immediately or forfeit your inheritance."

Cliff slammed the table with his fist. "I'd like to know how he found out where I was."

Kyra covered his hand with hers. "He probably found out like I did—hired a detective. I'm surprised he didn't do it years ago."

"You're right. Still, my gut instinct tells me there might be a connection between Jacques' pursuit and my father's note."

"We're going to have to leave here," Luke said. He looked from Shane to Kyra. "Wade told us he sent a message to Jacques before leaving Las Almas, alerting him to where he was headed."

Shane nodded in thought. "Well, the Lucky Number Seven is out of the question, as well as any hotel in Las Almas. We could travel to another town, but I suspect, the only way we're going to chuck these coyotes is to take the offensive." He rapped his fingers on the table as he glanced over at Cliff. "What do you want to do? Do you want to take Kyra to another town while Luke and I take care of it?"

"Hell, no. Sorry, Kyra." Cliff leaned over the table, his hands in fists. "I want to stop this *now.* If only there were someplace safe for Kyra to stay while we flush them out and finish this off."

Shane leaned back in his chair, taking a sip of coffee. "Well, there's one place, but you and Kyra won't like the idea."

Kyra blinked. "Where?"

He glanced at Cliff. "Let me tell Cliff outside. I don't want him having a fit in front of you."

Cliff raised his eyebrows in surprise as he lifted himself from his chair. He and Shane walked out, the door shutting soundlessly behind them.

When they reentered several moments later, Cliff was grim as he beckoned Kyra with his hand. At her approach, he put his arm around her, and guided her outside to sit beneath the big tree.

"What is it?"

Cliff settled on his haunches in front of her. He didn't know how to begin. "Well, I don't like this, not by any stretch of the imagination, but Shane does have a good idea." He grasped Kyra's hands, rubbing with his thumbs.

"So, tell me."

"Shane thinks, and after some thought I agree, that maybe the best and most unexpected place for you to stay is . . . Lucy's."

"Lucy's?" She gaped at him. *"Madam Lucy's?"*

"Now, honey—"

Kyra retracted her hands, screeching for all to hear, "Are you out of your mind? You want me to stay in a-a house of sin?"

Cliff almost blushed. "I'm afraid so. But hear me out," he added when she made to rise. "I know it's a distasteful idea, but it's also a good one. Lucy has an attic room she only lets very important clients . . . well, she has this room where you . . . we could stay. I think she'll allow it if I pay her well enough. You won't have to worry about being seen by anyone there, and that's the last place anyone would think to find a genteel lady."

Kyra's eyes watered to green pools. He felt like a cad. "My reputation is in tatters anyway," she said, "so just put me in-in a-a . . ." She bowed her head, unable to finish her sentence.

He tipped up her chin. "Hey, you know I'm going to fix that. As soon as we can, we're going to get married." He leaned down a little and narrowed his eyes. "What's really bothering you?"

She shrugged, looking away for a moment. "It's not within the realm of good taste for a future husband to flaunt his past mistress to his fiancé. There, I'll have to face any number of past paramours."

Cliff gathered her then in his arms. "Oh, honey, I'm sorry. Believe me when I say that if there was a better idea, I'd do it in a heartbeat." Something twisted inside him to see her sadness, and he vowed he'd do everything he could to make her smile every day of her life. "Hey, you're the only one I care about. They mean nothing to me."

"That may be so, but what if we're there and you can't help but compare me to a memory of someone else. I'm inexperienced, you'll wish—"

"Don't say it because it isn't true. *You're* the woman I want—the only woman that leaves me warm inside. You make my head turn, and no one else can do that. Understand?"

She nodded, and he took her hand again and kissed it. "You're the only woman for me. In my mind you became my wife when you gave yourself to me, and I won't dishonor you, ever. My father hurt my mother with his indiscretions. I won't do that, and I'll never want to because you satisfy me as no other woman can."

"Do I really?" she squeaked.

"Yes." Then he took her face in his hands and planted a soft kiss on her lips. He wanted to do more, but Shane and

Luke waited inside, so he restrained himself. He grimaced—he'd have to sleep with the boys tonight. He didn't want her fretting about what Luke and Shane might think. He sighed.

Cliff pulled himself up along with Kyra. "Come on. Let's head inside."

Once back in the cabin, Cliff told Shane and Luke that Kyra'd agreed to go to Lucy's. "You two can take Wade and the thief to the sheriff's office. I'll take Kyra to Lucy's. If we get there at the crack of dawn, there shouldn't be any witnesses. Most of the town will still be asleep." He glanced around at everyone—his gaze lingering longer on Kyra. "Any other ideas?" When nobody answered he nodded. "All right. That's the plan."

Fifty miles away, in Dallas, Jacques Delacroix tightened his fist, crushing the telegram he'd received from Oscar Wade. He'd waited for some good news, and finally he'd received it. She'd been found. He curled his lips into a sneering smile, the crumpled piece of paper dropping from his clutches to bounce off the mahogany writing desk onto the plush, red carpet beneath his feet. Soon—soon he'd have her back.

He walked around the most luxurious suite of rooms he'd found in Dallas. It was nothing compared to what was available in New Orleans, but it would do. A black walnut four-poster bed dominated the center of the room. He walked toward it, bending to retrieve the discarded telegram on the way. The smell of brandy drew his gaze to the empty tumbler on the nightstand. He pulled the bell for service, then stretched the note open to read once more. So, Kyra was somewhere near Athens—with Cliff Baldwin, exactly as his father had anticipated. Dread, and exultation, sliced through him at the thought of meeting him.

The main reason he'd courted Kyra in the first place was to obtain information regarding Clifford U. Baldwin *the Third*. And probably, if he were honest with himself, to exact a bit of long-distance revenge. He'd needed to take something away that had once meant so much to Baldwin. He hadn't expected to want her for himself, to need her to care for him. Her joie de vivre had tantalized him to hope for something better. Her compassionate and understanding nature had drawn him like a moth to a flame.

And now, like a moth to a flame, someone had to burn. She'd betrayed him—in more ways than one. He'd asked her more than once if she knew where Baldwin was. Although she'd loved recounting childhood memories of her *dear* friend Cliff, she'd claimed not to know where he'd gone when he'd left New Orleans. Obviously, the chit had lied to him.

She'd have made a fine politician's wife, despite her reputation for breaking engagements. Then again, his reputation wasn't exactly unquestionable. Obviously, she'd seen something when she'd lost her locket behind his gazebo. What else did she know? He wouldn't allow her to impede his political advancement.

Athens. He'd be on the stage in the morning, and if he didn't find Mr. Wade there with Kyra, he'd head to Las Almas Perdidas. Baldwin was sure to return there eventually.

An anxious knot churned in his belly. *His dear father* had blackmailed him to bring Baldwin back—dead or alive. Unfortunately, he'd learned that Baldwin had become a dangerous man over the years. He wasn't just anyone to trifle with, for Jacques's Dallas sources had confirmed Baldwin was skilled with a gun and deadly.

Jacques seated himself on the down mattress, the telegram again crushed in his fist. Somehow, he'd figure out what to do once he found her—and Baldwin. This time, *he* didn't plan to be the one to burn.

Chapter Eighteen

Cajun Surprise: Can't tell what wild ingredients are in this one. But it'll sure get your attention, and might even change your life.
From the *Sinfully Delicious Bakery Recipe Book*

Kyra studied Cliff's hard profile as their horses plodded toward Las Almas Perdidas and Madam Lucy's. His lips were tight and his eyes shielded beneath the brim of his hat. He was more upset about her staying in a brothel than she was. The old chivalrous Cliff was still there, deliberately hidden beneath his toughened cowboy facade. But the fourteen-year-old boy who'd protected her from the neighborhood bully, and the twenty-year-old young man who'd left home to protect her from himself, was now this hardened cowboy still shielding her from the harsher realities of life. He didn't want her to experience a place like Lucy's, much less the life-and-death game of hide-and-seek they played. He blamed himself for her situation.

She sighed as she transferred Bayou Kitty from his sleeping place in her arms to free one hand, then reached out to cover Cliff's fingers where they clutched Blackjack's reins. His startled eyes accused her of disturbing his brooding silence.

"This isn't your fault," she said. "You can't protect me from everything. And besides, I'm not that innocent anymore."

Lord, she really shouldn't have said *that,* she thought, noting the tic in his cheek. She squeezed his hand. "That's not what I meant and you know it. I've seen a lot these last few years, culminating in witnessing a violent murder. Believe me, staying a few days in a house of ill repute is the least of my worries. Besides, you'll be there with me, won't you?" Darn, she hadn't meant her words to sound so helplessly pleading. But it seemed to work. She had his full attention. His protective instincts were winning over his guilt.

Gruffly, he said, "Of course I'll be with you. As much as possible anyway. I'll spend time tracking Jacques, and Yancey, too, for that matter. But I won't leave you there alone. I won't let anything happen to you. I promise."

"I trust you more than anyone I know, Cliff. That's why I ran to you. However, I think I've matured a little in the last few days. I understand now that the ultimate responsibility for my safety and my well-being lies within me, with God's grace. I know you've promised to protect me. But neither of us knows what the future holds. You're not invincible. And I don't want you blaming yourself should something happen to me. Even more importantly, I don't want you putting yourself at risk for my benefit. Your life and happiness are the most important things in the world to me."

Cliff had turned away from her during her little speech, and now as he faced her, she was surprised to see a tear sliding down his cheek. She'd never seen Cliff cry before, not even when his mother died. A lump rose from her chest to settle in her throat.

"What's wrong?" she asked. "I meant to tell you how much I love you, to make you happy, not hurt you."

"Your words—the last bit. It's almost verbatim what my mother told me the last time I saw her, two weeks before she died . . . before she slit her wrists and killed herself."

Kyra was shocked. Coldness settled in her chest, then a gut-wrenching pain of sympathy for the deep-seated anguish she saw on Cliff's face. She'd never known, never suspected, there'd been no whispers of gossip. What pain Cliff had hidden all these years! Nausea rose to her throat, and she pulled hard on Poker, hastily throwing her leg over so she could slide down his side. Cliff was beside her in an instant, holding her as she emptied her stomach on the dusty ground.

"Kyra, I'm so sorry. I didn't mean to upset you." He took the yowling Bayou Kitty out of her hands and set him on the ground before wetting his bandanna with water from his canteen and pressing it against her lips and face. He should never have spoken the words aloud—the words that had tormented him for seven years, knowledge he'd never shared with anyone besides his father . . . and a few servants.

"Oh, please don't comfort me. Why haven't you ever told me this before? I can't imagine what you must've suffered."

He turned to motion to Shane and Luke, waiting for them far up the trail with Wade and the other outlaw tied to their saddles, to go on. Although it would be painful, he'd share his past. She'd be his wife soon, and he wouldn't hide his family secrets from her anymore.

Facing her fully, Cliff took a breath and said, "I found her. I'm sure she didn't intend that to happen. I think she tried to protect me even as she planned her own suicide. She did it while I was away at school. But I'd come home unexpectedly due to an outbreak of influenza on campus. I found her in her bedroom alone, her life bleeding away, a knife on the floor by the bed. There was a bruise still shining on her cheek from her last encounter with my father's fist. I remember pulling her into my arms, crying out to her. She peered at me through wet eyes, said, 'Oh, God, my son.' And that was it. Her head fell back against my arm." He inhaled raggedly before continuing. "I laid her down on the bed and went running through the door shouting for the servants, calling for a doctor. There was a rush in the hall. But I saw my father come out of a bedroom a few doors down, pulling up his pants, a half-naked maid behind him.

"I lost control, I punched him, over and over, blaming

him for Mother's death. As he lay on the floor bleeding, he whispered, '*Like father, like son. Enjoy your inheritance, Junior.*"

Cliff stood and turned away with a shuddering sob. Kyra pursued him, hugging him from behind. He grasped her hands, massaging them, and went on with his story. "After her funeral, I didn't see my father again until right before the Christmas Eve party. He had no remorse that he'd driven her to kill herself. I wanted to murder him—strangle the life out of him. I had to flee the violence within me. So I left. Eventually I met Shane and became a bounty hunter." His lungs emptied of breath. "I became even more violent. I sold my soul, or as my father suggested, inherited my destiny."

He turned in Kyra's arms, facing her, shaking with his intense emotions, his feelings of guilt. She hugged him tighter. "What am I doing, Kyra? I have no right to marry you. There was a lot of truth in what my father said. *His* father was very abusive toward his wife and children, as was *my* father to *us.* I beat him worse than he ever beat Mother or me. And since then I've lived a life of violence."

Reaching up, she took his face between her hands. Peering deep into his eyes, she said, "I think there's a big difference between beating an innocent, defenseless woman or child and beating a grown man who committed the unspeakable acts your father did, especially in such a moment of torment and outrage. I'm not saying what you did is right—just understandable. But the person who's suffered the most because of your actions over the years . . . has been you." She shifted one hand to his shoulder and shook him. "It's time to stop punishing yourself, Cliff, for what is past. You need to forgive yourself."

Cliff shook his head. "I'm not good enough for you. You should be free to choose someone better."

"I'm free *now,* and *I choose you.* This is the life I want. I desire nothing else but to be your wife, to make a loving home with our children, to work together building our ranch, creating our future—to help you leave your past behind."

"I don't know. I want to be with you, but I just can't trust myself." He stepped away from her.

She stepped forward, thrusting her chin up, her hands on her hips, her eyes glaring. "Then trust *me,* Cliff. *I'm not your mother.* I won't let you hurt me. If you ever raise a hand to me, I'll . . . I'll leave you quicker than fleas hoppin' off a coyote carcass." She grinned.

He couldn't help his lips quirking in response, wondering when she'd heard young Sammy's favorite expression. He didn't know what to say. Logically, he knew there was no choice. They'd made love and he'd promised to marry her. He cared for her tremendously and lusted for her even more. But he felt at war within. And honestly, he wasn't sure if he was more afraid of hurting her, or being hurt by her should her love falter as his mother's had when she'd killed herself, leaving him alone.

Throwing his hands up in the air, he turned back to Blackjack, grabbing his reins. This was just a bunch of nonsense, trying to understand feelings. Action was a lot better. They needed to be on their way if they were to reach Lucy's before sunup.

Motioning to leave, he grunted a noncommittal response, then waited as Kyra, sighing deeply, interrupted Bayou Kitty from his never-ending bath. Once she was mounted, he galloped off in a flurry of dust as if a pack of wolves was in hot pursuit.

They arrived at Madam Lucy's at dawn as planned, having separated from Luke and Shane a mile before town. It was dark, and their arrival should've gone unnoticed.

Kyra grimaced as she looked up at the back door of the beautiful Victorian home. She truly didn't want to stay here among these women she didn't know and couldn't respect. But she'd have to make the best of it, for Cliff's sake. He was determined to protect her as if she were a fragile angel. If only there were a way to protect herself without involving him.

She wasn't the same tame kitty her mother had ordered around for years. As if sensing her thoughts, Bayou Kitty stirred in her arms, purring and rubbing his head against her hand for her caress. It was amazing how well he'd traveled on horseback. Absently, she rubbed the kitten behind his ears, contemplating her circumstances, while she waited for Cliff to rouse someone to let them in.

Her mother had always controlled her life—telling her what to do, how to dress, where to go, even whom to marry. Kyra had submitted out of a deep sense of love and respect, as well as the ingrained teachings of New Orleans society, which dictated that young ladies follow the instructions of first their parents and then later their husbands. But her outward obedience had warred with her inward rebelliousness, which had resulted in her first submitting to, and then breaking, her six previous engagements.

It was time to let go of her childlike behavior and truly take responsibility for her own actions, as she'd proclaimed earlier to Cliff. Being out West, away from the strictures of the society in which she'd been raised, had opened her eyes. It was as if she saw herself for the first time, with the blinders removed—with a fresh sense of who she was and what she wanted out of life. Yes, she'd run away because of her fear and need for protection. And she'd chosen Cliff because he'd been her trusted friend and she'd known he'd take care of her.

But there'd also been a part of her that had longed for him in a completely womanly way. He made her feel so feminine, so special, cherished, and understood. She'd run for Cliff not only to escape her problems, but also to find *him* and the relationship they'd once been developing. She'd chosen for the first time in her life what and whom she wanted. She wouldn't let anyone interfere with this most important decision—not even Cliff. If he tried to run again, she'd hunt him down and drag him back by his hair.

Grinning at that image in her mind, Kyra felt lighter of heart, and more prepared to face the events sure to await her during her time at Madam Lucy's. Cliff opened the back door and ushered her into the dark and silent house. She wrinkled her nose at the musky smell. When her eyes adjusted, she made out Lucy's dim outline against the shadows. The older woman moved forward, into a beam of dusky daylight, wearing a white serviceable nightdress and robe that covered her so completely it was almost virginal. Her face, as usual, was carefully controlled and unreadable. She didn't seem pleased, but that was all Kyra could sense. Kyra started to speak, but Lucy motioned silence with a finger against her lips. As quietly as possible they made their way up two flights of stairs to an attic room on the third floor.

Once the door was shut behind them, Lucy turned to Kyra. "I'm told you're in need of a safe place to stay for a few days. You're welcome to use this room. It hasn't been lived in for some time and no one ever comes up here. I'll have to tell a couple of my girls you're here, of course, so you can use the water closet and have meals brought to you. Horace will also have to know—for your protection. I realize this isn't what you're used to, but I hope we'll get along well enough for a few days."

Kyra held out both hands, enveloping Lucy's within her thankful grasp. "Miss Lucy, you have my heartfelt gratitude for allowing me to stay here. I'll try my hardest to be as little a burden as possible."

She'd finally elicited some emotion from the older woman. Lucy's face was frankly surprised, and somewhat dubious.

"Yes, well, that's very nice. I'll leave you now to get settled." And she walked out the door, shutting it quietly.

Kyra turned to Cliff. "So, what do we do now?"

"You sleep, and I'll go to my ranch and check on things." He reached for Bayou Kitty, transferring the pet from her arms to his. "Let me take him. Emilio will look after him." She opened her mouth to protest, but he interrupted, "He can't stay here, Kyra. You wouldn't want to keep him cooped up in this small room all day. And besides, he might yowl and alert someone to your presence."

She let the kitten go, her fingers wet from where he'd licked them, and watched the pair leave, feeling totally alone.

Shaking her sense of self-pity, Kyra turned to survey her temporary abode. It was a lovely, girlish room, dressed in pink lace and ruffles. How charming and so totally unsuited to what she imagined a brothel room should look like. It was decorated almost like her room at home had been when she was a small child.

But her thoughts really weren't on the room's decor. They were on Cliff. Ever since he'd told her about his mother's suicide, a knot of fear had been growing in her belly. She understood why he protected his heart so much better now. She was scared—scared she would lose him. What if he started resenting her for forcing the seduction? Now that she'd found him, made him hers, how could she ever go on without him?

Her heart went cold. How could he even consider life without love? To her, life had no meaning without it. What was she to do? How could she touch his soul when he protected it behind an iron gate? She was too inexperienced, and as a consequence unable to understand the ways of men. They weren't like women, a fact she had only begun to truly understand. She'd thought to seduce Cliff with talk and memories, and instead all it had taken was a glimpse of her naked body.

She needed to learn more about men.

Her mind returned to her surroundings as she eyed the wide bed. Of course! Why hadn't she considered the possibilities sooner? She needed expert advice on men, and where else to get it but from a professional source? Surely one of the ladies in residence wouldn't mind instructing her on the male species.

She snapped her fingers in satisfaction. She was brilliant. Cliff wouldn't be running away from her this time. She wasn't the same naïve sixteen-year-old as before. She was older, more mature, knew what she wanted from life, and most importantly, was now strong and determined enough to get it.

"The bounty's on you this time, Bayou Baldwin. And the reward?" She drummed her fingers on the side of her chin then smiled. "Your very cautious heart."

"*Mon Dieu!* Where's that mule-eared, grasshopper-kissing, son-of-a-slug Cliff Baldwin? If you know the whereabouts of that toad-stabbing . . ." The words trailed off as someone closed the door.

Cliff recognized that cantankerous voice. Well, it was about time. A huge grin split his face. It sounded like someone hadn't changed over the years. Cliff would have to alter his plan to make room for this new development.

Glancing around, he saw Sammy jawing with some friends a couple of doors down. Cliff strode over to them.

"Can you take this pest back to the ranch when you go, Sammy?" He passed the kitten to his young hand, and it immediately pawed at Sammy's eye-patch. "Corral the rest of the men and I'll join you shortly," Cliff said as he turned back to the Sheriff's.

When Cliff entered the office, he found Grandpère swinging a walking cane wildly in the air while mumbling something about inept, cow-brained youngsters playing at being law officers. Cliff's grin spread. Sheriff Overby had to be at least fifty, but maybe that did seem young to Grandpère. Kyra's grandfather seemed a little shorter and grayer, but he still had his ruddy complexion and flashing green eyes—focused on Cliff.

"Well, it's about time you showed up! I've torn this town apart looking for you, and I'll be tearing you up in a second if you don't tell me where my granddaughter is. She better be unharmed, or I'll forget any fond feelings I once felt for you."

"Good to see you, too, Grandpère. I've missed you as well." Cliff cut through the old man's bluster as he hugged the man who was the closest thing to a true father he'd ever had. Grandpère pounded him on the back. He abruptly pushed away from Cliff and scowled, but not before Cliff noticed the wetness in his eyes.

"*Merde!* You'll not be making me cry now, boy." The old man shook his finger. "Not after you run off and left us like you did, without even a note good-bye or letters over the years. First thing I hear from you is a cryptic telegram a few days ago about Kyra being here and to watch that no-good fiancé of hers. What's going on? You better tell me now and it better be good."

"Yes, we need to talk, but not here."

The sheriff waved as he headed out the door. "Actually, Baldwin, you can have privacy here. I was just fixing to step out and do my rounds when this old coot showed up pitching a fit because he couldn't find you at your ranch or anywhere in town."

"Who do you think you're calling old, you snake-skinned, swine-smelling . . ." Cliff effectively shut off Grandpère's flowing tirade by placing one hand over his mouth as he motioned Overby out.

With one target removed, Grandpère turned to the other. "And just where have you hidden *ma petite*? I most certainly have been all over this town and haven't been able to locate either of you. Where've you hid her and why?"

"Good Lord, I hope you haven't mentioned Kyra's name all over town. We're trying to keep her presence a secret."

"*Sacre bleu,* I may indeed be getting a little old, but I ain't senile yet. Of course I haven't mentioned her name, only yours. So, where've you been?"

"I have her hidden in a safe place. I'll explain the whole situation to you, but it'll take some time. We've got two killers on our tail and I'm trying my damnedest to protect her until we can put a stop to them. First, where's Jacques?"

"I had an old friend's son trail him for a few days in New Orleans. He didn't do anything out of the ordinary. Then he got a telegram and hightailed it for the train depot. I followed as quickly as I could on the next train. I knew he'd purchased a ticket for Dallas, and found the hotel he stayed at, but lost him. So I headed here *tout de suite*."

Cliff scowled and nodded. "Here, sit down in the sheriff's chair while I catch you up."

Thirty minutes later, Grandpère shook his head, mumbling how he never did like that jackal-hearted Jacques. "Couldn't understand what my daughter saw in that man. Of course she never looks much farther than bank account and family credentials. She's a good woman, don't misunderstand, but she doesn't have my good sense in regard to understanding character, *ne pensez-vous pas?*"

"Well, I'll have to agree with you, at least where Jacques is concerned. But you do understand now why I had to hide her."

"And just exactly where do you have her squirreled away, son?"

Trust Grandpère to home in on what he least wanted to say.

"She's . . . she's staying with some . . . friends."

"Friends, you say." Grandpère's sharp gray gaze pinned him mercilessly. "And just who are these friends?"

"She's staying at Madam Lucy's over at the edge of town, in a third-story room." Better to spew it out and get it over with.

"Madam Lucy's? You better not be saying what I think you're saying, boy. 'Madam Lucy' sounds like a *madam* to me. *Dieu du ciel!* Are you telling me my sweet, innocent baby angel is staying in a whorehouse?"

Cliff winced at Grandpère's roar. "Yes, sir."

He sincerely hoped Grandpère didn't suffer from any heart conditions, as his face was blotted purple and red.

"And what gave you the idea there wasn't any other safe place in this whole dad-blamed area?"

Leaning closer, Cliff whispered, "It's a small community, sir, and people talk. I had to keep her presence an absolute secret, and if there's one thing the girls at Madam Lucy's can do, it's keep a secret. Besides, most of them don't know she's there anyway. Finally, Jacques would never think to search for her there."

Grandpère poked his cane at Cliff's chest. "There's a reason for that, son. She sure as hell shouldn't be sitting out in a whorehouse. Now what are you going to do about it?"

"What do you mean what am I going to do about it?" He pushed Grandpère's cane aside. "I told you my plan. I've got two friends and all my ranch hands helping me. We're going to flush those two weasels out and handle them. That's what we're going to do, and then Kyra will be perfectly safe to come out of hiding."

"*Ah, non,* that's not what I meant. I meant what are you going to do to protect her reputation now that you've ruined it?"

"Ruined her reputation! I haven't ruined her reputation. Whatever gave you that idea?" Grandpère was a good judge of character, but surely his lewd thoughts weren't that evident.

"You know what I mean. You can't let a girl of Kyra's class stay in a brothel and not have the story spread eventually. *Sacre bleu,* sometime, sooner or later, someone here will hear about it and the news will spread back to New Orleans. For that matter, her reputation is shot there anyhow after running away like she did and no one hearing from her for days."

"I can assure you, Grandpère, that I've already made arrangements to protect Kyra's reputation. She's agreed to become my wife. As soon as this ordeal is over and it's safe, we'll be married." He looked down, staring the older man in the eye.

"She has, huh." Grandpère's expression instantly changed and he stared keenly back at Cliff as if trying to see past the mask Cliff had made of his face. "And just what made you ask her to marry you?"

"As you said, sir. I realized how her reputation was at risk by our need to protect her safety." He wasn't about to let Grandpère make him stammer like a sixteen-year-old boy.

"I seem to remember you protesting, one of the last times I ever saw you, about how you'd never marry and no one could ever force you to, *oui?*"

"That's true, but situations change. People change."

There was a long, dreadful pause while Grandpère examined him from head to toe. Cliff felt as if he'd been turned inside out and thoroughly inspected. Finally, Grandpère seemed to come to a conclusion. He hoped it would be positive.

"*Tres bien.* I guess we better get going then. Seems like we're going to have a wedding *this afternoon.*"

Chapter Nineteen

Rose's Fried Chicken: Always best if you've raised and butchered your own. You'll never go wanting with home-grown freshness.
From the *Sinfully Delicious Bakery Recipe Book*

A light rapping on the door awoke Kyra. Prying her eyes open, she focused on a wood floor—and a trapdoor. Disoriented, she lifted her head to study the unfamiliar, pink room. "Madam Lucy's attic," she mumbled in remembrance. Someone rapped on the door again. Pulling the sheets up to her chin, Kyra called out tentatively, "Come in."

Lucy walked in with a pretty blond woman holding a tray in tow. "Miss Lourdes, I'm sorry to wake you, but it's near noon, and we thought you'd want to eat while the food is hot. This is Rose. She's one of my best ladies. You can trust her to help you while you're here."

Rose and Kyra exchanged a look. Kyra saw the wariness she felt inside reflected on Rose's face. Really, this was awkward, and her mother—for all her lessons on etiquette and deportment—had never instructed her on the proper greeting for a prostitute. *And one who may have "serviced" her future husband, no less.* What was she to do?

But her innate grace and empathy overruled any disdain as she smiled at Rose and murmured hesitantly, "Pleased to meet you. I'm sorry I'm not quite dressed yet so I could welcome you better."

A relieved grin flashed across the slight woman's face. "Aww, don't you be worrying about your clothes none. I'm sure you got more on than I do most times. Thought you might be getting hungry, and it wouldn't do for you to go traipsing down to the kitchen yourself yet. Would you like it there in bed?"

"Yes, please."

Madam Lucy stepped out the door as Rose helped arrange the tray over Kyra's lap. The whiff of fresh-baked bread made her stomach sound out a loud roar.

Rose laughed. "My, you must be even hungrier than we thought."

The tension was broken.

Kyra sat up straighter, unconcerned now with her appearance. "Yes, I haven't eaten in over twenty-four hours. Cliff was determined to get back to town as quickly as possible. He didn't want to stop to camp, and we rode through the night."

Rose smiled, but said nothing. Kyra's stomach lurched. Maybe she should steer the conversation away from any mention of Cliff. It was better not to learn something she might not want to know.

"Oh, this food looks so good. And the bread smells divine. Do you get it from a local bakery?"

"Shucks, no. We bake and cook our own food here. Some of the town businesses think our money's not good enough for them, even if the owners do come visit us frequently in the evening. Actually, I'm the cook today." Rose seated herself in a nearby chair, crossed her legs, and swung one foot back and forth.

Kyra's appetite got the best of her, and she dug into the tempting breakfast. "This bread has such an interesting taste. What kind is it?"

"Sourdough. It's my specialty."

"And the okra and butter beans have a fresh, delicate flavor."

"We have our own garden. Madam Lucy teaches us all about growing our own food and cooking, at least those of us that don't already know. She says it's wise for women to know all they need to take care of themselves. You can't depend on men—except for one thing, if you know what I mean. She also teaches us how to save our money, ride horses, hitch up carriages, and handle a gun."

"My, that is extensive training. She cares for you like a mother, it sounds like." Kyra spooned another bite into her mouth.

Rose rolled her eyes. "Ummph, a heap of a lot better than mine did, that's for sure. But you're right. I think that's actually part of it. She used to have a little girl, you know. This was her room. But something happened to her—to the little girl and Madam's husband. Don't really know what, she won't talk about it. Afterward, Madam started this business."

"Oh, so you mean she hasn't always run a-a . . ." Kyra floundered. What was the proper word to call a whorehouse when having a pleasant conversation with a prostitute housed therein?

"A brothel, you mean? Go ahead and say it. Don't be shy. Lord knows I'm sure not. I know how these things work and what proper young ladies think about me and my kind. I'm even surprised you're talking to me as you are. Maybe that's why I'm flapping my mouth so much. The proper ladies of Las Almas twitch their skirts and cross to the other side of the street if they happen to see one of us coming their way. Like they think whoring might be contagious."

Rose's face was carefully neutral, but Kyra sensed the hurt behind her words. Rose stopped swinging her foot.

"I'm sorry. That's so rude." Kyra set down her spoon and chewed on her lip, feeling guilty. True, she'd never acted in the manner just described, but then she'd never had reason to, not knowing how to recognize a prostitute from a lady in the light of day. At night she was never let out on the streets alone. Would she have acted the same way if the situation had presented itself? It was hard to say. But her mother would certainly have told her to do so. In fact, she did seem to remember having been instructed in such a maneuver. It must have slipped her mind along with many other of her mother's meaningless directives.

"But getting back to your question"—Rose's voice brought Kyra back to the present—"no, Madam hasn't always run a brothel. She used to be one of the proper young matrons of this town—until her husband died. None of us know what happened, but we figured he left her penniless and she had no choice but to start this business. It does make her sort of lonely and, well, maybe a bit lacking in trust. I mean, most of these ladies in town used to be her good friends. Now they treat her with the same disregard they do the rest of us."

"Why, how sad. Surely something could be done to make the ladies show a little more Christian charity."

The sound that erupted from Rose was a combination snort and groan. "You won't push that bit of logic by anyone here. The preacher in town condones such nonsense. We're frequently the subjects of his sermons, or so I'm told. They won't let none of us inside those precious church doors. They want to keep the sinners out, you see. But Madam takes care of us good enough. And she understands, too. When one of the girls has saved up enough money to start a new life, or decides she's had enough of whoring, Madam helps her get out on her own."

"That's quite amazing. Then if the girls have a choice, why do so many stay here?" She took another bite of chicken.

"Money. We make good money. But still it takes time to save up enough to move to an area where you can make a fresh start. This world just isn't a friendly place for a woman without a man."

Kyra understood that bit of logic. It was a truth that transferred across economic and social lines. A woman had a hard time making it on her own in Kyra's world as well.

She'd finished her fried chicken and sliced tomatoes as Rose finished speaking. "I'm stuffed. It was so delicious. You know, it makes sense for a woman to learn to provide for herself, even if she doesn't foresee being left on her own.

You never know what the future has in store for you, do you?"

"Ain't that the truth?"

"I have an idea, and I wonder if you'll help me with it."

"Sure be glad to if I can. Ain't never had a proper lady ask for my help before." Rose smirked—but not unpleasantly.

"I'm not sure I'm as proper as you think." Kyra blushed.

Rose snorted again. "I sure can't say the same, seeing as how my ma was the one who threw me at my first man when I was fifteen. She'd got too old for the customers to pay much."

Kyra was horrified, but masked her reaction by pressing her lips together. "Well, uh, I . . . umm, what I'm trying to say is that I've lived a pretty useless existence, and I'm only now learning how to be self-sufficient, as you say. I'm learning to cook. Truly, I am," she protested as Rose erupted into laughter. "I'm getting good at it, too, but nowhere near as good as you. I was wondering if you'd mind teaching me a few things while I'm here—like how to cook, and a little about gardening. That sort of thing. I'd be tremendously appreciative."

"How appreciative?" Rose's eyes narrowed.

She was referring to money. It took Kyra by surprise, but she understood as well. They weren't friends, after all, and she represented wealth to someone who hadn't had any.

"Oh, say, twenty dollars worth. Would that be all right?"

Rose's eyes widened. "Hell's teeth, that's good money for not being flat on my back. Sure enough, you got yourself a teacher. When ya want to start?"

Kyra bounded out of bed. "How about now. Let me get dressed and freshen up. Oh, I forgot, would it be all right for me to go below to the kitchen?"

"Sure, we can sneak you in. Like I said, today's my day to cook, so the other girls won't come anywhere near there. Just tiptoe down the back stairs when you're ready. They lead right to the side door of the kitchen. See you in a bit," she said as she shut the door behind her.

* * *

"The secret to making sourdough bread is to let the starter sit just long enough, and then knead it in good," Rose instructed Kyra as they worked side by side in the kitchen.

Earlier, while all the other ladies took afternoon naps, they'd spent some pleasant time in the walled garden, with Kyra's head enveloped by a large scarf. Rose had taught her the fundamentals of growing vegetables and herbs. It was fascinating. She hadn't received this type of useful instruction even from Grandpère. Rose explained briefly about soil type, weeding, fertilizing, and harvesting. The brothel garden was surprisingly large and well tended, and the smell of herbs and flowers gave a sense of homey warmth.

Rose had also shown her the henhouse, and together they'd found a few eggs. Raising chickens had seemed fascinating—until Rose demonstrated the different ways to wring a chicken's neck. She'd also mentioned that a few of the ladies were proficient fisherwomen. It was obvious the brothel was able to supply most of its own food.

Kyra felt comfortable now with Rose—even relaxed enough to discuss more personal matters. It was time to find out the information she needed to thaw Cliff's heart.

"You know a lot about men, don't you, Rose?"

Rose guffawed. "Yep, I reckon you could sure say that."

"I was wondering if you'd mind giving me some advice about—about Cl . . . I mean, men in general. You know what I mean?"

"Sure, honey, shoot your questions. I don't mind sharing from my vast knowledge. You're paying good money anyhow."

"Well, see, I don't know much about men and relationships. That is, um, beyond attracting a rich and socially prominent husband. What I need to know now is something more practical."

"That's me, practical Rose filled with lots of practical advice. Here, honey, while we're talking you knead this dough." She passed Kyra a wooden bowl.

"Oh, I've never kneaded sourdough before, just biscuits, and I learned that on my own." Kyra's fingers dove into the lumpy mess.

"Well, think of the dough like a man. In order to rise, it needs something to trigger it. In the case of the bread, either yeast or a sour starter will do the trick. But it's not enough to get a rise out of the dough. You have to add in just the right amount of stimulation and at the proper rate, so that it won't erupt in one big bubble. You do this by working—you could say massaging—the yeast through the whole mixture. Kneading is the key to success."

She winked slyly. "Now much the same is true with a man. It's quite easy to stimulate one—getting a rise rather easily. But if it's not controlled, then his bubble will shoot off early, giving neither one of you as much pleasure as is possible. So the trick is to learn to knead him in such a way you both enjoy the end result much better."

"How?"

"Honey, dear, I'm sure you've heard the saying: The way to a man's heart is through his stomach?"

Kyra nodded emphatically. "Oh, yes, especially during lectures on the importance of proper menu planning and chef supervision."

"Well, I want to tell you a little secret." Rose leaned closer to whisper in Kyra's ear, a mischievous grin lighting her face. "The quickest, most direct way to a man's heart actually exists a little lower—say, about ten inches lower."

"You mean . . . ?"

"That's right. Men have two heads and when it comes to matters of love and romance, they tend to do most of their thinking with their smaller one."

Kyra deliberately closed her mouth and tried to make her eyes a little less wide. She didn't want to seem naïve.

"Now," Rose continued, "what we'll do is cover both bets. I'll teach you how to season food *and* a man so you can rouse *both* his appetites. You follow my directions, honey, and your Cliff won't let you out of his sight for an instant."

"I . . . I didn't say anything about wanting to learn this for Cliff's sake."

"You didn't have to, hon. I got my own eyes and ears. I remember when you came looking for him, and I saw his face when he was told you were here. Behind the surprise, there was a yearning I've never seen on him before. He's always so cold and empty, but that evening I saw a warm feeling in his eyes—for you. I also saw him when he left here early this morning. He looked like a hunted man. Men can sense when they're about to lose their hearts, and they sure struggle against it at first. He wants you, Kyra, and he's fighting it, but he won't be able to fight you for long, especially with my help." Rose nudged Kyra with her elbow, chuckling.

Kyra's heart lifted with Rose's encouraging words, but then her breath left her with realization. "Y-you were with Cliff the night I arrived?" She kept her attention focused on the dough, unsure how to ask what she wanted to know.

"There's no need for me to try and keep it secret. You know he was here with one of us, and yes, it was me. But I think you know enough now to understand sex and love are two different things—at least they are for a man. I haven't been a whore all my life, you know, and I won't be one much longer." Rose's gaze left Kyra's face and focused on a picture on the wall. "I did have a brief period in which I lived with an older aunt and helped her out. I had a beau at that time, and I learned the difference between sex and love." She turned away to reach for a baking pan. "And I'll feel it again soon, if I can help it."

"I'd like to help you, too, Rose. I know we just met and, well, there's a lot of difference between us, but you're being a good friend, and if there's anything I can do to help you start a new life, I'd be honored." Kyra reached for the pan Rose held out.

Rose seemed taken by surprise, her eyes watering. Kyra quickly said, "What would you do if you were able to leave? How would you make a living?"

Rose brightened. "Oh, I have it all figured out. Like you said, I'm a pretty good cook, and I enjoy it, too. One day I'm gonna open my own restaurant and hire my own girls to help me run it. I'd thought about applying at the Lemonade and Bakery Shop down the road, but those ladies would never hire me. So I guess I'd have to go to another town to start out, you know, until I got enough experience and money saved to start my own. Then I'll hire any ladies, like myself, who want to leave *the business* behind and start a new life. Madam has inspired me."

Kyra listened as she dumped the dough into the bread pan. She sensed an emptiness and deep longing in Rose. She also felt guilty. Here she was, admittedly having earlier felt somewhat superior to this beautiful young lady standing before her, and now she felt low in comparison. While she'd grown up with all the luxuries of life, a loving family, social influence, a secure home, and bountiful food, what had she done with them? A long list of six fiancés—that's what. But here was this prostitute, having been thrown into her career as a child by her *loving* mother, living always on the harder side of life, without security, and yet she had plans to make a difference in the world, to help others out of the same misery in which she'd been forced to reside.

Kyra flung the last of the dough into the pan, and wiped her hands clean on a towel. Well, there was no reason why she couldn't do so as well. She could help. She was her own person, and in control of her life. But first she had to get out of this sticky situation. It would be better not to say too much now; not make any promises she may not be able to keep. She reached out and touched Rose's arm.

"I admire you, Rose. You're a brave and compassionate woman. I don't know when I've ever met anyone like you before."

"Aww, shucks, you're making me blush. And I can't believe it anyhow. Why, a fine lady like you—you meet quality all the time. Me? I'm just trash, that's what they call me."

"Then 'they' don't know the real you. You may not live the life I'd want to live, but you have a good heart and the desire to help others. I have a lot to learn from you, and not only about cooking and, uh, men."

Now she blushed as well.

"Well, speaking of men, I think it's about time I got back to my lessons with maybe a little more detail. Wouldn't want you to be short of ideas on exactly what to do with Cliff."

Kyra understood. Rose was uncomfortable taking praise from a woman, as she probably didn't get it often. It was time to return to a less sensitive subject—*sex and seduction.*

"Yes, please, give me lots of details. I want to know exactly what to do to catch my man—to catch my Cliff."

Kyra and Rose were engulfed in laughter when Cliff returned to Madam Lucy's. He was surprised, and nervous to say the least, to discover the two so obviously enjoying each other's company in the kitchen. They seemed startled to see him, and if he wasn't mistaken, they both tried to keep a straight face.

Cliff nodded a greeting to Rose and then turned to Kyra, flushed from cooking. The smell of baking bread made his stomach growl. He hadn't taken time to eat. "Kyra, I hope you got some rest and had a good morning." Could she see the twinkle in his eye? He couldn't wait to see her reaction to his surprise.

"Oh, I've had a wonderful time. Rose has been very friendly and we've had *so much* to talk about."

Cliff's heart sank with a dull thud to the bottom of his gut. This couldn't be good—but she *had* been laughing. Surely Rose wouldn't have told Kyra details about, about, well . . . them, together. Thank God he had the perfect distraction.

"Um, I have a surprise for you." Turning swiftly, he grabbed for the door he'd just come through.

"You do?" Her head jerked up, her eyes brightening.

"*Mon Dieu,* didn't you know no better than to hide out in a whorehouse?" Grandpère stomped in with a growl.

Kyra screamed joyfully, running to the older man as he castigated her for the fix she was in because she hadn't had enough sense to run to him for help instead of Cliff.

Cliff smiled as he watched them argue and hug each other. They were so alike it was scary. He shook his head. Maybe now was a good time to sneak away.

"Oh, Grandpère, what you must be thinking," Kyra wailed. "I'm a tarnished woman."

Grandpère snatched Cliff's belt loop before he could get away, shooting a squinting scowl that could put an outlaw's glare to shame. His legs turned to jelly. Imprisoned, Cliff forced himself to stop fidgeting, clenching his hands into fists.

"Well, *chérie,* after Cliff's wedded you right and proper, the tarnish will polish right off, won't it, Cliff?"

Chapter Twenty

Shocking Pink Wedding Cake: For those who dare the unusual.
From the *Sinfully Delicious Bakery Recipe Book*

"Are you crazy? You can't mean to get married right now! In complete secrecy? What's gotten into you, Cliff?" Lucy sputtered.

Madam Lucy looked horrified. It was the first honest expression Kyra'd seen from the older woman. She understood. When Grandpère had announced their impending nuptials, she'd suffered a moment of astonishment as well. She'd quickly regained her senses, however, and was now ready to seize the opportunity.

Kyra glanced around her temporary bedroom, where they had all gathered, finally focusing on her grandfather. She was thrilled to see him, of course, but was equally worried about how tired he appeared after his long journey. He seemed to favor his cane more than usual. She bit her lip, the guilt about involving Cliff in her turmoil now extending to Grandpère as well.

"I don't buy that nonsense for a moment," Lucy went on. "You were the one who brought Miss Lourdes to hide out here in absolute secrecy, and you want to risk blowing it by getting married right now? You better give me a better explanation than because this crazy old coot wants to see his granddaughter married on his own wedding anniversary."

Obviously Madam wasn't buying their quickly made-up explanation, which Cliff had delivered while Kyra was lost in thought—an explanation that, by coincidence, happened to be true.

"Well, then, would you believe it's because this crazy *old coot* has a shotgun pointed at my back? Figuratively speaking," Cliff added when Lucy attempted to peer behind him. "He says this wedding's going to take place today or I'll be sleeping with the earthworms come sunup."

Kyra noted Cliff's grin—he took Grandpère's threats about as seriously as she did. So why was he humoring the older man by going through with the wedding? She knew why *she* was—because it was the one thing she desired most on all this earth: Cliff Baldwin as her husband *right now.* But what were Cliff's reasons? Yes, he'd said he wanted to marry her, but why was he willing to hurry it and risk their safety?

She'd find out later. She surely wasn't going to let those questions or any other foolish nonsense stop them. That being the case, she'd better take charge and make things happen, since no one else seemed capable of doing so.

"Yes, Mrs. Tupper." Rose had informed her of Madam's last name since she hadn't wanted to keep referring to her as "Madam." It grated on her sensibilities. "We do indeed want to be married today. Now, if we could get down to business . . . We'll want to keep it small due to this whole secrecy thing," Kyra said with an airy wave of her hand.

She paced as she formulated her plans. "But there are four people I'd like to invite, other than yourself, of course. I'd like Rose to come, and I wonder if she'd mind going to fetch the minister. She can be trusted to contact the reverend without letting the news get out. Then would you send a messenger out to Shane Chandler, Luke Hampton, and Paco Mendoza at Cliff's ranch? The message should be worded vaguely enough so no one else understands what it means. Something like 'Group meeting at L.T.'s. Come immediately.' Yes, that should work." Kyra snapped her fingers as she resisted an urge to reach out and close Madam's hanging jaw. Cliff looked just as astonished, while Grandpère sat in a chair in the corner, softly guffawing.

At least *someone* was delighted with her wedding. Obviously the other two were surprised by her ability to take charge. But Kyra'd been taught since early adolescence how to organize social events, and she wasn't about to have a shabby wedding, even if it did have to be small and secretive, and in a wh—

"Cliff," she said, whirling, knocking him off balance. "We can't have the wedding he . . . I mean, can't we go to the church to get married? Mama will surely pitch a fit when she finds out I wasn't married by a priest in a Catholic church, but a Protestant church will be better than a br . . ." Oh, darn, she didn't want to offend Lucy.

"Absolutely out of the question," Cliff replied. "There's no way I will risk your safety anymore with this foolishness by taking you to one of the most public places in Las Almas. Would you like us to be shot on your wedding day?" he asked with a growl.

Noting the firmness of his jaw and the tic in his cheek, she knew there was no way she was going to change his mind. Oh, well, she'd have to marry in a brothel, but no one would ever find out about it!

"Grandpère, if you ever breathe a word of this to Mama, or anyone else back home for that matter, *you* will be sleeping with the earthworms. Do you understand me?" She craned her neck to peer behind Cliff's broad shoulders as she wagged her finger threateningly. Did that loud snort mean he'd taken her seriously, or not?

"Now, on to the dress." She turned back to Madam. "You or one of your girls wouldn't happen to have a wedding dress hanging about, would you?" she asked somewhat facetiously.

She was surprised when Lucy said, "As a matter of fact we do. Irene keeps one on hand. Has a regular customer who likes to play pretend, if you know what I mean."

No, Kyra didn't exactly know what she meant, but her mind ran wild with possibilities. She had to rein in her imagination, however, and get back to work.

"Do you think Miss Irene will let me borrow it?" At Lucy's affirmative nod, Kyra continued. "Good. That gives me something borrowed. Then I'll need something old, something new, and something blue. I have Grandmère's cameo locket with me." She reached below her neckline and pulled out the beautifully carved blue piece attached to a gold chain. "That will take care of something old and blue. Then I'll just need something new."

"I'll take care of that," Cliff said softly behind her.

"Thank you." She smiled at him over her shoulder and then moved on. "There's also the matter of rings. I'd prefer a double-ring ceremony."

"Well, now, I think I might be able to help with this one." Grandpère rose from his seat in the corner and, leaning on his cane, shuffled closer. "Here, *chérie*, these were your *grandmère*'s and mine. She asked me the day before she died to make sure you got these when the time was right. I've held off through six idiotic fiancés waiting for the right one. Now I think you've found your lucky number seven. I put these in my pocket when I left home, hoping Cliff would be as I remembered and that you and he had *truly* found each other. My greatest wish is that you experience the love, peace, and happiness your *grandmère* and I knew."

Kyra threw herself into Grandpère's arms as he tossed the pouch to Cliff. Nothing could have touched her heart more than having the deep well of love and commitment from previous generations flowing through her marriage. Whispering, "I love you," she pushed back gently from Grandpère's embrace as she dabbed at her eyes. The wedding had to go on. "Now then, the license—will we be able to get one on such short notice?"

Madam Lucy answered this one. "We'll let Reverend Worthington think he's marrying one of my girls. He'll be so delighted to rescue one of the damned that he'll do whatever it takes to get the license for you."

"Wonderful. It sounds like we've made our plans. Let's set the time for three hours from now. Mrs. Tupper, would you be so kind as to send out Rose and the messengers? Cliff, you need to get yourself ready"—she shot him a look clearly saying he better bathe and dress nicely—"and Grandpère, you rest." With that, Kyra swept out of the room toward the back stairs.

"And where do you think you're going?" Cliff's voice trailed after her.

"Why, to bake the wedding cake, of course."

Everything was perfect, or so Cliff had been told twenty-five times by a frantic Kyra as she rushed up and down Madam Lucy's back stairs from the kitchen to her bedroom, making preparations. She was certainly very excited about the impromptu event. It made him feel warm inside to see her glowing countenance, and he was proud to give her pleasure. *Please, God, let it last.*

Cliff was worried, though. With the last-minute preparations for the wedding, there was quite a bit more hustle and bustle around Lucy's house. All the girls now knew of Kyra's presence and the impending ceremony because of the heightened activity. Her safety could be at risk. The nuptials would be before supper so there'd be less of a chance a customer could walk in. He'd set Horace to guard the door, just in case, with strict instructions as to who was to be admitted. He'd taken the extra precaution of warning Madam Lucy to make sure her girls kept their mouths shut, but not all of them could be trusted. He would just have to be more vigilant from now on.

Hell, he'd gone momentarily loco when he'd given in to Grandpère's demands. But it did give him peace of mind to think Kyra would be left with the protection of his name should something happen to him. Maybe that was why he'd consented to the spontaneous affair; he couldn't figure out any other reason why he'd risk jeopardizing Kyra's hiding place.

Turning from gazing out the doorway of the "entertainment room," as Kyra called it, he paced back toward the window. The room was filled with a multitude of flowers and herbs, which Kyra had insisted on throwing about, whispering, *The place could at least smell like a church.*

It smelled like a hothouse.

At least he no longer smelled like a sweaty horse. He'd bathed at the local bathhouse and bought a new black suit at the mercantile for the occasion, as he hadn't had time to go back to the ranch for his own clothing. The new white shirt and black tie were starched and pressed. Rose had seen to that.

Where was the minister? And where were Shane and Luke, for that matter? It was almost time and here he was alone in the designated "chapel." His mother would turn over in her grave if she knew he was getting married in a whorehouse. But she'd also be very pleased he was marrying Kyra. She'd always had a soft spot in her heart for his young friend, and had encouraged Cliff to invite her over frequently. In fact, she'd seemed to have ideas of matchmaking during the last year of her life.

A cough caught Cliff's attention, and he turned in surprise to find Shane slumped on the doorjamb observing him curiously. "How long have you been standing there?"

"Long enough to know you weren't paying a lick of attention to your surroundings, and if I'd been Yancey you'd be dead." Shane moved further into the room, as silently as he'd appeared. "So, amigo, what was that mysterious message I received about a meeting? What's up?"

"I'm marrying Kyra in about five minutes."

Cliff felt a distinct pleasure at having, for the very first time, disrupted Shane's familiar placid composure. His face showed complete shock now. Cliff grinned.

"You—you're doing what? Have you been chewing on locoweed? Don't get me wrong, I think you and Kyra are spiritmates, but now's not the time or place for a wedding. What's gotten into you?"

"Apparently Grandpère and Kyra have, because everything is set, or *perfect* as I've been told, and as soon as the minister gets here we're going to be married."

They both turned toward the door at the sound of frantic footsteps down the front stairwell. Kyra rushed into the room, breathless, her breasts heaving with her hurried flight. "Shane Chandler, don't you dare try to talk Cliff out of this wedding if you want to live to see another day."

She was right up in Shane's face, stubbing her "poking" finger into his chest, and actually had Shane stepping backward in retreat.

Shane grinned, but Cliff felt like a stampede of frantic cows had gotten loose in his chest. His pulse raced, he couldn't breathe, and he was sure he'd broken out in a sweat—and all because Kyra looked . . . *magnificent* was the only word to describe her. Beautiful was far too tame a word for the way her glorious hair curled around her delicate face and shoulders, the way her daring green eyes defied Shane, and the way the rounded curves of her body were highlighted by the seductively cut wedding gown.

Seductively cut wedding gown! What the hell did she have on? Instinctively he reached to remove his coat to cover her, but stopped as she whirled toward him—her tirade at Shane halted.

"And don't you go thinking you can get out of this wedding now, Clifford Baldwin. You promised me and you're going to stick to your promise if I have to . . . to, well, I don't know what I'll do, but you better just listen to me. Let me know as soon as the minister gets here." And with that she swept from the room, leaving both men gawking after her.

"Interesting dress," Shane remarked pensively as he watched Kyra's swift flight back up the stairs.

"I'm too scared now to tell her she can't wear it," Cliff responded feebly. "It's a dress she borrowed from one of Lucy's girls. It's supposed to be a wedding dress."

"Well, it *was* white."

And that was about the only resemblance it bore to a wedding dress as far as Cliff could tell. He didn't know what kind of material it was made from, but it was almost see-through. Thankfully, Kyra'd had a chemise on underneath. The bodice had been cut into a deep V that went almost to her belly button, and the back had been cut equally low. The hem had reached just below her knees to show off some pink and white striped stockings one of Lucy's girls surely had to have lent her. But the worst part was the red roses embroidered at strategic points over her breasts. As much as he'd wanted to cover up the provocative dress so Shane and others couldn't see her in it, another, harder part of him had wanted to rip it off and feast on what lay beneath.

Shane's chuckle interrupted his thoughts. "I guess Kyra doesn't hold with the superstition that it's bad luck for the groom to see the bride before the wedding. Your wedding's starting to look interesting. Maybe it's not such a bad idea after all."

Cliff's tension eased at Shane's continued laughter, and, he finally joined in himself. "I think it will definitely be a one-of-a-kind ceremony."

A knock sounded on the front door, and Shane left to answer it. He returned with Reverend Worthington, who appeared "holier-than-thou" as he entered Madam Lucy's, undoubtedly for the first time.

"So, Mr. Baldwin, which one of Mrs. Tupper's girls is about to be made an honest woman? I'd like to say it's about time someone in this town started taking his responsibilities toward these girls seriously."

"I'm sorry to disappoint you, Reverend, but my bride, Kyra, is only visiting here for a few days. She isn't one of Lucy's girls. We found it necessary for her to stay here to protect her safety. I hope I can count on you to keep her presence here a secret." His tone implied the minister had better do so.

The Reverend, however, wasn't taking notice of Cliff's tone, and instead sputtered in rage. "You can't mean to tell me you've hidden a decent young lady here at Mrs. Tupper's and that now you plan to conduct a hurried wedding on these same premises. I won't have it. This is not proper!"

Shane stepped forward and murmured in Worthington's ear, "You'll do as requested or I'll let it be known I've seen you on Comanche land visiting a certain Indian lady—unchaperoned."

The minister shut his mouth and moved stiffly to the stage at the back of the room, his Bible clutched in his hand. Cliff nodded to Shane, who left to inform the others that it was time. Cliff had the presence of mind to follow the reverend and hand him a sheet of paper with his and Kyra's full names written out. If nothing else, they needed to get that part right.

Within a few short minutes there was a flurry of footsteps on the stairs as Lucy's girls hastened into the entertainment room. They were all dressed in their finery, as he observed vivid shades of purple, pink, orange, and red, lots of lace petticoats showing, and black fishnet stockings flashing beneath the raised hemlines. There was also an abundance of feather plumes sticking out of elaborately coiffured hair, and plenty of face paint. And if Cliff didn't miss his guess, they'd rouged their nipples as well in honor of the event.

They were excited about having a wedding in their midst, and had gone all out to prepare for it, although he did observe a few sullen faces. Madam Lucy, the only modestly attired one in the bunch, stood silently at the back of the throng.

The girls filed in and took their places standing on either side of the stage, facing the door, waiting for the bride to make her entrance. One lady sat at the piano and began the liveliest rendition of "The Wedding March" Cliff had ever heard.

Slow footsteps came sedately down the staircase. In a moment Rose appeared. She'd obviously been selected as maid of honor. She was dressed in a purple and green striped low-cut dress with a pink boa draped across her shoulders. She smiled at Cliff, winking suggestively, before moving on to her place.

He barely noticed his former paramour as he was captivated by the lovely vision standing in the doorway. Cliff's gut tightened as Kyra entered the room—her eyes focused on him. Someone had found a see-through lace shawl and draped it over her head to serve as a veil. The yellow roses he'd bought were clutched in her left hand. The pink wall sconces cast her in a rosy hue. She was absolutely charming. He forgot all about his worry over her dress. Grandpère leaned only lightly on his cane as he escorted her. If his grin were any wider, it would tear his face clear in two.

Cliff walked forward to meet them. "You're perfect," he whispered into Kyra's ear before dropping a kiss on her cheek through the veil and tucking her hand under his arm. Together they walked forward to face the minister.

"The Wedding March" finished on a loud bang, and Reverend Worthington cleared his throat. "We are gathered here today in the sight of God and angels . . . well, the sight of God anyway . . . to join this man and this woman in holy matrimony. Who gives this woman's hand to be married?"

"I do," a chorus shouted from around the room as all of the ladies and Grandpère responded.

Reverend Worthington was taken aback, but quickly recovered. He obviously wanted to finish with the service and leave.

"Uh, now then, marriage is a most honorable estate, created and instituted by God, signifying unto us the mystical union, which also exists between Christ and the Church. So, too, may the marriage of Cliff and Kyra be adorned by true and abiding love. If there is any man present who knows a reason why this couple should not be united in marriage, let him speak now or forever hold his peace."

Running footsteps pounded from the front door as the minister spoke. Then Luke appeared in the doorway. "I know a reason. Cliff, you've got to take Kyra and leave. A friend just saw a man fitting Delacroix's description leaving the church not ten minutes ago. I'm not sure where he's headed, but he could be on his way here. I'll stay and stop him while you take Kyra and run."

"No!" Kyra shouted as she swung to face Luke. "Jacques can't do anything in front of such a large group of witnesses. Why, there's even a minister present. I'm safer here than I'd be anywhere else. *And we are having this wedding now.* Please join us, Luke, and *keep your mouth shut.*" She turned back and smiled sweetly at the minister. "Pray, please continue, Reverend."

He cleared his throat roughly before proceeding. "W-would you please face each other and join hands? Kyra, do you take Clifford U. Baldwin the Third to be your wedded husband? Do you promise to love, honor, cherish, and obey him, forsaking all others and holding only to him until death do you part?"

"I do," Kyra whispered as she slipped the plain gold band on his finger. She'd like to have protested that "obey," but couldn't without slowing down the ceremony. It didn't matter. Cliff would learn soon enough that she'd obey only when it suited her.

"Do you, Cliff, take Kyra Dawson Lourdes to be your wedded wife? Do you promise to love, honor, cherish, and protect her, forsaking all others and holding only to her until death do you part?"

"I—"

A loud bang stopped Cliff before he could get the words out. Paco ran into the room. "Boss, you have to come quick. Some gunman hid out on the hill above the ranch and shot up the place. A couple of the men were hit, Sammy pretty badly."

Cliff whirled to leave, but a steely grip on his arm stopped him stiller than a fox in a snare. "You leave this room before saying, 'I do,' and you're a dead man, Cliff Baldwin."

"I do." Cliff said, and shoved Grandmère's ring on her finger.

The minister proclaimed, "Cliff and Kyra, as the two of you have promised your love for each other by these vows, the giving of these rings, and the joining of your hands, I now declare you to be husband and wife."

Cliff, Shane, Paco, and Luke rushed out of the house, the front door slamming behind them, to the accompaniment of: "Congratulations, you may kiss your bride."

Grandpère and Lucy's girls surrounded Kyra, offering their congratulations and good wishes. Kyra smiled, showed off her ring, and gave hugs, with tears in her eyes and worry in her heart. She was now Mrs. Clifford U. Baldwin the Third. But she feared for Sammy, and prayed she'd still have a husband by the end of the day.

Chapter Twenty-one

Double Fudge Banana Split: A decadent concoction, which will leave you drooling. But don't eat too much or pay the consequences!
From the *Sinfully Delicious Bakery Recipe Book*

It was past midnight when Cliff trudged up the back steps of Lucy's to Kyra's room. He reached behind his neck to massage his strained muscles as he quietly opened the door. An oil lamp flickered light across Kyra, sitting in bed reading. He stopped short. Damn, why wasn't she asleep?

She jumped out of bed and rushed to his side. "How's Sammy?"

Turning away from her, he removed his gun belt and hat. "Not so well," he finally answered. "I chased down the saddlebag doc and he's there with him. Along with all my men. He'll pull through," Cliff said, forcing himself to believe the words.

"I'm sorry. Do you want to talk about it?" Kyra laid her hand on his arm, forcing him to turn in her direction.

"No." He didn't even want to think about it. Not about young Sammy, whom he'd seen grow from a gangly boy in his teens to a young man. And certainly not about the deathbed promise he'd made to Sammy's father that he'd take care of his son for him.

But his thoughts wouldn't let him escape. They tracked him mercilessly, pursuing him with the vengeance of guilt. None of this would have happened if he'd . . . Hell, he didn't know what to do. He hadn't wanted to leave Sammy, but then he'd been filled with constant worry for Kyra's safety. It seemed either way he turned, he was letting someone down.

He needed sleep, to forget his worries for a short time. "Where's Grandpère?" He finally looked at Kyra.

"He left for the Hacienda a few hours ago."

She was in her nightdress, her face solemn and long, her gaze boring into his.

He sighed, and then sat on the edge of the bed, removing his dusty boots. It was then that he saw the table set for two, with a burner keeping a chafing dish warm. A fragrant candle was almost burned to the nub.

"You waited supper for me?" As she nodded, his stomach growled.

She grinned at him. "I think a little bit of food will do you some good, hmm? You look in need of some nourishment."

He watched as she leaned over the table, uncovering the tray, and fantasized about the well-shaped derriere outlined for his imagination. Sleep might not be the only way to forget his worries for a little while.

As they sat at the small, intimate table and ate the lake fish and fresh garden salad, Kyra asked, "What happened?" He rubbed his thigh. "By the time I got there, the gunman had fled. Most of the men were fine. One or two nicked, but really no problem . . . just Sammy."

He took a bite, forcing the corn bread down. "I organized the men into two groups—one to ask questions in town, the other to track the gunman. No one seems to know anything. I'll need to search harder tomorrow. This has to come to an end, and we can't wait for Delacroix to find us." He massaged his temples. "I was too tired to go on any longer, and with Sammy . . ."

"You poor baby."

He grinned at being referred to as her "baby," but quickly changed the subject. He didn't want to indulge in feeling fussed over. "This fish is delicious. Can't say I've ever eaten here at Lucy's before."

"Rose is a good cook. She taught me a lot this afternoon about how to prepare a pleasing meal."

"Oh, really?" Cliff's gut tightened. It was inevitable Kyra would find out about Rose. Would she understand? He gulped. *Only when south Texas froze over.* Women weren't rational about such things. Why should Kyra be any different?

Kyra picked up a banana and slowly peeled it as she talked. "This is our wedding night."

His heart slammed against his chest. It sure as hell was, now wasn't it?

"Do you like bananas, Cliff?"

Talk about changing the subject.

"Rose said they had a customer who came in this week from the Caribbean and paid them in tropical fruit. They're quite delicious. Here, try one."

She shoved the fruit into his mouth. As he chewed, she continued. "You know, one of my fiancés was fond of bananas. He had them imported regularly."

"Oh, really, and which deadly sin was he?"

"*Gluttony,* of course. His name was Pierre Gourmand, and he *did* love to eat." Kyra peeled her own banana and lightly touched her tongue to the fruit. "He was very sophisticated about what and how he ate. He always instructed me to savor my food, not inhale it as I normally did. For instance, take a banana. He said you must first smell the lush, sweet aroma." She delicately sniffed at the fruit. "Then stroke the silky, hard texture." Again her tongue flicked out, licking up one side and down the other.

Cliff started to feel uncomfortable down below. He had an image of where he'd like that tongue to be besides on the banana.

"Then you must let your mouth experience the whole of the fruit," she said as her lips surrounded the banana, forming an O, sliding up and down. "It's only after allowing all your senses to relish the luscious fruit that you can fully appreciate its delicate, sweet taste."

Lord, he'd explode right out of his pants. Surely she had no idea what she was doing to him. She was too innocent. But there *was* a devilish gleam in her eyes.

Kyra bit off half the banana and swallowed it in one big bite. Cliff resisted an urge to check his chin for drool. Something was going on. She was playing with him, and if he didn't miss his mark, she was blushing underneath her bold facade. What could she and Rose have discussed? His insides knotted in worry and anticipation.

She stood up, circling behind him. He stiffened when her hands massaged his shoulders.

"I know you've had a hard day, and no chance to rest. Why don't you let me ease your body's tension? I'm sure I can help you release a lot of pressure." She pulled his shirt free of his pants, then, releasing a few buttons, drew it over his head.

She was going to seduce him. And there was no way in hell he'd stop her. Her hands felt so good as they worked through his muscles in his shoulder and down his back. Her fingers found a tight knot and began to knead out the resistance.

Despite anticipation, he did indeed feel the stress ease from his body. Her hands were magic. She used her thumbs well to work deep into the source of his aches and weariness. He slumped forward, dropping his head to his arms resting on the table, affording her more access. Her fingers roamed up and down his back and across his shoulders, as his mind wandered into semi-slumber despite his full arousal. Slowly her fingers drifted lower and lower. Then they began to inch around to his front. He was almost asleep when she claimed hold of his shaft and started kneading through his pants. His eyelids flew open.

"Ohh." He groaned as his pelvis involuntarily ground against her hand. "Kyra, do you have any idea what you're doing to me?"

"Making you horny as hell, I hope," she whispered in his ear.

He opened one eye and turned to peer at her behind his shoulder. Her childhood mischievous grin was plastered across her face, but her look was pure woman. And a woman who knew what she wanted and was about get it.

"You've been talking to Rose, haven't you?"

"She has a lot of interesting information to share. Would you like me to demonstrate what an avid pupil I am?"

His lips curved. "I always did enjoy private lessons."

She placed her finger over his mouth, then shut him up even more effectively by straddling his lap and rubbing herself hard against his arousal. She wasn't wearing underclothes! He crushed her to him as his mouth claimed hers in a savage, passionate kiss.

But Kyra wasn't about to let Cliff take the lead in her seductive game. Her fingers worked to release the buttons on his pants as he fumbled with her dress. She had his rod released before he'd bared a breast. She didn't wait. She lifted herself and came down hard, forcing him deep inside her. It was a good thing Rose had convinced her to go without her bloomers.

"Oh, God, Kyra. So hot, so wet."

She lifted herself, moving up and down slowly. Fiercely he finished unbuttoning her bodice, and his mouth clamped down on one nipple. Desire shot through her, and her juices flowed. When Cliff's finger pressed on her button of desire, a strong orgasm released over her in waves. Cliff didn't stop; his mouth moved to her other breast, his teeth gently biting at her nipple, as his fingers prolonged her climax. With Cliff's mouth at her breast, his fingers on her sensitive bud, and his manhood deep inside her, she experienced pure bliss.

"Cliff . . . Cliff, please . . . don't stop." She thrust against him harder.

When her last shudder ceased, he removed his hands from her body and grasped the chair beneath his hips so he could force himself better upward and into her. Kyra reached behind him to wrap her fingers around the chair back to hold herself steady with the force of his moves. Incredibly, she grew aroused again as Cliff grunted and pumped into her. His sweat trickled between her breasts, their musky scent enveloping them. Groaning, he spilled his seed into her. Kyra followed in release.

She collapsed against his chest, recovering her breath. He'd lost as much control as she did, if the pounding of his heart beneath her ear was any indication. She smiled. Yes, Rose was a good teacher and she herself was an even better student.

"I'm surprised this chair didn't collapse." Cliff's words brought her gaze back to his face.

She leaned down and nibbled his ear. "I think they have to buy pretty sturdy furniture here."

A low rumble sounded in his chest. He should move, but couldn't bring himself to separate. Happiness pervaded his being. He couldn't want anything more out of life than to be with this woman always, together, connected in body and soul. He'd never felt as complete as he did right now. Maybe he should tell her. He hesitated . . . his emotions were too new, too strong, too sensitive. Tomorrow was too uncertain.

"Why don't we move over to the bed? You're exhausted." She lifted herself off him, placing a kiss at the corner of his lips.

As they lay in bed, curled up together, arms around each other, Cliff let the blissful contentment of the moment overtake him. Tonight he had peace and Kyra.

Tomorrow was another day.

"Chicken and dumplings, yum." Kyra lifted a wooden spoon, tasting the meal she and Rose were preparing. It was nearly noon and she'd lost count of how many times her thoughts had turned to Cliff. He'd been gone when she'd awakened shortly after dawn.

She turned her thoughts to Grandpère. He would eat with her after he returned from sending her parents a telegram. "Please let him show a little bit of tact for once," she murmured to herself, "and keep some of the details to himself."

"The table's set. I'm going to take a short nap," Rose called out.

"All right, I'll clean up here." Kyra stirred the food one more time, the sumptuous aroma drifting to her nose in a steamy wave of temptation. It hadn't been all that hard to prepare. She pictured Cliff then, at the table in their home. He'd smile and tell her how delicious her meal was, and follow his compliment with a kiss.

A lump in her throat, she stumbled toward the sink, and a whole pitcher of fresh lemonade keeled over the counter, splashing in a yellow gush across her white blouse and blue skirt. "Oooh, that man is liable to turn me into mush!" She mopped up the mess the best she could, and then stared down at her stained clothing.

She'd have to change. She flew up the stairs to her room. After removing her wet garments, she threw on her other blouse and skirt set, then marched down the stairs again.

As she descended, the back door creaked open. All the other ladies had left for the afternoon to do their weekly shopping in a neighboring town. Unsure of whom it could be, she grabbed hold of the banister and fled back to her room. Her heart beat wildly when the intruder climbed the stairs. Could someone know she was here? Where was Horace?

"Now what?" Kyra bit her lip in contemplation, the faint clopping sound of heavy boots coming closer.

She'd have to use the trapdoor on the floor. Frantically, she grabbed her gun off the bureau, and ran to the hatch, flying through it.

Closing the door above her, Kyra held onto the ladder for a moment, listening. The door to her room above clicked open and closed. Horace wouldn't come to her room, and it didn't sound like Cliff. This person shuffled quietly about, the ominous sound of spurs jingling. Definitely not Cliff—she'd never seen him wear the things.

Her throat tight, she hopped off the ladder in the back corner of one of the girls' rooms. Briefly, she noted the double bed and nightstand. Moving toward the door, she gasped. Silly, it was just her own reflection in the ornately carved mirror. Taking a big breath, she reached for the doorknob, but froze in mid-motion. Footsteps in the hall. Someone was coming. Then the hatch above her creaked open.

Kyra swallowed. Where to hide? She eyed the armoire and quickly deposited herself inside, snuggling behind the clothing, as far in the corner as possible. She shifted a folded blanket to cover her feet, and prayed.

Listening intently, she heard the bedroom door screech open. Palms clammy, she didn't breathe. The person entering the bedroom gasped in obvious surprise at the sight of whoever was on the ladder.

"What . . . doing . . . ?"

A conversation ensued, the muffled voices so low she couldn't make them out. She tried hard to understand what they were saying, and the fragments she picked up left her no doubt she and Cliff were the topic under discussion. One was obviously a woman, and the other a man. But who?

". . . men are gone . . . leave . . . Cliff Baldwin . . . this morning . . . Lucky Number Seven . . ." whispered the woman.

". . . the girl . . . hiding . . . you got your money . . ." The man seemed to counterattack, his spurs jingling toward the armoire.

The woman whispered, "Horace coming . . . out of here . . . now."

The jingling spurs receded, the next sound the attic room hatch slamming shut.

Kyra let out a long breath and swiped at the perspiration dripping down her brow. She had to get out of there. From the snippets she'd overheard, the man knew where Cliff had headed. What if he were Yancey?

She had to warn Cliff. It wasn't safe at the brothel any longer. If only she knew where to find Shane or Luke.

Poker! Praise God, Cliff had left the gelding in case of an emergency. She prayed she would reach the ranch in time.

Kicking Blackjack into a gallop, Cliff headed toward Las Almas, his gut coiling hotly. Sammy's condition hadn't improved. The ranch hand still fought for his life, but there was little Cliff could do for him now, and it was time. Time to draw out both Zach Yancey and Jacques Delacroix for a showdown. The sooner the better. He tugged at the cartridge belt he wore across his shoulder, then glanced at his pocket watch.

Damn, he was late. Shane and Luke were waiting for him behind the Rabid Wolf. They had information—and a plan.

He rounded the bend of the trail that hooked around a clump of cottonwoods, and the hair on the back of his neck stood up. It was a sensation he knew well, learned from years of bounty hunting. Someone was coming, and as close as he still was to his ranch, he wasn't taking chances.

He pulled out his Winchester rifle from the saddle scabbard, slapped his horse on the rump after dismounting, and headed for the nearest tree.

His shoulders tense, he held the rifle under one arm and one of his blued Colts in his other hand, both cocked and ready. Whoever it was paused. Then the footsteps resumed, coming his way. As the person approached, Cliff made ready to jump him. Stepping out from behind the tree, he gasped.

Kyra screamed.

Cliff uncocked his weapons and shoved the Colt back in his holster. "What the . . ."

"Cliff!"

"Kyra . . ."

She hurled herself into his arms with a resounding thud. Without taking a breath, she said, "Oh, Cliff, I'm so glad you're all right. I was so worried. I was at Lucy's when a man walked up to my room and I had to go down the trapdoor, and then as I was leaving one of the girls was coming, and I hid in her armoire and . . . and the man who was coming down through the trapdoor ran into her and they were talking . . ."

"Whoa, Kyra! It's all right." She took a couple of breaths and hugged him tighter, if that was possible. Getting a better grip on his rifle, he unwrapped her arms from around him with his free hand and said, "Now, slowly, what happened?"

Kyra's brow furrowed. "I overheard a man. I'm not sure who, but one of Lucy's girls told him that you'd left for the Lucky Number Seven, and they talked about me, too . . . and, well, I knew I had to warn you."

"Shhh. It's all right." He held her to him again, feeling her long shudder straight through to his bones. "Where's Poker?"

"I left him over there"—she pointed toward a clump of trees behind her—"because I thought I heard someone coming."

"Kyra, if you sensed danger, you should have run as fast as you could. Will you ever listen to my advice?"

She shrugged and smiled mischievously. "I suppose I'm not a very good listener."

Cliff shook his head in exasperation, planting a quick kiss on her lips. He pushed away, but she raised her arms to twine around his neck and pulled his mouth down for a more thorough greeting.

He tousled her hair. "Let's go. I'm already late meeting Shane and Luke. We'll figure out where to put you when we see them. Damn. I can't believe someone at Lucy's betrayed us. You couldn't tell who the woman or man was?"

"No. The man wore spurs, that much I know. From the armoire it was hard to distinguish the voices."

Cliff sighed.

A sound.

The click of a gun hammer pulling back. Cliff's experience-sharpened instincts took over. He pushed Kyra behind him as he turned to face their assailant, his chance to draw too late. He'd uncocked his rifle, too. *Goddammit,* he should've been more aware.

Masking his thoughts, he studied the impeccably dressed man before him. Sandy hair, blue eyes, and a mustache, exactly as Kyra had described. Judging by the trembling against his back, it could only be one person. Jacques Delacroix.

He narrowed his eyes at Jacques. It was time.

"Well, well, well," said Jacques nonchalantly. He arched an eyebrow as he tried to peek around Cliff. "Have you, Mr. Baldwin, perchance seen my dearly beloved fiancée?"

Cliff tilted his head to the side, surreptitiously gauging the situation. "Have we met?"

Jacques laughed. "No, but we should have. I've observed you countless times back in New Orleans."

Cliff refused to show his surprise. "Why is that?"

Jacques laughed again. "You mean your dear father never told you? Kyra!" he called out.

Kyra started to move, but Cliff prevented her from reaching his side. He shook his head.

Jacques laughed again. "You mean to keep her hidden, I see." His face twisted to a snarling scowl. "How about a bedtime story? I'll tell you one I was told at the tender age of six." Jacques paced a few steps, his gun aimed steadfastly at Cliff's chest.

"What do you want?" Cliff growled.

"My fiancée . . ."

". . . is *my* wife."

Cliff watched the hatred wash over Jacques' face. His animosity was greater than he'd expected. It was personal—pure hatred, as if he'd despised Cliff for a long time. But that was impossible, wasn't it? He'd heard of Jacques' family, but never met him.

"How interesting," Jacques sneered. "That changes things considerably."

Cliff eyed the surroundings, searching for ways out and possible cover. He had to keep him talking.

"Let Kyra leave, and we can discuss things. This doesn't have to end in bloodshed." He winced at his own words. He'd uttered very similar words to Tommy Yancey.

Clammy moisture covered his palms and upper lip. His head was also beaded with sweat. Something—some dark memory—threatened exposure, flashing in his mind, making him dizzy. Kyra. He had to be strong. She depended on his protection, and he was already failing her. Tommy Yancey's horrified face stalked him . . . and something else. Not now, *please.*

Jacques curled his lip. "No. I could have shut her up by marrying her here, in this godforsaken hole; she couldn't have testified against me then, could she . . . *brother dear?*"

Chapter Twenty-two

Judas Bread: Not what it appears to be, this bread is actually a poison used to bait rat traps.
From the *Sinfully Delicious Bakery Recipe Book*

A blinding, painful flash of light streaked before Cliff's eyes. He worked to keep his gaze as steady and indecipherable as possible. This was bad. What was wrong with him? He'd never faltered in the face of danger, but now his chest felt heavy, and his body wavered. He hoped the bastard didn't notice.

He'd tell Kyra to run while he covered her, even if it meant risking his life. He'd opened his mouth to speak just as Kyra forced her way around him to face her ex-fiancé.

"That's enough, Jacques. Put the gun down. I don't know why you're so determined to come after me. I wanted to break the engagement, but after five fiancés I knew the scandal would be fierce and so I ran. It's as simple as that."

Jacques glared. "And so you ran off to find my lost brother?"

"Why do you keep saying that? Cliff isn't your brother. You've never even met him."

"Paulette Delacroix . . ." Cliff whispered, his legs suddenly weak.

"I'd heard you were smart." Jacques smirked. "You see, Kyra, the whispers are true. I'm not truly a Delacroix. And I've paid for it my whole life, while Cliff had all the things I should've had. My *father* always hated me. He was a cruel man. I never understood until he came to me one night, drunk, and told me the whole sordid story. My mother was from Boston, you know?"

"What are you saying, Jacques?" Kyra sounded shocked.

"I'm saying, darling, that I was conceived in Boston by my *real* father, Clifford U. Baldwin Junior. I'm saying that my real father used her, and she was forced to escape the scandal of Boston society. Only, she made two mistakes—one to marry the first available man without telling him she was enceinte, the other to carry on with Clifford Baldwin again when he transported himself to New Orleans after the war. Who do you think suffered as the scapegoat? Who was beaten for not being my father's son? Me! Who was always threatened with being disowned? Again, me! I hated my mother, I hated my father—both fathers, but I hated Cliff most of all." He stared at Cliff. "I hated you for being legitimate, for living peacefully. I hated you for having the father who ignored me—his son, too. Now you think I'll let you have my fiancée as well? Why, when I can make her a . . . widow?"

Cliff felt his wits return, but he was stunned. It was all becoming clear—the fights between his father and mother over Paulette Delacroix. And his father's illegitimate child. It seemed his *brother* had lived the mirror image of his life. Only, Jacques didn't know it.

Cliff grabbed Kyra's arm and pulled her behind him. He needed to talk some sense to the man.

"Jacques, my life was nothing like you've imagined. My childhood was the same hell you've described. My father, our father, was and probably still is a drunk, only he functioned in society, so people didn't know. I was no stranger to his fists," he added hoarsely. "There's no need to do this. Put the gun down and we can talk."

"You expect me to believe that?" He chuckled sarcastically. "Oh, everyone knew your father had mistresses. Most men do. Otherwise, your family seemed very ordinary."

"Well, I'm sure yours did, too. My family was not ordinary. We just hid it well. My mother made excuses for him, blamed herself for his mistakes, helped him when he should have helped himself, lost her sense of self and dignity, and suffered his fists and cruel tongue. I suffered them, too."

"I don't believe you."

"You don't have to. But why do you think I disappeared from New Orleans? My mother died and there was no more reason for me to stay." He wouldn't tell him he'd been running from himself.

The emotions on Jacques' face were mixed. He seemed confused. Then he scowled. "It's too late now. Kyra is a problem. She witnessed something she shouldn't have, and *I* am not hanging. She decided her fate when she betrayed me with you."

"Why, Jacques? At least tell us why you killed that poor woman," Kyra pleaded.

Jacques arched an eyebrow. "So you admit you were there. That was most unfortunate for you to see."

"Would you have believed me if I'd told you I hadn't been?"

He waved his hand. "No. Your locket had no reason to be where I found it. You'd had it on the evening before, and you hadn't been anywhere near my town house since then, much less my gazebo."

Kyra's eyes watered. She was frightened—for herself and for Cliff. The memory of the poor woman being stabbed to death rose forth in its dark gore. She shuddered. But she also pitied Jacques and the childhood he'd had. It had twisted him because he'd been of a weaker spirit. Unlike Cliff. Cliff was still a good, honorable person. How clear it was to her. Was it clear to him? Would they even survive so she could point it out to him? She felt the weight of her derringer nestled in her pocket. Could she risk it? Did Cliff have a plan? She had to keep Jacques talking.

"Why? Why did you do it?"

"Many reasons. But let's start with my inheritance, *darling*. I had to secure it. My trump card was that in the eyes of society I was a Delacroix. The eldest, too. My father often threatened to leave me out of his will. He said he'd give it to his *real* sons, my younger brothers. But if I could follow in the family tradition and secure my political career, he wouldn't have dared besmirch my name—the family name. I had a goal to follow in my grandfather's footsteps, but Sabina threatened to ruin it for me."

Kyra clutched at Cliff's arm. "Her name was Sabina?"

Jacques smiled wolfishly. "Yes. She was my mistress, my dear. A man has needs, and I couldn't have you until our wedding, now could I?" He eyed Cliff with distaste. "To think I wasted my chivalry so you could whore for my brother."

Cliff lunged forward, but was checked by Kyra's restraining hand on his arm. "Watch your mouth," Cliff said.

Jacques aimed his gun with more precision. "You forget who has the upper hand. *You* are in a precarious position. I still haven't decided. Kill both of you, or just shoot you and make Kyra my wife." It was impossible to miss the longing in his eyes.

"Then hop to it," Cliff said with a growl, his voice menacing. "Take your chances. You can shoot, but I'm fast enough to draw on you while I'm going down. I hope you like lead for dinner."

"Ah, yes. I've heard you've developed quite a reputation indeed. Why, you may have more blood on *your* hands than I do. You're a famous killer, if I'm not mistaken. And you think you're better than me?"

"Shut up!" Cliff snapped.

Kyra froze at the scene unfolding before her. Jacques looked calmly crazed and Cliff was very angry. She'd never seen him so furious or disturbed, even when he'd faced Wade. It worried her.

"Jacques," she called out. "You were telling us about Sabina. Please. Why did you kill her?"

His stare squarely on Cliff, he drawled, "Diplomatic Kyra. You would've been—no—could still be a good politician's wife, with a firm hand, of course."

"I don't need a firm hand."

"Oh, you do. You've always been a little wild, but you do make life exciting. I like that in a woman. I've often wondered if it translates to the bedroom. Sabina was a lot like you in some ways, and she was a fiery piece. But alas, she went too far. She threatened me with her knowledge. She was my mistress for several months, and I made the mistake of telling her about my illegitimacy. Unfortunately, she'd also been playing the whore for Cliff's father."

"My father?" Cliff asked sharply.

Jacques' eyes twinkled. "Ah, yes, I bet you've never experienced the delights of sharing a mistress with your own father, have you, Cliff? I did so—unknowingly. See, I found out Sabina was quite the enterprising slut. After uncovering my illegitimacy, she formed a liaison with *our* father, and during afternoon tea sold my business and political secrets along with her body. Seems he thought he could control me if he knew enough about me. He feared my increasing political power and the retribution I might wager with my knowledge of his shady business dealings. He knew I'd made it my life's work to know his. After all, I loathed him and wanted to bring him down any way I could. Still do."

Kyra was horrified.

Cliff gaped in disbelief. "How did that lead to murdering Sabina?"

"Well, I discovered her leaving your father's one day, reeking of sex. She was a fool to think I wouldn't eventually find her out, especially as your father and I had been neighbors for a while—not by coincidence, of course. So I confronted her. I came to understand where the information in your father's little blackmail notes had been coming from—by way of Sabina's deceitful mouth. I did the only thing I could. I shut her mouth permanently. Unfortunately, in the heat of rage I, too, forgot what close neighbors your father and I are, and that he constantly spied on me. He saw the whole touching scene from his upstairs bedroom window." He sneered at Kyra. "See, darling, you weren't the only witness to my little peccadillo."

Kyra couldn't believe what she was hearing. She was mortified to have played any part in the woman's death. For the first time she almost hated a person. "You, Jacques Delacroix, are a vile man."

"That may be, but you've married an even viler one, I assure you."

Kyra glanced at Cliff, who surveyed their surroundings, all the while keeping an eye on Jacques's gun. She returned her gaze to Jacques. "Cliff is nothing like you. Do you hear? *Nothing.*"

"Oh, I think he's exactly like me. Which is why his father wants him back in New Orleans so badly. It seems Cliff's father needs both his sons under his thumb and in his image. I've been blackmailed to bring Cliff back willingly, or kill him." Jacques sneered and leveled his aim toward Cliff's chest. "I'm betting he's not willing, and I don't want to displease our loving father."

Kyra screamed, "No!" as she pulled Cliff back.

A shot kicked up dust in front of her feet, and another whizzed by her head. Cliff's heavy body threw her down on the ground with a quick roll. Fleetingly, she saw Jacques also hit the dirt. Someone else must be shooting at them, too.

Cliff half dragged and half pushed her ahead. With his body covering hers, they rushed to a large rock that rested on an incline. More dust flew to his left as another bullet hit the ground.

He thrust his rifle into her hands. "Keep your head down, and run for it. Go!" he yelled.

Cliff watched her sprint away, her body low. He followed her, protecting her back. Ducking, he twisted to return fire at their unknown assailants. Once Kyra was safely behind the rock, he lunged to join her, both his Colts barking all the way until they emptied.

He surveyed Kyra for injuries. "Are you all right?"

"Fine." Kyra knelt after handing him his rifle, cocked, and pulled out her parlor gun. "I'm ready," she said.

He shook his head. God, she was something else.

He inched his head over the rock and sucked in his breath at the sight of Zach Yancey joining Jacques behind a tree, some distance away.

Jacques shouted, "I'm not paying you to be stupid. You could have shot me, you imbecile."

"Yeah, well, you were taking your sweet time, and that ain't safe with Baldwin," Yancey coolly replied.

"Well, now he has *more* of a chance, doesn't he?" Jacques rebutted. "Where are the others?"

They stopped yelling, and Cliff couldn't hear the rest. Goddammit, Jacques and Yancey had help, and he was only one man. What to do? It was too much to hope Shane and Luke would come to the rescue again, although it was entirely possible they'd worry when he didn't show up. God, he was going to be sick. When he'd first started bounty hunting he'd suffered from nerves a few times, but he'd hardened. Now they were back. Jacques' story had shaken him.

But most of all, he was scared for Kyra. He couldn't lose her. He'd rather die, and if he got killed, he'd have to hope Jacques would want her to live so he could have her. That would give Shane time to save her if Cliff couldn't. The other gunmen might not care to keep her alive. Jacques was possibly, and ironically, her only chance. Cliff would give the fight of his life, but Jacques was staying alive as long as he himself was . . . just in case. There was also a niggling doubt in his mind. Could he kill Jacques, his own brother, who'd suffered like he had?

Yancey was another story. He wouldn't care who lived or died. That one wanted revenge. Cliff would have to kill him given the chance.

A bullet whizzed by his head, and he ducked before bobbing up to return fire. More shots from the right this time. He aimed his rifle carefully and shot at the head he saw incline forward. One down.

Returning to a crouch, he kept his eyes trained on Jacques' hiding spot, making sure the other man didn't move as he reloaded his Colts. He was surprised when he heard Kyra's derringer go off. He glanced over. "Head low, Kyra. I don't want to lose you." He fired again while Kyra rested against the rock and reloaded. He stooped low as more bullets ricocheted around them. Kyra grabbed hold of his leg, and he flashed his gaze at her.

Her eyes were moist and large. "I *won't* lose you either, do you hear me?"

For a moment he stared at her. Then he winked and proceeded to take aim.

A bloodcurdling scream sounded. "Take that, you son of a bitch," he muttered. "Two down." But there seemed to be yet one more besides Yancey and Jacques.

He glanced over to his left, twenty yards away. Jacques was slithering his way around. Cliff pointed his gun, the sting of sweat dripping into his eyes. Dammit. Couldn't his father have kept his rod in his pants for once? How many ambushes had Cliff been in? And here he was, feeling like a green kid.

He handed Kyra one of his six-shooters, slapping his cartridge belt down between them. "This is better than your derringer. Cover us on your right."

He waited to hear her fire. He wanted her busy so she wouldn't see him shoot Jacques if he ended up having to do that.

Aiming carefully, he shot around Jacques, pushing him back. "Back, son of a bitch, back," he rasped.

Jacques suddenly moved out from behind a tree and jumped into a run before falling onto his haunches, drawing a bead on Cliff.

Cliff aimed his Colt, his shaky finger pressed hard against the trigger. "You don't have to do this," he yelled.

"I do, I do."

Cliff's senses blurred. It was unreal as he stared into Jacques's cold blue eyes—his father's eyes. Jacques squinted in concentration, his finger squeezing on the trigger, and all Cliff could do was feel his own gun hand tremble with indecision. Then an explosion, loud and deafening, immediately followed by another, sounded in his ears, and he rolled. Coming about, he ignored the burning in his leg. Jacques' chest was spread in crimson as he stared incredulously—at Kyra.

"I didn't shoot," Cliff called out before turning to Kyra.

Her smoking gun was pointed at Jacques, the message in her eyes clear. She'd meant to kill him, and would shoot him again if she had to. Dazed, Cliff watched as Jacques teetered on his knees and slumped dead on the ground.

Cliff shook his head to clear it. *Don't think about it.* Yancey was still out there. Shakily, he returned to his post. Kyra was already returning fire.

It seemed like there were two left, Yancey to his left and another man to their right.

"Yancey! Give yourself up," he called out.

"And hang? I'll take my chances, you—"

Shots rang out from different directions. Cliff looked over at Kyra; then together they peered over the rock.

"Paco and your men!" Kyra exclaimed.

And what a gratifying sight they were, running Yancey and his ally out of their cover. Being on horseback, they easily had the two villains cornered and apprehended. Cliff watched, numbness setting in, then rested his forehead on the rock, his hands gripping the surface, granules chipping and showering onto his legs. Jacques and all he'd said flashed through his mind, the pain powerful and complete. His chest squeezed tight and his thigh burned. He was losing control.

Warm breath whispered against his temple. Sweet Kyra.

She embraced Cliff, planting kisses on his head as she held him to her breast. Her eyes misted. Tears fell for Cliff . . . and for Jacques. For what they'd both suffered. She laid her head sideways over Cliff's head, and stared at Jacques' lifeless body. Seeing it wrenched more grief from her heart. She'd had to kill him or risk losing Cliff. Her husband's life had been worth saving, but the pain was still deep.

Cliff stiffened. He lifted his head and clasped his hands around her face, straightening it to view his. "Don't. Don't look at him," he whispered.

Kyra sat on the sofa before the cold fireplace at the Lucky Number Seven, wrapped snuggly in Cliff's quilted robe. Luke and Shane had arrived and had gone to help Paco haul away a wounded Yancey along with the other survivor. Cliff's thigh, as it turned out, had only been grazed. Thank goodness.

She tugged the quilt higher, her hands smelling of gunpowder. Her life had changed irrevocably. The image of Jacques's lifeless body haunted her. With a blinding shot of empathy, she understood Cliff's inner torment, why his need for peace was strong. Her disarrayed emotions left her confused.

Where was Cliff? He'd gone to check on Sammy. She looked at the clock on the mantel. He should be back any minute.

"Kyra?"

She peeked her head over the back of the sofa to find him coming in the door. He limped slightly toward her.

"How's your leg?" she asked.

"It's just a scratch, and you took care of it as well as Shane would have." He slumped in the chair next to her.

"How's Sammy?"

"He's dead."

Kyra stared at him a minute. His eyes were somber, and there was another emotion she couldn't name. Something akin to desperation. "I—I can't tell you how sorry I am." Tears blurred her view, and she bent her head to say a silent prayer for the poor boy's departed soul as her grief doubled.

Silence loomed for a few minutes, except for the sound of the clock over the fireplace, loud and metallic.

"Kyra. I've decided you should go home with Grandpère," Cliff said in a low, empty voice.

She jerked her head up, her heart twisting. "I *am* home."

"No, this is my home."

"You married me. This is my home, too."

"New Orleans is your home."

"My place is with you."

"I don't want you."

Kyra felt the piercing stab straight to her soul. "Cliff, you can't send me away. I need you . . . you need me. I love you."

"You're better off without me. I can barely take care of my ranch and men—let alone you. I don't want you here . . . *I need peace.* Please give it to me."

He didn't look at her as he spoke. Maybe she had a chance. She'd play her last hand. Her voice breaking, she said, "Quinton Green would find all this very humorous. He was number five—*Envy.*"

Cliff sighed deeply, halfheartedly curious where this would lead. "Why? I don't recall him being the jealous sort."

"Well, maybe how one acts with one friend isn't always the same as with another, or a person he's engaged to marry."

"Maybe not. But he had nothing to envy. I'd say he had it all . . . looks, wealth, intellect. Actually, he was a very good catch."

"Oh, I'm still fond of him, but . . . He envied *you* greatly." Her voice cracked again, and his chest tightened.

"I wouldn't know why," he murmured.

Kyra lifted her teary gaze to him and whispered, "No, of course not. You've never seen the truth about yourself. What about *your* looks, wealth, and intellect? He saw all that and more. He may even have seen what I see—a man who's honorable and honest. You dealt with poor circumstances as a child and rose above them to be the good person you are, so concerned for others, so selfless you'd rather live your life alone than risk hurting me. The truth is Quinton thought you had it all, but you don't really, not until you commit to love."

Ah, that was it then—her attempt at checkmate. Only, she didn't understand the unfair ways out a desperate man with high stakes could find.

"Kyra, an honorable man doesn't run away from his troubles. I was a coward when I left New Orleans, plain and simple. I still am . . . and I don't know . . . about love, only what was done to me in the name of it."

"Then you must go back to New Orleans and face your past."

"*That* I will never do."

She leaned forward, her expression daring. "You tell me, Cliff Baldwin, that you don't love me and I'll leave. But you look in my eyes when you do."

He rose to his full height and limped over to her. When he crouched in front of her, his deep blue gaze was steady.

"I care for you, always have. . . ." He paused, then whispered, "I've lusted for you, but I don't love you. I never have."

Straightening, he turned and walked back to his room, the click of his closing door signaling his final move.

Chapter Twenty-three

Mother's Chicken Soup: An old-fashioned comfort food. This medicinal soup may appear simple, but looks can be deceiving.
From the *Sinfully Delicious Bakery Recipe Book*

Kyra stared at the Texas countryside as it raced by outside the train window. It was all a blur to her; she didn't notice anything about the various flowers and trees they passed. Even the longhorns left only a vague impression. Her thoughts were turned inward as she remembered her parting scene with Cliff. A heavy iron pressed on her chest, so great was her pain and fear. She faced the window so the other passengers couldn't see her tears.

Had it only been yesterday since he'd looked her in the eye and told her he didn't love her? It seemed like an eternity. She'd lived in something of a daze since then. Grandpère had taken care of all the arrangements—hiring a wagon to take them to Dallas and getting tickets on the next train. Even now he was off checking to make sure their luggage, what little there was, had been properly stowed. Kyra didn't know what she would've done without him—probably she'd still be in the living room at the Lucky Number Seven, staring at the spot where Cliff had last stood. She hadn't seen him since.

Despite her best efforts, a tear crawled down her cheek. Surreptitiously, she wiped it away. If one of the ladies sitting nearby were to express concern, she'd lose control and weep openly. She much preferred to suffer in silence.

She fingered the black armband she wore in memory of Sammy. It wasn't much, but time and circumstances prevented her from donning more black. With the way she was feeling, a widow's full mourning would be more appropriate.

Her heart couldn't accept Cliff's words that he didn't love her and never had. She couldn't believe his feelings for her were only lust when hers were now, and always had been, so much more. How could he be so cruel? Maybe she was being vindictive, but the shock she'd suffered at having killed a man was nothing compared to the shock and heartache of hearing her husband say he didn't love her. She felt so alone and empty inside. She had gambled on a dangerous game of seduction . . . and lost.

"Hey, there, *ma chère*, what do you find so interesting outside that window?" Grandpère slid into the seat beside her.

"Oh, nothing much. The countryside is interesting. Is everything all right with the luggage?"

"It's locked up as tight as a river captain's liquor cabinet. I'm sorry we couldn't get on a sleeper train, but there wasn't another one due for a couple of days, and you seemed pretty eager to be on the way."

Kyra came out of her self-absorption long enough to notice the lines of worry on his face. "Please forgive me, Grandpère. I hope you're not too uncomfortable, and I'm sorry I haven't been much help. I guess my feelings got hurt . . . just a little."

Grandpère cupped her hand where it rested on their shared armrest and squeezed it affectionately. "My guess is, *chérie*, that your feelings got hurt just a lot. It's hard to think logically when one's emotions have been chewed up raw and spat out hard. Give yourself a couple of days, and you might see things differently. At least that's what your *grandmère* always said when I went storming off mad at her. And I never would've admitted it to her face, but she was always right."

"You miss her a lot, don't you, Grandpère."

"I miss her like I'd miss the salt in my food—always and every day. But she's still living here in my heart," he said with a thump on his chest, "and will be as long as this old pump keeps on pumping.

"You see, Kyra, loving someone isn't just about feeling happy and sharing good times. Loving is about giving until it hurts, keeping on despite the pain, and discerning what lies beneath the surface of your mate even when your own innards are raw and bleeding."

"Yes, but what if he doesn't love you back?"

"That's where the understanding comes in. Give yourself time to cool down a bit before worrying too much about what Cliff said. Your perception is a little too cloudy from pain right now, *n'est-ce pas?* Wait until you can see things clearly, and then maybe you'll understand better why Cliff said what he did."

Kyra nodded to let Grandpère know she understood, even though she wasn't certain she did, then turned back toward the window to rejoin her solitary, melancholy thoughts.

"Kyra! My baby."

She and Grandpère had just walked through the door of her parents' town house, unannounced, when her mother entered the hall. Instant shock washed over her mother's features, replaced by a loud squeal, and the rush of feet as her father came to check out the ruckus. Soon, she was smothered with bear hugs and they were all laughing and talking at once.

"Mama, Papa, I'm so glad to see you both."

"Kyra, where've you been? Why didn't you tell us what happened? Do you know how worried we've been?" Her mother gave her a little shake with each question.

She was shocked to see tears streaming down her mother's face. Never had she seen her mother cry, not even when Grandmère had died. Oh, she knew her mother had cried—but only in private.

"Mama, Papa, I'm so sorry. I didn't mean to frighten you. It's such a long story. Please," she said, taking both her parents' arms in hers, "let's go to the salon and I'll tell you everything."

As they walked arm in arm, her mother glanced over her shoulder at Grandpère, and giving him a fulminating look, indicated he'd better follow and his story had better be good. At the same time she nodded to a waiting maid, requesting tea service.

A couple of hours later, after Kyra's and Grandpère's stories had been told, and all her parents' questions answered, there was finally a moment of silence. Each sat, with tea in their hands, mulling over what had been said. The biggest shock, it seemed, was that Kyra and Cliff had married and that Cliff wasn't with her. Kyra hadn't wanted to explain their parting scene. It was too painful, or perhaps her pride was still too hurt. Instead she'd simply said she'd come home for a visit to reassure her parents. She was formulating a plan, anyhow, that would make this statement true.

"One thing I'm still not clear on, *ma chère*, is exactly where you were married. And was the ceremony properly conducted by a priest?" her mother persisted.

"Oh, Mother, we were married in the most beautiful, charming home with lots of special friends in attendance. The minister was eloquent in his words and desire to see us wed properly. There were flowers everywhere and Grandpère gave me away. And we enjoyed a fine reception afterward." Kyra beamed with her memories.

"What I don't understand"—her mother's quavering voice drew Kyra's gaze—"was why you didn't come to us in the beginning? Why didn't you trust us? Alexandre has been most upset."

"Now, Nicole . . . who spent hours gazing out the window the last few weeks?"

Kyra was startled to see tears back in her mother's eyes. They seemed to threaten her father as well. "Oh, Mama. It wasn't that I didn't trust you. It's just that, well, I guess I was so worried and feeling guilty. I mean, I knew I'd told exaggerated tales to end my previous engagements, and I guess I felt a bit like the boy who cried wolf. I felt *you* didn't trust *me* anymore, and that I didn't deserve to be trusted." She ended on a whisper.

"Kyra, of course we trust you. You could never fool us with your outlandish stories and antics. You've always been a little bit full of a hurricane. We're used to your vivid imagination and rebellious ways."

"You've always reminded me of your mother in that regard," her father said from his seat beside Nicole.

Now Kyra was shocked. "Mama and I remind you of each other? How so?" In her mind she and her mother were two very different creatures.

"You both have the same enthusiasm for living, the same empathy for understanding others—except each other—and most importantly, the same rebellious streak."

"Mama is a rebel?"

"Ohhh, the worst sort of rebel." Grandpère joined in the conversation now, a gleam in his eye. "Why, the stories I could tell you of your mother when she was growing up . . ." His hand told the story instead, rolling around in a sweeping motion, indicating the wild antics of a mother Kyra now saw through new eyes.

"Why do you think she became so concerned with society and propriety? Because it went against everything I'd ever tried to teach her, that's why. She deliberately sought to be the exact opposite of her parents." Grandpère's steely eyes turned from his sputtering daughter to his laughing granddaughter. "Just like you've done yourself."

"Papa, you think you know me so well, but you just might be mistaken," Nicole said. She looked at Kyra. "They're right in many ways. But men must always be so limited in their view of the world. True, I've always been a bit of a rebel. But I didn't choose how I approached life for the sole purpose of thwarting your *grandpère.* I've much more sense than that." She shot him another thunderous look, her arms across her chest and her toe tapping.

"The world I grew up in was not the same as the one you experienced, Kyra. Times have changed a lot since the War. Society is relaxing its standards; the young, and especially young ladies, are so much freer than they were in my day. Women do so many things—some own businesses, some play sports like tennis, many travel alone—why, there's even talk of women getting the right to vote. When I was coming along, a woman's power was limited. My choices were few. A high position in society was the best choice for having power and control over my life"—Nicole paused a moment to pin Kyra with her gaze—"and for making your life better as well. Romping around with your *grandpère*, learning to shoot, play cards, and other such nonsense, might be a lot of fun for a young girl, but it won't get you anywhere as an adult. Believe me, I know. I didn't want you to experience the pain of being ostracized and ridiculed like I was. I wanted you to have your friends *and* your choices."

Kyra'd never before seen, or perhaps noticed, such strong love in her mother's eyes. Unfortunately, she also saw sadness and hurt—hurt that Kyra had never understood her properly.

"Oh, Mama." Kyra crossed over to her mother, took hold of her hands, and knelt in front of her. "I love you. I'm sorry if I haven't said it enough or showed you." Kyra reached for her father's hand as well, and brought both their palms to her lips. "I love you *both* so much. I guess I never realized how lucky I was to have two wonderful parents who loved and supported me. I took you for granted. But I've seen now that not all children are so blessed."

Her father patted her head as her mother squeezed her hand. Finally, Kyra stood and moved a short distance away. "I want to discuss a plan I have with both of you. I've met a few people lately, including Cliff, who weren't as lucky as I. There's a very special woman who lives near Cliff who has a plan to make a better life for herself and a lot of other unfortunate women. I'd like to help her, and I'd like to use my trust to do so. I know Cliff and I have control over it now that we're married. But since your mother left it to me, Mama, I'd like your blessing, *both* of your blessings." She stared at her mother and father beseechingly.

"Tell us your plans first," her ever-practical father requested.

"Las Almas is a rapidly expanding town. It's just a day's ride south of Dallas and is becoming more settled with new ranches starting and families moving into the area. There's a Bakery and Lemonade Café in town that's doing good business. Rose, my friend, is an excellent cook, and I might add I'm getting to be a pretty good chef myself." Kyra was quite pleased with her mother's look of astonishment, even though it was followed by one of doubt. She held up her hand to stave off any questions until she was finished presenting her plan. "I'd like to buy the Café, or start my own, and go into business with Rose. We'll hire any of those unfortunate women who want to work. I think it could make a big difference in their lives . . . and mine as well."

Kyra's father looked fairly surprised. Her mother, however, had pride clearly sketched on her face.

"I'll give you my blessing, Kyra, on one condition," Alexandre said. "I want you to meet with my accountant as well as my lawyer, and accept their help in analyzing your decision and formulating your plans. Is that agreed?"

"Agreed."

"My daughter—business owner and philanthropist. And by marriage to Cliff, now on the Social Register. Oh, Kyra, I couldn't be more proud," her mother exclaimed.

"Well, I guess I had two pretty wonderful examples to follow."

Three days later, Kyra bustled down the sidewalk of the Vieux Carré on her way back to her parents' town house. The sun shone brightly on the white-washed building she passed, glistening off the wrought iron balcony rail. An aroma of spiced seafood tantalized her nose as she passed an open doorway, and the lively sounds of a Cajun guitar quickened her pace.

Her heart felt lighter and she was pleased with herself. She'd just concluded her third and final meeting with her father's lawyer and accountant. Her plans were made, approved, and the money was ready. All she had to do now was go back to Las Almas and make the offer to purchase the Café.

She paused when she saw a black-haired kitten playing in the alley with its brothers and sisters. He reminded her so much of Bayou Kitty, which brought Cliff's image fresh to her mind. Grandpère had been right, of course. After the pain and betrayal caused by Cliff's hurtful words had lessened, she'd been able to think rationally about what had occurred. She could now understand Cliff's motives. Once again, he'd been protecting her. Any hope that had remained after their violent encounter with Jacques had crumbled with Sammy's death. He'd resolved to send her away before she—or he—could *really* be hurt. And he'd known that the only way to force her to leave his side was to deny his love and hurt her intolerably.

It had worked.

But it wouldn't work for long. She'd spend a few more days with her parents, leisurely pack her belongings, and say good-bye to a few friends. Then she'd be back on the train to Dallas. Kyra would stay in Las Almas long enough to put her plan into action before riding out to the ranch to confront Cliff. A big grin split her face as she fantasized about the surprise she was sure to cause him—until she remembered the last time she'd surprised him.

Shaking herself out of her reverie, Kyra continued down the sidewalk, a skip in her step. As she walked in the front door of the town house, she savored the aroma of the chicken soup she and her mother had prepared earlier in the day. Smiling, she noticed a letter lying in the silver tray on the parlor table. Her heart quickened. Could it be from Cliff? No, she saw as she picked it up—it was from Rose Evans. Now that was curious. Evans. She'd never asked Rose's family name.

Surprised Rose would write her, especially so promptly, Kyra tore open the letter.

Dear Miss Lourdes, I mean Mrs. Baldwin,

I know you're surprised to be getting a letter from me. Actually Paco is writing this down, as I never did learn how to spell. But I thought you should know what happened after you left.

Cliff came to Madam Lucy's after talking with the sheriff. He stormed into the house madder than a saint in hell. He was determined to find out who'd betrayed you. He questioned all the girls and searched through the house high and low.

Lucy was gone. Her room was in a shambles, clothes thrown all over the place.

Cliff found a letter from her father-in-law's lawyer. None of us knew it, but it seems that Lucy never owned this house. It belonged to her father-in-law, and he died over a month ago. The letter concerned his will. Old Man Tupper blasted Lucy in his will for turning his son's home into a brothel, and he disinherited her.

We found out later that Lucy had emptied her bank account and taken a stage out west. Don't know where she went.

I know it was a rotten thing she did betraying you and all, but I still feel sorry for her. I hope that doesn't make you mad at me. But I can kind of understand what she was going through. The lawyer's letter threatened all sorts of legal things for the kind of business she'd been doing in her father-in-law's house. She had nothing left and I guess she was desperate and scared. So she sold information for money and ran. But I'm still thankful to her for all she did for me and the other girls.

I know this may be none of my business, but I saw Cliff yesterday in town. He really looked sad. I don't know what happened between you and why you left, but if I know men, and I think I do, that man sure isn't happy that you're gone.

I'm not sure what I'm going to do now. I don't have enough money yet to do the plan I talked to you about. We girls figure we've got a couple of weeks before that lawyer shows up here causing trouble. So we're going to run the place ourselves while we can and try to save enough money to buy our tickets to the next town and the next brothel. . . .

Kyra skimmed the closing remarks of the letter. A couple of weeks . . . actually she probably only had a few days. She needed to finish packing. She wanted to get back before any of the girls left town, especially Rose.

Chapter Twenty-four

> **Sinfully Deviled Egg:** This hard-boiled egg has a golden core that is scrumptiously delicious. No other recipe will do.
> From the *Sinfully Delicious Bakery Recipe Book*

Had it only been a week since she'd left?

"Whoa." Cliff patted a lathered Blackjack on the nose. "Sorry, boy. I'm restless and working you too hard."

Waving to Paco, he sent the horse for a rubdown.

On the way to the house he saw Mr. Pip in the corral, bringing a somber smile to his lips. He detoured toward the mule.

"Hey, Mr. Pip." His chest tightened at the thought of Kyra. He missed her. Every day he'd imagined her in New Orleans; she'd be walking down the Vieux Carré at that moment, or riding her favorite mare across the rolling hills of Belle Celine.

The nights were the worst. He'd lie awake aching for her, dying to reach for her, but his bed was empty, desolate, and bigger than it had ever been. He'd never even shared it with her, and he regretted not having made love to her in his own home.

God, how he wanted her—he'd never imagined he could want a woman so much.

He patted Mr. Pip's neck. "You know, I kind of like your name now. It suits you," he murmured.

One final pat and he headed toward his bleak and empty house. The only warmth in the whole place came from a damn nightdress she'd probably left behind on purpose to torment him. Every night he'd hold it to his nose like a lovesick fool, searching for her scent. It had almost faded now.

Maybe in the morning he'd seek out Shane over at Luke's rented cabin where he'd been helping Luke with some sort of project. He needed a distraction.

He finally had his peaceful ranch, but his prize had lost its value.

As he neared the steps to the house, he saw Emilio playing with Bayou Kitty. The black armband around the boy's well-worn sleeve reminded him of the matching ones he and all his men wore in memory of Sammy.

"*Hola,* Señor Baldwin. *Como está usted?*" Deep brown eyes questioned him.

"I'm fine, Emilio. How about you?" Cliff spoke in English as Paco had been after the boy to practice the language more.

"Señor Baldwin, is it true Señor Sammy is playing with angels now? That's what Miss Rose say to me yesterday when she brought some *sopa de pollo* to the chow hall."

He took a deep breath. "Yes, I'm sure Sammy is making those angels laugh just like he did you."

Emilio's eyes turned browner as they looked away from him. "Señor Baldwin, the preacher man say we go to hell if we don't tell the truth. Do you think he be right?"

"No, I think God will forgive you. But he'll want you to tell the truth as well."

"Well . . . I didn't say truth. I knew Papa be mad at me because I wasn't listening, *again,* but it's my fault Señor Sammy got killed." His bottom lip quivered.

Cliff's gut wrenched in empathy. He crouched before him, bringing him eye-level with the boy. "What happened?"

"Papa told me to stay inside, to keep door locked, but I wanted to see what a 'devil bastard' looked like. So I snuck out and hid behind the wagon. Señor Sammy saw me and ran to me. Those bad guys shoot at us, but he took me back to our cabin. He was shot after he shut my door."

Cliff opened his arms, and hugged Emilio tight as the little boy sobbed all over his shirt. "Listen to me, Emilio. It's not your fault Mr. Sammy got killed. Now, I'm not saying it's all right that you didn't listen to your papa. But it's not your fault. Those evil men alone are responsible for killing Mr. Sammy."

"Señor Sammy is a hero, no?" Emilio's eyes filled with hope.

Cliff nodded. "Mr. Sammy's a hero. And I'm sure what will make him most happy is to see you do the best with the life he saved."

"He like you Señor Baldwin, no? My Papa say you're a hero. You took care of those bad brothers that killed Mama and little Evita. And you protected us when they came again."

Cliff broke out in a cold sweat under the hot Texas sun. Out of the mouths of babes. Him, a hero. Hell.

Cliff vaulted off Blackjack in front of Luke's cabin. Spotting Luke sitting under a tree, he ambled closer. Luke's legs were crossed, his eyes closed, and his breathing deep. Cliff stopped short, and waited to be acknowledged. Feeling awkward, he debated leaving.

Eyes still closed, Luke asked, "What brings you here, Cliff?"

"How did you know it was me?" Cliff arched his eyebrows.

Luke smiled. "The way a blind person would. I recognized the sound of your steps and your scent."

"That's . . . disconcerting."

Luke opened his eyes and grinned. "I had two great teachers during my time in Asia. They taught me that sometimes the enemy can't be seen and one must use his other senses to find him."

"Sounds difficult."

"With training and time it becomes second nature. So

long as your enemy isn't yourself." Luke's gaze was intense. "That one isn't only the hardest to see, but the hardest to defeat."

Cliff nodded, uncomfortable, then ran his gaze toward the cabin. "I'm looking for Shane. Thought he was helping you out."

"He is. He's out back. Go on, and I'll join you in another minute."

Cliff nodded again and walked around behind the cabin. He found Shane sitting on a stool, carving on an odd length of wood while he studied a map at his moccasined feet.

"Cliff," Shane acknowledged.

Cliff hooked his hands in his pants pockets and kicked at a loose rock. He watched it fly into a clump of bushes.

Shane set his carving aside, folded his arms, and leaned back against the cabin wall. "Anything new at the ranch?"

Cliff exhaled through pursed lips. "Yeah, Mr. Pip's been ornery, breaking out from the corral and getting into the garden. Bayou Kitty has caught onto bird- and mice-hunting and leaves presents at my doorstep." Cliff shrugged. "That's about it."

Shane chuckled. "You've got it bad, Baldwin. Don't you think it's time you went after her?"

Cliff scowled at him. "You and Luke are uncanny."

Shane smiled wider. "You made a mistake. If I were you I'd be on the first train to Louisiana in the morning."

"I don't want to go back there."

"Another mistake."

Cliff was startled. "How so?"

"You need to return and face those things that made you run in the first place. Your perspective may have changed after all these years, and you may find the peace you're seeking."

"Easy for you to say."

"Not so. I've also run from my obligations. After I finish helping Luke, I plan to go claim a wife."

Cliff choked. "You what?"

"You heard me. A wife. Like you, I once didn't see things clearly."

"Kat?"

"Kat."

"Will she be expecting this?"

"No. But she'll get used to it. I hope she will anyway."

Cliff grinned. "Should I feel sorry for you or for her?"

Shane drew a feral smile. "Her."

"I don't know if I can face my past." Cliff shrugged.

Shane stood, stepping closer to him, and rested a hand on Cliff's shoulder. "Let me help you. Right now, she's there . . . alone. She's living the life she had before coming here, going to those fancy parties and all, meeting people, in particular men who find her attractive, and vulnerable . . . and alone."

Cliff scowled and said, "All right, all right. I just hope I don't regret it."

Shane sighed. "Cliff, there's no sense fighting destiny. It'll come whether you like it or not. You can try to fight it or you can mold it to your needs."

"I'll leave tomorrow."

"Good. That's some woman you've got. If you didn't go after her, I'd have to think about hunting her down for myself."

"Only if you have a death wish."

It had been one hour since he'd stepped off the train in New Orleans. Amazing how it appeared as though he'd never left. All the buildings were the same, the shops, and even some of the street vendors he'd known since he was a child. Cliff breathed in a gulp of New Orleans' thick and sticky air. Yeah . . . the smell and taste was pure Mississippi River.

He found the nearest livery stable and rented a horse. Too many years in Texas. Riding in carriages had always felt confining to his long legs.

Thirty minutes later, he rode a gray gelding, trotting among the hustle and bustle of New Orleans. In some ways it felt good to be back. Very little had changed, he noted again as he passed an open market. Memories flooded his mind, and in many he found Kyra, the young girl who'd shared in his mischief on these same streets.

Would she still love him? Maybe she'd realized it was her good fortune that he'd sent her back—that he'd been right and her life was better without him in it. He bit his lip. He'd find out soon enough, but first things first.

Shane had been right. He needed to face his ghosts. He had to go back to Belle Époque, to his mother's bedroom, and finally, he had to see his father again. It would be hard, but maybe he'd be a better man for it. A better man for Kyra.

Leaving the city behind, he guided his horse into a canter, occasionally slowing down around jutting roots that extended like long fingers from the rich dark soil. Large deciduous trees formed thick nests hugging the trail that led to his father's plantation. The shade was welcome as the humidity was thick and stagnant in the city he'd recently left.

As he neared the old plantation, his heart beat faster and his stomach churned with anticipation. He passed the big magnolia Kyra used to head for when she'd visit, forever trying to hide from him or climb it. In some ways it seemed the tree had grown with her. His gaze clung to it until he had a crick in his neck, the forgotten memory of a thirteen-year-old Kyra seeking solace under that tree one hot summer day resurfacing. Was it still there?

Pulling his horse to a halt, he dismounted and cautiously stepped under the umbrella of the tree's large waxy leaves. He found the spot on the trunk where Kyra'd etched her secret as a young infatuated girl. His blood rushed at the sight. It was still there: KDL loves CUB. He'd ignored it then. Now he wouldn't. He traced the carving. It felt smooth . . . and good. Maybe Shane was right and there was such a thing as destiny.

But destiny could be created—or at least manipulated. Yes, maybe some cards were stacked against a person from birth, but what one made of those cards was one's own choice. They could become either a castle or a prison. He'd always thought that to love was to lose. But perhaps love wasn't always a losing proposition; perhaps it could be the ultimate victory.

Vaulting on his horse, he galloped the last stretch to the main house.

Belle Époque. The large white columns against the brick exterior seemed omnipotent in their presentation—timelessly elegant and bright. Its beauty warmed the coldness that had settled inside him at the dark memories surfacing in his mind. In some ways, he loved this place, although he'd come to prefer the wide-open spaces and simplicity of Las Almas.

Anxiously, he dismounted his horse and slowly climbed the front steps to the large wooden door. He grabbed hold of the brass handle and banged it against the brass plate beneath.

A minute later, his father's majordomo, Richard, opened the door, a little grayer than Cliff remembered, but otherwise the same. Richard had followed their family all the way from Boston, and had known Cliff all his life. He eyed Cliff, from the top of his hat to his cowboy boots, a confused expression on his face.

"May I help you?"

Cliff removed his hat, fingered back his hair, and said, "Hello, Richard, it's me."

The majordomo's eyes bulged. "My God! It can't be."

"It's good to see you." Cliff clasped his hand and stepped inside, taking in the opulent foyer and the staircase with the many oil paintings that hung on golden wallpaper. Extensive, plush Persian rugs still covered the floor. His father may have been a drunk, but he'd still managed to maintain his desired way of life. He'd also had a lot of help from his very capable and trustworthy accountant and attorney.

"Lord! Are you back in New Orleans to stay?" Richard continued to peruse Cliff from head to toe. "Where've you been, and why are you dressed this way?"

Cliff grinned. "I've been living in Texas."

"Oh, my, Texas." He smiled. "You look well. It must suit you."

"Thank you." Cliff turned serious. "Is my father in residence or is he in the city?"

"Yes, he's in the study, in a bit of a mood, if you know what I mean. He's not been well. The doctors say it's his liver."

"I see. If you don't mind, I'd like to go up to Mother's bedroom before seeing him."

"As far as I'm concerned, this is still your home."

"Yes. Thank you."

Cliff started up the stairs and paused. "Richard, why have you stayed here all these years?"

Richard shrugged. "At first it was to serve your mother, God rest her soul. Such a gentle lady with a good heart. After she left us, I didn't feel the need at my age to move on."

Cliff nodded, his throat tight. Lifting his gaze to the landing above, he climbed the stairs as though he'd never left. That was what it felt like. A few more steps forward, last door to the right. Mother's room.

He stood there a while, imagining her inside waiting for him. Shuddering with a cold sensation, he turned the knob. The door creaked ominously when he opened it. The room was dark and musty. It reminded him of those times before she'd died when he'd find her still in bed, in the dark, unwilling or unable to rise. He moved to the green velvet drapes and forced them open. That was what he should have done then, and he was doing it now. His last memory would be of light and love.

When he turned to study the room, the sunshine that filtered through the glass panes highlighted the eighteenth-century furniture pieces his mother had loved so much. His gaze drifted to the mahogany writing desk on which she'd spent many hours penning stories, poems, as well as letters. Eyeing the bed, he recalled how she'd become sick with melancholy, and with the aid of laudanum, had drifted away from all she'd loved, including him.

Ignoring the pain of seeing her bed, he concentrated on the desk again. It evoked pleasant remembrances at least. Maybe he'd find some of her writings. A warmth flooded his chest—he could bring them back with him to Las Almas to share with Kyra and eventually his children.

When he finally rifled through the drawers, relief poured through him. Her things had been left untouched. He pulled out several of her papers and leafed through them, pain sawing through his heart, overwhelming, yet joyous as well. He had something concrete to remember her by, something to hold onto and pass on. He couldn't wait to share them with Kyra. His heart beat with wary hope. *God, please let her want me still.*

He opened the lower right drawer and beneath an empty bottle of laudanum, he spotted his mother's well-read Bible. It was black with a cross etched on the hard leather cover, the pages gold-leafed and delicate. He thumbed through it, and a piece of paper glided toward the floor.

Bending to pick it up, he saw it was a letter . . . for him.

May 31, 1873
My Dearest Son,
If you are reading this, then I have finally left this earth . . .

Cliff looked up toward the ceiling, gulping for air. His mother had left a letter. She'd said good-bye. He choked down the emotion threatening eruption and continued:

How I have missed you since you left for the University, and how proud I have been to have you for my son. I hope you can forgive me for having brought you into a world that was often unfair, and sadder than a boy's life should ever be. Please forgive me for not having had the fortitude to alleviate the pain you had to suffer. I have often been too involved in my own trials and tribulations, fighting the darkness that has often threatened to encompass my entire being. I am so tired and so very desperate with the drowning feeling of defeat. My only consolation is to dream of the bright life you will lead after I am gone.

You are a very special young man with a gift. You have lived a childhood no one would want, and yet you have grown to be the decent, honorable young man that you are. How I wish I could see your life unfold. I know that it will be wonderful and that you will make it so.

Please do not be saddened by my leaving, darling. I have suffered long enough, and now is my time for peace. Just be sure to do one thing for me—always live your life to the fullest. Live the life I should have had, and dreamed. Give my life meaning by making the most of yours. And always remember that I love you.

Forever,
Mother

With a shuddering breath, Cliff placed the letter against his heart and spoke. "Thank you, Mother. I know you're here and wanted me to find this."

With that, he placed the letter along with the other treasures he'd found, and holding them, walked out the door. He passed his bedroom. Should he look in? No, that room held nothing for him now. It was time to face his father.

Descending the stairs two at a time, he headed toward his father's study, his steps faltering as he approached the door. He set his mother's things on a hallway table and knocked.

"What is it?" his father bellowed.

Cliff pushed open the door and softly crossed the thick Turkish carpet. He sought out his father behind the desk. Dressed in a heavy black sweater, a look of disbelief on his face, his father stared at him. The older man was thinner than Cliff remembered and bore a yellowish hue to his skin. He was sick, and yet the evidence he still drank was present in the many decanters and snifters that lined a service cart near the window.

His father stood then, speechless, bloodshot eyes bulging. Cliff took in the protruding bloated stomach that marked the man's disease. He glanced away, the strong smell of cigar drawing his gaze to the curling smoke from the Tiffany ashtray.

"Hello, Father." Cliff looked back as his father reached out.

"Cliff . . ."

Regret seemed to flit across his father's features for a moment, and then was gone, the unreadable wall in place as always.

For a moment, the familiar sense of hope had clutched his insides—the same feeling he'd always experienced at any morsel of kindness or emotion his father might display. As usual, it was followed by the plummeting sensation of dashed dreams.

His father sat back down, leaning forward a little and rubbing at his arms. August in New Orleans was hot, but he seemed cold. It had to be his illness. Pity curled in Cliff's belly, but he ignored it, heading for the window. Only this man could bring on so much emotional distress. Life in his father's presence had been like a wave that never calmed. It reached the shore only to roll back into another larger wave, the crash of devastation wider.

"I hear you haven't been well," Cliff said, pulling back a curtain to peer outside, his aim to display a calm facade.

"Is that why you came back? Or are you here for my money?"

Cliff shoved the drape closed, whirling around. "No. I didn't know you were sick, and I don't care about your money."

Hands shaking, his father reached for his snifter. "Would you like a drink?"

Cliff froze, completely silent.

"I don't drink."

His father snickered. "No, of course not. You always did think you were perfect and had all the answers. You and your mother . . . so alike. She used to think she could tell me what I should and shouldn't do, shoving her better judgment down my throat."

"If that's how you see it." Cliff shrugged. "Maybe she just cared about you and the family."

His father leaned forward, shouting, "You can get off your high horse. Do you think I haven't hired informants on my only heir? I have it on good authority that you're no better than I am. Last I heard, you were nothing but a killer." Then, as if the thought had suddenly occurred to him. "You're not here to kill me, are you?"

Placing his hands widely on the desk, Cliff leaned in, his father forced backward. "No. You'd like it if I were just like you, wouldn't you? Would it make you feel justified in being as you are?" He couldn't stop the sneer that curled his lip.

"I had no choice," his father said.

"Ah, but you did." Cliff could see clearly now. The moment he'd been most like his father was when he'd sent Kyra away—when he'd shut himself off to love. He wouldn't let his father win.

He'd thought to confront his father regarding what he'd sent Jacques to do, but he wouldn't. He wouldn't even tell him Jacques was dead. He didn't care about anything but his drink anyway.

Stepping back, Cliff couldn't help but add, "A small part of me hoped, as unforgivable as I find the things you've done, that perhaps you'd met with an epiphany of sorts. But even now, as sick as you are . . ." Cliff slapped his thigh and whispered, "I see that you're hopeless. But know this—it ends here . . . with *me.* My children will *not* inherit the family curse."

Clifford U. Baldwin Junior narrowed his eyes. "You leave here again and I'll disinherit you."

Cliff looked up at the ceiling with a tired chuckle, then stared back at his father. "Father, I have riches beyond compare, and they have nothing to do with money. I have someone who loves me and wants to share her life with me. I have my own ranch, which I worked for and built with men who are loyal to me. All you have is whiskey to keep you warm at night. You want to disinherit me? Fine." Bringing his face to within an inch of his father's, he succinctly said, "I don't give a shit." With that, he turned, walked out the door, grabbed his mother's things, and left.

His heart hammering an erratic tempo, he'd managed to get back on the main road toward the city. All these years he'd fought a battle within himself, only to realize how much time he'd wasted. He was nothing like his father. Somehow he could see it now. Kyra had been right. Why hadn't he listened?

Sweet Kyra. Where to find her? Most likely, her family would be in the city by now. It was almost fall, after all. *God, please let her want me still.*

Dressed in a deep-purple diaphanous evening gown, Kyra couldn't help but tap her foot with boredom. She'd disliked the idea of spending a stuffy evening at Laetitia Gressin's annual "end of summer" party, but Laetitia was a dear friend of the family and would've been offended had Kyra not attended. At least it was nice to see some old friends before returning to Texas.

Thoughts of Cliff intruded as usual. How she missed him. She grinned. What would he say when he saw that she'd returned and had no intention of leaving? *Just let him try to make me go.* Crossing her arms over her chest, she tapped her foot furiously.

Her view of the crème de la crème of New Orleans society was suddenly obstructed by Laetitia's older brother, Kristoffe—a handsome blond man with blue eyes, dressed in black tie. He wished to dance, and she accepted. After a few twirls around the dance floor, she thanked him and gracefully slipped toward the punch bowl and the food.

While she enjoyed her refreshments, she found herself chatting amicably with some of her finishing-school friends. They, of course, all wanted to know the details of her new husband, Cliff Baldwin.

One of the young women, Dora, tugged on her arm, begging her to tell them why Cliff had left all those years ago with no word. Examining each of her girlfriends' faces, she saw how eager they were for gossip. She wasn't sure how to respond, but then didn't have to. The room buzzed suddenly with the sound that only quiet speculation could make. Curious, she stretched her neck to see what the commotion was about.

Another girlfriend, Evelyn, grasped her arm. "My Lord, Kyra," she whispered, "Who is *that?*"

"He couldn't possibly have been invited, dressed as he is," chimed another one in dismay.

A painfully thin Clarice, Kyra's school bench-mate and still unmarried, moved beside her, a dazed look on her face. "I must be dreaming. A real cowboy, looking dangerously rugged . . . and coming this way. My mother would swoon."

"Yes, Clarice, he's quite something else," Kyra whispered.

She was dazzled. He'd come all the way to New Orleans, in his "Texas male uniform," looking very tall, dark, and . . . good enough to eat. Halfway across the great room, he removed his hat, which had been tilted over his eye, as he swaggered toward her. Kyra gulped. He was coming for her, his eyes possessive and shining with . . . love. She wanted to shout her joy for the entire world to hear, but she waited. She'd see what he had to say.

The group around her dissipated, mouths gaped open. Evelyn gripped her arm again. "Kyra, let's leave before he approaches us. He surely can't be respectable."

Kyra pulled her arm from the woman's grasp. "No, Evelyn. My *husband* has come for me, and I intend to stay right where I am. I'm about to collect my winnings." She ignored the chorus of gasps, and crossed her arms.

As Cliff reached her, her heart pounded with anticipation. Had he realized he loved her? She could see the dark emotion in his blue eyes, and his appeal for forgiveness was written on his face when he stopped solidly in front of her, his head cocked. He reached out then and took hold of her hand, raising it to his mouth, his lips lingering.

Kyra gave him a cocky smile and whirled, pulling on his hand to drag him to the veranda. The buzz of commotion raised an octave higher with the drama unfolding. She didn't care.

Once outside, she let go of his hand and leaned against the balustrade, the familiar music of the trickling fountain below soothing her racing heart. It struck her then that this was the same place where Cliff had kissed her seven years ago before walking out of her life. It had come full circle. A serene smile on her lips, she sought his gaze. He observed her with so much hope in his eyes, it made her heart skip a beat. She waited.

Cliff hitched his thumbs into his pants and stared at the magnolia behind them. "Mr. Pip and Bayou Kitty missed you."

"They did?"

"Yes." His gaze was intense.

"Well, in a few days I would've seen them when I returned."

"When you . . . what?"

"I'd already planned to return once I signed my trust papers."

"You did?"

"Yes."

Cliff drew a long breath. "I see." He shrugged nervously and said, "I went over to Belle Époque today."

"You did?" Her eyes widened.

He smiled. "Yes. I-I'm nothing like him, Kyra. And I'm nothing like Jacques was either."

Kyra's eyes watered, and she swallowed hard. "No, you're not."

"I was wrong to send you away."

"Yes. Well, I wasn't obeying."

Cliff chuckled huskily. "I guess not. Does that mean you still want me?"

She pursed her lips in feigned contemplation. "Perhaps. I don't know. It depends on you."

"In what way?"

She cocked her head to the side. "Do you remember the last time we were right here?"

"Yes," he whispered. "You were the most beautiful vision I'd seen all evening."

Kyra reached toward the overhanging branch of the magnolia, and plucked a large waxy leaf. She dangled it over her head. "It isn't mistletoe, but I'll pretend if you will. Do it right this time, won't you?"

Cliff exhaled a pent-up breath and grinned as he closed in on her, his arms bracing behind her on the balcony. "I can see I've married a bossy bit of goods," he said with a growl low in his throat.

"I've told you repeatedly that I'm always one step ahead of you . . . and my bets are good."

"You've definitely won this round."

She leaned up toward his lips, a hairbreadth away. "You may be holding three of a kind, but I've always got a full house. Don't you forget it, Bayou Baldwin."

Then gently, softly, thoroughly, he kissed her. She leaned into him, enjoying the feel of his arms around her once more, inhaling his familiar earthy scent. A moment passed, and he deepened the kiss, his hunger for her evident as he pressed against her belly. It excited her, reminded her he was hers.

Breaking their kiss, he tucked her head under his chin, as they both waited for their breathing to resume a more even tempo.

He kissed the top of her head. "I want you so much—"

"Oh, Cliff, I can't wait to have babies," she said with a laugh.

He clutched her tighter, chuckling softly. "Don't worry. We'll get busy tonight."

"Promise?"

He smiled lazily, eyes twinkling. "You can bet on it."

She returned the lazy smile. "Have I ever told you about my seventh fiancé?"

"No, which one was he?"

She gave him an impish grin. *"Lust."*

"Hmm. Did he not suit either?" He showered her face with kisses.

"No. He suited just fine—"

He placed a finger on her lips. "Shh. I know how it ends."

"How?"

"He lusted for you, convinced himself that was all he could feel or let you know. But the truth was that he loved you. He'd loved you in pigtails," Cliff said, raking his hand through her loose curls, "and he loved you when you carved that silly message on his magnolia tree, and when you stood here, seven years ago, in your high heels trying to impress him. But most of all, he loved you when you walked into a Texas brothel and turned his cold life into something warm and full of hope." He grazed her face lovingly with his knuckles. "I love you, Kyra Dawson Lourdes Baldwin . . . and I always will."

Epilogue

Christmas Eve 1880
Las Almas Perdidas, Texas
Sinfully Delicious Bakery and Restaurant

Fresh aromas of gingerbread, apple cider, and roasting chestnuts filled the air as the revelers joined together in yet another Christmas carol, "God Rest Ye Merry Gentlemen." The proud partners of the restaurant, Kyra and Rose, had called all their friends together for a good old-fashioned evening of carols and refreshments. The restaurant was decorated in green holly and cedar, with red ribbons around the table legs and red candles casting a charming glow.

As they started in on "Good King Wenceslas," Kyra slipped out to the kitchen, returning with a huge tray of mincemeat tarts—her specialty.

"I thought I told you not to lift anything heavier than a loaf of bread," Cliff said behind her as he reached to take the heavy tray out of her hands. His shiny new deputy's badge reflected the candlelight.

Sheriff Overby had pleaded for help, saying Cliff was the perfect choice to preserve the peace—even if it was only part-time. Cliff could spare some time from the ranch as his men had everything running smoothly.

"You've got to be more careful now that you're carrying my son." Cliff brought her attention back to his stern face.

"Your daughter, don't you mean," Kyra shot back as she made a face at him. Really, the man was being quite obnoxious about it all.

Kyra blushed whenever any of her waitresses, all former ladies of Lucy's, teased about the speed with which she had gotten pregnant. But Cliff just grinned and boasted about how he'd always been quick with a gun. He delighted in embarrassing her. She was already into her fourth month and growing round.

She gazed at the crowd, warmth filling her inside. Although a few of the town "matrons" had boycotted the restaurant to show their disdain for her employees, most people had accepted them enthusiastically as the food was superior.

"You know, Kyra," Luke said, claiming her attention, "I got to observe some unusual birthing rituals during my travels in the Far East. In one community the mothers actually give birth to their babies while sitting in a tub so the child is delivered into the environment it's most accustomed to—water. I'd be happy to help with your birthing if you'd like to try it."

Kyra was horrified; she didn't know what to say. Grinning, Luke winked at her.

"No, no. If anyone's going to help with the birthing, it's going to be me." Shane roughly pushed Luke aside as he crowded in on Kyra. "My mother told me all about delivering babies from the time I was little. We'll rig up a thing for you to hold onto and you can give birth standing up. I promise you it's a lot easier and more effective."

Kyra's feeling of horror changed to one of dread.

"No, no, *Señor.*" Paco squeezed into the crowd now gathered around Kyra, dragging Rose behind him. "I have delivered many a foal and calf and know just what to do. I'll help—"

Rose elbowed him in the side, grimacing at her fiancé. "None of you men are going to be anywhere near Kyra when the time comes. That's women's work. *I'll* be her midwife."

Laughingly, Cliff pulled Kyra away from the group as they argued amongst themselves as to who'd help deliver the baby and with what approach. "Come with me, I have a surprise for you," Cliff whispered into her ear. As they left, he grabbed an orange from the basket of Christmas fruit Kyra'd set on the counter.

Outside in the cool December air, he tugged her into his arms, kissing her tenderly. "Have I told you yet today how much I love you?" He wore that disarming half grin, which she loved so much.

"Let me see, I think you might have. Yes, I'm sure you did. Right after you finished sending a *message* to the baby."

"Well, I want him to get to know his father as soon as possible. I can't get much closer to him than that at the moment, can I?"

Kyra chuckled. "I guess not, but do you have to communicate with him so frequently?"

"Listen, I think they've settled the argument," Cliff cocked his head as the partyers inside joined in "Silent Night." "Do you want to go back in?"

Kyra shook her head. "I'd rather go on home with you. Let Rose and Geraldine clean up."

Cliff tucked her arm under his and together they walked to their wagon. Looking up at the vast, clear Texas sky, Kyra saw a light streak across the heavens. "Look, Cliff, did you see that shooting star? It was aimed straight for the Lucky Number Seven." Grinning up at him, she reflected, "Grandpère used to say shooting stars were angels sending their miracles to earth."

"I can believe it." Cliff looked deeply into her eyes. "I got shot by one about six months ago. But I kept the angel as well as the miracle."

Unable to speak for the lump in her throat, she hugged Cliff fiercely. He held her silently as "Oh, Holy Night" wafted on the breeze.

"Let's go," he finally whispered into her ear.

Helping her up onto the seat, he held the orange up to her. "Would you like an orange?"

Kyra leaned down and whispered in his ear, "I'd rather have a banana."

RENEE HALVERSON

If André DuBois were a betting man, how would lay odds that the woman in red is robbing his dealers blind. He can tell beauty's smile disguises a quick mind and even quicker fingers . To catch her in the act he deals himself into the game, never guessing he might lose ghis heart process.

Faith O'Malley depends on her wits to succeed at cards, and experience tells her the ante has just been raised. The new gambler's good looks are distracting enough, but his intelligent eyes promise trouble. Still, Faith will risk everything—her reputation, her virtue—to save the innocent people depending on her. It won't be until later that she'll stop to learn what she's won.

Dorchester Publishing Co., Inc.
P.O. Box 6640 __5062-5
Wayne, PA 19087-8640 **$5.99 US/$7.99 CAN**

Please add $2.50 for shipping and handling for the first book and $.75 for each additional book. NY and PA residents, add appropriate sales tax. No cash, stamps, or CODs. Canadian orders require $5.00 for shipping and handling and must be paid in U.S. dollars. Prices and availability subject to change. **Payment must accompany all orders.**

Name: ____________________

Address: ____________________

City: ____________ State: ________ Zip: ____________

E-mail: ____________________

I have enclosed $__________ in payment for the checked book(s).

For more information on these books, check out our website at www.dorchesterpub.com.

____ *Please send me a free catalog.*

Ronda Thompson

Although Violet Mallory was raised by the wealthy, landowning Miles Traften, nothing can remove the stain of her birthright: She is the child of no-good outlaws, and one day St. Louis society will uncover that. No, she can never be a city gal, can never truly be happy—but she can exact revenge on the man who sired and sold her.

But being a criminal is hard. Like Gregory Kline—blackmailer, thief and the handsome rogue sent to recover her—Violet longs for something better. Gregory is intent upon reforming her, and then his kiss teaches her the difference between roguishness and villainy. She sees that beauty can grow from the muddiest soil, and Violets don't always have to be blue.

Christine is shocked that she's agreed to marry. Her intended, Gavin Norfork, is a notorious lover, gambler, and duelist. It is rumored he can seduce a woman at twenty paces. The dissolute aristocrat is clearly an unsuitable match for a virtuous orphan who has devoted her life to charity work. But Christine's first attempt to scare him off ends only with mud on her face. And, suddenly finding herself wed to a man she hasn't even met, Christine finds herself questioning her goals. Perhaps it is time to make her entrée into London society, to meet Gavin on his own ground—and challenge him with his own tricks. The unrepentant rake thinks she's gotten dirty before, but he hasn't seen anything yet. Not only her husband can be scandalous—and not only Christine can fall in love.

___4805-1 $5.50 US/$6.50 CAN

ENTER TO WIN
A *SINFULLY DELICIOUS* COOKBOOK!

Now you can cook up your own romance with twenty-four mouth-watering recipes inspired by those featured in *Sinfully Delicious*. Just correctly answer the three following questions based on the book by Lora Kenton. Be sure to give your complete and correct address and phone number so that we may notify you if you are a winner.

(Please type or legibly print.)

1) What type of establishment does Kyra accidentally enter in her search for Cliff?

____

2) What memento has Cliff kept on his bedside stand?

____

3) What piece of fruit does Kyra get creative with on her wedding night?

____

NAME: ______________________________

ADDRESS: ______________________________

____

PHONE: ______________________________

E-MAIL ADDRESS: ______________________________

MAIL ENTRIES TO:

DORCHESTER PUBLISHING CO., INC.
SD CONTEST
276 FIFTH AVENUE, SUITE 1008
NEW YORK, NY 10001

OFFICIAL CONTEST RULES: No purchase necessary. Must be at least 18 years old to enter. Only one entry per envelope. Only one entry per household. Use of a photocopy of an original entry form is acceptable. Entries must be postmarked by October 15, 2002. The contest is open to all residents of the U.S. and Canada, excluding employees and families of Dorchester Publishing Co., Inc., and the Comag Marketing Group. A random drawing for all contestants who correctly answer the above questionnaire will be held at the offices of Dorchester Publishing on or before October 30, 2002. Odds of winning are dependent on the number of correctly answered entries received. Any illegible, mutilated, altered, or incorrectly filled-out entry forms will be disqualified. Not responsible for lost, late, misdirected, damaged, incomplete, altered, illegible, or postage-due mail. Entries become the property of the sponsor and will not be returned. The Grand Prize certificate will be mailed to the winner on or before November 15, 2002. Void where prohibited by law.